THE HAVEN

A LIGHT IN THE DARKNESS

MARK ALLEN HOLBROOK

ZAMIZ PRESS

FICTION / Christian / Contemporary

FICTION / Christian / Suspense

Special discounts are available on quantity purchases by corporations, associations and others. For details, contact the author.

DO YOU HAVE A MESSAGE TO SHARE WITH THE WORLD?
ARE YOU INTERESTED IN HAVING YOUR BOOK
PUBLISHED?
VISIT ZAMIZPRESS.COM

Cover design by Nathaniel Dasco

Editor John Irvin - Proofreader Rebecca Black

The Haven: A Light in the Darkness — 1st Edition

ISBN: 978-1-949813-26-5 and 978-1-949813-27-2

CONTENTS

To all the pastors who fight the good fight and stay true to the Word.

The Lord will be our God, and delight to dwell among us, as His own people, and will command a blessing upon us in all our ways, so that we shall see much more of His wisdom, power, goodness and truth, than formerly we have been acquainted with. ... For we must consider that we shall be as a city upon a hill. The eyes of all people are upon us. So that if we shall deal falsely with our God in this work we have undertaken, and so cause Him to withdraw His present help from us, we shall be made a story and a by-word through the world. We shall open the mouths of enemies to speak evil of the ways of God, and all professors for God's sake. We shall shame the faces of many of God's worthy servants and cause their prayers to be turned into curses upon us till we be consumed out of the good land whither we are going.

But if our hearts shall turn away, so that we will not obey, but shall be seduced, and worship other Gods, our pleasure and profits, and serve them; it is propounded unto us this day, we shall surely perish out of the good land whither we pass over this vast sea to possess it.

Excerpt from the sermon "A Model of Christian

Charity" by John Winthrop, governor of the Massachusetts Bay Colony which became the third settlement in the New World, after the one in Plymouth, when it was founded in 1630.

PROLOGUE

Mitch and Mary stood on the house porch with their realtor Derrick. As they surveyed the front yard with its 225 feet of gravel driveway, they were unaware that they were being watched.

Mitch said, "Derrick, I think this is definitely the one."

Mary nodded and added, "Yes, this is the place we've been looking for. I like the house layout and there is all the room we need and more."

"I am glad to hear that," Derrick said. The Harrison's search for a new home in the country had started back in June and it was now September. Derrick had shown them no less than twenty-five homes, most of them overpriced and in need of repair. The hot real estate market had made it difficult to find a house to place a bid on before it was gone. This particular house had been on the market one week, an eternity in the market, but no one had looked at it yet. Mitch and Mary had spotted the house on their way home from another day of driving around looking and immediately called Derrick to set up a showing. That was Tuesday and this was Friday.

Mitch continued, "It has everything we were looking for. Five acres, a perfect spot for our garden, few trees to deal with, and the house itself is perfect."

Derrick responded, "I get that the property is to your liking, but are you sure this isn't too much house for you? It just seems like a four-bedroom home for a couple soon to retire is overkill."

"Not at all," Mary replied. "There is plenty of room if the girls come to stay for a weekend or holiday or if we need to accommodate others who may need a place to stay."

"Others?" Derrick asked. "Are you thinking of opening a Bed & Breakfast? I don't know if the zoning will allow that."

"No, not a B & B," Mitch explained. "More like a retreat. We wanted a home with enough room to be able to welcome anyone, family, friends—whoever—if the need arises."

"Okay," Derick responded. "I can't argue with an attitude like that. Did your pastor say something that led you to think along these lines?"

"No," Mary replied as they started down the porch steps. "Not our pastor. A higher authority."

As the three made their way to their cars, the two who had been watching from their perch on the roof smiled. The larger of the two, Elias, turned to his subordinate,

Zera, and said, "These two will do well for our Lord. Their hearts are pure in His will."

Elias and Zera had been at the home since it first went on the market, shielding it from other potential buyers. This home was destined for the Harrisons.

Zera replied, "I do believe you are correct. But will they be able to withstand the enemy's attacks? They have no idea what is coming."

"Perhaps not exactly, but we have heard their conversations with each other. They are preparing for the difficulties ahead even though they cannot see them clearly. Such faith will see them through."

"I pray you are right, Elias. The plan for them and for this place is ambitious. Much depends on their commitment and courage."

"As it always does with men and women, Zera."

With a nod from Elias, the two lifted from the roof and faded out of this world, returning to the one from which they had come.

1

MARCH 28

THE FOLLOWING YEAR

It was his morning routine. Up before dawn when the stars still shone and most of the world around him was still asleep. Coffee cup in hand, he scanned the various news sites searching for the all-but-ignored tidbits of information. Most people, when reading or watching the news let the information roll over them without much thought. Their comprehension focused on the headlines, not the details. For Mitch Harrison, the devil was in the details, literally. As he continued to peruse news stories that morning, he could not help but wonder how much time was left. The world was spinning out of control and he knew it could not go on much longer. His country's debt was rising at an alarming rate. Public discourse, whether through social media or on the streets, was escalating from disagreement to hatred. Violence was becoming the norm and losing its shock value as a day without a shooting was now worth reporting.

He particularly watched for news of shootings and violence to the South in the city. The city he grew up in and knew almost street by street was fast becoming a war zone. It was not a question of if violence would erupt each day, but simply a matter of how much and where. Shootings in the poorer neighborhoods, drive by shootings, the discovery of murdered bodies, and those taken by overdoses were accumulating daily. He remembered how, many years ago, the local news covered the story of when the city first recorded 100 homicides in a year. That number was now reached before Father's Day or sometimes sooner.

For this reason, among others, he and his wife, Mary, had decided to leave the city for the relative safety of rural Ohio. They had not gone far, thirty-five miles north of the edge of the city, just outside the small village of Mt. Olive. The previous year, as a pandemic gripped the nation, a tumultuous election loomed, and the voice of hatred swept the country, a quiet resolution to make the move had developed. The need to move was not born out of fear or panic. No, both Mitch and Mary had a peace about their lives that was their foundation. A peace known only to those who knew, regardless of how bad things got, the world was a temporary place and to be viewed simply as a bump in the road on a journey of God's making.

At sixty, Mitch was entering what he hoped would be his golden years. Always active in sports and working around the house, he had aged well, but for a few nagging injuries from his youth. Not tall, just under six feet, he was now mostly gray and could stand to lose a few pounds.

If pressed to describe him, his friends would say he was intelligent and somewhat pensive. Mitch had an innate curiosity that had served him well professionally and had also made him a voracious reader. Aside from his Bible, he read history mostly, but enjoyed a good mystery as well. His years in the news business during the first half of his career had developed a need for information daily.

Mitch finished the last swig of coffee and headed upstairs just as the first early streaks of dawn illuminated the clouds. *It is going to be another beautiful sunrise*, he thought as he headed up to the second floor to check on the newest additions to the Harrison household. As he entered the spare room and flicked on the light, he could already hear the chirping of the fifteen chicks they had recently picked up from the local feedstore. He settled on the edge of the bed and looked in on the yellow balls of fluff and began counting. "...twelve, thirteen, fourteen, fifteen." Satisfied all the chicks were doing well, he watched them frolic, eat, and drink as his mind drifted back over the past twelve months.

One year ago, they had just celebrated the wedding of Mary's youngest daughter. Elaina and Eric made for a storybook couple. And both Mary and Mitch felt good about the union. Eric was from farm country, about an hour north of Mt. Olive. A solid, no-frills kind of man who believed in hard work and honesty. Elaina had told them long before she met Eric that she wanted to get out of the city. Her job in the superficial, fast-paced life downtown was just not for her. Eric was an answer to prayers. Now they were settled into their home and their jobs and making plans for the future in Tipton. They were happy and content and starting a family did not seem that far off. The elder daughter, Abbigail, was now in Tipton as well, commuting back to the city where she worked at the same hospital as Mary.

Mitch often reflected on his new family. He and Mary had been married just three years and Mitch had no children of his own. Now, with Elaina and Abbigail, he found himself a step-father for the first time. He discovered he enjoyed the role and looked forward to the coming years as the girls started their careers and families.

The news of the pandemic came the week of the wedding. Then, it was something that was coming, but not here yet. The Tuesday after the wedding, the governor shut the state down. It was surreal. A once thriving state economy stopped in its tracks by some unknown virus that they were told had the potential to kill millions. The governor and his Health Department director warned that, even if everyone followed the rules, fifty thousand people in the state would die from the virus in the first few months. Mitch and Mary dutifully monitored the news and watched the press conferences to learn as much as they could. As the weeks turned into months and the people stayed at home, it seemed the crisis had been averted. The numbers of deaths and cases were far lower than predicted and many believed the state would reopen before summer was over. But as spring became summer, the messages out of the Statehouse began to change. Instead of flattening the curve, they were now told that everything had to stay closed until a vaccine could be developed, and that could take a year or more.

As this was going on, Mitch and Mary continued planning for their retirement. Not in response to the virus as their plans were in place and retirement was coming at the end of the following year. As they talked about it, they realized that they did not want to retire in the city. True, they were pleasantly ensconced in one of the city's comfortable suburbs of Wadesville. Their house was not large or elaborate but situated on a quiet street and had room enough for what they hoped would be many visits from the girls and grandchildren. It was an ideal place to retire and become grandparents. But something did not feel right to Mitch.

Then, one day, Mitch received the strongest of messages—a clear and definite command, "Get out!" The message seemed to come from inside him, but with the effect of hearing it out loud. When Mitch shared this with Mary, she simply nodded and said, "This is so obviously from God and is a clear message for what we are supposed to do."

Finally, after months of searching, they found the perfect place. It sat on five acres on country road with only three other houses nearby. The land was open, so plenty of room for the large garden they wanted to plant. The house was a newer cape-cod style with three bedrooms upstairs and a master suite on the first floor. Most of the basement had been finished into two rooms. Mitch used one as his office, while Mary took the other for hers. The house had a great sitting porch on the front and a two-tiered deck on the back. When they moved in, they could envision family gatherings, having friends over, and making lots of memories in their new home. Shortly after moving in, they had a small barn built to house lawn and garden equipment. Mitch planned to build a chicken coop in the back corner as well.

Mitch and Mary had met in church four years ago, introduced by their mutual friend, Liz. Both had experienced the tragedy of a failed marriage and were still weighed down by the sense of loss. God did not intend for marriages to fail and neither could shake the feeling that they had failed God. Mitch had been on his own for sixteen years, Mary only four. Their first meeting at church was followed by dinner with their mutual friend. Mitch recalled how Mary seemed pleasant enough. She was pretty in a simple way that did not turn heads, but rather pulled you into her sparkling eyes and quiet smile. She was petite with beautiful brunette hair just to the shoulder. Her brown eyes seemed to always be as open as possible, to catch everything going on around her. The dinner was nice, but neither thought much about the other after.

That summer, Mitch got word from two of his closest friends and spiritual mentors that they were starting a new Bible study group. He was excited. Mitch had known Dave and Denise Anderson since his marriage broke up and their presence and support had been a rock through tough times. The group would include church friends, Jim and Betty Jackson, Maggie Mason, Joanna Tyler, and surprisingly, Liz Cook. And Liz had asked Mary to be a part of the group as well. Liz, Dave, and Denise knew each other because they were neighbors.

Mitch smiled as he remembered how, at the group's first meeting, he had sat next to Mary. As he settled in for the meal, his arm lightly brushed Mary's and an unexpected sensation ran through him. At first, he was surprised. The slight touch was unintended, but the feeling was electric. All through the dinner he wanted to look over at Mary. He was anxious to look with new eyes. The last time he had seen her, they had not really talked. But now he wanted to learn more about her.

As the summer wore on and the group began to meet, it seemed Mitch and Mary were destined to come together. At their pre-study dinner, they always seemed to end up sitting together. Then, Mitch asked Mary if she wanted to have dinner and a movie sometime. He could still remember that first date. Yes, it sounded trite, but it was magical. The following Sunday, they met at church and Mitch came over after. By the time he left, they both knew that they had found the "one." They were engaged that fall and married the following April.

Now, as Mitch sat waiting for the sunrise, he could not believe it had been almost two years since they were married. It had been an eventful two years. Their wedding, Elaina's wedding, and Mary's oldest daughter, Abbigail, graduating from college. Then the move to Mt. Olive. Mitch thought, as he often did, about how simply amazing it all was. He was now happily married to a wonderful woman who shared his faith and beliefs, had two stepdaughters who were beautiful, vibrant young women. And now preparing for a retirement that he had been looking forward to for a long time.

Mitch Harrison, before meeting Mary, had his life all planned out. He was a planner after all and having everything in order made him feel good. His plan was to work until he was sixty-four, then retire in a nice, small condo near his friends, Dave and Denise. He would play golf, be involved in his church, and live a comfortable, uneventful retirement. He had had a good life despite his failed marriage. A rewarding career, two actually. He had worked for twenty years in the radio and television news industry. The work was rewarding and adventurous. But the business began to change, and Mitch started to question if he wanted to be a part of an industry that no longer served its viewers and listeners. He began to realize that, instead of informing the people of the news, the broadcasts were becoming nothing more than sensationalized tidbits designed to elicit strong emotions—negative emotions that spurred panic, hate, and mistrust. He switched gears and was blessed to land at the state historical society in the marketing department and enjoyed ten years promoting history, a passion he had developed as a young man. And now, he had spent the last five years directing the visitor's bureau in the adjacent county, a job he enjoyed as much for the people as for the work.

But everything had changed in the last few years. Mitch had no doubt that those changes were no accident. He could see how God had led him through life, closing some doors and opening others to bring him to where he was now. On the verge of retirement three years ahead of schedule and at complete peace with his life, he could not have imagined a better situation. But he also knew that, as much as life was good and pleasant now, a darkness was approaching. He did not fear the darkness for he knew they were protected from it by their faith. He often recalled Jesus' warning to be prepared for the thief in the night. And that is what they were now doing as the second year of the pandemic was beginning.

The sound of Mary moving about caught his attention and he rose to go downstairs and pour his wife's first cup of coffee for the day. It was something he enjoyed doing every morning, greeting her with a kiss and a cup. As he was pouring the coffee, Mary padded into the kitchen with a "Good morning" and, after they spent a few minutes in each other's arms greeting the day, she asked, "So, what is the news I need to know this morning?"

"Not much today, except that the state legislature is being very vocal that they will not allow for a vaccine passport. Some are talking about writing a bill to specifically ban any form of vaccine proof, saying it could lead to discrimination for those who aren't vaccinated."

"Like us," Mary added.

"Yes, just like us," Mitch replied. "And I hope they are successful. For your sake."

Mary had become increasingly worried that her job was in jeopardy. She worked for the large state university at the hospital. She had always worked from home a few days a week, but since the pandemic, she was at home full-time. Her boss had been pressuring her and others to get vaccinated, even though the university had not made it mandatory. She feared it would be soon and she would have to make a difficult decision.

Mitch and Mary had talked about the vaccine and were likeminded. They were disturbed that all discussion about possible treatments for the virus had been quashed in favor of the development of a vaccine. It seemed obvious to them that this was nothing more than opening the door for the pharmaceutical industry to make billions. They also were concerned that the new vaccine was RNA based. The thought of being injected with something that could alter their God-given make up was simply out of the question. Mary had pointed out recently one evening as they sat reading their Bibles a scripture that seemed to speak to their concerns about the vaccine.

"It says here in Genesis 1:26, 'Then God said, "Let us make man in our image, in our likeness."' So, if we are made in God's image, doesn't that mean that we should avoid altering what God has made? I mean, think about it, if this vaccine, an RNA vaccine, alters our DNA, we are changing our bodies in a way God never intended."

"I think you are absolutely right," Mitch agreed. "Even more so since, no matter what the experts say, no one knows what this vaccine will do to us. Not to mention that we have no idea what exactly is in it. And I do not trust these claims for effectiveness. There simply has not been enough time to determine if it even works. How can they say it is 80% effective when it is so new? It sounds more like a politician's promise than sound medical information."

The entire virus situation and the government's reaction to it made no sense to Mitch and Mary. They had talked often about how it seemed that real information was being buried or ignored by the news. They recalled how, last year, doctors were reporting great success with a regimen of hydroxychloroquine, an existing drug that was on the market, cheap to produce, and readily available. Almost immediately, the Centers for Disease Control (CDC) and government health officials mounted a campaign denying the doctors' claims and discrediting them. Mitch had even read reports that some of the more vocal doctors had been quietly fired from their jobs for not recanting their claims. Of course, such news was not found on the popular news media. You had to go looking for it as the big news operations were in lock step with the government.

Mitch and Mary were also concerned with what they saw as deceptive practices by the government and the CDC. The CDC had issued a report last summer which clearly indicated that, of the reported virus deaths, only four percent were from the virus alone. The remainder had an average comorbidity rate of 2.9. This meant that the patients had other factors contributing to their deaths. Mitch strongly suspected that, in fact, those deaths were not caused by the virus at all. Most people who contracted the virus were asymptomatic. There was no reason to think that a patient suffering from COPD, liver failure, or any number of conditions could not be asymptomatic as well. While not reported by the news, Mitch and Mary knew that hospitals were getting federal dollars for every virus patient they treated. So, it was not a stretch to assume that a hospital would report as many deaths as possible as virus-caused to increase their bottom line.

What was also disturbing was the fact that this information was not secret, yet the news outlets ignored it. Just like they had ignored reports last year of people receiving letters that they had tested positive when they had not even been tested. Mitch and Mary knew firsthand that this was true. Jim and Betty's daughter had gone with two friends to be tested last summer. The wait was long and they decided to leave before being tested. Each had received a letter in the mail from the testing site indicating they were positive for the virus.

Mitch could not imagine where all of this was headed, but he knew it would not be good. It felt like the world was traveling full speed down a hill with no brakes and bad steering. "At least," he thought, "I know where Mary and I are headed and that is a comfort."

2

———

APRIL 10

It was a typical April day in Ohio as Mitch worked on their newly built mini barn. There was a hint of warmth, but it was far from hot. The heat would come in May as the temperatures and humidity rose. For now, he enjoyed the pleasant weather as he worked to build the chicken coop in the back corner of the building. The garden just behind the building was coming along—the tilling was almost done, and planting time was approaching. He reflected on all the work ahead of him this spring and smiled. Nothing improved Mitch's mood more than being outside, doing basic work, and enjoying the sunshine. He nailed another stud into place and heard his cell phone ring, so he stopped his work to answer.

"Hello."

"Hey Mitch, how are things?"

It was Matt Reed, Mitch's best friend. Matt and his wife, Kate, were in Wyattsville. Even though they now lived two hours apart, Mitch and Matt were still as close as brothers. Closer even because they were brothers in Christ.

"Things are good. Working on the coop today. It won't be long until those chicks become hens and need to move to their permanent home."

"I still can't believe you and chickens. You are becoming a gentleman farmer!"

"You know me, can't take the country out of the boy."

Mitch had come from an Appalachian background and had spent many a summer during his youth at his grandparents' farm in the southern part of the state. Those were some of his fondest memories and he had always wanted to recreate that sense of satisfaction in working the land and supporting himself. That was part of the reason he and Mary had moved to the country. Many who knew Mitch were surprised. Being a college-educated career professional made people assume he was an intellectual. That was something that annoyed Mitch often. It rankled him that many people stereotyped hill folk as uneducated and uniformed. He saw himself as an intellectual. He had co-authored a book on the Civil War, wrote numerous articles on history, and was a member of the state's Speakers Bureau. But that did not mean he had forsaken his roots or forgotten the lessons he had learned from his family. The most important of which was faith is the answer to every challenge in life.

Matt responded, "That I know too well. Say, I wanted to get your take on something."

"Sure. What's up?"

"Well, I read an interesting article last night and it has me worried."

"Go on," Mitch replied, his concern now growing.

"It seems the Pentagon has announced they have created a microchip that can detect the virus. The plan is to insert it into sailors so they can detect the virus early."

"Ouch."

"Exactly. We know there has been talk of some sort of vaccine identification, but this is something altogether different. Coming at it from an early diagnosis approach is going to appeal to a lot of people."

"I think you're right. Something like this will circumvent the vaccine ID laws. They can argue that it is not proof-of-vaccine, but virus detection that will save lives. But we know it's a small step to use that chip as a form of identification and a quick slide down a slippery slope."

"I hear you. So, what can be done about it?"

"Honestly, nothing. Like I have said before, we cannot prevent what is coming. God's plans are inevitable, only our response to those plans is not. If this chip takes hold, I have no doubt it will be accepted worldwide, and its use will be expanded beyond its intended purpose."

"Amen! I agree, but it still concerns me. My boys are not believers, and I cannot sleep at night for fear that they will be deceived. If this chip is what we think it is, they will not hesitate to take it when the time comes. And that will seal their fate before God."

"Agreed. I feel for you Matt. Any sign that your boys are understanding any of this?"

"I wish. They are so caught up in their lives and careers, they just do not have time to look at things beyond that. I keep trying to find a way to get through to them, and they must take it seriously. They just don't want to hear it."

"What about Erica? Will they listen to their sister? Maybe she can talk to them and try to help them see the truth?"

"We've talked about that and she is trying. But you know that brothers do not take a younger sister seriously. They just think she is following what Dad and Mom are doing just like always."

"Well Matt, keep praying and we will here as well. It is in God's hands anyway."

"Indeed. Thanks, Mitch. So, how are other things on the farm?"

"Things are good. Getting ready for the season. I am ready for some nice summer weather."

"You have a regular Green Acres there!"

Mitch laughed. "Well, I think Mary would argue with that. She is no city girl dragged into the country. We did decide to name the place though."

"Really? And what is it?"

"We call it Harrison Haven."

"The Haven. I like that."

3

MAY 9

Mitch was a bit tired as they sat in church that Sunday morning. Yesterday had been a busy day. The chicks, now young chickens, had been moved into their new home. The garden had been planted. Well, most of it anyway. They still needed to plant their corn for the chickens, but that would come later. The garden had both sweet corn and field corn. To keep both species from cross-pollinating each other, they had to be planted a few weeks apart. Other than that, everything was in the ground. Sweet peas, potatoes, tomatoes, peppers, cucumbers, green beans, cantaloupe, onions, sweet potatoes, and the sweet corn had been planted.

The garden was large, certainly bigger than what it needed to be for the two of them. But they had decided they had the room to plant enough to share. The food pantry up in the county seat could certainly use fresh produce this summer. And they planned to can and freeze the excess to use through the winter. They also knew that there may come a time when what they grew in the garden and the eggs from the chickens would be their sole source of food. They were not preppers like some out West. No plans to build a bomb shelter or other drastic measures. But they did recognize that the world was becoming a fragile place and assuming the grocery shelves would always be stocked seemed naive. If anything, the first year of the pandemic had clearly shown how quickly basic human needs could be hard to find.

As the pastor came to the pulpit, Mitch thought to himself how blessed they were to have found this church. It was only a few miles away and it felt like home. The spirit was strong here and not tainted by worldly views. The message was clear from the leadership, they did not preach the gospel of prosperity. Life was hard, the world was broken, evil was gaining ground, and our focus should be on God's saving grace. It felt like a breath of fresh air to Mitch, especially after leaving their previous church in the city.

They had actually stopped going to their former church before they moved. The previous year, they had come to realize that the church they were attending had lost its way. The message from the pastors were less about God's plan for them and more about creating a better world. That somehow, if they just worked hard enough, they could right all the wrongs going on in their community. And if they did, God would continue to bless them and make them happy.

Happy, Mitch thought at the time. *When did God get into the happy business? The Bible does not mention happiness. It tells us life is hard, but salvation brings us joy in the midst of trouble. Peace when all around us is in chaos. Contentment in laying up our treasures in heaven instead of this world.*

Next, politically correct phrases began to crop up in the sermons. The calls for members to be more "woke" in their lives. The church had traded evangelism for advocacy. The breaking point for Mitch had come that June when, while watching the service online in the midst of the pandemic scare, the pastor had told the story of God's revelation to Peter to now include the gentiles into the faith. He had used the example, he said, "to show that even Peter had his prejudices." Mitch was outraged. How could a supposed man of God twist and manipulate scripture this way? Peter had been preaching God's Word relentlessly and suffering for it. He was following the teachings of Jesus, including his admonition that he had not come to deny the law, but to fulfill it. Peter was not prejudiced against the gentiles; he was following God's laws and instructions. And now God had chosen him to reveal His plan to welcome all into the faith. That was the last time Mitch and Mary attended the church, and the search for a new one began.

Mary had attended their present church a few years back and suggested they try it. Mitch agreed and they began to watch the services online. Mitch immediately felt at home there. Geneva Baptist Church was as large as their previous one but had a more intimate feel to it. The singing was more sincere, and spirit filled. The preaching was unapologetic about the fact that there was only one way to salvation, through Jesus Christ. And politics were nowhere to be found. While it was true that the sermons could be interpreted as anti-government, they were not political. Instead, they were anti-world. Pastor Fred did not mince words. He cautioned the congregation constantly to not let themselves get drawn into the immoral culture of the nation. To avoid becoming embroiled in political side-taking and debate, he reminded them often, regardless of what was going on around them, peace could only be found in God's love and salvation. It was a message Mitch and Mary identified with and it became their foundation in all things. This church was close enough to their new home that they felt connected with the people and the work the church was doing in the community.

Mitch came back to the present as Pastor Fred began the day's sermon.

"Today, I want to talk about how God meets our needs. Not our wants, but our needs. Think back if you will to biblical times. Whether we are talking about the days of Abraham, Isaac, Jacob, or Jesus. Look at these times in human history and ask yourself if people had all they needed. Did they? Certainly not by today's standards. Why, they did not have cars, or televisions, or cell phones. There were no sports to watch. No vacations to go on. No stores to shop at. No movies to go see. None of those things. Did they need them? Do we feel sorry for the Apostles because they could not share the message of salvation on Facebook? Wouldn't Paul have been better off if he could have texted his followers and encouraged the churches he founded?

"And what about Noah? He could have simply shown the people the forecast on the Weather Channel app and maybe they would have listened to him. The point is, the people we read about in the Bible had all they needed. Noah did what God commanded with what he had. He built this massive boat with only his three sons to help. The Apostles spread the Word of God by personally testifying to others—a testimony that has reached millions over the last two thousand years.

"So, my question to you today is, 'What do you need?' What do you truly need? Now, I am not suggesting you go through your home and throw out everything. We live in a time when we have many things that are useful. We have devices and tools that let us live every day without laboring to produce our own food and clothing. We have cars to travel around at speeds people two thousand years ago would call a miracle. We have large homes that sit mostly empty with extra rooms.

"We have just gone through a difficult year. Store shelves emptied. Jobs were lost. We were isolated in our homes for months. People were afraid. I am here to tell you today, God did not tremble when the virus came. So why should we? Instead of watching the news and worrying about what is going to happen, should we not ask God what He wants us to do in this situation?

"When it comes to our abundant lives today, we should be asking, what would Jesus do? If Jesus stepped into your life and ran your household, what decisions would He make. Would He worry about replacing a car that was not shiny and new? Would He debate adding to His wardrobe to stay fashionable? Would He ponder remodeling the master bathroom? Getting the latest technology? Upgrading His cable TV package?

"I think we all know the answer. Jesus would evaluate His resources and figure out how to use them to help others. I believe He would determine what He needed and be content with that. The rest of His resources and time He would minister to those in need. So, as we sit here in this beautiful church building and contemplate the week ahead, I ask you to do so with that simple question in mind. What would Jesus do? The truth is this question is less about what you do than how you think. Jesus did life differently than the rest of us because He thought differently. He did not worry about the future. Remember, He charged the disciples to go out and spread His Word, carrying not even one coin because God would provide all they needed. And they did and God did."

Mitch left church that morning thinking about what Pastor Fred had said and wondering what it meant for Mary and him. They were not extravagant by any means, but they did lead a comfortable life. It was rare that they denied themselves something they wanted, they could afford it. But were they doing enough? Was life too comfortable? How did they determine what changes they should make to be better servants to others and to God? What resonated with Mitch most was Fred's admonition to change how they thought, not just what they did. Mitch had believed he had become a caring person. He was content with what he had. Perhaps he was content because he had so much? How would he feel if things were not as good for them? It was something he was going to need to pray about and discuss with Mary.

Later that evening, Mitch and Mary sat on their front porch after a peaceful Sunday dinner, enjoying each other's company. They often sat on the porch in the evening, talking, reading, or just sitting like this in quiet contentment.

Mary looked over at Mitch and asked, "What is on your mind this evening? Something's stirring through your thoughts. You've very pensive today."

Mitch replied, "You know me so well." He looked out at their front yard and the field beyond, continuing, "I have been thinking about Pastor Fred's sermon this morning. What we have versus what we need and, more importantly, what we do with what we have."

Mary sat up in her rocker and agreed, "It was a powerful message today. I've felt convicted to consider our resources here and strive to find God's will for how we use them."

"Exactly, we have so much, and retirement is coming, so where does God want us to put our efforts? We've already decided our goal to travel in retirement is no longer important. The world is too violent, and we just aren't that interested in being far from home anymore. So, what does that mean for us? What do we do with ourselves?"

"I have been thinking the same and I have an idea," Mary remarked.

Mitch turned toward Mary in anticipation. She did not speak often about their direction in life, but when she did it was certainly God inspired. Mitch knew that whatever came next was likely to be meaningful and apparent in its simplicity.

"And what have you been thinking, dearest?"

"Well, here we sit in this wonderful home. We have more room than we need, and the land has so many possibilities. We call this Harrison Haven, but what if its proper name should be God's Haven? True, this place has been our personal haven from an ever-deteriorating world. Here we can get away from the hate and violence, an immoral culture, and all that comes with that. And yes, we are thankful for what God has provided us in this home. But I just feel this place is about more than just us."

"I've been getting that same feeling. So, where do you think God wants to take us with this?"

"I think... no, I know God wants us to make this a place for others as well. He did not put the word 'haven' on our hearts without a purpose. I am not sure exactly what that purpose is, but He has one."

"I agree. But who is this haven for? Are we supposed to open our home to those in need through our church? Or through this community? And how do we do that? I don't see how we go about making it happen. There are logistics to consider in setting things up to accommodate people. And what do we do to provide for them? How do we change the way we run the household if we have other people here? And how long will they be here and how do we help them when they are? There are just so many things to consider."

Mary smiled at Mitch and replied, "My dear husband, don't you think that, if God is asking us to do something, He will take care of the details? Ours is not to concern ourselves with the whats and hows, but to follow His lead and be open to where it takes us? I think our job is to prepare this place and ourselves and wait for God's timing. He already knows who is coming here and when. Ours is to be ready for them when they arrive."

"Of course, you are right. Forgive me for getting so worked up about the details and 'what ifs.' You know I can't help myself with planning too much and not letting God take care of making things happen in His way."

"There is nothing to forgive, my love. That's one of your gifts. Look at all you have done here. Without your careful planning, we would not be in a position to answer God's call to us to make this a haven for others. And we will need your planning skills for what God has in store for us. I have a feeling His plans will be a challenge for us to carry out."

4

MAY 15

It did not make sense. Most would say it was crazy. As Mitch and Mary watched the drilling rig go deeper, they both wondered if they were going too far in their quest to be more independent in their lives. Drilling a water well on their property sounded like a great idea last fall when Mitch had called to get quotes. But when the quotes came in at more than five thousand dollars, they had quickly set aside any plans for a well. They had no idea it would be that expensive. Besides, they wanted to put in a hot tub this year and spending money on a well would delay that purchase. But here they were watching the hole get deeper and deeper, seeing the dollars rack up with every foot. The hot tub was crossed off the to-do list for being too extravagant.

The discussion about whether to go ahead with the well was more of a debate. When Mitch first brought it up, Mary was incredulous.

"You want to spend that much money on a well? I thought we already discussed this? It's too much for something we don't need. Sure, we both like the idea of a well and all, but really, Mitch. Do you think it is wise to spend that much of our savings on something so frivolous?"

"I wouldn't call it frivolous. A bit of a reach, sure. But just like we discussed before we knew how much it would cost, having a well insures we will always have water, no matter what happens. What if the water company stops working? We have a back-up generator in case the electricity goes out. Why not the same for water?"

"That's different. We could lose power during a thunderstorm or a snowstorm. Those are real possibilities. But water? It would take a complete breakdown of everything for the water to stop. Do you really see that happening?"

"Maybe, maybe not. I just feel uneasy knowing we are vulnerable in this area. I agree it is a lot of money for something we may never need. But think of it this way. We can survive without electricity. We can get by for a while on the food we have stocked up. But, without water, we won't make it more than a few days."

"That's why we have cases of bottled water in the basement," Mary responded. "I just think this is going too far. I do like that we are living off our land, the garden, the chickens, milling our own grain and all. But Mitch, a well doesn't make sense."

"Mary, do the math. Even with all the water we have stored, it would last us only three weeks at three bottles a day each. That does not include water for cooking, just drinking. And forget about bathing or washing clothes. And then there are the chickens. They drink two gallons a day. Where would that come from."

"Okay, I see your point. But you are talking about a major 'what if' that may never happen." She paused, looking at Mitch, and saw in his eyes that, although he was arguing for the well, there was no sense of self in him about it. "Listen, let me think about this some more. You know how I am about spending chunks of money. I know we are blessed that way, but it still makes me uneasy to see the savings account go down."

The discussion ended there as Mitch and Mary agreed to seek God's guidance for this decision. Mitch prayed for clear direction, he wanted to be sure he wasn't trying to make a decision out of fear, but one that would serve God's purposes. Even if he couldn't see what that purpose was at the moment.

Then the news of the drought in the West became ugly. What had been an annoyance for many, had now become a disaster. Water was being rationed in homes and businesses. Irrigation water was being heavily restricted and farmers, realizing planting a crop may be useless, left their fields empty. And now there was talk of shipping water to the West. And not just truckloads of bottles like during a disaster. FEMA had announced a plan to divert water from the Midwest reservoirs, as much as 20 percent through a proposed pipeline. It sounded good on paper, but just a 20 percent reduction in the water supply meant that any sort of drought in the Midwest would bring the reservoirs down to dangerous levels. And that could mean rationing and more. Of course, the problem was not really the drought. It was the fact that West Coast cities had grown so large without natural supplies of water.

Before the industrial revolution, a century ago, cities developed near water for obvious reasons. But the development of ways to store and deliver water anywhere meant cities could now be located anywhere and were not limited in their growth by the local supply. This had led to larger cities growing an increasing distance from where their water came. It was a recipe for disaster that was now coming to fruition.

Mitch watched all of this and debated whether he was right about digging a well. He didn't say anything to Mary about it, not wanting to pester her on the subject. But he saw the situation getting worse and wondered if others were thinking the same and how long it would be before the well-drilling companies were booked up for the rest of the year. He prayed for a clear answer on the subject, something that would make it plain to both of them on what to do.

A few days later, as Mitch and Mary were starting their day, the answer came. Mary was in the shower and suddenly the water stopped. Toweling off, she called to Mitch, "Hey Mitch, the water stopped. What's going on?"

"What do you mean stopped?"

"I was in the shower and the water pressure went down and then was gone."

"Let me see what I can find out."

Mitch went online, checking all the usual news and

information sites, but found nothing about a water problem. He kept checking all day, but still no word on why the water was out. Late that afternoon they received an email from the water company. A pump in the water tower had died. An alarm was supposed to go off to tell the company so they could replace it. But the alarm had also failed and the tank in the tower had run dry. The company said it would take a day or two to replace the pump, and then five more days for the tank to refill. Seven days in all, but only if everyone kept their taps off. If they tried too soon, it would just delay the filling of the tank.

Seven days with absolutely no water. Was this the sign Mitch and Mary were looking for? Mitch thought it had to be. They needed a plan to get by for the next week. They called Dave and Denise to see if they could come down every other day to take showers. They could get by for a week without doing laundry if they had to. And they should probably get more bottled water as what they had on hand would dwindle quickly. Mitch stopped in at the grocery store in Mason where he worked to find the shelves empty. He was surprised as he was in the next county and, he thought, far enough away that their local outage would not affect things there. The same was true of all the stores they tried within forty-five minutes of their home. With a few thousand water customers now trying to stock up, the shelves emptied quickly. Their biggest concern was the chickens. They needed at least two gallons of water every day. Add to that another five gallons for cooking and washing dishes and they were looking at fifty gallons of water for the week. Mitch decided the best idea would be to fill containers at work to bring home every day. It was a chore hauling that much water, but it was the only option they had.

Mary had grown quiet during this time and Mitch knew she was worried. The sudden interruption of a basic need had shocked them both. As they sat at the dinner table the third day of the outage, Mary said to Mitch, "I have been fighting this situation ever since the water stopped."

"Fighting it?" Mitch asked. "Mary, I haven't seen that at all. You dove right in to planning for how we will get through this. You calculated how much water is required for each need and plotted it out for the whole week. It is a great plan, and we are in good shape because if it."

"That's not what I mean. Of course, we needed to come up with a way to get through this. No, what I have been fighting is accepting the fact that you were right about the well. I do not want to admit that this water outage is a clear sign from God about what we should do. I do not like it and, quite honestly, I am mad at God about it. I don't want to be mad, but I am."

"I understand completely. I know I have been arguing for a well these past few weeks, but in my mind, it was mostly theoretical. It was something to check off the list, so we would be prepared for everything. Deep down, I did not really think we would be faced with a situation like this. Yes, this is temporary. But now I ask myself what if it wasn't?"

"And so have I. This is only affecting our area, but there is nothing to say it could not happen on a larger scale. Like the whole state or beyond. And it could be for longer, not just a week. As much as I hate to admit it, I think you need to make the call and we need that well."

Mitch made the call the next morning. As expected, the well drillers in the area were terribly busy. The company Mitch spoke to said they were getting dozens of calls a day from frantic people wanting them to come out immediately. That demand quickly ebbed as they learned just how much drilling a well would cost. But enough were booking dates that Mitch and Mary would have to wait six weeks before their well could be drilled. But then, a few days after the water came back, the company called to tell Mitch they could dig the well in a few days if they still wanted it. The day after the water came back, most of the company's appointments had canceled. As the water flowed again, they forgot about their worries and decided they were just overreacting. Mitch made the appointment and now, as they stood watching the drillers do their work, he knew they were doing the right thing.

5

——————

MAY 19

"You really had a well dug," Joanna asked.

"Yes, we did," Mitch replied.

Mitch and Mary had just shared with their Bible study group that they had a well drilled on their property. Up to this point, everything they had done made sense to everyone; it was just country living. But the well was something else. And it was no surprise that Joanna had seemed incredulous. Mitch had known Joanna as long as Dave and Denise. They had all served together in a previous church and had become close. Joanna spoke her mind often but did so with courtesy and respect. The group, Mitch and Mary, Joanna, Dave and Denise, Maggie, and Jim and Betty were sitting in Dave and Denise's living room to start their study after sharing a potluck dinner.

Joanna continued, "So, explain to me how you decided you needed a well."

Mary offered, "You remember a few weeks ago we had that water outage when the water tower went dry?"

"Yes, I remember, but that was a failed pump or something, wasn't it?"

"It was, but it got us to thinking. What if it was more than that? What if something happened that caused the water to dry up in the entire county, or even the state?"

"I don't think that would ever happen," Joanna responded.

"Maybe not," Mary said "But it could happen. Look at the drought out west. People do not have enough water to bathe or wash clothes. Crops are drying up and dying. And it seems to be spreading eastward into the plains states. It may not reach us, but even so, water could be diverted to the West and then there would be shortages here."

"I guess," Joanna said. "But it still seems a stretch. It is a big 'what if'."

"You're right, it is. We thought long and hard about doing this. Let me explain it this way. We all know that there have been shortages in the grocery stores ever since the virus hit. And they seem to be getting worse. And aren't we all stocking up when we can because we know it could continue? Even the news is saying these shortages could last another year or more. And isn't water even more important? Mitch did the math and just for the two of us to have enough water to drink and stay healthy, we would need one and half gallons a day. That is forty-five gallons a month. In bottled water that would be 180 each month. And that does not leave any left for cooking, bathing our washing."

Joanna sighed and looked at Mary. "Well, when you put it that way, I guess it makes sense. It's kind of scary to think of though."

"It is scary," Denise said. "A lot of what is going on in the world is scary. The shortages, the violence, the virus. It can be difficult to know how to react to what is going on. Some, like Mitch and Mary are able to take steps, like they have, to minimize the negative effects of what seems to be a deterioration of our society."

Jim jumped in. "And what about all this violence? I mean, I guess I was not too worried when the shootings and other things increased in the city. It is getting so big, that just comes with the territory. But now it is spreading and affecting us here in the suburbs. It has gotten to the point that Betty and I don't go anywhere alone."

Maggie, who had been listening to the discussion intensely, sat forward, a look of concern on her face as she added, "I hear what everyone is saying, but don't you think that this is just temporary. We keep hearing on the news that the government is working to solve these problems. The shortages, the violence. Shouldn't we trust that it will calm down and get better?"

"Should we?" Dave said. "Or should we look at all that is going on from a biblical perspective. I think for too long, we Christians have only used the Bible to relate to our personal challenges. We look to it for ways to deal with our own frustrations, fears, and weaknesses. Maybe it is time we stepped back and see what God has to say about the times we are living in. And what He says we should be doing as Christians and not just as people."

Mitch had been silent during the discussion. He wanted to get a sense of what the group was thinking about current events and how it related to their faith. He was gratified to hear Denise and Dave steer the conversation in the direction it was going. He shifted in his chair and took a breath before starting a conversation he had been dreading but knew now was the right time.

"There has been something on my mind for quite a while now that I haven't shared with this group. In fact, I have only shared part of it with Mary. And it has to do with exactly what we are talking about. You all know Mary and I moved to Mt. Olive because we wanted to retire in the country. And that is true. We wanted to enjoy more space, plant a garden, and get away from the city traffic. To live in what we have called Harrison's Haven. That is exactly what it has been for us. A place where we can enjoy life together at a slower pace."

"But there is more to this than our retirement home. Last summer when we started talking about moving, I received a very clear message from God. At first, I chalked it up to my impatient nature to complete a task. We had decided to look for a country home and I just wanted to get it done. But, as our search continued, there developed in me a sense of urgency. I got the feeling that this was important. Far more important than just our retirement home. And then one day, I heard a voice. It was not a physical voice, but it was spoken to me as loud and clear as if it were. The message was simply, 'Get out!' It startled me and I questioned whether or not I had really heard anything, or if it was just a feeling. As I thought and prayed about it, I came to realize that the message was indeed real, and it was telling us to go."

Mitch looked around the room at his friends and wondered if what he was about to say would damage his and Mary's relationship with these people. He paused and wondered if he should continue. Just then, Mary reached over and squeezed his shoulder in support. Without words, she was saying, "Speak your mind and heart. You know from where this comes."

Mitch nodded and continued, "In Mathew 24, Jesus says, *'And many false prophets will arise and lead many astray. And because lawlessness will be increased, the love of many will grow cold. But the one who endures to the end will be saved. And this gospel of the kingdom will be proclaimed throughout the whole world as a testimony to all nations, and then the end will come.'* I have read this scripture over and over, along with others speaking to the end of the age and believe these words from Jesus were spoken for those of us living today. Not in theoretical terms, but because they are talking about what is happening now."

Denise, in her role as the spiritual leader of the group spoke up. "Mitch, I have no doubt of what you say and your experience hearing God's message to you and Mary. Can you talk more about how Matthew 24 is speaking to us today?"

"Sure, Denise. Let's look at the first line, *'And many false prophets will arise and lead many astray.'* We tend to think of this in terms of famous, or infamous, false teachers. People like Jim Jones, David Koresh, and the many others who ended up killing their followers or getting them killed. But, as horrible as those were, I think today's false prophets are even more dangerous. More dangerous because they are not fatalistic. We shake our heads at the gospel-of-prosperity preachers with their mansions, private jets, and expensive clothes, but the reality is that they are leading people astray. People who are genuinely looking for something meaningful in their lives. And they cannot get to God's true message of hope and redemption because these false preachers are so good at manipulating their fears and desires. But it goes beyond these obvious shysters. It appears to me that the gospel of prosperity has crept into many of our churches without any notice."

"What do you mean?" Betty asked. "Wouldn't we be able to detect it? I mean, it is not hard to spot these pastors. All they talk about is money and that 'live your best life' nonsense."

"I wish it were that simple," Mitch replied. "But from what I can see, it is more subtle than that. You see, our churches have become more like social institutions than places of worship and salvation."

"What's wrong with doing good in the community?" Joanna asked. "I enjoy the ministries I'm involved with."

"Nothing wrong at all, Joanna. We know salvation does not come from good works, but we are still charged with doing them because our faith compels us to. The problem is when it becomes more about advocacy than salvation. For example, look at how many churches across the country are standing up and making strong statements about social justice. Not necessarily a bad thing, but why now? Where were all these churches the past few generations when abortion became law, God was removed from public life, and the entertainment industry was permitted to infiltrate our children's lives with their filth? Nowhere! That's where they were. And still are. Pastors won't state publicly their opposition to these things because our worldly culture favors them."

Maggie spoke up, "I see what you mean. Those are touchy subjects, but why would pastors avoid them? Isn't their job to speak out against sin? All sin?"

"Of course it is, Maggie. It is every Christians' responsibility. Why don't they? I cannot say what is in every pastor's heart but do believe that they are afraid of getting in trouble with the media and having protesters in front of the church. So, they avoid any mention of the really difficult topics so they can operate under the radar of a society that is growing suspicious of the church. Another reason, I believe is that they do not want to upset their congregations. Let's face it, the contemporary churches don't ask for a commitment like churches once did. You don't need to become a formal member. You don't have to have a personal relationship with church leadership. You can come on Sunday, put your check in the offering plate, send your kids to the church activities, and go about your life. And, if the pastor happens to preach a sermon on Sunday you disagree with or find too challenging to your personal weaknesses, you can simply move on to the next church. Many of our pastors today are more concerned with keeping the congregation happy than challenging them to live out their faith as Jesus taught. They don't want to risk offending anyone. They want their people to be happy."

Jim asked, "I hear what you are saying, and I guess I can certainly see this taking place, probably some in our own church, but what's wrong with a pastor talking about happiness? Doesn't God want us to be happy?"

Mitch paused. This was a question he knew was coming and the topic was a thorn of contention with him concerning churches today. "Jim, let me ask you a question. Where in the Bible does God say He wants us to be happy? You can look, but you won't find it. The opposite is actually true. The stories in the Bible are not about happy people, but rather about people who endured great hardships. All the way back to Noah, then Abraham, Jacob, Job, Daniel, Ruth, Esther, and so many more. And the point of the stories of these people was how their faith carried them through a difficult life. Think of the Apostles. They all suffered for their faith and all, but John, died for it. Their lives were full of hardship, danger, stress, and poverty. And yet, every one of them suffered gladly. And that is the message we should be hearing from the pulpit. Not about happiness, live your best life, or even make the world a better place."

"There is something I read the other day that has me greatly concerned," Denise said. "I read this article about a church in Tennessee that announced they believe the Bible is not the Word of God. They say it is a response to

God and nothing more. This church says the Bible cannot possibly address the problems of the modern world, so it is the church's responsibility to interpret the Bible, discarding what they see as irrelevant."

"Whoa," Joanna responded. "I hadn't heard about that. Where is this church in Tennessee and, honestly, how can they call themselves a church if they are just going to make up whatever they want to?"

"I believe it is in Nashville," Denise answered. "They call it Progressive Christianity. I call it no Christianity at all. In 2 Timothy the Bible says, 'All Scripture is breathed out by God and profitable for teaching, for reproof, for correction, and for training in righteousness, that the man of God may be competent, equipped for every good work.' These people seem to be saying they will decide what in the Bible is useful and ignore the rest."

"You know," Maggie chimed in, "I think I am going to look into this some more. I want to find out if this sort of thing is going on in other places. I can see how dangerous it is and how easy it would be to slip in false teachings without anyone realizing it. It's kind of scary."

"It is," said Mitch. "What scares me most is that so many young people without any upbringing in the faith are being deceived by these heretical churches. What they are teaching sounds good to them and the fluidity of their doctrine lets them believe whatever they do is okay. It's just more of the blurring of the line between right and wrong. Obedience and evil."

"Well," Dave said, "this wasn't our planned topic for this week, but a good one, I think. Mitch, thanks for sharing this. I know it was difficult. We tend to think of our time together as a group every two weeks as a refuge from the crazy world out there. A chance to just be together in a safe place with people we trust. Maybe it's time for us to begin to look at our time together from a new perspective."

"I agree," Denise added. "So, what if next time, we talk about the next verse Mitch read to us? Remember, it was 'And because lawlessness will be increased, the love of many will grow cold.' Ouch! Not something pleasant to think about, but certainly relevant to the times in which we live. Is everyone okay with that?

Betty offered, "I am. Maybe it is time we talk about these things. I am beginning to think there is a lot going on in the world I am not aware of."

"Me too," Jim said. "I want to figure out what is going on out there. I don't want to be blindsided here in our suburban bubble."

"This all sounds a bit crazy," Joanna said. "I don't know that I want to spend our time every two weeks talking about this stuff." She paused. "But then again, I guess we should. I'm not sure things are that bad, but what do I know. Maybe they are. If so, I suppose we should try to figure it out."

"And what about you Maggie?" Dave asked. "How do you feel about discussing these topics?"

Maggie had turned quiet during the discussion. At one point, Mary had looked over at her and Maggie had withdrawn physically. She had her arms wrapped around herself and her head was bent downward. She looked up at Dave and said, "Honestly, this scares me. I just want to crawl up in a ball and wait for Jesus. If the world is really this bad and only getting worse, what's the point in talking about it?"

"A fair question," Denise said as she leaned forward, trying to get Maggie to reconnect with the group. "It is scary. And stressful. And hard to talk about. So, do you think these are things that have to be talked about eventually? Is it better to talk about them now or maybe later?"

Maggie shifted in her seat, thinking about the question. "I suppose now is better than later. But I am going to need everyone's help with this. You know how I am with talking about bad stuff. It makes me lie in bed at night worrying. I don't want to worry."

Mary turned to Maggie and said, "And that is exactly why I think we should face these issues, Maggie. As Mitch said, the Bible teaches us how to get through the hard stuff in life. Not just the worldly hard stuff, but the stuff that comes from Satan. The false teachings, the violence, the depravity. Jesus wants us to be prepared to face a world that is broken and falling, never to get better. It has been broken since Adam and Eve and we shouldn't expect it to get better. God's Word tells us it will get worse and worse until His Son returns to reign. We can't be prepared for Jesus' return if we are ignorant of the evil around us and don't know how to lean on God to get through it."

"You are right, Mary. Okay, let's talk about this stuff. I'll get through it as best I can. But can we still laugh and have some fun when we get together? I do like to do that with all of you."

"Of course, we can," Denise said. "After all, laughter comes from God. He makes us laugh, not just from our mouths, but also from our hearts. So, next time we will tackle the subject of lawlessness in our world. Let's all read up on our scriptures and commentaries. Dave, will you lead us in our closing prayer?"

6

MAY 23

The sun was high overhead and the humidity continued to rise as Mitch and Mary worked in their garden. It was late to be planting, but the cooler temperatures and constant rain the first half of the month had caused the delay. Finally, the weather broke and shifted from cool and wet to hot and humid almost overnight. Mitch had been impatient waiting for the weather to finally break and had busied himself getting the chicken coop and its outside run ready for their birds. Now, as they worked to get seeds and plants into the ground, Mitch thought back to a time a few years ago and another garden.

Before he had met Mary and before he had moved to Mason for work, Mitch lived with his brother, Jason, in an old house out in the country south of the capital. They were good years as the two brothers had similar interests. Jason was retired, even though he was only a year older than Mitch. He had worked for the local library system straight out of high school and retired when he was only forty-seven. At the time, Mitch envied his brother as he did not expect to retire until he was sixty-five.

One of the brothers' favorite parts of their country place was the garden. Both had grown up spending summers on their grandparents' farm and had fond memories of their time helping to work the fields, gather eggs, and do the daily chores of farm life. So, there was no question when Jason retired to the property and Mitch moved in shortly after that they would put in a garden.

The year Mitch moved in, as they began to prepare for planting season, Jason seemed to fatigue quickly. By the time planting began, he couldn't work the garden at all and sat in a lawn chair watching while Mitch did the work. Jason visited his doctor to try to discover what was causing the fatigue. A series of tests followed over the next several weeks until finally in June a diagnosis. It was cancer of the liver. Untreatable.

Mitch was stunned. The doctors said Jason had only a few months left. He would not see Christmas that year, and probably not Thanksgiving. Then the cardiologist called them in for an appointment and they learned that Jason's cancer was causing a condition known as Amyloidosis. His body was creating an extra protein that was settling in his heart where it would eventually stiffen the muscles and cause it to stop beating. The doctor could not say how long it would take the protein to do its work. It could be a month, a few weeks, or even just a few days.

Mitch and Jason came home and prepared for the

inevitable. Family was informed of the diagnosis. Mitch worked feverishly to run the household, coordinate visits from family and friends, and make sure Jason had every comfort he needed. But most worrisome to Mitch was the fact that Jason was not a believer. He had faded away from church in his teenage years and not returned. It worried Mitch now and he struggled to broach the subject with Jason. Talking about it would be emotionally difficult and Mitch was trying to maintain a semblance of normalcy in the house for Jason's comfort. As the weeks progressed and Jason's condition worsened, he developed a calmness that surprised Mitch. On several occasions, Mitch could hear Jason listening to gospel music in his bedroom and had hope that his brother was coming back to God. Mitch began to realize that his purpose was to serve his brother's physical needs during this time so Jason could reconnect to his faith privately.

On Jason's last day, the family had gathered on a Wednesday evening for a big dinner. There was a lot of laughter and teasing, just like always. It was a great time, and they all relished the moment. Mitch and his three brothers and two sisters had lost their mother when they were all young. Their father had died seven years previous to this day. So, the six of them had held on to each other and were closer than most families. They took their strength from that unity. They were a family of orphans but had each other. Jason's death at only fifty-five made them all numb for quite some time.

As Mitch came back to the present, he looked over at Mary carefully planting tomatoes and was grateful for how God had blessed them. Years of loss and loneliness had been replaced with a daily joy of living. The simple pleasures of life seemed like more than enough now. Just like it had been when Mitch and Jason had lived together.

Mary looked up from her work to see Mitch staring off in the distance. "Mitch, what has you so captivated? You look like you're someplace else."

Turning to her, Mitch responded, "I was. I was just thinking about my days with my brother and how peaceful they were. Just like our time now. That place Jason and I shared was so quiet and comfortable. The world could not interfere with our lives there. Much like it is here. And I am just now realizing that one of the things I was looking for when we were house hunting was a place like that. A place that would be our retreat from the craziness of this world. A place that required our attention and hard work. A place where, at the end of every day you felt like you had accomplished something meaningful. Like planting a garden, cutting the grass, tending the chickens. Doing basic things for basic reasons. A simple life."

"I understand," Mary said. "There is something special about this place. I've felt it ever since we moved here. It's like I have no great desire to be any place else. It feels like more than just home. It is truly a haven."

Mitch smiled. He and Mary often shared the same thoughts without realizing it. This was one of them. The more time they spent in their home, the more it felt consecrated somehow. It was more than a house; it was a gift. A gift they were meant to share. They were not sure exactly what that meant but looked forward to finding out.

The planting was almost done and none too soon. The sun was getting lower, and the air was getting a bit of a chill. Mitch stood from his work and surveyed their property. He prayed silently, *Lord, you brought us here for a reason. I don't know what it is, but you do. All we ask is that you guide us where you want us to go. Show us what to do and how to do it. And I pray we have the strength to endure what is coming. You have placed upon me a burden. I can feel it in my soul. I can also feel the danger coming. Not to our trust in you, but from this world. I pray for your protection for us. And if harm should come to either of us or our family or friends, I ask for your peace to help us through. Amen.*

When Mitch opened his eyes, Mary was there beside him. She had a slight smile on her face, and he knew it was because she enjoyed seeing him in prayer.

"So, can you tell me what you were praying for? Or is it just between you and God?"

"It's no secret. I was just asking the Lord to give us the strength to do what He has planned for us. And thanking Him for this place."

"Amen to that. It is a lot of work and I know we have struggled some days with that work. We are not as young as we used to be." She sighed and then continued, "Some nights I can hardly move. But then, I think about the results of our labors and know it will be worth it. Actually, I am excited to think about later this summer when we can bless people with the fruits of this place."

"Me too. Now let's go check on our hens and see how they like living in their new coop."

They had moved the young chickens, now two months old, to the chicken coop within the barn two weeks ago. They seemed to like the added room and the new places to play and cavort. In a few days, once they had acclimated, they would start letting them out into their run. It would be their first time outdoors and Mitch and Mary were looking forward to seeing the birds explore the open spaces. Of the fifteen chickens, three actually belonged to Dave and Denise. When they had first told them of their plan to raise chickens for eggs, Dave immediately declared he wanted to buy in to the operation. Mitch and Mary had planned to get ten chicks. Dave's three would make thirteen, so Mitch rounded up to fifteen when he picked them up at the feedstore.

Fifteen chickens, each laying an average of five eggs per week meant the flock would generate seventy-five eggs every seven days. Dave and Denise's share would be fifteen, leaving sixty for Mitch and Mary. They planned to give away to family and friends as many as they could but knew there would still be more than they needed. So, at least three dozen every week would go to the food pantry. The eggs would complement the weekly donation of produce from the garden.

It was all very ambitious. The large garden to tend, the chickens with their coop and run to be built. Mitch sometimes wondered if he was trying to recapture his younger years, and this was too much for a man of sixty. Those nights he fell into bed tired and sore, he questioned the wisdom of what they were doing. Everything had seemed easier before. Tilling and planting were fond memories. Now the work brought an aching back and stiffness in the morning. But then, accomplishing anything worthwhile took work and no one ever said work was easy. Mitch looked forward to their meeting with Pastor Fred in two weeks to discuss how what they were doing at the Haven could help those in their area.

7

JUNE 4

As the group settled into their seats in Dave and Denise's living room for the bi-monthly Bible study, the social chit-chat died down in anticipation of the topic for the evening.

Denise opened the conversation as she usually did with a prayer, then said, "Last time we began to discuss a section of the book of Mathew. We will continue that discussion this evening, but I would like to first read again the scripture to refresh our memories of what Jesus said.

"Mathew 24, verses 10 through 14, 'And many false prophets will arise and lead many astray. And because lawlessness will be increased, the love of many will grow cold. But the one who endures to the end will be saved. And this gospel of the kingdom will be proclaimed throughout the whole world as a testimony to all nations, and then the end will come.'"

Dave looked around the room and said, "Last week we talked about the false prophets and being led astray. Tonight, we will concentrate on the next verse, 'And because lawlessness will be increased, the love of many will grow cold.'"

Dave continued, "Let's take a closer look at the first part. What does it mean that 'lawlessness will be increased'? I am not looking for a great biblical definition here. What does it mean to you in your life? Where have you personally seen an increase in lawlessness?"

Joanna leaned forward and said, "Well, I can see it everywhere. I mean, every time I go out to shop or something, I see it. It can be something as simple as when you are approaching a door to a store or restaurant. I had it happen the other day. A man was a few steps ahead of me and he just walked right in, didn't even think to hold the door. I know it's not a big deal, but something like that used to be considered rude. Today, people aren't even paying attention to others. It's like the people around them don't matter."

"I know what you mean," Maggie added. "You know, Jesus says lawlessness here and everyone thinks that means committing crimes. But I think God's looking at this from a totally different perspective. Sure, we are seeing more crime, more murders, and things like that. Even if those crimes went away, the world would still be a mean, rude place. I cannot tell you how many times I have passed a stranger on the street or in a store. When or eyes meet, I say 'hello' or something to be nice. And almost all of the time, they don't say anything back. Sometimes they act like I did something wrong. I guess you would say that is a heart grown cold!"

Denise asked, "Do you think this is what the Bible is referring to? The way we treat each other?"

"In a way, I think it is," said Mary. None of these little incidents by themselves are that big a deal. But I think they are a sign of what is in people's minds and hearts. It is like speeding in your car. Sure, people have been going over the speed limit since cars were invented. But we all know that, lately, it has been getting worse. It used to be two or three miles over. Then five or six. It kept going up and now, if you are on the freeway going less than ten miles over, cars are flying past you. Most people will say it isn't a big deal. Just people in a hurry. But I think it is more than that. First off, it is dangerous and shows a blatant disregard for the safety of others. Secondly, driving recklessly says a lot about someone's character."

Dave asked, "Their character? How do you mean?"

Mary responded, "It's like this. When you go to get or renew your driver's license, you have to sign a form, right?"

"Right," Dave answered.

"And that form includes a statement that you will abide by all of the traffic laws when driving. Most people do not even read the form, but they do know they are agreeing to be a responsible driver when they sign. Well, if you sign that form and have no intention of obeying the traffic laws, you are a liar. And not just lying in the heat of the moment. But a deliberate lie, the worst kind."

"I see what you mean, Mary," Dave said. "I think we are on to something here. These little things indicate a breakdown in our society. I could add to the examples already given. I had a friend the other day who bragged about how a clerk mistakenly charged him less than the price of an item. He thought he made out. All I could think of was that my friend is a thief. If he knew the price of the item was more than he was charged, he should have told the clerk and paid the honest price. Now, my friend would never walk out of a store without paying for something. But isn't what he did just the same?"

"I think it is, Dave," Mitch jumped in. "And I think we are on the right track here. To jump straight to the really bad things going on misses how we got to this point. And Mary was right to bring up character. Character has been on my mind a lot lately. I can remember when character mattered. When schools taught children how to be honest, respectful, self-disciplined, and compassionate. And our society in general valued character. The message once was, 'regardless of your station in life, being a person of good character is worth more than worldly success.' Sadly, that isn't the case anymore. Children are taught they must succeed in the classroom and achievement is more valuable than character."

Maggie started to speak, but Mitch waved her off, "Present company excepted of course, Maggie. I know you try to teach your students the importance of character, but I think you are an exception. The point is the goals have changed. No longer are people trying to grow in wisdom and intellect. The only thing that matters now is to achieve, achieve, achieve."

"I see what you are saying, Mitch," Denise said. "And I think that ingraining to achieve has produced something else that is troubling. The absence of humility. The Bible tells us boastfulness is a sin, but nowadays, it is rare to see someone on a screen speak humbly and modestly. Whether it is actors, athletes, or politicians, there is an arrogance about their achievements. Of course, it is refreshing sometimes to hear a famous person thank God for their achievements. But look what usually happens to them. Tim Tebow was practically run out of the NFL because of his faith."

"And maybe that's okay, Denise," Mitch said. "While I agree it was wrong what the league and the media did to him, maybe he is better off. Once these industries, organizations, or leagues become so sinful, so evil, it is better for people of faith to separate themselves from them."

"This makes me think that I need to spend some time looking at what and who I am supporting with my time and resources," Joanna said. "I don't want to contribute to companies who are anti-Christian or that support things I don't believe in."

"Exactly," Mary responded. "That's why Mitch and I decided not to get cable TV when we moved to Mt. Olive. There is just too much violence and immorality on most of the channels. We also canceled one of our streaming services. You know, the one that was recently in the news for a show that portrayed children in adult situations." She shivered and continued. "We realized that we were supporting a lot of things we shouldn't have without knowing it. So, we started evaluating everywhere we spent money. The stores we shop at, what we watch on TV, where we eat, everything. And it amazed us at how widespread the sinfulness was."

Maggie asked, "Where do you find out all of this? I don't want to contribute to this stuff, but how do you know?"

Mitch responded, "It isn't easy. First is to completely stop watching the television news. I stopped years ago because I could see how the news was being manipulated. When I was in the news business years ago, we tried to honestly convey what was going on as best we could. Then there was an explosion of news channels on cable. Everyone was trying to get viewers, so the focus shifted from honest reporting to sensationalized stories. Then the 'analysts' started to show up on the news programs. And that is nothing more than someone's opinions. But people started to take these opinions as fact because they had always relied on the news shows for their information. They did not notice the shift from facts to opinions. Today, most of what is shared on a news program is opinion or an interpretation of events, not the actual facts."

"So, how do you figure out the truth of what is going on in our world?" Denise asked.

"Again, it isn't easy," Mitch responded. "My best recommendation would be to turn off the news on TV and the radio. Go online and read the news on websites. And read the news on a variety of websites, so you can compare what they are saying. When you do this, it is amazing how different the same news story can appear on different sites. And by comparing them, you will be able to pull the facts out of all the sensationalist noise."

"Good advice, Mitch," Dave said. "So, let's get back to our topic, lawlessness."

"Sorry," Mitch said. "Sometimes I get carried away."

"That's okay," Dave said. "These are important things to think about. Even though we are charged as Christians to not be of this world, we still live in it and need to know what is going on so we will not be deceived. Are there other examples of lawlessness you think relate to what Jesus said?"

Before Mitch could respond, Joanna asked, "Mitch, I know you were in the news business years ago, but do you really think they are lying to us? Why would they not just tell us the truth? I am having trouble believing an entire industry would do something so dishonest."

"A fair question," Mitch said. "Let me explain it this way. Here in America, we have our own culture. Now, it is a more diverse culture than anywhere else in the world because our country is made up of people from literally everywhere. But we still have a culture unique to our country. We have shared experiences—shared entertainment, shared recreational activities, shared traditions, and a shared history. We also have a shared set of values. Those values can and do change over time. Since its founding, our country had a shared value that embraced slavery and considered African Americans less than whites. It took a Civil War and years of effort afterward, but that value has changed completely. And it impacted not only African Americans, but all non-white people in our country. Today, as a culture we see everyone as equal, regardless of race. We have made that equality into law. But those laws could have never been made if our culture had not first changed. You see, a nation's laws are a reflection of its culture. And culture is the shared beliefs of a society."

Joanna jumped in, "Okay, that all makes sense. But what does it have to do with truth and with the news media?"

"I am going somewhere with this, trust me."

Joanna nodded her assent and Mitch went on.

"What I just described is the macro view of society, culture, and its laws. But under the surface there is a constant series of dynamics that can coalesce into major cultural shifts. For example, we have all seen in our lifetimes a shift in our entertainment culture. I can't imagine anyone arguing that our entertainment has not changed drastically. Movies and television programs used to depict situations where people faced difficulties in life and those stories almost always ended with the main characters learning something about themselves and becoming better people. Precious few still contain that valuable life lesson element. Instead, our entertainment devolved in to programs and films about personal achievement, sexual pursuits, and sensationalized violence. The industry calls it examining the human condition. But the reality is that it is nothing more than evocative entertainment designed to get viewers emotionally stirred. And as the exposure to these themes continues, viewers begin to adopt the values portrayed in the movies and shows. And eventually, those values assume a place in our national culture. How else can you explain the fact that cage fighting is now mainstream entertainment?"

"Cage fighting?" Maggie asked. "What is that? I've never heard of it."

"Good for you that you haven't, Maggie," Denise said. "We saw an ad for it the other day. I was stunned. All I could think of was the arenas of ancient Rome and the gladiators. I just don't understand why people want to watch something like that."

"I don't either," said Mitch. "But it wasn't like it happened overnight. Boxing used to be very popular, but then the public lost interest. Watching people beat on each other for money just wasn't valued anymore. Then, over the last several years, movies and TV shows kept adding more violence. Unfortunately, people responded positively to the increased violence and we saw a cultural shift toward acceptance of violence in our entertainment. And the cage fighting is really just a real-life version of the violence in entertainment. To answer your question, Maggie, cage fighting is two people, sometimes women even, in a literal cage fighting. Not just boxing, but kicking and whatever else."

Maggie responded, "That is disturbing."

"It is," replied Mitch. "Even more disturbing than the

actual fighting is that there are enough people willing to watch it to make it profitable."

Joanna piped up, "I see what you're saying, but what about the media and truth? What does all of this have to do with that?"

"Sorry again, I tend to go off on tangents easily. Okay, so back to our culture and how it perceives truth and leads to national values. So, the entertainment industry is a subculture that we see can impact our national culture with its activities. There are other subcultures. Professional sports and, to an equal degree, college sports. Corporate culture is another. Not the corporate culture a particular business has inside its walls, but the culture of professional achievement that drives people's perception of their worth. Then there is the culture of education. Mostly our colleges and universities and how they work together to train young minds into a particular way of thinking." Mitch continued.

"But I will stop there and get to the point to address Joanna's question. The news media is a subculture as well. What I saw happening when I was in the business was a gradual shift in how people in the business saw themselves. When I started in news back in the 1980s, we saw ourselves as gatherers whose job was to then pass along the stories we discovered to viewers, listeners, and readers. Over time, perhaps because news became more profitable and the on-air reporters and anchors became famous, news people started to see themselves more as the gatekeepers of information. They were now stars and highly paid ones. So, that must mean they were smarter than the average person and it was their job to decide what people needed to know. And that arrogance would naturally evolve into a belief that they not only should decide what information people should have, but also what they should think about that information. Now, if a group of people take it upon themselves to determine what others should think, and act on that belief, they are deciding what is true about any particular thing. Their truth becomes to them the only truth. They do not believe the public has a right to receive information and decide for themselves what to think about it. The media have already done that for them. So, this subculture, the media, is determining what the country should think and what it should value."

"Wow," Jim exclaimed. "I never thought about it like that. But it makes perfect sense. It does seem like the news is more about experts giving their opinions than it is about actual facts. But how does this relate to the lawlessness that Jesus talked about in Matthew 24?"

"Okay," Mitch relied, "I better bring this around to a conclusion. I really am sorry for the rabbit holes I keep going down. Mary knows all too well that, when I get started, it is hard to stop me. Getting back to the truth and lawlessness—so the news media has developed their own version of the truth. They have decided what is morally right and wrong and then use that as their foundation for how they report the news. There is no doubt that their perspective is anti-biblical. And here is how that contributes to lawlessness. The media has picked sides. Politically, religiously, and morally. The way they choose to portray newsmakers they agree with is with complimentary words and phrases. They will also convey the opinions of those newsmakers as being mainstream. Conversely, newsmakers that the media disagree with are labeled with negative terms and as representing a minority of Americans."

Denise said, "I see where you're going, Mitch. This is how right is called wrong and wrong is called right. How lies are called truth and truth is called lies."

"Exactly, Denise. There's more to it than that too. This manipulation of society by the media does something else. The total discrediting and malicious name-calling by the media of those they do not agree with has created an adversarial element to our culture. We see this clearly in social media where civil conversation is non-existent. People act is if anyone who disagrees with them is beneath contempt and not worthy of living. And this attitude is reinforced from other parts of our culture. The fanatical following of sports has deepened people's animosity toward anyone not on their 'team.' People are picking sides on everything. With this type of perspective, it is not hard to see why our culture is breaking down. The common experiences, values, and traditions that are the glue of a society are being swept away. What is left is a population of people bouncing from one cause to another, all the while believing those who are not part of their causes are to be hated and despised. A perfect storm that can only lead to lawlessness."

"This seems like a good place to stop for the evening," Denise said. "Mitch, thanks for your insights on what is going on around us. There is a lot to think about and even more to pray about. Next time, we'll look at a verse that contains some hope in these troubled times, but also a warning I think for Christians like us in a broken world. We'll discuss verse 13, 'But the one who endures to the end will be saved.'"

8

JUNE 8

"I am sorry it has taken so long for us to get together," Pastor Fred remarked as they sat outside a small restaurant in Sullivan. "I know you both have been anxious to talk about how you can minister to others. So, let me say grace and we'll dig into lunch and what you're doing up in Mt. Olive."

After Fred blessed their meals and they began eating, Mitch said, "Pastor Fred, we appreciate you taking the time to talk with us. We know how busy you are with the church."

"Not too busy to do God's work, Mitch. So, tell me what it is you are thinking. I know you said you have a big garden and some chickens but give me the details."

"Sure," Mitch replied. "As we mentioned before, we moved to Mt. Olive last fall. Mary and I are both retiring at the end of this year and we decided we did not want to retire in the city. So, we started looking for a place in the country last summer. At the same time, we were becoming concerned with the teachings and attitude of the church we were attending."

Mary added, "And that's when I suggested we attend Geneva. Remember, I attended a few years ago and really enjoyed the services, so we started watching the online services. When you reopened the church, we attended in-person."

"I do remember you both when we reopened. In fact, we had a lot of new attendees when we reopened the church."

"I can understand," Mitch stated, "The sermons were so powerful, still are, and we could just tell that this was a church that was not afraid to shine Christ's light on the world. I am not surprised others felt the same as us."

"Thanks for the kind words, Mitch. We are certainly blessed at Geneva. God has provided so many opportunities to serve Him. And there are so many in the church out serving their communities. I think that is what makes our church so strong in the spirit, our commitment to service. And I have a feeling that commitment is something you both want to be a part of."

"We do," Mitch replied. "I'll start at the beginning. When we moved to Mt. Olive, we were pleased we had so much room. Five acres is a big change from our postage-stamp lot in the city. I immediately started thinking about a garden. My brother and I had always had a garden and I couldn't wait to have one again."

"This was the brother who died of cancer?" Fred asked.

"Yes." Mitch nodded. "He became ill just as we were planting the garden that year. So, I suppose part of what I wanted to do was capture some of those great memories with my brother, and make some new ones with my wife."

Mary then spoke, "I was all for a garden too. We had small ones when I was younger, and I love cooking with fresh, home-grown vegetables. But when I saw the stakes Mitch had put in the ground to mark where the garden would be, I thought we were going to need a tractor!"

Fred laughed and queried, "So, this is a big garden then?"

Mitch replied, "It seemed big at the time. But honestly, as we planted seeds and plants, it did not seem so big anymore. We knew we were planting so much more than we needed. But then we thought of family and friends we wanted to share the harvest with, and the size made sense. And then, as we talked about it, we also realized, even sharing with our friends and family, we would still have quite a bit left. Then you mentioned the food pantry up here in a sermon several weeks ago and we knew that's where the surplus would go."

"Definitely sounds like a God thing." Fred grinned.

"No doubt about it," Mary responded. "And that's why we wanted to talk with you. We know the church is ministering to people here in our area and we thought the best way for our garden to contribute is to use the system already in place."

Fred had finished his lunch and pushed the plate away as he replied, "We do have a great ministry around Mt. Olive. It is mostly the southern half of the county, down where you are. I am sure we can find the best way to get your offerings into needy hands."

"Oh," Mary exclaimed, "The eggs too! We figure we should have four to five dozen a week to give away. That'll be an important protein source for those in need."

"Yes, it will," Fred said. "So let me talk to our ministry leaders and get things started. Now, I know you both will be so busy tending to everything there at your place, so I have a suggestion. We will determine who needs what in the way of groceries, make the lists based upon what you tell us will be available each week, and then our ministry leaders will come and pick everything up to distribute. That way you two won't feel burdened with the time and energy to deliver the food."

"That is perfect, Pastor," Mitch said. "We were worried a bit about getting everything into the hands in need. Although, I think we would like to come along sometimes so we can meet the people the church is serving."

"Of course," Fred responded. "I think that is a great idea. I think the people of your community should know who is helping them."

Mitch replied quickly, "We are not looking for credit or thanks, Pastor. Just knowing people will have healthy food on the table is all we want."

"I understand, Mitch. But I was thinking more along the lines of the people receiving the food understanding that Christian people have set aside part of their personal harvest to help others. Not about you two specifically, but about the love of Christ shared in this way."

"That makes sense," Mary said. "Now, Pastor, you also have to tell us how many eggs you want each week. We would love to provide them for you."

Pastor Fred chuckled. "No, those are for the people in need. I don't want you taking from them for me."

"We should have plenty," Mary replied. "Really, our estimates are conservative, and we expect, especially in the summer, to have more than we told you."

"Well," Fred responded, "I suppose a few every now and then would be okay. I do miss the taste of farm-fresh eggs like when I was a child in West Virginia."

"Great," Mary said. "As soon as they start laying next month, expect a dozen on your desk that Sunday."

Mitch changed the subject. "Pastor, I wanted to ask you about something else."

"Please do," Fred responded.

"Well, it is about the governor's new health orders concerning the virus. I think everyone was glad to hear that the restrictions were being lifted this summer. But the announcement that those restrictions will still apply to those who have not been vaccinated is troubling."

"It sure is," Fred replied. "This is something we have been discussing at the church. Trying to find the best way to respond to these potential obstacles to people attending services."

"Mary and I have talked about that too. But I have another worry. It is that making those who are not vaccinated still wear a mask will make them, make us, potential targets for harassment and eventually being banned from entering stores and other places."

"I share your concerns, Mitch. While I know some pastors have been encouraging their congregations to just obey what the governments are telling them to do with regard to the virus, I believe we have reached a point where faithful Christians must ask themselves if doing so will contradict their beliefs."

"That is exactly what we have been thinking," Mitch responded. "We believe our healthcare decisions should be private and not impact where we go and what we do. I am worried that this is heading down a slippery slope to something worse. To me, it seems like the virus is being used to take advantage of people's fears and get them to accept things they normally would not."

"I think you are correct, Mitch. Who would have thought that the powers that be in the country could have demanded everyone stay home and isolate for so many months and everyone went along with it? But that is what happened and is still happening. At Geneva, we have tried to be responsible when it comes to the health and safety of the people who enter our building. We did the online and outdoor services most of last year. But there comes a time when God's people must gather to worship and support each other. Honestly, I am surprised we haven't received any negative reactions to opening the church building last fall."

"I am as well," Mitch responded. "But don't you think it is just a matter of time? Especially, if these new orders will require all public buildings to ask for proof of vaccination."

"Yes, this will come to a head very soon. I expect we

will be hearing from the health department telling us to implement some sort of vaccine check at the doors."

"What will you do?" Mitch asked.

"I can tell you what we will not do. We will not turn away anyone who wants to enter the Lord's house of worship. The very thought of that infuriates me. Jesus accepted everyone who came to Him. He did not reject anyone who wanted to follow Him and we will not either."

"I am glad to hear this," Mitch said. "But I think our church and others who think the same are headed for some difficult times."

"I agree," Fred responded. "But the church is no stranger to persecution. If the day comes when we are prohibited to meet in our building, we will meet in secret just as those in the early church did. Remember, in places like China, Iran, and Turkey, Christians meet secretly to worship because being a Christian in those countries is illegal and, in some cases punishable by death. And here in our country, while we have challenges coming our way, we can still practice our faith without that kind of worry."

"Very true," Mitch said. "At least for now worshipping together is not a life-threatening activity here. But it could change in the future."

"It probably will," Fred replied. "That's why it's so important for us to stay strong in our faith and realize that this world hates us. They hate us because people have allowed their thoughts to be controlled by Satan. We are seen as narrow-minded, mean people who want to tell everyone else what to do. But of course, the truth is, God's people only want to share the amazing news of the Gospel and Jesus' love for every person. We are being attacked for preaching Jesus' plan for salvation as being exclusive and discriminatory. We are accused of denying people's right to make their own decisions about who they are. Nothing could be more inaccurate. As humans made by God, we are endowed with the freedom of choice. We can choose to follow Him or not. And with that choice comes accountability. We as the Christian faith do not tell anyone they don't have the right to choose, we simply relay God's message about the consequences of those choices.

Now, there are some churches that have chosen to avoid talking about many of these controversial topics concerning faith and the world. It grieves me to see some pastors preaching only of happiness and community and ignoring God's call for us to be apart from the world and to lead lives that exemplify God's commands. They do this to try to get more people in the building. But our purpose as Christians is not to increase our membership, but to save souls."

Mary commented, "That's why we now attend Geneva, Pastor. We were so disappointed that our previous church was choosing to get involved in political causes and cater to the gospel-of-prosperity crowd. It just felt so empty there and we were not challenged in our faith."

"And we are glad to have you both at Geneva. I'm so excited about this new feeding ministry you are starting. Jesus' feeding of the five thousand with five loaves and two fish wasn't just about nutrition. It was about serving others and showing the amazing things God can do for us. I am positive you both will have a similar impact in your area."

Mitch and Mary drove home from their meeting with Pastor Fred feeling a mix of energy and caution. They were energized about the potential to serve others with what they would produce at the Haven. They were cautious about the future of their church and other churches in a world that was straying so far from God's intent.

As they pulled into their driveway, Mitch looked over at Mary and said, "I am excited about our new ministry. It feels so right." He paused to wait for the garage door to open, pulled the car in and shut it off. He took the key out and turned to Mary and added, "At the same time, I'm worried about all this hate toward us and the church. It is not going to get better, only worse."

Mary smiled and replied, "Mitch, my dear, I know that we will get through whatever is coming. I agree that hard times are ahead. But remember, we are here in this place because we followed God's calling for us to create a haven for us and for others. I truly believe these coming months, while scary, will also be a blessing, and I cannot imagine dealing with all of this without you."

9

JUNE 11

It was a perfect summer evening in Wadesville as the Bible study group settled in on the deck at Dave and Denise's home. Maggie was in a good mood—her school year had ended and with that the beginning of her retirement. Denise was on summer vacation, her duties as a music teacher done for the year. Mitch was also in good spirits, his countdown to retirement had just gone under six months.

After an opening prayer, Dave opened with a reminder of their previous sessions and the topic they would now discuss.

"So, as we take a look at the twenty-fourth chapter of Matthew, specifically verses eleven to fourteen, recall that verse eleven spoke about false prophets and how many will be deceived. Then verse twelve explains how that deception leads to wickedness and a cold heart. And this evening we will talk about verse thirteen, 'But the one who endures to the end will be saved.' The question I have for us regarding this verse is two-fold. First, what does it mean to endure? And second, what does it mean 'to the end'?"

Jim started, "Well, to endure, I would say, means to not waver from our faith. To stay true to God and His ways."

Dave responded with another question, "I agree, but what do we think it is we have to endure? Temptation? Pressure to conform to the world?"

Joanna spoke up, "Temptation, of course. We are all tempted every day. Tempted to speak harshly, be selfish or lazy, judge others. But I think the real danger is to conform to worldly things."

"And what are some examples of how we conform to the world instead of to God's will?" Denise asked.

Mary responded, "We could do that by watching shows or movies that violate our Christian principles. Or gossiping about others just to fit in with the crowd. Or being coerced to accept a vaccine because the government tells us to, even if we believe it is wrong to do so."

Maggie added, "And we could be obsessed about money or material things. That can be a hard one for me. I watch my portfolio way too much sometimes. I am working on that, but it can be difficult to find the balance between obsession and just being mindful of your resources."

"I am right there with you, Maggie," Mitch responded. "I also think we can conform to the world by what we choose not to do. I was reading the other day about a lady in Finland who is being prosecuted for publicly stating her biblical beliefs. Just a minute, let me pull up the article so I get the facts right. Here it is:

"'Päivi Räsänen, a medical doctor who was Finland's Interior Minister between 2011 and 2014 and a leader of the Christian Democrats, has been charged with three hate crimes against homosexuals.

"The General Prosecutor of Finland has confirmed that, after an investigation of nearly two years, enough evidence was collected to open a penal process. Since 2019, Räsänen has been interrogated by the police on three different occasions.

"The politician will have to defend herself in courts for social media posts in which she quoted Romans 1:24-27 to criticize the participation of the Finnish Lutheran Church (of which she is a member) in the 2019 LGBT Pride festivals, for the content of a booklet about the Bible and sexuality, titled "Male and Female He Created Them" published in 2004, and her words in a radio talk show in the Finnish Public Broadcasting System, where she was invited to speak about the issue: "What would Jesus think about homosexuals?".'

"So, this lady, a former national government official is now facing a possible jail sentence for simply sharing her faith."

"That's crazy!" Joanna said. "I had not heard about this. It's kind of scary to think about."

Dave added, "I read the article as well. But there is another case, this one in the UK. A chaplain at Trent College in England has been reported to the British government's antiterrorism program for delivering a sermon in which he told pupils that it is acceptable to question and disagree with far-left LGBT ideology being taught at the school. Trent College claims it supports the evangelical principles of the Church of England but had invited an LGBT organization to help incorporate their beliefs into the college."

Jim responded, "So, this chaplain is in trouble for voicing what he believed, but the other group is invited to try to coerce the students to believe what they want them to? Does anyone see the illogic in this? It's free speech only if you speak what the government approves, otherwise, you go to jail."

"Exactly," Mitch replied. "And I think this is what verse thirteen is talking about. To 'endure to the end' does not mean to the end of our lives. In this context, where Jesus is speaking about the end times, I believe 'the end' means the end of this world. He is making the point that we will have to endure much more than we have before to stay true to our faith. As these prosecutions and persecutions increase, it will get harder and harder to avoid taking a stand. And how long will it be before something like this comes to our country? These cases are probably giving people ideas already about who they can target with similar charges."

"So, what does that mean for us?" Denise asked. "We are not in positions like these public figures, but will that protect us from potentially being targeted and accused of hate crimes?"

"Eventually, no," replied Mary. "I think it will get to the point that anyone who posts anything on social media that is Bible related will be targeted. The media created the label 'the Christian right' years ago to make people believe that Christians who hold to the Bible's teachings are ultra-conservatives who are racist, homophobic, and anti-science. And then the labeling of churches who hold to biblical teachings as 'fundamentalist' started. This was after the incidents with Jim Jones in Jamestown and David Koresh in Waco —where those cults were called Christian fundamentalist churches. So, now we have millions of people who associate Christian churches with those monsters who were controlled by Satan. It's frustrating, all we want to do is stay true to Jesus' teachings and love our neighbor. But today, doing that will get you labeled and in trouble."

Dave then said, "Okay, so obviously, to endure is a heavy thing that is only going to get harder. And when I think about that, I realize this is not something that just happened recently. I think we can all remember, when we were younger, going to church, vacation Bible school, and other faith related activities was considered normal. Of course, that was back when public prayer was considered just a part of our society."

"You are absolutely right, Dave," Maggie said. "When I started teaching years ago, mentioning God was no big deal. Now, we didn't evangelize to students, but we didn't have to hide our faith either. I can remember saying grace with my fellow teachers at lunchtime. If I did that now, I would get in big trouble."

"What are some other ways we have to endure to the

end?" Denise asked. Maybe some things we have to do or not do that are not so obvious."

"Well," Betty responded, "Jim and I always say grace when we are at a restaurant. Sometimes, I get the feeling that people are watching us and making judgments about us, just because we are praying. It can be uncomfortable, but I am not going to stop thanking God for my food and for His grace."

"A great example, Betty," Denise affirmed. "What are some other ways?"

Joanna stated, "Sometimes I find myself starting to say something to a friend who doesn't go to church that is church related, and I don't because I think it will make them uncomfortable. But this same friend may talk about a TV show that is immoral or say some curse words in front of me and that makes me uncomfortable. So, why shouldn't I express what I want to? Afterwards, I feel ashamed that I didn't speak my mind and say what I wanted to or even to challenge my friend when she says things that make me cringe. I guess I don't want to endanger our friendship. But that makes me think I am valuing that friendship more than I do my faith in God." Joanna turned her head in thought and continued, "But I do value my faith more than anything. So, if a friend is offended by my mentioning something about my beliefs, I guess they will just have to be offended."

"It is a challenge, Joanna," Mitch responded. "In my job, I have to remain neutral about so many things because I am a community leader. I self-regulate anything I say publicly or on social media. Sometimes it is frustrating, but it comes with the job. That's why I am so looking forward to retirement and being able to speak my mind more freely."

"So, Mitch," Maggie asked, "Do you feel like you are compromising your faith because of your job?"

"I don't think so," Mitch replied. "It is frustrating sometimes, but I am paid to do my job, which is politically and culturally neutral. Thankfully, I don't have to address any issues that would cause me to deny my faith. If that were the case, I would not hesitate to resign. I am just praying that nothing comes up in the next six months to change that."

"We will all pray for that for you, Mitch," Dave said. "This has been a good discussion this evening. We covered a lot of ground and hit on some challenging things going on in the world. Next time, our topic will be a bit more positive. Verse fourteen in our section of Matthew 24 is, 'And this gospel of the kingdom will be preached in the whole world as a testimony to all nations, and then the end will come.'"

10

JUNE 17

It was the kind of summer morning that you would dream of in the winter. Sunny, but not hot. A slight breeze, just enough to keep the air fresh. Mitch could not think of a better place to be than here at his favorite local golf course with his best friend, Matt. He and Kate had come up last Friday evening for the weekend. Mary and Kate were hitting the local antique shops and garage sales, while the two men were at the course.

Looking out over the expanse of deep green grass and the mature trees as they waited for their tee time, Mitch felt at peace. Golf had become a therapeutic getaway for him. He often played by himself and used the time to talk to God and, more importantly, to try to listen to Him. As he would make his way around the course, enjoying God's creation, it somehow helped to make things clearer in his mind. He knew the insights and new perspectives were a result of letting God into his heart and mind to guide him. The disconnect from the world that came with a round of golf didn't hurt either.

As the two sat in their cart watching the group ahead of them tee off, Matt asked, "I did not get to take a close look when we got in yesterday, how is the garden doing?"

"Really well," Matt answered. "Everything we planted came up, except for a few corn seeds which we replanted a few weeks ago. And the wheat and field corn in the back of the garden are up. I am looking forward to harvesting both this fall."

"You sure are ambitious. I can't blame you for milling your own wheat for bread. Not after having some at dinner last night. But to grow, harvest, thresh, and winnow it will take a lot of work."

"True, but we have come to the conclusion that spending more time with our basic needs will keep us healthier, both physically and spiritually. Besides, I think it will be fun. And, we won't have to worry about finding the wheat berries in the stores as things get harder to find."

"I understand. I think you're wise to grow the corn for the chickens. I just saw that the price of corn has more than doubled since last year."

"Exactly. We decided to grow the corn as feed before the prices started to go up. I wanted to because it reminds me of my grandfather's farm and how he did the same for his chickens. But now I wonder if it wasn't a prompting from God."

"That could be. We usually think God only nudges us

about big things. But the truth is, He is constantly guiding us in the right direction. That is, if we will let Him."

"Amen to that. Looks like we are up."

Both men stepped out of the cart and approached the first tee. Matt was the big bomber of the two. Mitch contented himself with staying straight and making the best of his limited abilities. As he prepared to hit his ball, Mitch wore a smile. Life was indeed good. He swung and hit the ball down the middle of the fairway a little more than 200 yards. *A good start*, he thought.

"Nice shot," Matt commented, then stepped up to his ball and took a mighty swing. The ball soared high in the air and passed Mitch's ball before it began its descent, finally landing and rolling almost 100 yards past Mitch's.

"Looks like your swing likes you today," Mitch said.

"Let's hope it lasts the entire round," Matt responded as they returned to their cart and headed down the cart path.

"Mitch," Matt then continued, "What do you make of this effort to bring together the world's religions? I am hearing some pastors say it is just good people trying to make the world a better place. But our pastor last Sunday said he believes it could be the beginnings of the false church and the false prophet spoken of in Revelation."

"I think your pastor is right, Matt. I have always been in favor of churches in a community working together to aid those in need. But this is something altogether different. What these people are talking about is fundamentally changing their beliefs to create something new. As I understand it, they say that the major religions should not be so exclusive. Even the Pope said last year that he believed Christians, Jews, and Muslims were all praying to the same God."

"That doesn't make sense. The god of Islam instructs followers to persecute and even kill Christians and Jews. It's simply illogical to say the three have the same god." Matt remarked.

"I agree. It doesn't make sense. But the problem is, to those who don't study the Bible or the Torah or even the Koran, it sounds so appealing. Look, I think this is about people wanting to genuinely find common ground and reduce the tension between these three religions. They sincerely want to do some good. The trouble is it is exactly those beliefs that are in conflict that are the foundation of each religion."

They arrived at Mitch's ball and he continued as he pulled a nine iron from his bag.

"The Jewish faith believes they are God's chosen people who should obey His law and await the Messiah. Christians believe that Jesus is the Messiah and His instructions supersede the old law. Muslims believe Mohammad then brought a new set of rules to the game that now should be followed. So, you have the Jews who believe Christians are following a false Messiah in Jesus. The Christians believe Muslims are following a false god in Allah. And the Muslims believe the Jews were not God's chosen people and should be eliminated. Add to that the fact that the Jews see Muslims in the same way they look back at the Babylonians, and the Muslims see

Christians as literally Satan, and Christians see Jews as a people who crucified their savior."

Mitch approached his ball and got ready to hit, but he paused and looked up at Matt to add, "Now everything I just laid out is not just each religion's perspective. How they view the others is an expression of their fundamental beliefs. Yes, if you take those conflicting views away, the three groups should get along. But let's be honest. If you remove what each group believes is their orders from God, you are not left with a religion. I don't know what is left, but it certainly isn't a religion."

Mitch took a breath and eyed the green up ahead. He swung his club and the ball arched skyward, landing about ten feet from the hole. As he came back to the cart, he looked at Matt and said, "Don't get me wrong, I would love to see the religions of this world stop all the violence and hate between each other. And honestly, who wouldn't. But if it comes at the cost of me watering down Jesus' message of salvation, no way. You might achieve some peace on earth for a time, but it will have nothing behind it."

"I agree with you," Matt said. "I wonder, too, what impact it would really have on all three. I mean for people who are committed followers. I don't see dedicated Jews, practicing Christians, and devout Muslims changing the way they think about God. What I do see happening is that this world religion effort will appeal to people who don't already attend a church, synagogue, or mosque. And if enough people around the world do that, the other three will be pushed aside and their beliefs minimized, if not outlawed someday."

"Good point, Matt, it could very well happen that way. Here is something else to think about. One of the powerful parts of our faith is the way Jesus minced no words about what it takes to get to heaven. In the Gospel of John, He said, 'I am the way and the truth and the life. No one comes to the Father except through me.' Nothing ambiguous about that. But that is what people don't like about it. There is no room to maneuver. Academics in our universities have been teaching for decades that there are no absolute truths. Everyone has their own personal truths based upon their experiences and perspectives. I see this effort to create a new global religion as an extension of that thinking. I have read some of what these proponents say. They believe the new religion should accept all forms of belief simultaneously. Sort of an 'I'm okay, you're okay' philosophy like back in the 1960s."

"And we know what came of that. Drugs, pornography, violence, immorality, and abortion," Matt offered.

"Sadly, yes. And this effort to make a new religion that can appeal to everyone around the world will be no different. It will have to rely on relative truth for its foundation. And relative truth is nothing more than a house of cards, ready to collapse at any moment. But it does fit in nicely with the rhetoric we have been hearing lately that is all about living your best life and being your best self. Not to mention the warning in the Bible when Paul wrote to Timothy,

"'People will love themselves. They will love money. They will talk about themselves and be proud. They will say wrong things about people. They will not obey their parents. They will not be thankful. They will not keep anything holy.

"'They will have no love. They will not agree with anybody. They will tell lies about people. They will have no self-control. They will beat people. They will not love anything that is good.'"

"Amen to that," Matt responded. "It can be discouraging sometimes to think about all of this. I can see the downward spiral and do not understand why so many cannot. Like my two sons."

Mitch responded, "Or my siblings and their children. It can be distressing. All we can do is try to be the best example we can and hope someday they will think back on our words and care for their souls and make the right choice."

"Looks like you made the right choice with that nine iron," Matt said as they arrived at the green. "Nothing better than a birdie putt to start the round."

11

———

JUNE 28

As Mitch scanned the headlines while enjoying his morning coffee, he stopped on one that read, "Western U.S. may be entering its most severe drought in modern history." Clicking on the story, he read scientists claimed the region is on the precipice of permanent drought. Starting in the year 2000, the Western US entered the beginning of what scientists called a megadrought—the second worst in 1,200 years. The US Drought Monitor placed 60 percent of the western states under severe, extreme, or exceptional drought. It wasn't just the lack of rain in the summer. Winter totals for the preceding winter were only 25-50 percent of normal for California and the Southwest.

Mitch sat back and pondered what he had just read. He had been following the story of the drought for a while, so the news was not a total surprise. Experts had been claiming the severe drought was from human-caused climate change, but Mitch wasn't so sure. He remembered the passage in 2 Chronicles, Chapter 7, verses thirteen to fourteen: "When I shut up the heavens so that there is no rain, or command the locust to devour the land, or send pestilence among my people, if my people who are called by my name humble themselves and pray and seek my face and turn from their wicked ways, then I will hear from heaven and will forgive their sin and heal their land."

Violence, lawlessness, immorality, drought, what would it take for people to pay attention to what God was saying. The violence and lawlessness were a natural result of society's turn toward materialistic things. Gone were the expectations that people would act kindly and respectfully to each other. All that mattered was getting as much as you could as fast as you could. People were living lives of comparison instead of lives of compassion. Idolizing celebrities, athletes, and business leaders had resulted in a hunger for more money, fame, and stuff. It did not matter how you got it, as long as you did. But there could never be enough of any of the three to fill the empty spot in people. They were trying to insert worldly things into the place God had intended to live in each person's heart. The more people crammed into that space, the worse the world became.

Mitch sighed and wondered how much longer things could go on like this. He was glad they had decided to bite the bullet and have the well drilled. While he did not necessarily expect the drought to move East, the continued dryness in the West would call for some drastic measures—like diverting water from the Midwest.

Mitch was about to go back to the headlines when he heard footsteps on the stairs leading to his office. Mary appeared, cup of coffee in hand and a smile on her face.

"Good morning, Mitch," she greeted.

"Good morning, my love. Sleep well?" It was a question he asked often as he was always concerned his early risings would disturb her.

"Slept just fine," she replied as she settled into the leather chair next to Mitch's desk. "So, what is the news this morning?"

"Water," Mitch responded. "Or rather, the lack of it. The drought out West is getting worse and no one expects relief any time soon. Water rationing is tightening and I think it is a matter of time before tempers are short and things explode out there."

"I am sorry to hear that. I just think of all of those people struggling. Not the ones whose lawns are drying up, that is just superficial stuff. I am thinking about the farmers, nursery owners, and others who need water for their businesses. It has to be tough."

"I am sure it is," Mitch said. "I can't help but wonder if this isn't all connected to the state of our country. I mean, this drought has now been going on twenty years and experts say it will only get worse. While the water in the West has declined for those twenty years, so has our nation's morals."

"Sounds like the Jews of biblical times. When they

turned from God, things started to go bad. How many times did that happen and they never learned?"

"I am not sure," Mitch replied. "But I know every time they did, it cost them as a nation. It eventually resulted in their utter destruction by the Romans for not accepting Jesus as Messiah."

"Mitch, do you think this virus is another of God's punishments? This one for the entire world."

"I don't know. It could be. Or it could be a mechanism for God's overall plan for mankind."

"How so?"

"Well, and this is just my opinion, it could be that the fear the virus has caused, which has led to a blind obedience to authority, and then a willingness to get vaccinated, is a practice run for the mark of the beast."

"Really? Like conditioning people for it ahead of time. I can see that. This talk of an international proof of vaccination is scary. It doesn't take much of an imagination to see it evolving to some sort of permanent identification."

"Exactly, what could start as a means to determine if a person is medically safe could quickly become a form of a global ID system."

"The worrisome part of this," Mary added, "Is most people will not give it a second thought. They're so afraid of getting sick, they will do anything to feel safe."

Just as Mitch was about to respond, an alarm went off on his computer. He had set it up to receive alerts about certain news items and this one showed a financial warning. He quickly maneuvered to the news story link and began to read. As worry creased her husband's forehead, Mary asked, "Mitch, what's going on?"

"It's a financial alert for a story." He quickly scanned the article, then switched to a screen monitoring the stock market. What he found there was disturbing. The market was in freefall, heading down faster than he had ever seen. It wasn't just the Dow or Nasdaq, it was everything. Stocks, bonds, gold, silver, everything.

Mitch turned to Mary and said, "The market is taking a nosedive. A big one. Actually, all of the markets."

"Oh no," Mary responded. "That's not good. Did something happen?"

"I'm not sure," Mitch replied. "Let me check." He scanned through and a pattern began to emerge. It wasn't obvious at first, but as he read a variety of stories, it became clear.

"It doesn't look like one specific thing, but a combination. And that makes it more dangerous. The market knee-jerking to a specific event is usually very short-lived. But this looks like a fundamental loss in confidence. The consumer price index is still rising, as is inflation. Materials and parts shortages are shutting down production lines around the country, and interest rates are continuing to rise. Combined with the recent tax hikes, you have the perfect storm for a quick slide into recession."

"So, just a recession? We've been through that before."

"Yes, we have. But there are some disturbing circumstances along with what I explained."

"Like what?" Mary asked.

"Well, new housing starts have slowed to a trickle. The

rising cost of building materials have finally had an impact and people have stopped building. That and fears of food shortages. Remember how we read about the cost of corn doubling almost overnight from demand? That led to a subsequent rise in meat prices. So, naturally, as meat prices rose, people started buying more non-meat products and that demand has caused those prices to rise. Add to that the high cost of fuel and the lack of drivers to move freight around the country, and our entire economy becomes very fragile."

"Sounds like a very complex situation."

"It is. It is so complex that most people cannot see how it all ties together. The climate change people celebrate high gas prices because they think it will help the cause. The folks who do not like the stock market say all it does is make the rich richer and do not understand how it funds pensions in this country. The food situation could be better if we as Americans did not throw away about a third of the food we purchase. And finally, our decadence and desire for more has pushed our economy into a position where the luxuries drive more of our GDP than the necessities do. And that means that, when the economy slows down, the luxuries go first, creating the downward spiral."

Mary looked at Mitch, taking in what he had just said. "So, what does that mean for us? You keep track of our investments, are we in trouble?"

"Too soon to tell. Things could settle down and be okay. The markets could rebound tomorrow. But remember, our advisors switched us to low risk investments this year since we are retiring in December. That should protect us from the worst of it."

"And if it doesn't stabilize and continues to go down, what then?"

"Then we trust in God to see to our needs. We have been careful with our decisions and we've set up this place so we can live with minimal outside supplies. If worse comes to worse, we'll get by."

12

JULY 4

What had for over 200 years been a celebration of a nation's founding had become a day of protests and hate-filled speeches. Somehow, the founders of the country had now been transformed from wise men who valued freedom to nothing more than rich, entitled old men who succeeded at the expense of others. No one could point to exactly why the founders were now perceived as bad people, but the mantra continued every day. Mitch saw it for what it was. Evil doers had known for centuries that a lie repeated often enough would become truth to the people. Hitler practiced it to deceive the Germans. And communists had used the technique effectively in many countries. And now the American media and academia were doing the same.

As Mitch read the news coming across his computer screen, he was saddened. *When had people become so disillusioned?* he wondered. Why were people focused on viewing through a contemporary lens those from the past? Why not celebrate all the nation had accomplished? It had been a long struggle to achieve the equality expressed in 1776, but they had done so. And the work continued to eliminate discrimination and inequity. But it seemed that was too much to ask. It caused Mitch to consider why so much dissent and trouble existed in his country. Why did America hate itself so much?

Mitch sat for a while, thinking about the condition of the world when a scripture verse came to mind. He grabbed his Bible and opened to 2 Timothy where he read:

"But understand this, that in the last days there will come times of difficulty. For people will be lovers of self, lovers of money, proud, arrogant, abusive, disobedient to their parents, ungrateful, unholy."

There it was. The answer to his question. People today were proud, believing themselves smarter and better than anyone who had come before them. Arrogant in their thoughts, assuming that they knew better than their ancestors. Abusive to anyone who did not agree with them and their interpretation of history. Disobedient to their parents by forsaking the values they had been taught by their parents and grandparents. America had become a land of lovers of self. And, if a person loved themselves above everything else, they acted accordingly. *Enough negative for the day*, Mitch thought as he shut off the computer and headed upstairs. *Time to get ready to celebrate the holiday.*

Their little village of Mt. Olive was too small for a

parade, but Gerard, the county seat to the north wasn't. Mitch and Mary settled into their lawn chairs on the main street and awaited the parade's start. All around them were American flags, bunting in store windows, and neighbors chatting with each other. Mitch smiled and thought, *This is what July Fourth is about.*

"You look happy," Mary said. "Care to share?"

"Oh, I was just enjoying the atmosphere. It is amazing when you look around. People are glad to be together again. The isolation of the virus made people forget that others are just like them. We all go to work, cut the grass, have dinner, and all the other things we do every day. Being separated meant people's knowledge of their neighbors near and far was limited to what they were told by politicians and the media. But here, today, what those people say is irrelevant. They can see for themselves that we are all part of one community. Not divided, not hating each other. This feels good."

"I agree," Mary responded. "It is so nice to be out and see people together. And what better day to see it happen then today? Isn't it in the Constitution about the freedom to gather?"

"It is," Mitch replied. "It is part of the first amendment. Just like most of the Constitution, it was a radical idea at the time. Along with the right to assemble, the rights to follow your own religion, free speech, and to defend yourself. In 1776, governments were monarchies, with a King or Queen who made all the decisions. The people had no say."

"Well, I am certainly thankful we live in a country where we enjoy so many freedoms."

"Agreed," Mitch responded. "At least for now."

"Now don't go down that road today, dear. Let's just enjoy the parade and have a good time."

"You're right. No negative thoughts today."

They both turned to look as they heard a marching band begin to play. As the parade went by, Mitch enjoyed the smiles on everyone's faces. Waving flags were everywhere and other patriotic signs abounded. Thinking back to the first July 4th, Mitch realized that, despite the condition of things that day, it was truly a miracle that the country had survived for more than 200 years under the principles established by the founding fathers. But then again, how could you go wrong when your premise rested upon the inalienable rights granted by God?

13

JULY 10

The Bible Study group had decided to meet at Mitch and Mary's for the evening and both hosts were happy their friends were there. The garden was in full bloom with some of the earlier vegetables already being harvested. The group's meal included fresh lettuce, sweet peppers, and onions from the garden. Tomatoes were only days away from ripening and the sweet corn was filling out nicely. As the group settled in after the meal, Mitch ran down to his office and returned with a stack of papers.

"What do you have there, Mitch?" Maggie asked.

"Some things to share for this evening's discussion," Mitch responded.

"I am looking forward to talking about tonight's verse," Betty said. "It certainly is more pleasant than the first three we have discussed."

"Indeed, it is," Denise commented. "So, let's get right to it. We have been looking at four verses in Matthew 24, eleven through fourteen. This evening, verse fourteen, which reads, 'And this gospel of the kingdom will be proclaimed throughout the whole world as a testimony to all nations, and then the end will come.'"

Mitch stated, "Betty, I agree with you in some sense that this verse is more positive than the others, but I did some research, and the numbers say something different." Mitch began distributing the papers he had printed the previous night. "There are a number of international mission organizations that are working to identify peoples who have not been reached by the Gospel. You'll see on the page that Global Media Outreach's recent study indicated forty-two percent of the people on earth have not been exposed to the message of salvation."

"Forty-two percent," Joanna commented. "That is amazing. With all the missions going on, I would think that number would be lower."

"I thought that too," Mary said. "But what Mitch found out is that many of the places that are unreached are that way because those in power prevent it. Like it says here lower down on the page, the Joshua Project report indicates only about ten percent of Muslims in Asia personally know a Christian, whereas about seventy percent of Muslims in North America know a Christian. Only about fifteen percent of all Muslims worldwide personally know a Christian. And Asia is the most isolated continent with less than twenty percent of the more than

4.5 billion people claiming to know a Christian. Eighty seven percent of all Hindus, Muslims, and Buddhists have limited, if any, contact with a Christian."

Mary continued, "The main reason these people don't know a Christian is because, in most cases, it is illegal to be one."

"Turn to the second page," Mitch asked. "Here is some information on what is called the 10/40 window. The 10/40 window is an area on the map in northern Africa and Asia that's northern border is at 10 degrees north of the equator, with a southern edge at 40 degrees south of the equator. It is a large rectangle that contains the overwhelming majority of those unreached by the Gospel—ninety percent."

"Wow!" Maggie exclaimed. "So, is anything being done to reach these people?"

Dave spoke up, "From what I have been reading, the worldwide missions have begun to shift focus to this area, but it is a challenge. In some of these countries, if you are found to be a Christian missionary, you will be killed. The least you will be punished with is to be kicked out of the country. And some of the cultures are so hostile to the Word, just having a conversation about Jesus is dangerous."

"Exactly, Dave," Mitch responded. "But there is good news as well. Look at the bottom half of page 2. There you will see what has been going on in the last twenty years to preach the Gospel. As a result of the 2000 Billy Graham Conference on Evangelization, reaching unreached groups has become a priority. And since 2005, in the 10/40 range, 409 organizations have sent 29,500 full-time workers in 4,957 teams to engage 3057 unique people groups for the first time with the Gospel! They have planted 139,671 new churches and report 3,237,647 believers among these groups."

"It goes on to say, 'today there are only 261 people groups with populations of more than 500 people that remain unengaged.'"

"It sounds like we are getting closer to reach the entire world then," Betty observed.

"We are," Mitch replied. "And I think the point is, we won't know when that happens. Only God will. He is the only one who can monitor the progress of the Gospel in real time. Which means, Jesus' statement that the Gospel of the Kingdom will be proclaimed throughout the whole world could happen at any time."

"Amazing," Joanna said. "What you said about God being the only one who will know makes sense. I get the statistics, but I don't think God is waiting for the statistics people to declare the Gospel has reached the whole world. Only He knows when that will happen and exactly what qualifies to meet what Jesus said."

"A good point, Joanna," Denise said. "So, as we sit here this evening in the middle of a country where we can hear the Gospel freely, what does all of this mean for us as believers? What do we do with this information?"

Jim had been carefully listening to the conversation up to this point, but he finally spoke up. "Well, for one, I think it means we should consider supporting missionary efforts more. Especially those in the 10/40 area." He paused and thought a moment. "But it seems a little strange in a way."

"How do you mean," Dave asked.

"It's like, we want everyone to be reached with the Gospel, of course, but doing so brings the end of the world. I mean, I look around at all the craziness going on—the violence, immorality, and such—and see it's leading us to the end times. It never occurred to me that something good, like preaching to people would also do that."

Dave responded, "That is an interesting observation, Jim. I had not thought of it that way either. It reminds me of the hymn, 'Come, Lord Jesus Come.' If we do want Him to come, there is something we can do to help that happen."

Maggie sat up and said, "Now this is interesting. Sometimes, when I get really down about the world, I pray for the rapture. I just want to be taken away from all of this evil. And what you are saying, Jim and Dave, is that, instead of just praying for it, I—we can do something about it."

"So, what do we do then?" Mary asked. "Perhaps we should think about supporting the missions as Jim has suggested. I can talk to our pastor and see where our resources will be most helpful."

"That's a good idea, Mary." Denise said. "We'll look forward to hearing what you find out."

"There is something else I would like to talk about," Joanna said.

"Please go ahead," Dave said.

"Well, remember a few weeks ago when we were talking about the people in Finland and England who were being prosecuted just for being Christians and sharing the scriptures?"

"Yes," Denise responded.

Joanna continued, "I remember when we discussed it, we thought it could not happen here in America. Well, it is happening."

"Where?" Maggie asked.

"In California. A pastor there has been charged with hate speech for preaching a sermon explaining that God intended marriage to be one man and one woman. And the government there says that is hate speech against people who live a different lifestyle."

"Seriously," Betty said. "So, just sharing what the Bible says about marriage is a crime?"

"According to the article, yes. The accusers say that the Bible's teachings are anti-LGBT, anti-abortion, and intolerant, so they should be classified as hate speech."

"Intolerant?" Mary asked. "How is the Bible intolerant?"

Joanna responded, "On that one, they say it is less the Bible than it is Christians who say Jesus is the only way to salvation. The claim that believing that is being critical of other religions and thus intolerant."

Mitch responded, "The very basis of Christianity, and for that matter any religion is its belief that it is the only true belief. Are they going to go after Islam as well?"

"I don't know about that," Joanna replied. "The article didn't mention any other religions except Christianity."

"Disturbing," Dave added. "Actually, I found a startling statistic recently. The most persecuted religion in the world is Christianity. The report said in 2019, 340 million people were persecuted for their Christian faith. It also said that thirteen Christians are killed every day, twelve churches attacked every day, and that these numbers are an increase of sixty percent over the previous report."

"That is troubling," Mitch said. "340 million is a huge number. But, when I think about it, maybe it shouldn't be such a surprise. Let's say you are a Christian and share your faith on social media. Then you apply for a job and the company looks at your pages and sees you are a Christian and decides not to hire you. That could be because the hiring manager is an atheist or had a bad experience with Christianity in their youth. Or it could even be because they don't want to endanger the reputation of the company by hiring people that could get attacked on social media. Any way you look at it, it is discrimination bordering on persecution."

"I agree, Mitch," Denise said. "It's one thing to push God out of public life, as has been done lately, but what is going on now with Christians being ostracized is more than that. It is a form of persecution."

Dave then said, "I think we have reached the conclusion to our discussion this evening. But I would like to briefly look at the last few words of this verse. 'And then the end will come.' While I think it is good that we have been discussing for several weeks now Jesus' words regarding the end of days, the reality is, none of us knows when our personal end will come. I would like to think we would all be together until Jesus calls us home. But that is just a wish. We don't know what the next days, weeks, or months hold in store for us."

Dave paused when he noticed the group was listening intently and wearing somber faces.

"Sorry, didn't mean to end on a down note, but thought I would just mention that. We have all suffered the loss of loved ones in our lives and have been blessed that this group is still whole. I hope it stays that way for a long time."

Later that night, as Mitch and Mary lay down to sleep, Mary said, "I have been thinking about what Dave said." She propped herself up on an elbow and continued. "Mitch, I do not think I could endure it if something happened to you."

"Same for me, Mary," Mitch replied. "That caught my attention too. I wonder what prompted Dave to say what he did?"

"I don't know," Mary replied. "He always seems to bring up a perspective on a topic that gets you thinking. I just don't want to think about this one. It is too scary to contemplate."

"Agreed. After my mom died when we were all so young, we clung to each other. And when Dad died, my siblings and I grew even closer. We took strength from the fact that we still had each other. When Jason died, it was like something shattered. For the longest time we were just going through the motions at our family gatherings. We knew we needed to keep them going, but the absence of Jason made them feel hollow."

"Oh, Mitch, I can't even imagine how hard that was."

"It was. Over time, it got better. The family dynamic changed; it was different. But the feeling of family returned the way it was before. For me, knowing I will see my mother, father, and Jason again is a comfort. I just wish it was the same for the rest of my family."

Mary responded, "There is always hope and we will continue to pray that they turn to the Lord. What else can we do?"

"Prayer is definitely the right thing to do. I just wish they would at least consider returning to church. But it seems like, the longer people are way, the harder it is for them to come back. And, what really bothers me is, if they do not repent now, doing so after the rapture will mean suffering and danger like has never been seen before. I know, after the rapture, my siblings will see it for what it is and know what happened. I'm fairly confident they will come to faith. But the thought of them going through the tribulation scares me."

"Mitch, I share your concerns and have the same for some of my distant relatives. I am thankful my girls, and other close family are believers. All we can do is pray and try to be a light in the darkness."

"Of course, you are right. And I have been thinking, this place, our haven now can be the same for my family after we are gone. At least, I hope it will be."

"It will, Mitch. We know that one of the reasons God

brought us here was so that we could provide just such a place."

Mitch took Mary by the hands and looked into her eyes. "Another reason why I love you so much. Your caring heart is a constant reminder of God's love for us and my family. He sees what we need and what they will need in the times to come."

14

———

JULY 17

As Mitch watched the numbers quickly climb while he gassed up the pickup truck, he wondered how much worse things would get before God called His people home. At $4.75 per gallon, gasoline was now a major expense for them and for everyone. America's commuter society relied on affordable fuel and he knew the constant rise in gas prices was beginning to take a toll on the economy. The relief everyone had been feeling as the virus receded during the summer was now being replaced with an unease over the slowing economy and inflation. And Mitch's job as a tourism director was feeling the pinch. The optimism of the spring when people began to travel again after a year of isolation was beginning to wane. The summer months were supposed to be the busiest for travel and had been so until gas prices steadily increased.

And the growing call for a chip implant program in

Europe was cause for more concern. Even though the virus was following its natural course and new case counts were plummeting throughout the world, European leaders were still pushing for vaccinations and the implant as a reliable means to verify those vaccinations. Mitch knew it would only be a matter of time until the same effort would start in the US. He hoped it would delay long enough for his scheduled retirement in December. If not, he wasn't sure what he would do. He was certain he would never accept the vaccination, regardless of the consequences. He had little trust in the people telling everyone the vaccines were perfectly safe. A recent article he had read detailed how vaccine after-effects were only being tracked if the patient reacted within the first fifteen minutes at the vaccination site. No monitoring of side effects was being done in the following hours or days. And a more disturbing news item he had just read explained that the CDC was looking into multiple cases of fluid buildup around the heart in young men who had been vaccinated. He wondered how many more problems existed with the vaccines that were being covered up or under reported.

Hanging up the gas nozzle and seeing he had just spent $104 to fill up his tank, Mitch shook his head and said a quick prayer, "Lord, as much as this expense pains me, I know there are so many who simply cannot afford to put gas in their cars. Please be with them and comfort them and help them find a way to get by during these awful times. Lord, I pray that our leaders turn from their current ways and look to you for guidance. I pray they seek to serve you and those in this country who are struggling, instead of their misguided efforts to turn our nation away from You and Your way. Amen."

As Mitch got in his truck and fastened his seat belt, he noticed an SUV squeal its tires as it took off from two pumps away. An attendant came running out of the gas station yelling at the driver. Mitch quickly realized that the driver had taken off without paying for the gas. And he noticed as the vehicle sped away that it did not have license plates. *This was planned,* he thought. He wondered if it wasn't simply a case of theft, but one of desperation. Perhaps the driver was out of work and needed a full tank to look for a job? Whatever the case, it was obvious things were deteriorating quickly.

Mitch pulled away from the station and headed for home with a sense that this was just the beginning. People would become more desperate, and the rules of a civilized society would break down. As he drove, he thought about what more he and Mary could do to prepare for the difficult times ahead. One thing he realized was that gasoline would become an issue. Perhaps they should consider doing something about that soon.

When Mitch arrived home, he relayed to Mary what had happened at the gas station.

"I don't think the gas problem is going to go away, at least not anytime soon."

"What can we do?" Mary asked.

"I was thinking about that. We could get one of those elevated gas tanks like you see on large farms. Some of them hold 200 gallons of gas. And I expect that, buying it in bulk would be cheaper than at the pump."

"Then I think that is what we should do. I know we don't drive that much, but who knows how bad this will get. We could see shortages like back in the 1970s again."

"We could. I will do some checking in the morning and see if we can't get a tank and get it filled this week."

Mitch let out a large sigh, prompting Mary to ask, "What is it, dear? You seem deflated."

"More like disappointed. I was just thinking about a year or so ago. We were dreaming about retirement and the places we would go and things we would do. Remember? We talked about taking off for several weeks and just driving across the country."

"I remember," Mary responded. "It was going to be our great adventure."

"It was. But now, our world has grown so small. The idea of driving around the country seems too risky. With violence escalating and the threat of an economic collapse, it just doesn't make sense to travel too far from home."

"Perhaps not. I understand your frustrations. I wanted to see my stepbrother and his family in California, but no way do I want to go out there now." Mary looked aside as she furrowed her brow. "And it makes me a bit angry to think about it. We should be able to go wherever we want whenever we want. This is the United States after all."

"I agree, dear. We should, and for some people, that is still the case. We could, too, if we choose to ignore what is going on in this country—and around the world for that matter. Let's be honest, most of our friends and some family would say we are being paranoid. We are overreacting to the news. But we know that is not the case.

We are not blind to the lawlessness that has spread everywhere. Our country is a tinderbox just waiting for a spark to ignite a firestorm of hate and violence."

Mitch rested his hands on Mary's shoulders and continued. "We don't know when our society will go over the edge, but we both know it will be sooner rather than later. Much as we are trying to live our lives here on earth in preparation for eternity with God, we are choosing to make decisions about what we do and where we go in the same way. Yes, we could throw caution to the wind and travel, shop, eat out, and go wherever we felt like. We certainly can afford it. But we both recognize our place is here. God has put us right where we are supposed to be. On this land doing what we are doing."

"You always seem to see through the clutter of things, Mitch. You start out being frustrated about something and, by the time we are done talking, you've cleared away the debris to find what really matters."

"I don't know about that, but I do know that what we are doing here is important. We are getting prepared to do God's work and serve others. Do I sometimes get frustrated? Sure. But I guess I've learned to accept the way things are. Our lives might not be turning out the way we expected, but I wouldn't trade it for anything."

"Nor would I," Mary responded. "We have a good life here at our haven in the country." She gave Mitch's arm a quick squeeze. "You go check on getting that gas tank. I have to go collect some eggs from the barn."

15

AUGUST 1

Abbeyand Mitch had just finished dinner when Mary's phone rang. She answered it to Abbigail's usually fast talking kicked up several notches.

"Slow down, Abbey," Mary said. "I can't understand what you are saying."

"Mom, what am I going to do! Did you see the notice from the hospital?"

"Yes, I received it today by email," Mary responded. The email came late in the afternoon announcing that all hospital staff would be required to be vaccinated. The email explained that, by October 15, all staff were required to provide proof of vaccination to their Human Resources departments for continued employment. Failure to do so would result in immediate dismissal. There were exemptions, Mary had read, but they were narrow and few. One was for religious beliefs, but that exemption only applied if one's religion banned all vaccinations. In other words, you could not claim an exemption based upon your personal belief. So, Mary's argument that she did not want to inject her body with something that would alter God's creation was meaningless. Mary sighed and returned to the phone.

"Abbey, dear—we talked about this a few weeks ago. We knew the day was coming."

"I know we talked about it, but I didn't think it would actually happen."

"The important thing now is to try to stay calm and come up with a plan."

"I am trying, Mom, but I can't lose my job. What else can I do? I can't go to another hospital; they're all going to have the same requirement. Maybe I should just get the vaccine."

"Do you really mean that, Abbey?

"No. I don't. I can't go against my convictions. Both medical and spiritual. There is a reason why so many of the hospital staff have not been vaccinated. We know there is something not right about this. And, of course, I will not compromise my faith by getting injected with something that could alter my body."

"I am glad to hear you say that. Stay strong in those beliefs."

"I will, Mom. But what am I going to do? We don't have much time before the deadline. What are you going to do?"

"I'm still thinking on that. I had hoped to make it to December when I retire, but that doesn't look like an option now. I will probably look for something here near Mt. Olive."

"Will you try for an exemption? That might work."

"I will try. My doctor may write one for me if I can convince him it could be risky with my asthma and allergies. But I am not counting on it."

"Well, at least you don't have to worry about working for long. I, on the other hand, have an entire career ahead of me. Or at least I did until now."

"Abbey, I know this is frustrating and you cannot see a solution. But you know where your help comes from."

"Yes, from the Lord."

"Right, so I think our best course at this point is to turn it all over to the Lord. He will have a solution for both of us."

"You are right, Mom. It won't be easy. With Nick and I planning to get married next year, this just makes it more complicated."

"Perhaps not. You were planning to move to Tipton when you got married, right?"

"Yes."

"Why not move early? Start looking for a job there now. Sure, it may not be what you had in mind, but you would be close to Nick and your sister."

"That does sound appealing. It isn't what I planned, but it could work."

"Abbey, do you remember when Mitch and I bought the house in Wadesville? We said this would be our retirement home. No more moving. And look at us now. We thought we were content there, but we are so much happier here in the country. It wasn't something we could have foreseen, yet it has turned out better than what we had planned."

"Good point, Mom. I will think on it. And pray, of course."

"That's the best we can do, Abbey. Pray and be open to whatever God has for us."

"Thanks, Mom. You always talk me down off a ledge."

"You are welcome, dear. So, you are good now?"

"Yes, I'm good. I'll talk to you tomorrow and we can discuss options for us both."

Mary hung up the phone and sighed. She turned to Mitch who had just entered the room.

"You know, Mitch, when the news came today, I wasn't so much worried about my job. I was more concerned with Abbey's. She is just getting started in her career. She is good at what she does and has such a compassion for her patients. It makes me angry that it is being taken away from her by these people."

"I know, dear. It all seems so ridiculous to us. But we live in a world where people are scared. They have moved so far away from God that everything that happens causes a panic. People are so fragile today. Without the peace and contentment of God's grace, they see everything as a crisis and it must be solved. Even when there isn't really a crisis at all."

"I guess all we can do is pray. All we can do! Listen to me. I talk like prayer is a last resort when it is actually the first and best option. And you know what, Mitch? How many people are in worse shape than us? Sure, leaving my job four months earlier will be inconvenient, but it won't be disastrous. How many others will have to go from good paying jobs to minimum wage just to keep working at all?

"I suspect many will. Healthcare is such a specialized field that the skills don't transfer to other sectors easily."

"Correct. And I was planning on working somewhere local, not in healthcare, when we retire. I can just do that a little earlier."

"A very good point. I will still be working full-time through the end of the year. Nothing like this will happen with my job. I think we'll be okay."

"Yes, we will. By the grace of God."

16

AUGUST 15

He knew it was coming. Had read about it for a few years, but it was still a bit of a shock to see it in print. The World Economic Forum had met in Singapore and announced their effort to move the planet to a one-world currency, followed by a one-world government. It was all being pursued, they said, to deal with poverty and discrimination throughout the world. But Mitch knew that the real reason the powers behind the forum were escalating their plans was to consolidate their power. The Forum had labeled their plan the Great Reset. The plan called for reworking the global financial systems into one system with one currency. The problem with that, Mitch realized, is that a global currency would mean a global economy. And a global economy would be susceptible to catastrophic events. Since the industrialization of the globe, the separate economies acted as a buffer when one nation, or even a few, went into a recession. Other economies in the world would chug along and provide global stability while those in recession could rebound. A one-world economy would be so large, recovering from a recession would take decades instead of months. And the depth of such a recession that was world-wide would devastate far more people than one more regionalized.

And what was amazing was the fact that so many people around the world were welcoming the plan. They had bought into the argument that the world should be one large community. They believed the contention that a world-wide community would eliminate racism, poverty, discrimination, and environmental damage. On the face of it, it seemed to make sense. But Mitch knew that the reality was something far different. Combining the world's unique cultures, governments, and regional traditions into one would create a homogeneous society that would quickly lose its diversity. The effort to make everyone feel a part of the same global society would erode the differences that made life on earth fascinating. Mitch shook his head as he thought about the ultimate extremes of a global society. You would not be able to go to an Italian or Chinese restaurant. Or a Greek festival. Or anything that celebrated uniqueness.

But what concerned Mitch more than the threat to cultural richness was the threat to freedom. A one-world government, by its very nature would be a totalitarian government. The old axion that nothing corrupts more absolutely than absolute power would be played out in the coming months and years. What had kept the world as free as it had been for the past century or so was a diversity of cultures and economies. Like some free countries acting as examples to others and leading the people of a nation to demand their freedom. Not to mention the tension inside a country between its people and the government. That tension—the people holding government accountable through the ballot box—was the mechanism that maintained a balance of power in a country. A one-world government would have free reign to do whatever they decided was best for the planet. Dissenters would be ignored at best. At worst, persecuted or even jailed.

Mitch sighed in resignation as he recognized that another of Satan's steps in destroying the earth was being accomplished. And then he thought about the millions of people around the world who would suffer because of it. Some could see where things were heading and felt helpless to fight it. Others were welcoming it, but would realize, much too late, that the promises were all lies. And Mitch's heart ached for the ones who did not know Jesus and whose despair would be so deep that they would be hopeless. All the more reason, he thought, to reach as many people as possible with the Gospel.

Later that evening, Dave and Denise joined them for dinner. They had come up for a visit and to pick up their share of the eggs. Of course, Mitch and Mary sent them home with fresh produce from the garden as well.

When they settled down at the dining room table for coffee, Mitch asked, "Dave, Denise, how are things in Wadesville?"

Dave responded, "Not good, Mitch. We went uptown

the other evening for dinner like we usually do and the sight was depressing. Many of the restaurants and shops have closed. There were few people on the sidewalks. It just had a feeling of abandonment."

"That is so sad," said Mary. "I have so many great memories there with you both. So, what is causing these closures?"

Denise replied, "We talked to some of the places still open and they told us it's several things. Some of the businesses simply couldn't keep enough employees to stay open. With government income subsidies and the growing feeling of entitlement, no one wants to work anymore. And many of the ones who do get hired act as if they should get a paycheck for just showing up, not actually working."

"That is very disappointing to hear." Mitch commented. "Are there other reasons?"

"Yes," Dave said. "We were also told that the coming requirements to have vaccine certification checks in place added more cost to operating than the businesses simply could afford."

"I guess we shouldn't be surprised," Mitch said. "The powers that be do not value our local businesses in this country. The large corporate retailers and restaurants chains have been so aggressive in dominating the markets, it is a wonder small business has held on as long as it has. And then there are the online retailers. They spend so much money marketing their shopping experiences that people forget what it is like to shop in-person. And that means all the money in our economy will eventually pass either to the corporate world or the government. A scary thought."

"It is indeed," Denise said. She paused and looked at Dave before she continued. "We are also noticing something else equally as disturbing."

"What is it?" Mary asked.

"It's at our church. You both know we have not felt connected to the church in Wadesville for quite some time."

"Yes," Mitch responded. "We do, and we've been keeping you in our prayers about that."

"Thank you," Denise said. "What has us concerned is that the church is hinting that it will soon require all attendees to be vaccinated and provide proof of vaccination."

Mary responded, "I can't believe a church, of all places, would deny entry to anyone for any reason. That is so not Christian!"

"I agree," said Dave. "But our larger concern is that some of our friends think it is a good idea."

"Are you talking about Maggie and Joanna?"

"Yes, and Jim and Betty as well."

Denise said, "We're struggling with how to handle this. With how to talk with them about it. We feel we have to say something, but don't want to push them away because we think differently about this."

Mitch responded, "That's exactly what Satan wants. He wants to divide us in every way he can. For centuries he has been successful dividing the church with the different denominations and beliefs. None of those differences were important, but he got millions over the years to buy in to the belief that their version of Christianity was superior to all others."

"Now he is working inside the churches to deceive and divide," Dave said.

"Exactly," Mitch replied. "It goes back to what we talked about in our group earlier this summer. False teachings that sound good on the surface but are nothing more than worldly pursuits. I was reminded of this the other day when I was reading in the book of Job. The Bible is full of stories about people struggling in life. And the main message is that life is a struggle, but all worth it if we have faith and believe in Him. Not the faith that is taught in many churches today. They teach members to have faith that God will give us what we want. But the Bible does not teach that at all. It says we should have faith in God's promise of eternal life. That eternal life with Him in heaven is perfect. Life on this earth is far from that. Sadly, many have been deceived into believing that we can create a better world here and now. And our churches getting so involved in social justice are doing just that. Our call is to save souls, not right the world's wrongs"

Denise commented, "I agree, Mitch. We have seen opportunities to directly serve others through our church drying up. Everything now is about protests and yard signs and using social media to influence change. And with that has come some clear political messages as well. It isn't feeling much like church anymore."

"I am so sorry, Denise," Mary responded. "I know this must be difficult. Especially since you've told us how unsatisfied you are with that church but feel obligated to remain there for our friends' sakes."

"Thanks, Mary. I'm not sure how much longer we can in good conscience keep attending. But we will wait upon the Lord and He will show us the what and when in His time."

"He certainly will," Mitch replied. "In the meantime, I will repeat the offer I made earlier this summer. You're always welcome to join us for services at Geneva whenever you like." Mitch looked at Mary and she nodded, knowing what was next. "And I will also let you both know that you are also welcome here at our home when things in the city get too dangerous. You know we believe God brought us here for a reason and that reason is to be a haven for those who need it. I never thought things would happen so quickly that we would even be talking about it now, but I'm glad we listened last year and came here."

Dave replied, "Thanks, Mitch. Denise and I have talked about Geneva and your offer to come here. I don't think now is the time though. Our place is still in Wadesville, ministering to our friends and doing what we can there. Honestly, I hope it never gets so bad that we would have to leave our home. We've been there for so many years, it would not be easy to walk away."

"I understand," Mitch said. "I realize what I am suggesting is no small thing. We both just want you to know that this place is here if and when you need it. I feel like you do, I hope things do not keep deteriorating. I truly do. I would much rather ease into retirement and enjoy life for a while. If that is God's will, then I will enjoy every moment of it. If not, I will try to enjoy every moment of whatever He has planned for us."

"A great way to look at things, Mitch," Dave said. "We so appreciate you and Mary as friends and supporters. We'll keep you updated on things in Wadesville. You just keep things going here. I have a feeling it won't be too long until you will have to put up with us every evening for dinner."

"And that would be our pleasure," Mitch replied.

17

AUGUST 25

Now that the garden was finally in full harvest, Mitch and Mary kept busy delivering food to needy families around the county. Pastor Fred had connected them with other churches in the area as well as senior organizations to identify the greatest needs. They delivered the fresh sweet corn, tomatoes, cucumbers, peppers, green beans, potatoes, and cantaloupes on Mondays, Wednesdays, and Fridays. Of course, every home received a dozen eggs as well. Mitch and Mary enjoyed delivering the groceries each week and getting to know the people they were helping. And, when it felt right, they asked if they could leave a Bible for the family. Surprisingly, not one family they had asked had said no. In fact, they seemed touched by the offer. One young mother, Jenny, told them that she remembered reading the Bible in Sunday School when she was a little girl, but never had one of her own.

As they made their way home on that Wednesday, having stopped at five homes, Mitch said to Mary, "When I first mentioned the idea of helping others with our little mini farm, I never dreamed it would be like this"

"Like what?" Mary asked.

"So much not like work. Even though I knew it would be rewarding and satisfying to do, I also knew it would be hard work. But none of this is work. It is a joy to go into the garden every day and bring in the vegetables knowing where they are going. It makes me smile just to think about it."

"Oh, Mitch, I know what you mean. This is so much more fun than anything else. But there is one thing that concerns me."

"What's that, Mary?"

"Well, it's just that there are so many more families who need help and encouragement. We can get to fifteen families a week, but we know there are so many more."

"I've been thinking about that lately as well. We certainly have the time to visit more families, but I don't think the garden is producing enough for more. Maybe we can find some others with gardens who are willing to contribute. If all they have to do is harvest and we deliver, I am sure they will want to help."

"Yes, I think they will. I can ask Nancy and Tim next door if they can help with more eggs."

"Great idea. We'll start on that as soon as we get home."

They were just pulling into their driveway when

Mitch's cell phone rang. He glanced at the screen and saw it was Matt.

"Hello, my dear friend, how are you and Kate?"

"We are doing well, Mitch. What about you and Mary?"

"Just getting home from delivering produce to our neighbors."

"That is a great ministry you have going, Mitch. Wish we were closer so we could help."

"Me too," Mitch replied. "But I sense that's not why you called. What's up?"

"I take it you haven't been tracking the news this evening since you've been on the road. Something has happened in California."

"Well, if it happened in California, chances are it is not good."

"Not good at all. A pastor in Sacramento has been arrested and charged with hate speech."

"Hate speech? Is this about marriage again like in Sweden and the UK?"

"Not this time. He was arrested for a sermon in which he stated that the only way to heaven is through faith in Jesus Christ."

"Seriously? How in the world can they call that hate speech?"

"The article I read said that authorities have interpreted the pastor's words as denying others their right to practice their religion. It says that the pastor is free to promote his own beliefs but cannot disparage the beliefs of others."

"Let me get this straight," Mitch said. "Repeating what the founder of our faith, Jesus, said about getting to heaven is now illegal? That is insane."

"I don't think sanity has anything to do with it anymore. In this age where inclusion is the only thing that matters, saying anything that excludes people from something will not be tolerated. What's ironic about all of this is that many of the people who call this hate speech don't even believe heaven exists."

"Then why do they care what a pastor says in the pulpit?"

"Honestly, I think it is more about shutting up Christians. They don't want the message of the Gospel shared publicly because they don't want to hear it themselves. Evil doesn't want to be reminded of their enemy. If they can shut us up, fewer people will come to Christ."

"Well, I hope the case gets thrown out of court," Mitch replied. It has to. If this pastor is convicted, that is the end of the church publicly. We will all have to go underground. I expected this during the tribulation, but not now."

"I agree. But the reality is that things are moving quickly and all the momentum is on the side of evil."

"Okay, I will take a closer look at this tonight. But for now, we need to get the word out and activate some prayer chains for this pastor."

"We'll do so down here, Mitch."

"Thanks, Matt. Talk to you soon."

Mitch sat in the garage, staring at the steering wheel.

This is all happening too fast, he thought. Mary put her hand on his shoulder.

"Mitch, I heard enough to know what happened. Don't let it rattle you. We can't fight this from here. What we can do is continue our work and help those in need and share with them the Good News, and trust there are believers in California who will get on their knees and be strong for God."

Mitch placed his hand on top of Mary's and said, "Of course they will. As bad as things are in that state, there are still many Christians who are courageous and faithful. You're right. We have our job here to reach as many as possible."

18

SEPTEMBER 7

The Labor Day weekend had come and gone and Mitch, on his way home from work, wondered if anyone had even noticed. Sure, people enjoyed the three-day weekend, but did they stop to think about why? For Mitch, Labor Day had special meaning. His father had worked his entire life in construction. Locally at first, then with a company that built large buildings throughout the Midwest. Those buildings were a constant reminder for Mitch of his father's commitment to his family. When he drove into the city, the state capital, Mitch would drive past a hospital, hotel, state office tower, and more that his father had worked on. He had worked hard, not stopping until a heart attack, at age fifty-eight, forced him to retire.

While Mitch did not follow in his father's footsteps for a career, he had learned the value of honest work. He wondered what his father would think of the world today.

It seemed to Mitch that the thirteen years since his father died had brought so many changes, most for the worse, that his father would barely recognize it. People no longer visited each other, and when they did, they spent all of their time looking down at their screens. Neighborhoods like the one Mitch grew up in were long gone. Mitch's family lived in a neighborhood of whites, blacks, and Latinos—and everyone got along. Kids played in backyards regardless of color. Neighbors helped each other and socialized together. Today, those same neighborhoods had a tension in them that was palpable. They had been told for so long that they could never be equal, never live together in peace, they had forgotten they once had.

As Mitch pulled into his driveway, Mary was hanging clothes on the line to dry. When he parked the truck, he thought about how the sun was getting lower each day at this time and soon fall would be here. The garden had done well and the pantry was stocked with canned tomato juice and sauce, pickles, potatoes, and, soon, sweet potatoes. The freezer held dozens of quarts of corn, green beans, and peppers. They were ready for winter, but what about next year? Would they be able to find seeds and plants for the garden? Would they even be allowed to buy them without a proof of vaccination?

He figured they had enough for next year's planting, but not beyond that. They could hold back seeds from whatever they grew, so that would help. He was glad he had done the research and they had only grown organic and heirloom vegetables. Seeds from those varieties could be planted successfully. Seeds from hybrid varieties could not. The seed producers claimed the hybrids grew better and were more nutritious, but the truth was, hybrids were developed so people could not keep seed back for future use. Rather, they would have to buy more each year. *Just one more example of how we are being manipulated,* Mitch thought.

When Mitch entered the kitchen from the garage, Mary was just coming in the back door. Her smile prompted one of his own as he enveloped her in his arms and kissed her.

"So, how was your day, my dear?" He queried.

"It was good. Work was tolerable and I sent out five job applications today."

"Good for you. Something will turn up before the deadline at the hospital."

"I know it will. Still, it is stressful with only five weeks left before I have to leave my job."

"Any word from your friend in Vernon Heights?"

"Not today. That possibility would be perfect for us. Vernon Heights is close by and I've known Bonnie for years and would enjoy working with her. She is a good Christian woman."

Mary had lunch with her friend, Bonnie, a few weeks ago and shared that she was looking for a new job. Bonnie then told Mary her company was looking to expand to Weirton to the North and she would need someone to run the Vernon Heights location. Mary had never thought of working for a Heating & Cooling company, but somehow, it seemed like the right place.

"Well, if it's supposed to be, it will happen."

"Of course, it will. So, did you see the email from Pastor Fred?"

"No, when did it come?"

"About twenty minutes ago. Oh, right, you were on your way home."

"Have you read it yet?"

"Not yet. Why don't you go down to your office and read it while I finish dinner?"

"Sounds like a plan."

Mitch went down to his basement office and booted up his computer. While he was waiting for it to do so, he wondered what Pastor Fred's email was about. *Probably not something good,* he thought. Mitch speculated that it was probably in response to the news today about the pastor in California who had been arrested for the crime of saying Jesus was the only way to heaven. Or hate speech as the prosecutor had called it. The criminal court had convicted the pastor and that had been appealed to the federal appeals court—which had announced today that they had upheld the conviction. Mitch knew the appeal process would likely go all the way to the Supreme Court, but also realized the final outcome would not change. True Christianity had been so demonized by politicians, the news media, and others that the very culture of the nation had changed and so many people, including judges, no longer respected the teachings of the Bible.

Mitch sighed as he opened his email account and found the message from Pastor Fred. He began to read the email:

My dear friends in Christ,

As I write to you today, it is with a saddened heart. Our once great nation, founded on Christian principles and the belief that God is our creator and provider, is in a tailspin toward destruction.

We have long known that the number of true believers in our country has been shrinking. As false churches have arisen, preaching the gospel of prosperity or of a distorted interpretation of God's love, fewer and fewer churches are left that are faithful to the scriptures as written. Today, one of the pastors of those faithful churches seems to be headed to prison for simply repeating what our savior told to us many years ago when he said, 'I am the way and the truth and the life. No one comes to the Father except through me.'

Never did I think we would be on this earth to see such a day as this. I will admit to you that I thought such persecution of the faithful would happen after the rapture of the Church. But it is clear that God's plan for these times is otherwise. So, my brothers and sisters, what does that mean for us at Geneva Church? First off, it means we will continue to gather and to worship as we always have. I can assure you, I will continue to preach the Word of God the same as before. We will not avoid saying or doing what we are called to just to avoid trouble with the authorities. I am prepared to face the same as our brother in California if that is what it comes to.

My question to you today is this. Are you prepared to do the same? Today, evil is focused on pastors. Tomorrow, it may be all Christians. And that means you. I ask you to pray diligently for strength and courage. I ask you to assess your own personal situation and think about how you can be prepared for what is coming. I also ask you to think about how you may be able to help others who will find themselves in difficult situations because they will not deny their faith.

We do not know where this is headed. Jesus may call us home any day, any moment. But, until then, let us prepare ourselves calmly and with resolve.

Any wishing to help others who may soon be jobless or in need, please contact the church office and we will let you know how you can help.

I leave with these verses from scripture:

Romans 8:18

"The pain that you've been feeling, can't compare to the joy that's coming."

Isaiah 41:10

"Don't be afraid, for I am with you. Don't be discouraged, for I am your God. I will strengthen you and help you. I will hold you up with my victorious right hand."

Jeremiah 29:11

"For I know the plans I have for you, plans to prosper you and not harm you, plans to give you hope and a future."

And that hope and future are not of this world. Our treasure is in heaven and our eyes should be there as well.

With Christ's love,

Pastor Fred

Mitch sat and stared at the screen. Pastor Fred had written exactly what he had been thinking about lately. Mitch had always thought that, even though the world was turning evil, those in Satan's grasp would wait until the faithful were gone to begin their evil task in earnest. But now, it was clear that evil was out in the open and moving fast. Satan was trying to turn as many as he could from the faith before the rapture. Before they were beyond his reach. And sadly, it seemed the plan was working. More and more churches were following worldly values and not biblical ones. More people, even those who attended faithful churches, were starting to believe the lies of the feel-good culture. More were getting vaccinated and believing the lie from the government that they were doing so for our own safety and security.

What was worse, many of these same Christians were now shaming those who did not take the shot. Their accusations were laced with hate and cruelty. Perhaps they had been fueled by the ever-growing number of businesses that now required proof of vaccination to enter. The herd mentality was in full force and people were rushing headlong toward a totalitarian nightmare. Mitch thought, many of these same people, when evil finally revealed its true nature, would realize they had made a mistake.

Mitch realized that it had been naïve to think the world would go on as normal until they were called home. More accurately, he had wished and hoped things would be okay until then, but deep down he knew they were getting worse. Mitch also realized it had to be this way. After the rapture, those who were left behind and chose to believe would face unthinkable persecution. And that would not happen out of nowhere. Satan had been laying his foundation of hate for many years. He had lit the pilot light with the cultural revolution of the 1960s and was about to turn on the burner. Now was the time that Christians were being set up as radical, wrong-thinking troublemakers. Then, after the church was gone, it would be so much easier for Satan and his followers to hunt down and destroy any who dared to defy him.

Well, Mitch thought, *if this is the way it will happen, so be it. We'll face it as best we can. And,* he said to himself, *we had better be ready to take care of ourselves and others too.* With that he climbed the stairs and entered the kitchen. Mary looked up from her phone and said, "I just finished reading pastor Fred's email. What do you think?"

"I think it was right on point and a good reminder of what is coming."

"A reminder to be prepared as well," Mary replied.

"Yes, prepared for the worst. So, I'm thinking we need to do a complete inventory of everything in the house and barn and start stocking up now before prices go up more and the shelves are empty."

"I agree. I can do a food inventory. Just the non-perishables since we can't buy more than a week's worth of fresh foods."

"Good idea. But we can get canned or frozen vegetables and fruit. Greens are a problem though. I guess we will have to make do without them."

"Maybe not," said Mary. "We can plant lettuce in pots inside by the windows and at least have that."

"That will work. Great thinking."

"So, what are you going to work on then?"

"I think I'll expand the garden. Give us a little more

room next spring. We have to think in terms of not going to the grocery store at all."

"Do you think it will come to that?"

"I don't know for sure. There are a lot of people in Washington talking about a vaccine passport requirement for all public places. But if we prepare for the worst, we won't get caught short. And not just for us, but also to have an abundance, so we can help others."

"Well, in that case, we also need to find more canning jars and lids. More garden means we will be putting up more in the pantry."

"Agreed."

———

THREE DAYS LATER, Congress passed and the president signed a new law that mandated all public places require proof of vaccination for entry. This included all retail stores, including grocery stores as well as restaurants, doctors' offices, and hospitals. In fact, the new law required hospitals to vaccinate any incoming patients who had not received the shot. Protests broke out across the country with enraged citizens decrying the government's intrusion into their private lives and personal medical decisions. But little could be done about it. The few members of Congress who vehemently opposed the law were ignored by the media, essentially stifling opposition within the government and leading the public to think there was no opposition. And the social media outlets compounded the suppression of free speech by deleting any posts critical of the law by labeling them "misinformation."

Mitch watched it all unfold and knew that the country had taken a step down a path from which there was no return. Government never relinquished any control over the people once obtained. Just the opposite. As the politicians and bureaucrats gained more power, they hungered for even more.

19

———

SEPTEMBER 12

Digging potatoes out of the ground was hard work. Mitch had done it often enough, but not for several years. He and Mary toiled under a typical mid-September sun and humidity. But, as Mitch surveyed the growing pile of potatoes, he did not mind the aches and pains in his back, arms, and shoulders.

"Mary," he said, "Just look at that."

"Yes, it's impressive."

"Not only that, but it's also a living testament to how gracious God is. A year ago, we had just found this place and one of the things we said was best about it was plenty of room for a garden. Here we are harvesting every day. Yesterday, it was more sweet corn. The day before that a dozen cantaloupes."

"And don't forget all of the tomatoes this past week!"

"Yes, those too. God placed it on our hearts to plant this garden, and to make it bigger than what we personally needed so we could provide for those who are in need. Now, He's blessed this garden for that use."

"Yes, He has. We can also see that blessing in the basement. I don't know where I am going to put any more jars down there. I suppose we shouldn't worry about that though. I suspect we will be giving them away very soon."

"Yes, soon. With this latest tax increase and inflation, people have less money to buy food. Well, to buy anything. But what worries me most is the thought of families going hungry."

"I know, Mitch. It worries me too. I think we are doing all we can to help. Between the abundance of this garden and the dry goods we have stocked up on, we not only have enough for ourselves and our friends, but also for feeding several families for a long time."

"But how long is long enough? Three months? Six? A year? I don't see these difficult times ending soon. Maybe never."

"Mitch, you may be right. Life may never get easier. At least not in terms of the standards we once lived by. But wouldn't you say our lives are so much better now than they have ever been? Aren't we more content, more fulfilled, more joyful?"

"Absolutely. Every day is a bit of an adventure and everything we do is so simple and straightforward. This is so much better than going to a job and earning a paycheck. I can't wait for the day when going to work means stepping outside the house."

As they continued to dig potatoes, Mitch could not help but think about what lay ahead for them. He wasn't worried about their physical survival. They were in good shape with food and water. Financially, they had plenty of resources and a healthy portfolio. Of course, that could all disappear overnight as their money was mostly virtual unless they cashed it in. But Mitch thought, if things got so bad that their portfolio became worthless, money would no longer have any value anyway. What would have worth would be the essentials of life. Food, water, clothing, gasoline, and other necessary things. Ultimately, as Mitch knew, the only thing that really mattered, the only thing of value, was their faith.

———

As the vaccine passport system integrated itself into the country's economic system, Mitch and Mary's options for shopping for essential items diminished. The small local grocery store in nearby Carrington was the last in their area to require the passport for entry. They didn't need much from the store, just dairy products and a few other perishables. Things they could do without if necessary. They had just arrived home from the fruitless trip to Carrington when Mitch's cell phone rang.

"Hello," he answered.

"Hello, Mitch, Dave here."

"Hi, Dave. How are things? How's Denise?"

"She's fine, we both are. Say, the reason I called is that Denise and I were talking earlier today and realized that you and Mary are probably having a hard time getting some of the things you need at the grocery."

"More than a hard time. Impossible now with these new restrictions."

"That is what we thought. So, since we did get the vaccine, we thought it would make sense if you gave us your grocery list and we could go pick up what you needed."

"Dave, that's very generous. But also, an inconvenience for you and Denise to drive all the way up here."

"No problem. It isn't that far and you can return the favor with more of those wonderful eggs."

"Okay, sounds like a deal. We'll text you our list when we get home. And Dave, thank you. We do really appreciate the help."

"Again, no problem. It is a small thing in our eyes."

Mitch disconnected the call and Mary asked, "What was that about?"

Mitch replied, "It was about dear friends thinking of others and following God's leadings. Dave and Denise have offered to pick up what we need at the grocery for us."

"That is so kind of them."

"It is. Not a long-term solution but will certainly help right now. It does make me wonder about other people without the vaccine. We are blessed to have people like Dave and Denise in our lives. Not everyone is so fortunate."

"So true. Why don't we talk to our friends in our home group from Geneva and see if we can't get something going to help people in Mt. Olive? I am sure Jenny and Burt will want to help."

"Good idea. We'll call them and see what we can come up with."

————

Mitch called Burt when they arrived home and learned that he and Jenny were already working on the problem. Word had gone out to all the Mt. Olive home group members with the news that they were creating a grocery-shopping ministry for those in the area who were no longer able to buy anything without proof of vaccination. Burt expressed to Mitch his frustration that the latest restrictions were inhumane and downright evil. They ended their call agreeing to seek the Lord's guidance and assistance in finding those in need and doing all they could to help.

20

SEPTEMBER 25

Mitch stood with his brother, Steve, on the back deck of the Haven, watching their family enjoy a sunny fall day together. Mitch and Mary were hosting the annual family gathering for the first time and everyone seemed to be having a good time. The little ones were fascinated by the chickens—and the garden. Mitch's many nieces and nephews were also gathered around the firepit in conversation.

Mitch looked at his brother and stated, "I'm really glad everyone wanted to come up today. I know it is a bit of a drive for some."

Steve waved a dismissive hand. "Not that far, really. I think we are all just happy to have a great place like this to get together. We all loved Jason's place in the country and this feels like home here."

"Glad to hear you say that, Steve. You know, if it ever

became necessary, this could be home to our family. All of them."

"What are you talking about? The entire family here? Why?"

"Steve, we have talked about this before. The world is getting crazier every day. Violence, immorality, inflation, and now all of this power grabbing as a result of the virus. And you should know—you work in the grocery industry—shortages are starting to happen more and more. At some point, the only option will be to consolidate resources."

"I think you are overreacting, Mitch. It just seems worse because of technology. We have more information than ever, so we know everything that is going on now. As for the shortages, that it is just temporary. Everything is still recovering from the virus lockdowns. It will get better in a few more months."

"Will it?" Mitch asked. "I am not so sure. The problem is beyond getting the supply chain back up to speed. Especially for food. The drought in the west hasn't let up and crop failures are running ninety to 100 percent in some states. I have read articles where industry experts say we will start seeing shortages by the end of Spring next year. And it is not just here in the US. South American agriculture has been devastated by the weather. Flooding, freezing temperatures, even snow in the coffee groves that never get snow."

Steve responded, "That all may be true, but that is why we have food reserves. Those reserves will last until the harvest rebounds."

"I hope you're right, Steve. I'm not so sure. Corn

reserves are down thirty-six percent over last year, and other grains are in a similar situation. Factor in the low harvest this year and we could be looking at a serious situation. But forget that, let's say food shortages don't happen. Is the city still a place you want your grandchildren to live in?"

As Mitch said this, they both turned their attention to the youngest generation, Mitch's great nieces and nephews. Some were watching the chickens; others were throwing a football. While some of the girls were coloring at one of the tables under the large canopy. Their voices and laughter seemed to make the sunshine a little brighter.

Mitch continued. "Think about them, Steve. The city is no place for a child anymore."

"I really don't see things the way you do, Mitch. All of these problems will be worked out. The world has been going on for years, and it will continue on for many more. You really need to lighten up and not be so worried."

"Could not disagree more. What you see as progress, I see as a headlong race to chaos. Yes, technology has brought us many good things. But the truth is, it has brought more bad things than good."

"And exactly what is the bad?"

"For starters, we can make or do just about anything today. There are so many products to buy that it creates a sense of need that is false. We think we need every gadget and convenience to make our lives better. People rush around buying up the latest thing, only to find it does not make their life better, so they move on to the next wonder product. But ask yourself this, if all of this technology and advancement is so great, how come more people are depressed than ever before?"

"True, I have read where depression, anxiety, and worry are at an all-time high. But that is because the world is so complex and challenging."

"Yes, but that complexity is manufactured. It is self-imposed. We are old enough to remember when life was simpler. When we were young, not kids but young adults, life was more basic. Not just for us, but for everyone. Now, our society tells us we have to have all the technology to be happy. We have to keep our children busy with all kinds of activities. We have to have new cars, nice houses, and on and on. But the truth is, we don't need any of that. The things we are told we need are nothing more than distractions from what really matters."

"So, what does really matter, Mitch," Steve asked.

Mitch looked out at his family in his backyard—the kids playing, siblings laughing, and the blue sky above and turned to his brother and said, "What really matters, Steve, the only thing that matters is that we are prepared for the next life. This one is only temporary. You know that. We were taught the same things growing up. We know where Mom and Dad are now. Don't you want to be there with them? What matters is that we are ready when this world ends and God sends Jesus for His followers."

Steve stood there not looking at Mitch. This was his usual response to spiritual matters. Total shut down. Mitch knew it was difficult for Steve to think about faith. His children and grandchildren had not been raised in the church like they had. They had no concept of heaven other than as some nice place that everyone would go to eventually. Deep down, Steve knew some day he would have to face the reality and make a decision. But, like he had many times before, he put off the decision. He had time. Things were not as bad as Mitch believed. Maybe when he was older and it wouldn't cost so much, he would consider going to church again. But not today.

Mitch knew his brother had shut down and further conversation was pointless. But he had said what needed said. He withdrew the envelope from his pocket that he had planned to give to Steve and handed it to him.

"What's this," Steve asked.

Mitch replied, "Just something I want you to have for when the time comes."

"What time? Was does this mean on the envelope? *To my family. Only to be opened in the event I am no longer here.*"

"It means I want you to keep this until I am no longer here. Honestly, I hope the day will come when I ask for it back. That all depends on you."

Steve did not respond, but simply continued to look away, deep in thought.

21

OCTOBER 14

Mary had just returned from meeting up with Denise for their groceries and Mitch was helping her unpack as she said, "Well, we couldn't get several things on my list. Denise says the store was out of fresh vegetables and fruit. There were empty shelves scattered throughout the store."

Mitch responded, "So, not the normal occasional empty shelves, but more widespread than what we've seen the last year or so?"

"Yes, she said about one-third of the shelves were empty or nearly so. The strange thing though is that Denise says people didn't seem upset about it. I would have thought they would be worried or even angry, but she says they seemed resigned to it."

"Not surprising. They have been told that periodic shortages are just a result of the virus's impact on the economy. So, they accept it without question and assume it is temporary."

"We both know better. This talk about a disrupted supply chain is a ruse. Something more is at work here. It just feels intentional to me."

"I agree. But of course, no one can prove it. I expect we'll see it get worse next year when the real problems from this year's harvest kick in. For now, the fear mongering will achieve what they want it to."

Mary responded, "Mitch, I am worried. Fear never leads to anything good. It feeds on itself. Where will it all end?"

"Well, I guess it will lead to the beginning of the end. The rapture. The tribulation. Jesus' second coming."

"I get that," Mary said. "But until then, what do we do?"

"We just keep doing what we have been. Trying to make the best decisions we can and serving others."

———

That evening, Mitch and Mary sit down to check on the news close to home and around the world. They gave up watching the news on the television long ago. The twenty-second stories contained no useful information and the sensationalist nature of what was reported was insulting.

Mitch found an article online updating the state of the economy. Unemployment was nearing 12 percent, a figure that made no sense to them. Mitch, in his work at the visitors bureau, knew that employers were desperate for workers. Why, he wondered, if so many people were without jobs, did businesses have so much trouble finding workers. Just another nonsensical part of the world they lived in. The news of the economy was no better. Inflation was at 16 percent with no indication it would get better. The government had printed so much new currency the last two years to combat inflation, it now was impossible to do anything to stem the rapid devaluing of the dollar. Mitch thought about their portfolio and realized once again how fragile it was. He could look at the numbers on the screen, but they meant little. Unless converted to cash, they had no real value. Maybe they should think about pulling all of their money out of the market now before things got worse. Yes, their financial advisors would be against it. "The market will come back," they would say. "It always does." But Mitch wasn't sure that was true anymore. He had always been a student of history and one thing was clear, every great civilization of the past eventually crashed and burned. No reason the same would not happen to the United States. Of course, now in an even more global economy, the collapse of one country would have a domino effect.

It was clear to Mitch that, the only things that had any real value were the basics of human existence. Food, water, shelter, and clothing. Everything else was superficial. He contemplated the people he read about in the Bible. In those days, people were focused on the basics. A man was considered well off if he did not have to worry about food and shelter. It was actually considered inappropriate to have more than you needed. Having enough was all anyone should want. How far from that mindset had humanity strayed? It wasn't enough to have a solid house. It had to be in the right neighborhood and filled with the latest gadgets. Food was no longer a matter of sustenance. It now was an experience. Dining out in America was one of the country's most popular activities. In fact, fewer and fewer households even knew how to cook. Not to mention, making repairs to their homes.

Mitch's study of history had led him to realize that now, more than any other time in history, people were better off materially than ever. Sadly, they did not realize it because they had become so accustomed to life's luxuries, the perception was that they were necessities.

22

OCTOBER 20

The quiet of a pleasant fall Saturday morning was shattered by the sound of gunfire. Mitch and Mary almost jumped at first, but then realized it was their neighbors to the North. Periodically, the Garretts would trot out their semi-automatic rifle and blaze away. They were not target shooting like Mitch and Mary did on their range, just making noise. Mitch could not see what they were shooting at on the other side of the old barn in the back of the property, he just hoped they were firing in a safe direction. It was a strange household. Tom Garrett lived there with his teenage son, Johnny, and daughter, Susan. Normal enough, but it was the presence of many other teens on several occasions and the loud music that came from the house, often until the later hours, that worried Mitch. There just seemed to be an unsettling feeling about the place. Mitch would always give a friendly wave when he saw someone from the Garrett household but could not seem to get a conversation going. Tim next door had told Mitch that the Garretts had been this way since he and Nancy had moved there.

Mary said, "Mitch, I really have a bad feeling about the Garretts. The noise from the guns and the music is annoying, but I am not too worried about that."

"What are you worried about, Mary?"

"It's just that, as things get worse, people who don't have respect for others are the ones who will cause trouble. If food becomes scarce, people will get desperate. Desperation leads to poor decisions. Decisions that could affect us here."

Mitch replied, "I agree. The Garretts are a bit wild, but I'm hoping that their behavior is nothing more than blowing off steam."

"I hope you are right," Mary said. "I still think it best we keep an eye on them though. You can't be too careful."

———

LATER THAT EVENING as Mitch checked online for the latest news, he read that President Benjamin Jordan had announced a new initiative to combat hate speech in America. Jordan explained that much of the violence the nation was experiencing was due to radical beliefs and something had to be done to stop it. He had ordered the NSA, the National Security Agency, to begin monitoring citizens' communications for what he called hate speech. The president went on to define hate speech for the purposes of the new initiative. Not surprising, it included expressions of violent intentions, racial discrimination, and efforts to subvert government functions. What was most disturbing to Mitch was the inclusion of what the president called radical religious beliefs. While he did not go into much detail, Jordan's comment that, "beliefs that are intolerant of the lifestyles and beliefs of other Americans will not be tolerated." It did not take much interpretation to see that the president's comment was aimed at Christians. His past rhetoric about the destructiveness of fundamental Christians to the nation and its future was made clear now who would be targeted by the NSA.

A few minutes later, Mitch came upon an article by Pastor John Hicks decrying this latest effort by government to silence the Gospel. In the article, Hicks reminded his readers that the message of salvation had been attacked since Jesus first delivered it 2,000 years ago and it did not work then and would not work now. Hicks was one of Mitch's favorite pastors to read and was encouraged by the message, although he worried for the pastor. It would no doubt lead to some reaction from the government.

While Mitch sat contemplating these latest developments, Mary entered his office.

"I know that look, Mitch. What has you so concerned?"

Looking up from the computer, Mitch responded, "I was just reading that our president has ordered the NSA to monitor citizens communications for hate speech."

"Hate speech?" Mary said. "Well, based upon what he and his administration have been saying, I assume that includes real and true Christian teaching."

"It does. We know that the government and many people in this country think it is intolerant and discriminatory to teach the only way to heaven is through Christ. They want a world where all faiths have their own truths and can coexist."

"But that is contradictory. The world's religions are diametrically opposed to each other. They, by their nature, proclaim theirs is the only way. Which, by the way, is as it should be. Religion without exclusivity isn't a belief system at all."

"Agreed," said Mitch. "That is true of religion as it has been practiced since the beginning of mankind. But, in today's crazy world, more and more people are diluting the various religions so they can exist without absolutes. So no one feels left out."

"Then what is the point?" Mary asked. "If your religion is that weak in its doctrine, what use is it?"

"Not much, Mary. But then, it does make sense if this is a precursor to a one-world religion. If the world's existing religions are stripped of their exclusiveness, it is an easy step to consolidate them into one belief system where everyone is included. But with that comes the absence of any true commitment to believing anything that matters. It will become a religion of feeling good about yourself without any call to obey a higher authority."

"Can there be any doubt that we are living in the last days?" Mary asked.

"None that I can see," Mitch responded.

Mary sat down in the chair next to Mitch's desk. "There is something I wanted to talk to you about, Mitch."

"Okay. What is it?"

"Well, I've been thinking. Our world is changing so fast, it is important we try to stay ahead of all the craziness as best we can."

"Absolutely," Mitch agreed. "Any way we can try to mitigate the difficulties we face now or on the horizon, we should pursue."

"Exactly. So, I am thinking that we should look for ways to mitigate against inflation. Our dollars are not worth as much as they were a year ago, and it will only get worse. The only things that will hold value are those necessary to survive. Like this house for instance."

"True. So, I take it you have a recommendation."

"I do. While the stock market is still stable, inflation is making the dollars in our portfolio worth less every day. When inflation is at three to four percent and our portfolio rises eight to ten percent, we are gaining ground. But now, the numbers have flipped and we are losing every day. So, I think we should consider stemming the tide and moving our money where it will not lose value."

"Makes sense," Mitch said. "You have a plan in mind, I can tell."

"Yes, I think we should take out enough to pay off the

house. This house is our largest real asset. Paying off the mortgage will ensure we will keep it as things get worse."

"Good points and we should think about this. Maybe we plan to pay the house off at the end of this year? Let's give it more thought and see what we think in a few weeks."

23

NOVEMBER 11

As Mitch and Mary pulled into the church parking lot that Sunday morning, Mitch thought to himself how he liked it when Veterans Day fell on a Sunday. It somehow seemed appropriate. Jesus sacrificed His life that all might be saved. American soldiers had done the same so that their country might remain safe against its enemies. Mitch had a deep appreciation for the nation's military members.

As they parked in front of the church, Mitch and Mary noticed something unusual. By the doors, there men and women were standing whom they did not recognize. These were not the church members who greeted people as they entered. They were all in suits and did not have a look of welcome on their faces. Something else strange was going on as several people who approached the church doors were now returning to their cars.

"Let's see what's going on," Mitch said as he opened the car door for Mary.

As they came to the doors, they could see that the people in suits were all wearing badges. Clearly visible on the badges was the logo of the World Health Organization, the WHO. *What is this all about,* Mitch thought.

One of the WHO people demanded to Mitch and Mary, "I must see your proof of virus vaccination for you to enter this building."

"Excuse me," Mitch said. "This is not 'a building,' it is our church. A private building that you have no right to bar entry to."

"Actually, we do. Last night, the President signed an agreement with the WHO to enforce vaccine compliance. One of the measures to do so includes monitoring public gathering buildings. Only those who can prove they have been vaccinated can enter."

"This is ridiculous!" Mitch demanded. "I want to speak to my pastor. Let me in so I can talk to him about this."

"Your pastor is not in the building. He did not have proof of vaccination."

"What! I see. You really don't care about vaccinations; you just want to close this church down."

"Not at all, sir. Anyone with proof of vaccination may enter."

Mary grabbed Mitch's arm. "Mitch, let's go back to the car and try to reach someone to find out what this is all about."

Mitch was about to respond when Assistant Pastor Kevin came out of the church and approached saying, "Mitch, Mary, good morning. Look, I am sorry about this, we had no warning. They just showed up here and stationed themselves at all the doors."

"And you are just letting them do this?"

"There is nothing we can do to stop them, Mitch. It's the same all over the country. This order that the President signed has turned over all matters concerning the virus to the WHO." He almost whispered, "These people are armed."

"Unbelievable!" Mitch exclaimed. "Wait, you just came out of the church. Does that mean you showed them vaccination proof?"

"Well, yes I did. When Pastor Fred was turned away, he asked me to go in so I can talk to those inside."

"Are the WHO people here going to monitor what you say?"

"When Pastor Fred and I talked in the parking lot this morning, we agreed the best thing to do is to explain the situation to everyone and send them home."

"So, we're caving to this outrage and canceling the service?"

"I know it looks like that, but no, we are not. We just have to figure out the best way to deal with this. We won't give in to this persecution of our faith, I can assure you of that. Just go home and wait for a message from Pastor Fred later today."

"All right, Kevin. We'll go home and wait." As he

turned to go back to the car, he said, "I can't believe it has come to this. I am truly ashamed of this nation."

With that, Mitch and Mary returned to their car and drove home. It was silent the entire way as both were reeling from what had just happened. They knew the world was continuing on a downward spiral and that the Bible was clear that things would get very bad. But they had thought things like this would not happen until after the rapture. After believers had been called to heaven. The persecutions and troubles, they thought, were supposed to happen after they were gone. They were obviously wrong.

Later that afternoon, a message came via email from Pastor Fred. Mitch and Mary had been waiting impatiently for the message. They hoped to read of a plan to reopen the church, or even to meet in secret somewhere. As they sat next to each other on the couch, Mitch scrolled down the email on his laptop and they read:

Dear brothers and sisters in Christ,

I am sure by now you are aware of what happened at our church this morning. Without any warning or communication, agents from the World Health Organization came to our church early this morning to restrict access to only those who could present proof they had been vaccinated for the virus. I can assure you we had no prior knowledge this was going to happen. In fact, I was denied entry into the church by these agents.

I am assuming that you all have the same reaction I did to this blatant infringement on our right to freely worship as we choose. Our attorneys are looking into the situation but are telling us they doubt there is a way to get around it. It is expected that many churches, and ours will be one, will appeal this order to the courts as soon as possible tomorrow. I hope and pray our appeals are successful and we can be back together worshipping next Sunday.

In the meantime, I ask you to gather together in your homes today on our Sabbath and worship on your own. We don't need to be in the church building to worship. We don't need the music team to sing. We don't need videos on the screen. All we need are faithful hearts and our desire to worship the one and only King who rules everything... in heaven and on this earth. And as you worship today, I ask you to use the following scriptures to pray upon and reflect on what they say to us in these troubling times.

1 Peter 4:12-14

Beloved, do not be surprised at the fiery trial when it comes upon you to test you, as though something strange were happening to you. But rejoice insofar as you share Christ's sufferings, that you may also rejoice and be glad when his glory is revealed. If you are insulted for the name of Christ, you are blessed, because the Spirit of glory and of God rests upon you.

Matthew 5:10-12

Blessed are those who are persecuted for righteousness' sake, for theirs is the kingdom of heaven. Blessed are you when others revile you and persecute you and utter all kinds of evil against you falsely on my account. Rejoice and be glad, for your reward is great in heaven, for so they persecuted the prophets who were before you.

John 15:18

If the world hates you, know that it has hated me before it hated you.

Remember members of Geneva church, our strength comes from the Lord. Whatever happens in this situation, our faith and the promises of God will not change. Do not despair, but with rejoicing celebrate the love of Jesus Christ.

Pastor Fred

Mitch and Mary sat on the couch in silence. All the times they had talked about how evil was spreading in the world were no longer theory. It was fact and it was now. Mitch thought, *How can any true Christian not believe that we are living in the times approaching the end? The days of ignoring the world are over. It has come crashing into our lives and our churches and will not go away.*

Mary looked over at Mitch and asked, "So, what is on your mind about this? What do we do?"

Mitch replied, "Beyond doing as Pastor Fred asked and worshipping on our own, I don't know."

Mary paused, deep in thought, then spoke with a conviction that Mitch had learned to appreciate, "This is not going to stop with church services. It is just the beginning. Next will be proof of vaccination requirements to get gas or groceries. This church requirement they say is because they are mass gatherings. But soon eventually, it will extend to everything."

"No, not everything Mary. That would be like the mark in the Bible. This is just about showing a document to enter places. A document, not a permanent mark."

"True, but this is the lead up to the next step."

"Okay, I see what you are saying, and I agree. But

what of it? If the mark is next, we know we will be gone by then. We will be in heaven. It won't be our concern."

"That is true, Mitch, but don't you see? This place, this haven does not end with us. It has to go on for those who are left behind after we are gone."

"Like my family."

"Yes, like your family. Everything we are doing here is for two stages of God's plan. The first is for us and our friends—and for whoever needs our help. We have food, shelter, water, and more so we can survive here with others, plus send out food to others in need. But after we are gone, God wants this place to be a sanctuary for the people being hunted down for their faith. I truly believe that that means your family. Surely your siblings will see what it all means after the rapture. They will know where we went and what comes next."

"Okay, I see your point and agree completely. I've always hoped my family would turn from sin before it was too late. But lately, I have come to realize that will not happen. If they do come to faith after we are gone, they will need a place to live outside of the city. It will be too violent and too risky for a believer there."

"Exactly."

"But how can they live here after we're gone. When the mark comes, how will they pay the bills? The mortgage? Buy food?"

"I was thinking about that and there is only one solution. We have to pay off the house now. We should not wait any longer."

"Agreed. It will use up a large chunk of our finances but is probably the right thing to do."

"Yes, it would. But what good is all that money if we are not here to use it? And even if we are, even if God doesn't take us home soon, without a mortgage and utilities to pay, we won't need much to live on. I say we take out enough to pay off the house. Then we take out enough to pay the property taxes for the next seven years, no, make it eight years to be sure. Then we overpay our utility bills so there are enough credits on the accounts to last several years."

"I see. If we do all of this, the house can maintain without having to pay any bills. No mark, no problem. Everything is already paid up for the future. Mary, you are one brilliant person. I would've never thought of this, but it's perfect!"

"Well, I don't know if it is perfect, but I think it'll work."

"You have no worries we could be wrong, and the world goes on as normal? The virus thing fades away. If that happens, we will have reduced our retirement to a point where it won't support us."

"Worried, no. I realize there is a risk, but a small one. Even if this current situation eases, I do not see life going back to normal. We don't go many places now because of all the violence. We are becoming more self-sustaining every day, so we don't need much from the store. If this all blows over, I think we'll still be content and retire as planned. Yes, our plans to travel, do certain things, and enjoy life to its fullest will have to be changed. But really,

Mitch, haven't we already been doing that? We have said many times how we are content here in our haven in the country."

"Okay, like I said, brilliant. Let's start the process tomorrow. Our financial advisors will think we are crazy, but it is the right thing to do."

24

NOVEMBER 16

It was a Saturday afternoon; Mitch was in the barn checking the wheat stalks to see if they had dried enough to be threshed and placed in storage. He heard a car pull into the gravel driveway and wondered who had come. Stepping out of the barn he saw not one, but two cars. Dave and Denise's SUV and Jim and Betty's truck had pulled in. Mitch was surprised to see them unannounced. As he walked toward the house, he saw that Joanna and Maggie were also with them.

Stepping up to shake Dave's hand in greeting, Mitch said, "Did I forget about a get-together today? We weren't expecting company."

Dave responded, "No, you didn't forget. But I ask you to remember an invitation you made to all of us a few weeks ago. We are here to take you up on it."

Just then Mary came out the front door with a

quizzical look on her face, "Well, what a pleasant surprise! Hello, everyone, and welcome. Is everything okay?"

"If you mean for us personally, I think I can say we're okay. As to things in general, not so much," Denise said.

Mitch wondered what she meant, then offered, "Why don't we go inside, and you can tell us what that means."

The group made their way to the living room, and once everyone was settled, Mitch asked, "So, we are certainly glad to see everyone, but to what do we owe this visit?"

Dave responded, "I would say this is more than a visit. This past week, Denise and I have been having conversations with Jim and Betty, Joanna, and Maggie."

"Conversations about what?" Mary asked.

"Conversations about the community we live in. Or, more accurately, used to live in," Dave answered.

"Used to live in," Mitch said. "As in you don't live in Wadesville anymore?"

Jim responded, "No, we don't. And, if you will have us, we would like to come here to live with you and Mary."

Mary said, "Well, of course you all are welcome, but what prompted this? Did something happen?"

Dave looked around at the group and said, "It is more like a series of some things happened. Mitch, I know you follow the news, so you are aware of all of the things that have been going on down in the city. The shootings, the break-ins and robberies. The violent protests in the streets, and some of that has expanded into the suburbs as well. In the past week there were three shootings in Wadesville. Protests in front of the police headquarters have been happening the last four nights."

Joanna offered, "It's to the point that I don't feel safe going downtown anymore. I mean, you can't go to dinner or shopping without worrying about your purse getting snatched or worse."

"I didn't realize it had gotten that bad," Mary commented.

"It has," Dave said. "Our quiet little suburb is no longer quiet. So, these happenings have made us all feel uncomfortable in our own community. But that wasn't what prompted us to get together last night to talk about coming here."

"What did prompt your decision then?" asked Mitch.

Dave replied, "It was an announcement delivered via email from our church. The email stated that the church supports the government effort to verify vaccinations for entry into public buildings. That is bad enough, but what came next was worse. The church announced that, as soon as it is on the market, all attendees will have to prove they are vaccinated by having the chip implant."

"Seriously," Mitch exclaimed. "Don't they have any idea what that chip is? It couldn't be more obvious that this chip in the right hand is leading to the mark of the beast. What exactly did the pastor say about it?"

Denise responded, "He said he knew that some people claim it is the mark. But he disagrees and suggested the mark isn't a literal mark in the Bible. He says it is symbolic and the chip is about staying healthy."

"Amazing," Mary said. "So, he says it isn't the mark,

yet more and more businesses are saying they will only serve customers who have the chip. And the government plans to offer the chip at no cost, so everyone can get it. And the government is encouraging people to get the chip when it is ready because it can also be used like a credit or ATM card to buy and sell. How in the world can your pastor say this isn't the mark?"

"Because he doesn't really care about the mark," Betty chimed in. "It is obvious to me that all he cares about is keeping the seats full on Sunday, and the collection baskets too! First, he started in on social justice last year. Then it was church online for our safety. And now this chip thing. I always believed a church should be separate from the world, not embrace the world."

Mitch sighed. "You're right, Betty. A church should be separate from the world. We as Christians should lead lives outside of the current popular culture. I am sorry for all of you that it has come to this. Mary and I have been praying for your church that it would stand up for biblical principles and not get sucked into the storm of self-righteousness that seems to be driving the social justice crowd."

"We have been praying too," Dave said. "We tried to overlook some of the things that were going on in the church. But now it is a matter of truth. I don't think you can believe in the truth of the Bible and attend a church that caters to the world."

"That's why we're here. We realized we had to get away from the violence, the false teaching, and the spiritual danger in the city." Denise explained.

Mitch looked at his friends and felt for them. Their lives had been disrupted. They had left their homes. They had left friends too. And now, here they were at the Haven. It felt right to Mitch that they were here. *It's where they belong,* he thought. He looked over at Maggie who had been silent during the conversation.

"Maggie, you haven't said anything about all of this. Tell me what's going on in your mind right now."

She responded, "There is a lot going on." She sighed. "Everything they have said is true. And it makes me feel betrayed. That was my church. The place I went to worship. The place that I relied on to guide me through life and grow in my faith. And now there is nothing for me there. I'm mad about this. Mad that my life, our lives where we lived, has been taken away from us. I'm grateful to you and Mary for opening your home to us, but I don't like leaving everything behind."

"Oh, Maggie," Mary responded. "I am so sorry that this happened. I know you worked hard to make your house a home and were just starting to enjoy your retirement, and I know how you feel about leaving a place you called home. When Mitch and I moved here last year, it was a bittersweet time. We were excited to move to our dream home in the country, but sad that we were leaving Wadesville and all of you. But I can tell you we are happier here than we have ever been. I hope you," she looked around the room, "All of you, will come to be happy here as well."

"Thank you, Mary," Maggie said. "Don't get me wrong, I don't ever want to go back. I know I must start over. I can't think of any better people to get through this with than all of you."

"I agree," said Mitch. "We've been friends for quite a while. We'll now be even closer than before."

"Quite literally," Dave added.

Mitch stood. "Exactly, Dave, and to that point, let's get all of your things unloaded and in the house."

Jim piped up as he stood, "I hope you don't mind; we brought a lot of stuff. I think we all figured we should bring anything that might be useful, so the truck bed is piled high."

"I can see that," said Mitch. "I'm sure everything you brought will be needed."

They spent the rest of the day unloading the vehicles and distributing everyone's clothes and personal items to their rooms. Mitch put Dave and Denise in the West bedroom, Jim and Betty in the middle room, and Joanna and Maggie shared the East bedroom. It would get interesting in the mornings with six people sharing one bathroom, but Mitch figured they would work it out. Besides, it wasn't as if anyone was dashing off to work. Jim and Betty were retired, as were Joanna and Maggie. Mitch assumed Dave would continue in his job since he worked from home anyway. But he wondered about Denise. She was a school music teacher. He hoped she wasn't going to commute back into the city.

As Mitch came back outside to get another load, Denise was at the back of her car, so Mitch asked, "Denise, what about your job? I know how much you enjoy teaching music to those children."

Denise stopped what she was doing and sat down in the back of the open SUV. Mitch joined her as she replied, "That is the hardest part for me in all of this. I am going to miss teaching. I was thinking about last year when the virus hit and we were shut down for most of the year. At first, I missed the children and my job. But as the lockdown went on, I adjusted my approach to my days. I found plenty to do to keep me occupied. I suppose it will be the same here. Besides, I'm sure you have plenty of chores to be done here. That should keep us all busy."

Mitch chuckled. "Yes, it is a lot of work keeping up with this place. I'm grateful to have the help. The work is harder than I had anticipated, and I'm not as young as I once was. In fact, with so many hands here now, we might consider expanding the garden next year."

"As long as that means more sweet potatoes!"

Mitch laughed. He and Denise shared a love for baked sweet potatoes.

"Of course. We will add an entire second row next Spring."

25

NOVEMBER 17

The next morning, the residents of the Haven began to get organized. Everyone had put away their personal items in their rooms, but the food and household items had been left in a pile on the kitchen counter. Likewise for another pile in the garage. Mary and the rest of the women began sorting through the items in the kitchen. Maggie offered to make an inventory so they would know what they had on hand.

Mary replied to the offer, "Thanks, Maggie. Could you also go down in the basement and inventory our back-up goods down there? They are in the white cabinets."

"Sure," Maggie replied.

"I will help," Joanna offered, and they headed down the stairs.

Mary, Denise, and Betty began sorting through the stacks of food and cleaning supplies, separating each into smaller piles. As they worked, Betty asked:

"Now this is something I worry about. There are eight of us here. It will take a lot of food to feed eight people. Mary, I know you said you and Mitch keep an extra stock of food, but I doubt you have that much extra."

"Maybe not," said Mary. "We keep enough to feed us both for six months if we had to. I figure with that, and what you all brought, we will be good for those six months. Don't forget, we have all the food from the garden we canned. That's all on the other side of the basement. Maggie's inventory won't include that, but we will add it in for a grand total. So, I think we will have enough for maybe eight months or so."

Betty responded, "That sounds good. We can also be frugal about portions. Not like our potlucks in the past."

"True," said Denise. "We'll be careful to prepare just enough for each meal."

Mary looked at the two and said, "I'm certainly glad you're here. Mitch and I have been working so hard around this place. Don't get me wrong, we've enjoyed it. There is something about working to produce your own food that is very rewarding. But I have been concerned about Mitch. He works so hard and doesn't seem to want to admit he isn't a young man anymore."

Betty laughed, "None of us are young, that's for sure. Well, we're all here to help, so no one should have to work too hard. Everyone will pitch in."

"Thank you, Betty. It is a relief to finally see this place full of people. And not just any people. Our people."

Betty came over to Mary and gave her a big hug.

Before they could move apart, Denise joined in, shouting, "Group hug!"

Out in the garage, Mitch, Dave, and Jim were sorting through the items the Wadesville group had brought with them.

Jim was saying, "... so I figured we could use an extra propane tank. I think it is mostly full and we can use it on the grill."

"Excellent!" Mitch exclaimed. "Thanks, Jim. We have two extras and I keep them both full, so that will make a total of four. There may come a time when we will cook on the grill instead of the stove so we can save on propane from the big tank. We'll need that for heat this winter."

Dave rummaged in the pile and pulled out a strange device that look more like an iron plant stand than anything else. "I brought my wood splitter. I know you don't have any trees to speak of on the property, but I brought it anyway."

"Thanks, Dave. True, no trees on our land, but across the road there are plenty of dead trees along the edge of that farm field. I haven't been able to determine who owns it, but I don't think they will mind if we clear out the dead wood."

They continued to sort through the pile. Three gas cans were set aside to go in the barn. Mitch had three himself that he kept full for the lawnmower and tiller. Other odds and ends were sorted—some rope, sleeping bags, matches, and a variety of useful items. They were just finishing and getting ready to head to the barn when Mary came out with Maggie and Denise.

"We've put away all the food and done an inventory. I'm happy to say, we all can eat like kings and queens for the next six months at least. Well, maybe more like princes and princesses, but we won't go hungry."

"That's great, Mary," Mitch said. "That gets us into May of next year."

Mary then added, "There are a few things we need to stock up on. We are going to the grocery to try to find some canned meats, more pastas, and other staples like rice and beans."

"Are you sure that is a good idea?" Dave asked. "Don't you have to go into the city to the store?"

"No," Mary replied, "There is a grocery down in Sullivan and it's less than twenty minutes from here. Sullivan is a smaller town, so I don't anticipate any problems."

"Just the same," Mitch remarked, "Be careful. I assume you are protected?"

"Yes, as always."

Jim and Dave looked at each other wondering what "protected" meant as the women headed toward Dave and Denise's SUV.

The grocery store in Sullivan was always busy but seemed even more so as they searched for a place to park. Denise finally found a spot and the three headed into the store. Maggie suggested they divide up the list so they could save time, but Mary insisted they stay together.

"I understand what you are saying, Maggie, but I think we should stay together. I know I said it should be safe here in Sullivan, but let's be extra cautious."

So, the three headed down the aisles. Mary was shocked at how many empty spaces had appeared since her last grocery shopping trip only two weeks before. She worried they would not be able to find what they needed. Rice and beans were no problem. It seemed people weren't interested in something that took too long to cook. When they got to the pasta aisle, it was jammed with people grabbing whatever they could. Mary couldn't get the cart into the aisle, there were so many people.

"What are we going to do," Maggie groaned. "We'll never get through here."

"No worries," Denise said. I'll make a run for it and grab what I can and meet you both at the other end of the aisle."

"I don't know," Mary said. "I don't like the idea of you in there by yourself."

"I've got this," Denise replied. "Remember, I'm a runner, so I will just breeze through and grab what I can."

"All right," Mary conceded. "We'll see you at the other end."

Mary and Maggie turned to go down the next aisle, which was filled with kitchen utensils and practically empty. They watched Denise enter the mass of people and hoped she would make it through. When they got to the other end, Denise was just emerging out of the fray, her arms loaded. She walked up to the cart and, a little out of breath, started dropping the items in one by one.

"We've got three spaghetti, two rigatoni, one penne, two elbow macaroni, a fettuccine, and three old-fashioned noodles."

"Amazing!" Maggie exclaimed. "You did that so fast! How'd you even carry it all?"

Denise replied, "Well, we're talking about food here. I just dove in where there were gaps and grabbed."

"Thank you, Denise," Mary said. Let's go over to produce and see if we can't get a few fresh vegetables.

As expected, the produce area had been picked through and not much was left. They were able to pick up some carrots and asparagus, plus some brussel sprouts. They went through the checkout without any difficulty. Mary had brought cash from the safe at home, figuring it would be best not to pay with a card that would have to be paid off later.

As they exited the store and headed toward the car, Mary noticed three young men in the parking lot. When they saw the three women, they started walking their way. Denise and Maggie were busy chatting and didn't notice. Mary kept watching the three men as she asked Denise to please push the cart. Denise took over, still talking to Maggie. They were almost to their car when the three men approached. The men were dressed casually, but neatly. One was in khakis and a hooded sweatshirt, another in jeans and a sweater, and the third wore jeans, a blue coat, and a baseball cap. But Mary saw something in their eyes she didn't like. As she slowly opened her purse on her left, away from the view of the men, the one in the ballcap spoke.

"Hello, ladies. Fine day, isn't it?"

Maggie and Denise looked up in surprise. They had not noticed the men until then.

"It is a fine day," Mary answered. "Is there something we can help you with?"

"Not much," the man in the cap said. "It's just that we noticed you have quite a cart full of groceries there. So, I think to myself, 'I bet these ladies are pretty well off. Maybe so well off they would help those like us who are less fortunate."

"Exactly what is it you want?" Mary asked as her hand went inside her purse. She noticed that the other young men didn't seem as threatening as ballcap man. He was obviously the leader of the group.

"What we want," the man said as he stepped closer to the three women, "Is a donation. Yes, I am calling it a donation... of the cash you have, all of it. And we'll take your cart too. I am sure you ladies won't mind."

Denise and Maggie moved away from the men, Denise trying to keep the cart between them.

Never taking her eyes off the three men, Mary said, "Let me just reach in my purse here and see what I can find for you."

Before the three men, and for that matter, Denise and Maggie, knew what was happening, Mary had drawn her 9mm Taurus semi-automatic pistol out of her purse and aimed it squarely between the eyes of ballcap man.

Mary said in a firm voice, "The only donation you will get from me will be nine millimeters in diameter. How many would you like? I have enough for three for each of you, with some left over."

The result was immediate. The other two men started to back away in a rush, one tugging at ballcap's sleeve as he went. Ballcap finally backed off, but not before glaring at Mary and her gun.

As the men turned and hurried away, Mary kept the gun pointed at them. She muttered to Denise, "Put the groceries in the car and let me know when you're done."

Mary never took her eyes of the three men who were now fifty yards away and still moving, but not fast enough. Denise called to Mary when the groceries were loaded.

"Start the car, Denise. Maggie, get in the back seat." As soon as Mary heard the car start, she jumped in and Denise pulled away quickly. No one said anything for several minutes.

Finally, Maggie couldn't stand it any longer and said, "That was scary. I didn't even see those guys until they were right there. Did you see them, Denise?"

"No, I didn't see them until the one in the ballcap talked to us. Did you see them, Mary?"

Mary replied, "I did. I spotted them as we were coming out of the store. Something didn't look right about them."

"I am glad you did," Maggie said. "At least one of us was paying attention."

Mary let out a big breath to release the built-up tension and said, "A few months ago, I wouldn't have noticed them either. Mitch has been constantly reminding me to watch for danger. He says to always be aware of your surroundings. Most people get in trouble because they don't see danger until it's too late."

"Well, good for Mitch, and good for you," Maggie said.

"But wait, when did you get a gun? Can you legally carry that in your purse?"

"I've had a gun for years. This one is actually newer. Mitch and I picked it out just before we moved to Mt. Olive. Yes, I can carry it in my purse legally. Mitch and I both have concealed carry permits. We never go into the city without bringing our guns. I don't usually bring it when I'm going into Sullivan, but for some reason today, I did."

"Well, I am glad you did, Mary," Denise remarked. "I guess we're going to have some story to tell around the dinner table tonight!"

26
___

NOVEMBER 18

Jim and Maggie were sitting on the porch of the barn shelling corn for the chickens. Mitch fed the chickens special feed he bought at the hardware store in Mt. Olive that had the nutrients they needed to remain healthy and lay good eggs. The corn was a supplement so he did not have to spend as much money on the feed. The work was hard. He had to grasp an ear of corn in one hand and twist the kernels off the cob with the other. They had tried to use gloves, but they just slid across the corn. So, they worked slowly so as not to rub their hands raw.

As they worked, Maggie asked Jim, "Do you think things will ever get better? I mean, so we can go back home."

Jim stopped his work and looked at Maggie. "No, I don't think so, Maggie. I wish it were so, but nothing we are seeing makes me think it will go back to the way it was. Or even close."

"I suppose you're right. It just seems like such a waste. Everything was good for us all back in Wadesville. Now here we are, all in one house trying to figure things out. I miss my house, my street, my neighborhood."

"I know what you mean, Maggie. Betty and I had everything in our house just like we wanted it. Life was good. But, in some ways this is better."

"How do you mean?" Maggie asked.

"Well, life here is so comfortable and relaxed. Yes, we work hard every day, but I don't feel rushed like I did in the city, and my stress level has dropped since we came here. Before, I was always reading and watching the news and worrying about everything. Now, we keep up on the big things so we are not caught unaware, but the details of it just don't matter anymore."

"I see what you mean. I would always turn the news on in the morning and watch or listen most of the day. All that did was make me anxious and afraid. And now, I really don't give it much thought. I am enjoying myself too much to worry about the rest of the world."

"Exactly, and I think we're better off, too, because we have gone back to the basics. Working the land for food, doing all of our own repairs and maintenance, spending time together as a group in the evenings instead of watching television. Of course, working to help others in this area. It just seems like a purer life than we had before. At least that's how I see it."

"Jim, I agree with you, but don't you ever get homesick for Wadesville? Don't you ever miss home?"

"Sure, I do. Sometimes. But I've been thinking about that and found an answer in Isaiah. In chapter six, it says, 'In the year that King Uzziah died, I saw the Lord, high and exalted, seated on a throne; and the train of his robe filled the temple.' God then told Isaiah that He would bring destruction to Israel and the towns and cities would lie in ruin."

"How does that apply to our situation here?"

"Well, first off, when King Uzziah died, it was a terrible shock to Isaiah and the Israelites. He had been a good king and worshipped God. Then he got prideful and tried to burn incense in the temple, a task only priests were supposed to perform. God struck him down and chaos ensued. But, amidst all of this, God was still on His throne in heaven. Isaiah was shown this in a vision. So, I got to thinking about how our situation is similar."

"It is?"

"Yes. This country for many years followed God and was blessed by God. We became the wealthiest and most benevolent nation on earth. But then we became prideful and said we didn't need God anymore. We said we knew better how to deal with everything. We would decide gender, right and wrong, what is marriage, and a host of other things that previously were based on God's divine creation. So, much like King Uzziah who decided he was above God's laws in the temple, the people of this country decided they are above God's laws and, really, above God."

Maggie responded, "This all makes sense, Jim. But

isn't there a way for us to turn this around? 2 Chronicles says, 'If my people, who are called by my name, will humble themselves and pray and seek my face and turn from their wicked ways, then I will hear from heaven, and I will forgive their sin and will heal their land.' This could still happen."

Jim replied, "Of course it could happen, and I hope it does. But I really wonder if that opportunity has passed. Maybe a few years ago it was possible. It just seems that now there are too many people who don't even believe God exists to expect them to see what they don't want to see."

"Maybe you're right. Several times God has given people what they wanted, even though He knew it wasn't what they needed. Perhaps He has hardened their hearts because it's time for the latter days to take place."

"I think it is," said Jim. "Over the last year or so, as I watched the world getting crazier and crazier, I hoped that it was just a temporary thing. That everyone would calm down and go back to normal—or at least more normal. But, if we look around, it is easy to see that everything is moving faster and faster toward chaos. It's everywhere. I just don't see it turning around."

"I suppose I don't either. It still makes me sad to think about walking away from everything I had known for so long."

"I get it, Maggie. It was hard for all of us to just pick up and come here. Sometimes at night I lay awake and think about what may be happening in my neighborhood. On my street. Even my own house. And then I remember that we are only here for a little while. A short time compared to eternity."

Jim had filled his basket with corn, so he got up and placed it on the shelves in the barn, returning with an empty basket. As he sat down and picked up another ear, he continued.

"I look at it like this, Maggie. We are about the same age, mid-sixties. What's the most we could hope for in this life if things were normal? Another fifteen years? Twenty? Twenty five even."

"I would hope twenty-five."

"Okay, let's say twenty-five. That would be ninety years living on this broken planet with all of its wars, diseases, immorality, and every other way we have messed it up."

"That certainly puts a negative spin on life."

"Maybe it does but consider this. After the rapture and the seven-year tribulation, Jesus comes back and sets up His kingdom here on earth. Plus, the Bible says He will reign for a thousand years."

"Something to look forward to for sure."

"Absolutely. So, if we know we get to live a thousand years with Christ on a now perfect earth, why should we cling so tightly to ninety years on a very imperfect planet?"

"When you put it that way, I guess it does sound like my priorities are off."

"Oh no, I am not criticizing your wishing things had not gone so bad. I feel the same. It's just that, as Christians, we have to work to keep our eyes on the Lord and what He has planned for us. We can do that because the Holy Spirit is in us to remind and guide us. That is, if we get out of the way and let Him do so."

"Jim, you are right. Whenever I let the Spirit loose in me, I feel so strong and confident, no matter what is going on. Now that you mention it, I don't worry about the world then either."

"Good. Now we just need to hold on to that thought in the coming months and days. I have a feeling we'll need it in order to survive."

27

NOVEMBER 27

It was almost a traditional Thanksgiving Day dinner. They had sweet potatoes, green beans, pumpkin pie, and mashed potatoes. What was missing was the turkey. Finding one at the grocery would have been impossible if they had even tried. With store shelves going empty and the mood in the aisles getting dangerous, they opted to forego a turkey in favor of a pork roast from the freezer. When the eight friends who lived at the Haven gathered around the table, it felt a bit awkward. On this day of giving thanks, it was difficult for them to think of things to be thankful for. Of course, they were grateful for each other, food to eat, and a home to live in, but the condition of things in the world made them more concerned than thankful.

As was their tradition when dining together, Dave would say grace. His ability to deliver insightful remarks in giving thanks for a meal was something they always looked forward to.

Dave cleared his throat and began to speak. "I have spent most of today thinking about what I would say before we eat this meal, and honestly, I've got nothing."

Dave paused and the others looked to each other in surprise.

He continued, "It is tradition to go around the table and say what we are thankful for. But, as I stand here before you, we all know these things already. We are thankful for this food, this home that Mitch and Mary have so graciously opened to us, and for each other. We are of course thankful for our savior, Jesus Christ. Beyond these things, what? Maybe that is enough? With evil seemingly encompassing everything and people all over the world, displaying the worst of what they can do to each other, maybe, just maybe we should be thankful simply for God and each other."

Denise squeezed Dave's arm.

He thought a moment then countered, "No, that's not true. It is not enough to be thankful for what we have. I think we all believe we are here for a reason. God has something planned for us. Mitch and Mary moved here, and God brought the rest of us here. So, why did He? I don't have an answer, but I know, when God is ready, He will reveal our purpose for being here. I'm thankful that God has a purpose for me, for all of us."

Dave then thanked the Lord for the food and all their blessings and the group at the Haven enjoyed a happy, if unusual, Thanksgiving.

———

LATER THAT EVENING, Mitch was in the barn feeding and watering the chickens when Dave came in.

"Hey, Dave. Just about done here."

"No rush," Dave said. "I just thought I would come out here and enjoy the peace and quiet."

"Getting a little too noisy in the house for you?"

"Just a bit. The ladies are playing a rousing game of dominoes. Poor Jim got roped in, but I was able to beg off and slip away."

"I get it. I don't think I know anyone so kindhearted as those five women. But get them competing in something, and the game faces go on!"

"True. They're having fun, that's for sure."

Mitch closed the chicken coop door, made sure the lid to the feed can was secure, and remarked, "It's a pleasant evening, let's sit on the porch."

The barn had a nice porch across the front, and it was one of Mitch's favorite places to sit and relax. As they got comfortable, Dave started.

"Mitch, I've been thinking about what I said at dinner earlier. You know, about God having something more for us here."

"I've been thinking about it too, and I agree with you, Dave. There is something more. Something beyond our helping the food pantry. But I can't see what it is."

"I couldn't either, until now."

"I am excited to hear, go on."

"I was reading in the book of Romans earlier this

evening and I stopped reading because I felt a prompting. I closed the Bible and sat looking at it. And the thought that came to mind was this. Paul wrote his epistle to the Romans to bring to them the message of salvation. He and other Christians in Rome, mostly Jews, were just trying to survive under severe persecution. But Paul decides to try to reach the Romans, their oppressors, by explaining God's path to everlasting life. That's pretty amazing."

"It certainly is, Dave. I sense that realization led you to how the Haven can reach others."

"It did. As I sat there looking at my Bible, I remembered that I own several Bibles. Study Bibles, Men's Bibles, various translations. I think, in all, I probably own ten or twelve Bibles. But I can only read one at a time. And then I started to think of the Romans during Paul's ministry. The Christians had their scrolls of the Old Testament and copies of the Apostles' writings, but the Romans had nothing. Nothing to teach them that there is a better way. I started to wonder how many people around us here also don't have that knowledge. Don't have a Bible in their home."

"I have no idea how many don't have a Bible, Dave, but with the way the world is today, I would guess quite a few."

"Yes, perhaps most. So, I suspect that, if all of us pooled our extra Bibles, we would have quite a few that we could deliver to the people here in this county."

"I like this idea. Among the eight of us, we could probably come up with at least forty Bibles to give away.

But, Dave, you didn't bring all your Bibles with you, did you?"

"No, sadly not. I would have to go back and get them."

"I am not crazy about that idea. You have only been here a short time, but it won't take long for someone to notice your house is empty and break in looking for valuables."

"True. I could take Jim and we can stop at his house, too, and get their extras."

"That makes sense." Mitch paused, an idea forming. "We could ask Joanna and Maggie if they have extra Bibles at home as well. I tell you what, why don't I go with you and Jim. We'll get Joanna and Maggie's house keys from them. It will be much safer with three."

"Agreed. I'm assuming you will be armed?"

"Yes, reluctantly so. I hope I never have to use a gun on anyone but won't hesitate to defend myself and others if forced to. It is something I pray about often. Yes, I grew up around guns and hunted for many years, but the thought of actually shooting a human being is not something I want to experience."

Dave said, "I understand and agree with you. I appreciate that you and Mary have them and are trained to use them. I'll never carry one, but that's just me."

"You are sort of like Sheriff Andy Taylor from Mayberry."

"I suppose you could say that."

"Does that make me Barney Fife," laughed Mitch.

"No, I don't think so. More like a guardian."

"Okay, I'll accept that. Come on, let's share your plan with the group."

28

DECEMBER 1

They had decided to take Jim's truck to Wadesville to gather the Bibles. It was black and would be noticed less than Mitch's red truck. Besides, with its tinted windows, they were hoping people would assume those in the truck were dangerous and leave it alone. Mitch felt bad about the deception, but he was more concerned about getting in and out of the city safely than what people thought of them. Maggie and Joanna had given the men a list of additional things they wanted from their homes. Jim and Dave would also pick up some items in theirs.

Mitch, Dave, and Jim had also decided to take the backroads into Wadesville. Freeway shootings had increased of late and they preferred the two-lane roads for safety. As they entered the northern part of Wadesville, traffic was lighter than normal. In fact, most of the parking lots they passed were virtually empty. Except for the grocery stores where the lots were full and lines extended out the doors. They also noticed that the Wadesville police were in those parking lots. Even driving by, they could feel the tension as people stood in line to try to get food. They continued toward Jim's house to see the neighborhood was different. At first, they were not sure what it was that had changed.

When they drove onto the road to Jim's house, he stated, "Something is not right here."

"I feel the same," Mitch agreed.

Dave nodded. "Something is different, but I can't put my finger on it."

Then Jim questioned, "Where is everyone? No cars on the street or in driveways. No one out walking. It's like everyone is gone."

"Not quite," Mitch informed. "I just saw someone peeking out a window in that house up on the right. He looked scared."

"I say we get what we came for and get out of here," Dave said.

Jim replied, "Yes, get in and get out."

As they pulled into Jim's driveway and got out of the truck Mitch said, "Why don't you two go in and get the Bibles? I'll stay out here and keep an eye on things."

"Good idea," Dave said. "Never hurts to be too careful."

"I just don't want to leave the truck unattended. Nor do I want us to all be in the house together and risk getting surprised from the outside. Jim, get your gun out and you and Dave do a thorough search before you get the Bibles. Make sure no one is inside."

"Will do," Jim replied.

Mitch had given Jim his Ruger Mark IV .22 caliber pistol. Although the rounds were small and light, the gun itself would act as a deterrent and was effective at close range. Mitch was carrying his 1911 model Colt .45 semi-automatic. It was his favorite pistol. The 1911 was carried by American soldiers in WWII and was just as popular today as it was in the 1940s.

As Jim and Dave entered the house, Mitch took up position on the porch where he could see up and down the street. While he stood watch, he shook his head at the situation. *How could it have come to this so quickly,* he thought. Yes, Mitch had seen bad times coming, but the speed at which society had deteriorated was stunning. But, then again, remove people's trust in the future and they become desperate. Make food hard to get and tempers become short. Take away their jobs, and they do things they never would have considered doing. Mitch's heart ached for those he knew were suffering. Most of the people in Wadesville were totally unprepared for the current chaos. When he and Mary had lived here, they had joked about living in the Wadesville bubble. But that bubble had burst and the evil of the world had entered. Mitch did not know if the evil had come from outside of Wadesville or if it simply came to the surface in those who lived here. Probably some of both. Regardless, it was here and it was palpable.

Mitch heard the front door open and turned to see

Dave and Jim coming out, loaded down with boxes. "Everything okay in your house, Jim?" Mitch asked.

"Yes, but I get the feeling it will not stay that way very long. I shut off the electricity and the water, hoping that will prevent any potential damage from a fire or broken pipes. But the strange thing is, Mitch, it didn't feel like my home anymore. That surprised me. We have only been at the Haven a few weeks, and this house and this neighborhood feels like a foreign place to me."

"Perhaps that's because you, and the rest of us, are realizing more and more this world is not our home. We are only here for a little while. Maybe a very little while at that."

Dave said, "Jim and I talked and we think I should take over driving his truck. That way you two can stay alert for trouble and use your guns if you have to."

"Good idea," Mitch replied. "Of course, if you carried a gun, too, that would make things easier."

Dave responded, "That may be true, Mitch. But, as I've said before, I'm fine without the gun. Just doesn't feel like the right thing for me. Not that I have a problem with you or Jim, or anyone else having one. Just not my thing."

"Understood and I respect your feelings on this, Dave," Mitch replied. "Okay then, let's load up and get over to Dave's house."

The drive to Dave and Denise's house revealed more of the change in Wadesville. Mailboxes hanging open, no traffic, and the flutter of curtains as they drove past. Pulling into the driveway, Dave commented, "When it snows, it is going to become obvious which houses are not occupied. That, I'm afraid will mean houses like mine here will be targets for people looking for food and valuables. I don't like the thought of this place getting broken in to."

Mitch responded, "I am sorry, Dave. This must be hard for you. And for you, Jim."

Jim replied, "Yes, it's hard, but we did the right thing in leaving here. This is not the Wadesville we used to know."

The rest of the visit to Wadesville reinforced Jim, Dave, and Mitch's fears for the area. Joanna's condo was intact and they did see a few people out, but only in pairs. They had a worried look as if they were expecting something bad to happen. Their last stop was Maggie's, just outside of Wadesville on the way back north. Maggie's neighborhood was a little older and the houses were set back off the street a bit. As they pulled into the driveway, they could see the front door was open. Pulling their guns, Mitch and Jim approached the door. They could see where it had been smashed open.

Jim said, "Do we want to go in or maybe just go back to Mt. Olive? What if someone is in there?"

Mitch replied, "I suppose there is some risk Jim, but what do we tell Maggie? I would at least like to go in and see what we find so we can tell her. That would be better than her not knowing."

Jim responded, "Okay, you are right. She needs to know."

Mitch turned to Dave who was by the truck and said, "We're going to investigate. Keep out of sight in case anyone flushes out. We don't want them taking the keys from you and making off with the truck."

Dave went to the far side of the truck as Mitch and Jim approached the door.

Mitch said, "I'll go in and move to the left. You move to the right. Keep your gun in front of you and ready, but I am hoping the house is empty."

They entered, Mitch peeling to the left and entering the living room. Jim moved right into the kitchen. As Mitch surveyed Maggie's living room, his heart sank. The place was a mess. Furniture had been overturned and it looked like anything that could be, was broken and smashed. Making his way through the room, he exited into the hallway that led to the bedrooms on the left and the kitchen and dining room to the right. Mitch quietly made his way toward the kitchen and called softly to Jim, "Coming your way."

"I'm in the dining room," Jim replied.

Mitch joined Jim to discover the dining room looked much the same as the living room. Only, it seemed worse as Maggie's dishes were strewn around the room, all broken. It was either a case of maliciousness or anger at not finding what they were looking for. It didn't really matter why, Mitch knew Maggie would be heartbroken to know that this house, her house that she had worked so hard to make her own had been violated.

Jim asked, "What about the bedrooms, did you look there yet?"

"Not yet," Mitch replied. "I wanted us to do that together. Come on."

Approaching the hallway, Mitch stopped and turned to Jim. Quietly, he explained, "Here is how we are going to do this. When we get to each door, I want you to stand next to the door on the knob side. I will crouch down in front of the door, gun drawn. If we surprise someone, they will be looking high. I'll be near the floor and you'll be to the side, so hopefully, we'll be safe. No talking until we clear all three bedrooms. Got it?"

Jim nodded his head and the two moved carefully to the first door. Mitch got into position as Jim moved to the side. With a nod from Mitch, Jim swiftly, but quietly, opened the door. When the door opened, Mitch eased forward, staying low. It was immediately apparent the room was empty. More damage like the rest, but empty. The same was true for the other two bedrooms.

When they made their way back to the front of the house, Mitch remarked, "Whoever was here must have left as soon as they realized there was nothing worth taking. I am thankful for that. Last thing I wanted to do was to have to point a gun at someone."

Jim responded, "You and me both. I am not ashamed to say I was scared."

"Right there with you, brother," Mitch replied. "Many people don't understand that those of us who choose to be armed do not do so because we want a confrontation. Far from it. We just want to be prepared if we have to defend ourselves and our loved ones."

Jim responded, "I'm beginning to understand that. I

was never much for guns, but the world has changed and we have to do what we must. I do wish I knew how to use this better, though."

"We'll work on that when we get back. For now, let's get Maggie's Bibles and other things and get out of here. I'll take the bedrooms and you look in the rest of the house."

As Mitch and Jim exited the front door, Dave came around the truck and asked, "You guys were in there a long time. Everything okay?"

Mitch replied, "Yes, except that the house is a wreck. Everything is smashed up. I don't look forward to telling Maggie."

"She'll be okay," Dave assured. "I know Maggie loved this house, but she is strong and not into material things. It may bother her for a little while, but I think she'll get past it quickly."

"You're probably right, Dave," Mitch responded. "I think we could say the same for everyone in our group."

Jim added, "I wouldn't worry about Maggie. She and I had a good talk a few weeks ago."

"What did you talk about?" Dave asked.

"About the condition of the world. How bad everything is and how much we've lost in such a short time. But we also talked about how much we have to gain beyond this world. She even talked about this house and how much it means to her. But, in the end, Maggie is more focused on her permanent home with Jesus than this one."

"That's good to hear," Mitch said. "I'm just so glad you

all chose to come to the Haven. I don't like to think about what would have happened to Maggie if she had stayed here."

29

DECEMBER 4

As Mary updated their inventory of extra food in the basement, she realized that their stock was depleting quickly. While Mary and Mitch had worked hard over the last several months buying extra beans, rice, pasta, canned goods, and more, the inventory was evaporating with each day. With eight mouths to feed and trying to provide for needy families in the area, they would run out of food long before spring. Just as Mary was finishing her inventory, Denise came down into the basement.

"Hi, Mary, what are you doing down here?"

"Taking a food inventory, Denise. It doesn't look good."

"Oh no. I didn't realize we had a problem. But it looks like there is a lot of food here."

"Yes, it does look like a lot," replied Mary. "But if you

think in terms of all of us here, plus the twelve families we're helping, it will go fast. By my calculations, what we have on hand will last us three to four weeks. Maybe five or six if we stretch it."

"Not good," Denise responded. "Well, I guess we'll just have to go get more."

"Somehow, we will. Mitch and I can't go. Most stores won't let you in anymore without proof of the shot."

"True, but some of us did get the shot and we can go. But I am not so sure I want to go back into the city. It was scary enough going down to Sullivan last month. If you had not been armed, I hate to think of what might have happened."

"But we were fine, Denise. Nothing happened because we were prepared." Mary set the clipboard with the inventory down on the table in Mitch's office and said, "There are grocery stores in several of the towns around here that we should be able to still buy food. I think they are far enough away from the city that they should still be getting deliveries. Of course, we may have to stop at more than one to get what we need. I suspect there are still restrictions to prevent panic buying."

"Probably so. Let's go up and work out the details with the rest of our group."

As Mary and Denise explained the state of the food inventory and Denise's suggestion to refill the pantry, Mitch said, "Excellent thinking, Denise. And that ties in with something we all were discussing when you two came up. I have been reading some reports of stores only taking cash now. Seems some of the owners are worried that the credit cards systems will go down and not come back up. If that happens, the store owners could be left with thousands of dollars of credit and debit transactions not fulfilled."

Jim added, "And we were talking about how none of us thought to get cash before we came up here last month. I guess it never occurred to us that things as basic as credit and debit cards would become a problem."

"Oh," Mary said. "That could be a problem. Even though Mitch and I stockpiled some cash, I doubt it is enough to deal with our current situation."

"Agreed." Mitch nodded. "So, we need to address that issue sooner rather than later. I think we should tackle both issues at the same time, and do so today if possible. If one thing is certain, we don't know what tomorrow may hold."

The group divided into four teams of two. Each team mapped out a route that would take them to stores and banks in the nearby towns. They all followed the same routine. Stop at a bank and get as much cash as the ATM would allow. Then they would stop at the grocery store and get as much food and supplies as they could. Some stores let them use their credit or debit cards, others were cash only. Mitch had instructed each team to buy as much food as possible. "Don't think in terms of weeks," he said. "Think in terms of months and the fact they needed enough for several families."

When everyone had made their stops and returned to

the Haven, the process of unloading and moving everything into the kitchen took a little more than an hour.

"I can't believe all this food," Maggie said. "Where are we going to put it?"

"Good question," Mary responded. "That's why Mitch and Dave are downstairs rearranging the basement. Let's see what they've done."

When they entered the unfinished side of the basement, Mitch and Dave were just finishing their project. The two had cleared all the shelves that Mitch and Mary had used to store kitchen appliances, coolers, record boxes, and other items to the crawlspace at the other end of the basement. This freed up their six shelving units for food. They had purchased ten more shelving units that day and they were now arranged next to the first six.

"Nice work," Mary said. "Now to get everything down here."

"I have a plan for that," said Dave. "Let's form a bucket brigade down the stairs. That way, we won't be making a bunch of trips up and down. I know these old knees aren't up for that kind of exercise."

So, they did. Mary anchored the line in front of the shelves, being the excellent organizer she was. Within an hour or so, all of the food had been shelved according to type. When they were done, the group looked at the piled-high shelves and the impact of what it represented struck them. Stockpiling food to last several months meant their lives were now changed drastically. No more weekly trips to the grocery. No more going out to dinner. No more of the comfortable routine they had grown used to. Everything they ate and everything they did now had to be thought out carefully. It wasn't a matter of preference now. It was a matter of survival.

30

DECEMBER 8

Early December had been unusually warm. All the harvesting was done, and the garden prepped for the next spring. So, the residents of the Haven had been enjoying some much-deserved rest.

The group had been talking, without Mitch and Mary, about it for a few weeks. It wasn't like it was a secret, just something that they needed to decide before they brought it to their hosts. They decided. At dinner that evening, Denise shared with Mitch and Mary what they had been discussing.

"Mitch, Mary, we have been talking and there is something we would like to ask you both."

"Okay," Mitch responded, not sure what was next. Denise sounded very serious.

"We," she motioned around the table, "Have decided we would like you to teach us how to shoot."

Mitch looked at Jim who responded with a shrug, saying "not my doing."

"What brought this on?" Mary asked.

"It wasn't any one thing," Joanna offered, "But it just makes sense. Too many scary things have been happening and we want to be prepared."

"I understand," Mitch replied. "So, all of you want to learn how to shoot? What about you, Dave? Any change to your perspective on this?"

"Not me," Dave said. "I understand the need to defend ourselves and I have no problem with anyone, even Denise, learning how to fire a gun. But for me, it just isn't something I feel called to do. I have prayed about this, and that is where I am on it."

"I can respect that," Mitch said. Turning to the others he asked, "So, when do you all want to start?"

"Tomorrow would be good," Jim replied. "Before it turns too cold."

"Okay, but we should start tonight actually. We could just take you out tomorrow and let you shoot at targets, but it is important that you do some learning before that, classroom-type learning."

"Like what?" Joanna asked.

"Well, we need to go over gun safety, how a firearm works, how to hold a pistol, a rifle, and a shotgun. Then you will need to learn how to take apart and clean each of the guns. Then, when everyone is comfortable with all of those things, we can go out back and shoot."

———

AFTER DINNER THAT EVENING, Mitch took everyone down to his office in the basement for their lesson. He made sure all of the guns were unloaded, and then showed each person how to hold them, had them pull the triggers to get a feel for how much effort it took, and then had them learn how to take them apart and put them back together. The session took almost three hours and the group was a bit overwhelmed by it all.

"Maybe we shouldn't go out and shoot tomorrow," Maggie said. "There is a lot to remember and I don't want to make a mistake."

"Normally, I would agree with you." Mitch shrugged. "I would prefer to work with each of you one-on-one until you were totally comfortable. But everyone did a great job and I think you'll do fine tomorrow. We will go slow and take our time out there. I have talked about safety precautions on the gun range and you will only have one bullet in the gun to start. You will all do just fine."

31

DECEMBER 9

The warm weather held overnight, and the thermometer was approaching fifty-five at ten that morning while Mitch finished setting up the gun range. When Mary and he had bought the property the previous year, there was a large mound of dirt in the back near the fence line. He thought it would make the perfect backstop for a small shooting range. He and Mary had made some improvements to the mound and set the posts and plywood for targets. As the group approached the table Mitch had set up fifteen feet from the targets, he thought to himself, *Never did I imagine this. My friends learning how to shoot in my backyard.*

"We are going to go slow through this process. Not because none of you have ever handled a gun, but because this is the right way to learn how. Before we even get to handling the weapons, we need to talk about the mental part of gun use. Now, I am not worried about any of you having a cowboy attitude toward shooting. That's for the less mature. But it is important to have the right frame of mind when handling a gun. When practicing like this at a range, our mental approach is one of discipline and concentration. That's how we eliminate mistakes. And mistakes can be deadly."

Maggie, ever the schoolteacher, raised her hand.

"Yes, Maggie," Mitch responded.

"Mitch, I know I said I wanted to do this, but I am bit afraid. Does that mean I shouldn't be trying to learn to shoot?"

"Not at all. A healthy fear of any potentially dangerous activity is good. Think of it this way, when we were young and first learned to ride a bike, wasn't there a fear of falling over?"

Many nodded and Denise remarked, "Oh yeah, definitely for me."

"This is no different," Mitch assured. "Like any new skill we attempt, the more we practice, the more we feel comfortable and confident doing it."

Jim then said, "I am okay with shooting at targets like this, but I am not sure I could actually shoot a person. I guess I am more hoping that having a gun and looking like I know how to use it will keep something bad from happening."

"An excellent point, Jim. That is exactly what I was going to talk about next. Think about this, police officers often go through their entire careers without firing their guns. It is a rare thing when they even pull their guns. The gun they carry at their side is mostly a deterrent, and that is how we will treat them. But I think you all should be aware, carrying a gun does come with a responsibility. If you are faced with a dangerous situation and you are armed, don't hesitate to pull your weapon and take control of the situation. If a bad guy pulls a gun on you, he won't wait for you to decide whether or not to do the same."

Mitch could tell everyone was totally focused on what he was saying. And that was good. There were no unimportant parts to safely handling a weapon.

He continued, "Finally, I want you to think of being armed like you would having an insurance policy for your house or car. Both are something you need to protect yourself, but you really hope you never have to use it." He paused, then turned to Mary, "Anything else before we get started?"

Mary stepped in front of the group and looked specifically at the women.

"I want to reiterate what Mitch said about taking the initiative. Normally, the right course is to try to negotiate out of a dangerous situation if possible. That's why we carry concealed, the presence of the gun can itself be a provocation. But if threatened, it is vital to take control."

"Like you did at the grocery store?" Maggie asked.

"Exactly," Mary responded. "The element of surprise can throw off your attacker. Most people with bad intentions look for those who they think are vulnerable. For us, ladies, that makes us a prime target. However, when faced with a superior force and exuding confidence with that force, the bad guys are almost always going to take off."

"But if they don't," Mitch added, "Be ready to defend yourselves. Now, let's all step up to the tables and we'll get started."

Mitch and Mary took the group through the process of getting familiar with the weapons. On the table were Mary's 9mm Taurus and Mitch's 1911 Colt pistol. The array also included the .22 Ruger pistol, a 20-gauge Ithaca pump shotgun, a 9mm Baretta pistol, and a .22 caliber Marlin rifle. Next, they went through dry firing, pulling the trigger with an unloaded gun. They spent a lot of time with this drill in order to make the steps to handling a gun safely second nature. After Mitch and Mary were satisfied that they had the process down, they began to fire live ammunition at the targets. They started with only one round in each gun. Then three. And finally, a full magazine. After about twenty minutes of live firing, Mitch then took the group through the process of cleaning each gun. Cleaning, he explained, was just as important as learning how to shoot. An improperly cleaned gun would not fire. And that, he explained, could make the difference between living and dying.

As Mary helped the group stow the weapons and ammunition in the cases, Mitch walked over to Dave who had been watching the entire process from a distance.

"Any change to your thinking about learning to shoot?" Mitch asked.

"No, Mitch. No change. I appreciate you and Mary teaching everyone how to shoot. I really do. It's just not for me. Although I do have to say, my wife seems to have taken to it quite well."

"That she has," Mitch replied. "I think she is the best shot in the group. I do have to ask, is there a specific, underlying reason you don't want to learn to shoot? Or is it just a philosophical thing?"

"Good question, Mitch. I would say neither. After the incident at the grocery for the ladies, I thought a long time about this. Prayed about it mostly. I received a very strong feeling from the Holy Spirit that this is not something I am to do."

"Fair enough. We should always heed the leadings of the Holy Spirit. Speaking of leadings, I am being led to believe it is about dinner time. Hungry?"

"Yes! Now on that, I am always willing to participate."

32

DECEMBER 15

The sun had barely risen as Mary stepped quietly downstairs and into Mitch's basement office, she saw him busy on his computer typing away.

"What are you working on so furiously this early in the morning, Mitch?"

Mitch looked up from the computer and turned to his wife. "Oh, good morning, dear. I am working on a manual for the Haven."

"A manual?"

"Yes. I got to thinking about how we have talked about this place after we are gone and that others will find their way here to escape the chaos that is coming. When that happens, they will need instructions for how to run the house, take care of the chickens, the garden, and everything else."

"Yes, that's a good idea. Anything I can help with?"

"As a matter of fact, there is. You can work on the

sections that deal with food, the grain mill, maybe even canning instructions for next harvest."

"Next harvest, you talk as if we will not be here then."

"I did not mean next harvest as in this year necessarily. Just the harvest after we're gone."

"Okay," Mary replied. "Mitch, do you think we'll not be here next year? It seems like things are rapidly moving toward the end. Is this it?"

"I don't know, Mary. Only God does. Jesus spoke about this in Matthew, chapter 24, I think." Mitch reached for his Bible, thumbing the pages until he found what he was looking for.

"Here it is, Matthew 24, verses 45 and 46. 'Who then is the faithful and wise servant, whom the master has put in charge of the servants in his household to give them their food at the proper time? It will be good for that servant whose master finds him doing so when he returns.'"

Mitch closed the Bible and looked over to Mary. "While it seems like the rapture and the tribulation are imminent, ours is not to concern ourselves with the when of it all. Instead, we are to faithfully go about our lives, doing God's work until that time. Now, I'm with you, it does seem like the end is so close. But this isn't the first time people have thought the same thing. No, I'm not talking about the crazies in the past who gathered people and stood on mountain tops waiting for the end. But there have been times in history when the world was so evil and awful, many Christians thought the end was near."

"But why does it feel so different this time, Mitch?"

"Probably because, in many ways, it is different. In the past, the world that people saw was smaller. It wasn't really global like it is now. Things might be terrible in a country or a larger region, but okay elsewhere. Today, though, for the first time in history, these are not regional issues. The entire planet is facing evil, pestilence, violence, and more. And consider this. Jesus also said in Matthew 24, 'And this gospel of the kingdom will be preached in the whole world as a testimony to all nations, and then the end will come.' Never before has the gospel been able to reach the entire earth. But now, through missionaries, technology, and the fact the Bible has been translated into almost every language spoken, that is occurring."

Mary sat thinking, then said, "So then, when the Gospel reaches everyone, that is when the rapture and tribulation happen. Seems like that could happen any time now."

"It does. So, best to be prepared. I will say this, though. God's timing is His alone. While it may seem like the rapture is right around the corner, it may take years before we actually get to that point. As bad as things are, as accelerated as evil is working in the world, we simply don't know how long before God says, 'Enough!'"

Mary responded, "Well, for me, it can't come soon enough. This world is becoming such an awful place that there really is nothing here I will regret leaving behind."

"Amen," Mitch agreed.

33

DECEMBER 24

Snow would have been nice. Christmas just seemed that much more special when there was snow. As the group at the Haven gathered in the living room after dinner this Christmas Eve to read the Christmas story in the book of Luke, the drab, rainy day reflected their mood. One of Mitch's favorite things to do for Christmas was to put up lights outside. The cheeriness of the colors seemed to amplify the good feelings of the season. But Christmas lights were an expense that they chose not to make in light of the ever increasing cost of everything. Not to mention the periodic electrical outages that were coming more frequently now. Mitch worried that the power would go out for more than the usual few hours and cause problems at the Haven. While they could still keep the house somewhat warm with the woodstove, a loss of electricity would endanger the food in the fridge and freezer. An extended outage would likely cause panic for most people, resulting in who knew what kind of behavior. At least they were far enough from the city that any ensuing chaos would not likely reach them. But not far away from the neighbors, the Garretts who had shown a definite lack of wisdom in their behavior.

As the group settled in, Mary noticed that Maggie seemed distracted. She could guess why. This Christmas was difficult for the group, and especially for the mothers who were missing their children.

Mary sat down next to Maggie and patted her on the knee. "I know this is hard. Missing our children this time of year."

Maggie responded, "Thanks. Yes, it is hard. I am really struggling with not seeing my boys and their families for Christmas. I don't like that we can't get together and enjoy our Christmas traditions."

"I understand. It is so different this year. Mitch and I wanted to visit my father over in Vernon Heights this week, but he is so afraid of the virus he doesn't want anyone coming who isn't vaccinated. Mitch's family Christmas gathering was canceled because his aunts and uncles are afraid also. But what hurts the most is not being able to see my girls."

"I am with you on that," Joanna stated as she joined them on the couch. "Most days, I'm doing okay with this new life here. But right now, at Christmas, I just feel so depressed. There just doesn't seem like there is anything to celebrate this year."

Mary responded, "Yes, Joanna, it does seem that way. At least we were all able to talk to our kids this week. I am thankful for that. And I know Abbey and Elaine are okay up in Tipton. Still, I wish I could see them."

Maggie said, "Me too. Maybe you will this spring, Mary. But I don't see how I will see my kids with them so far away. Chicago and Pittsburgh might as well be on the other side of the globe."

Joanna put her arm around Maggie and said, "I know it's hard, Maggie. But we all have one thing going for us. Our kids know the Lord and will be all right. If not in this life, definitely in the next."

Dave walked to the front of the room as everyone settled and asked, "Did everyone get a chance to read the news article Mitch told us about?" Everyone nodded. "Good. Before I read the Christmas story, I think we should talk a bit about what was said. Mitch, can you recap the article for us and tell us what else has transpired since the Pope's Christmas Eve message was broadcast?"

"Sure, Dave. Well, as you know, the Pope's message today was shocking, to say the least. Not really a surprise to those of us who can see where the world is headed. But still hard to take in. So, in short, the Pope announced that he has been in talks with other world religious leaders and they have all agreed that what they call intolerance has to stop. He said that the world can't go on allowing religious extremists to exist. And he defined religious extremism as those who believe their religion is the only valid one. This isn't new. This Pope has been insinuating the same perspective for a while now. What is disturbing is that today he called out two groups. First, Muslim extremists. He said their terrorism represents not religion, but violent evil. I could not agree with him more on that. But the other group he attacked is what he called intolerant Christians. In his words, 'Christians who adamantly contend that following Christ is the only way to heaven.' He went on to say that, while many Christian churches around the globe have moved forward with their thinking and are open to other's beliefs, these fundamental Christians are a danger to us all."

"That's a bunch of hooey!" Jim said. "Since when is following Jesus wrong? Who does he think he is kidding anyway. No one is going to buy these lies."

"I wish that were true, Jim," Mitch replied. "But the truth is, most people are buying it. I did some checking and practically every major religious leader around the world has endorsed the Pope's comments. All the long-time Protestant denominations have put out statements of support. As have the Muslim leaders in countries outside of the Middle East and northern Africa. The Buddhists and Hindus have signed on to the Pope's stance as well."

"What about the Jews?" Betty asked.

"Now there is some encouraging news," Mitch said. "The Jewish officials in Israel have put out a statement strongly disagreeing with the Pope. Of course, that has caused a backlash, not only from other religions, but governments as well."

"Nothing new there," Joanna commented. "Hatred of Israel seems to be as popular as hatred of true Christians."

"I agree, Joanna," Mitch said. "There are some interesting developments. Protests have sprung up around the world at Catholic churches, and these are Catholics doing the protesting. One article I read quoted a protester as saying the Pope does not speak for all Catholics and his message today is anti-biblical. Another said it was time to break away from the Catholic church because it has become more of a government bureaucracy than a church."

"What about all of the non-denominational churches?" Denise asked. "Any word on a response from them?"

"Some," Mitch answered. "That will take more time as they are independent and the stance they take will depend on their local pastors and elders. I suspect we'll see where each church stands in the coming days when they make their statements in response. And one thing is true, every church will respond to this call for a unified faith. No church will be able to ignore it. I think we will see the news media go after independent churches or more fundamental, small denominations demanding they make a statement."

"Mitch, what about our church?" Mary asked. "Any word from Pastor Fred?"

"Yes, Pastor Fred sent an email just a little while ago. He was very clear in stating that the Pope's message was not of God, but of Satan. He warned that the Bible clearly foretold of the apostasy we are now seeing. He reminded us that the vaccine entrance requirements mandated last month for churches are an effort to keep true believers from meeting and encouraging each other. He went on to encourage us all to keep the faith and not let these difficult times sway us from belief in the one true God and His purpose for us."

"Wise words, indeed," Dave affirmed. "While we're all confident in our faith, my concern is for those who may be deceived by this development. They will be drawn in by the inclusiveness of a united world religion, and they cannot see that it is no religion at all. It won't have any substance or true meaning. It reminds me of the free love movement of the 1960s. Whatever you feel is okay. Whatever you believe is your truth. Or like people say today, 'You do you and I'll do me.' Somehow, they think, that will get you to heaven."

Mitch responded, "So right, Dave. I'm guessing that this new religion will attract many people. Some will be from existing religions and some will be those who don't even believe in God. It will all be so 'feel good' and undemanding that it will be very appealing."

"And yet," Mary offered, "All of those people searching for the missing something in their lives will still have the empty spot deep inside. The spot we all know can only be filled by Jesus."

"Amen to that," Dave blurted. "And with that, let's take some time to recall the true substance of our belief in a savior called Jesus Christ. Our reading is from the first chapter in Luke, I will start with verse 26. 'In the sixth month, God sent the angel Gabriel to Nazareth, a town in Galilee, to a virgin pledged to be married to a man named Joseph, a descendent of David. The virgin's name was Mary. The angel went to her and said, "Greetings, you who are highly favored! The Lord is with you...""""

34

JANUARY 1

The New Year had always been a day to look back and forward at the same time. This New Year's Day was no different in one sense, but completely different in another. One year ago, the virus was supposedly raging across the globe and the promised vaccine was coming soon. The contentious election was over and everyone was waiting to see what the results would be of the shift in political power in the country. The shortages were still a problem, but people were hopeful they would ease. People were just as hopeful that, if they could just get through winter, spring would bring an end to the virus and return life to normal. That was the looking back.

The looking forward was an entirely different matter —mostly because the hopes for the future had fragmented into a myriad of different dreams. Some hoped for increased vaccinations that would finally end the virus.

Some hoped for a global economy that would stabilize currencies and prices. Some hoped for an ill-defined era of equality that would make the world a happier place. Some hoped for an end to violence through the banning of private weapons. Still, some hoped simply that they would be left alone to live their lives without interference.

For Mitch, his hopes had narrowed drastically from the previous year. Gone were thoughts of post-retirement travel, weekly golf outings, and some serious antiquing. No, these things were from his past, not his future. All of Mitch's hopes now could be categorized into three things. Food. Shelter. Faith. Maintaining the Haven was a challenge with eight to feed, plus their efforts to help others in the area. Constantly working the mini farm and figuring out ways to make the house continue to function was a source of concern. Keeping a strong faith during the most challenging time in his life required more effort than the other two combined. But doing so was made that much easier by the presence of his friends—and his dear wife. Thinking of them reminded him that it was his turn to make breakfast and the sun would be up soon. He better get at it and figure out a new way to cook eggs. They had become an almost daily food for the group and he could tell some were getting tired of them.

———

"MITCH, I don't know what you did, but these eggs are great," Joanna commented as she placed another mouthful on her fork.

Mitch replied, "I just got creative, I guess."

"We can see that," Denise said. "These are delicious. Where did you find the recipe?"

"Right in here," Mitch replied while tapping his temple. "I just made it up. I was thinking of French toast while I was making breakfast and thought a little vanilla makes French toast taste good, so why not in scrambled eggs to."

"I can taste the vanilla," Denise said. "But there is something else there I can't quite identify."

Mitch grinned and said, "You are not going to believe this, but it is cornmeal."

"Cornmeal?" Joanna said. "In scrambled eggs?"

"Yes, cornmeal. As Mary knows, I love cornmeal pancakes, so after the vanilla, I thought, why not get a little crazy and try something new."

"Well, I can say I think your experiment is a success," Dave commented. "A new dish for a new year."

Mitch replied, "I wish there was a secret ingredient I could add to our lives that would make them better."

"What do you mean, Mitch?" Dave said. "I think our lives are just fine as is. We have all we need here. I can't think of anything we lack that really matters."

"Maybe not," Mitch replied. "I just think about how things were before all this started and wish we could get some of it back. No, not the material things of the world, but some sense of normalcy."

"I understand what you are saying, Mitch," Dave replied. "It can be tough some days when we think about what we have lost the last two years. But I am reminded of the thirty-seventh Psalm where the author wrote, 'Fret not yourself because of evildoers; be not envious of wrongdoers! For they will soon fade like the grass and wither like the green herb. Trust in the Lord and do good; dwell in the land and befriend faithfulness. Delight yourself in the Lord, and he will give you the desires of your heart.' I think we are doing just what is written about in the Psalm. We are dwelling here in the land and staying faithful the best we can."

"So true, Dave," Mitch responded. "An excellent reminder." He pushed his plate away and dabbed at his lips with a napkin, then went on. "I just sometimes get a bit down thinking about all it takes just to survive. But then, I suppose I should be thankful. Our lives have been pretty easy until recently. We live in a time where every luxury and convenience is at our fingertips. Well, used to be. So, now that we have to put a little more effort into living, I suppose I shouldn't complain."

"Mitch, I understand what you're saying," Maggie chimed in. "It can be hard some days. But you know, I don't think I've ever felt so fulfilled in life as I have since we came here. There is something about spending each day doing things that matter. I am busier than I've ever been, but don't feel hectic like I used to. We just go from task to task every day and it feels so natural. It's like a totally different vibe than before."

"I know what you're saying, Maggie," Betty said. "Jim and I used to have to think about how to occupy ourselves each day. Keep ourselves entertained so we wouldn't get bored. But now, living here, there is plenty to do and it doesn't even feel like work most of the time. Nor does it feel like we have to rush to get things done. It's funny, before it always felt like there wasn't enough time in a day to do what needed done. But, as I look back on it, the things we were trying to do were just things to fill the day. Now, we do things that need to be done to provide for our basic needs, and that is enough. There is a peace in knowing that your days are spent doing important things."

"I could not agree with you more, Betty," Mary said. "And Mitch and I are so happy you're all here. Yes, we could probably get by on our own, but we could never help others like we can with all of you pitching in. Speaking of pitching in, who wants to help with the dishes?"

"I will," Joanna said.

As the group took their plates to the kitchen, Jim approached Mitch and asked, "Mitch, I'm assuming you checked the news this morning. Anything of note on this first day of the new year?"

"As a matter of fact, yes. Quite a few things. I was planning on giving an update after breakfast. Let's bring in some more firewood and we'll get everyone together in a few minutes."

The morning dishes done, the group gathered in the living room, enjoying the warmth of the wood fire and settling in to talk. Mitch opened the conversation with an update from his news gathering.

"As expected, our leaders here in this country and around the world have issued statements about the year ahead. They are optimistic as usual this time of year, but what they are optimistic about is concerning."

"Like what?" Joanna asked.

"For starters," Mitch responded, "To a person, world leaders are talking about this as the year of unity. A good idea on the surface. But the unity they are referencing is one that continues the intolerance of any religion that is exclusive in favor of this concept of an open religion that welcomes all beliefs as having equal merit. They don't mention true Christianity specifically, but we all know that is the target based upon previous statements."

"Just more of the same," Jim stated.

"Yes, more of the same," Mitch replied. "The problem is any lie told often enough becomes truth for some. That is what will happen here. The same is true for the promises that food will become plentiful and gas prices will go down. They don't say how, just that it will happen. But that is not what concerns me most."

"What does concern you, Mitch?" Maggie asked.

"It is this. Each and every world leader talked about the need to become one globally. Not just religiously, but in every way. Some even referenced the World Economic Forum's 'Great Reset' plan as a road map to a new path to peace and safety. We all know that plan involves the loss of each country's sovereignty and each person's loss of personal property. They've said so. Now, more and more leaders and everyday people are embracing the concept."

"But surely it won't happen this year," Denise said. "That is a big leap from where we are now."

"I agree, Denise," Mitch replied. "Unless there is a catalyst that triggers a worldwide call for a unified, global government."

"What kind of trigger?" Joanna asked.

"There is only one thing I can think of that will accomplish that. The rapture. I think everything that has been happening and will happen is moving the world toward a new order. That order will happen shortly after the rapture."

"That makes sense," Dave said. "Once we're all gone, the Holy Spirit leaves this world with us. Chaos will break out and the ensuing effort to bring order will result in a global government."

"So, Mitch," Mary asked, "Why does this concern you so? If we are gone to heaven, what is the worry?"

"Just this, we are now helping a few dozen families. Through our efforts, all have Bibles, but many are still just learning God's truths. We are running out of time to help them see that salvation is possible, and to avoid the coming tribulation. I am afraid too many of them will wait until it is too late."

Jim spoke up. "Mitch, I understand your concern and it is valid. But remember, we are doing all we can and the rest is up to each person and God. I just believe that He has placed us in this work to bring people to Him and it will happen. It's happened already for so many of the families we minister to. I'm confident it will with the rest."

Mitch replied, "Thanks, Jim. I appreciate the reminders and the encouragement. That said, I think we all need to rededicate ourselves to our work here and make sure we do not miss one opportunity to share the Gospel with everyone we encounter."

"Amen," they replied in unison.

35

JANUARY 9

Mitch awoke to the sounds of a full-fledged winter storm. As he looked out the window in the pale dawn, he could see they already had about three inches of snow and it was still coming down. He thought how fortunate they were to have had the propane tank topped off just before Christmas. The propane company had suggested they wait, the tank was only down to sixty percent and should last into March. But Mitch had been insistent. He wanted to make sure the tank got nowhere near half empty. They had adopted the same approach to the gas tanks in their cars. The uncertainty of everything meant you had to be prepared for things to fall apart at any moment. At first, the constant guarding against catastrophe was stressful. But, as they fell into the rhythm of daily life together, it began to feel normal. Well, as normal as it could be.

It wasn't just about fuel for the furnace. The propane

tank also fueled the generator that would supply electricity in case of an outage. If they had learned anything over the past few months, it was that the things everyone took for granted to live life everyday could be disrupted without notice.

The electric had gone out between Christmas and New Year's. After determining there was no outage in the area, Mitch called the electric company to find out what the problem was. The representative took a while to come back with an answer. She told Mitch that the power had been shut off because the bill hadn't been paid in two months. Mitch explained that there was no bill to pay because they had a credit on their account.

She replied, "I can see that, sir, here on my screen. But it also shows you did not pay your bill for October and November."

"How can I pay a bill if we have a credit on the account? There is no bill to pay."

"I don't know, sir. I haven't encountered anything like this before. Let me check with my supervisor."

Mitch listened to on-hold music for several minutes until the representative came back on the line.

"Sir, I have spoken with my supervisor and she says that we can issue you a check for the credit on your account, so this won't happen again."

"I don't want a check. Look, you are applying the funds from the credit every month, so the bills are getting paid."

"That's true," she said. "But my supervisor says that is

what is causing the problem. Issuing you a check will clear it up."

"I realize you are trying to help, but my wife and I overpaid on the account, specifically so we wouldn't have to worry about paying the bill if something went wrong for us. Isn't there some way to make this work?"

"Let me see. Well, this might do it. I will set it up as an automatic withdrawal from your checking account. It won't actually take the money from there because of your credit. But that should fix the situation."

"Thank you. Thank you very much!"

Mitch and Mary set up a similar arrangement with the other utilities. Life at the Haven was certainly getting interesting.

Mitch pulled back from the window as he wondered how much snow they would get. As usual, the weather forecasts were all over the map. Literally. The predictions were for anything from three to ten inches. Well, the three was a sure thing, but how much more? Mitch walked into the kitchen for his first cup of coffee. As he poured, he dreaded the idea of bundling up to go out to the barn and feed and water the chickens. He shivered at the thought. Sitting down at the kitchen table, Mitch pulled his Bible to him and started reading in Psalms. He used to read a lot of Ezekiel, Daniel, and Revelation. Those books provided insight into the coming events. Of late, he felt guided toward the Psalms. It seemed fitting as these poems and songs provided comfort and assurance. Mitch needed support during these times.

This morning had brought him to Psalm 27. The first

three verses seemed like they had been written directly to him.

"God, You are my light and my salvation, whom shall I fear? You are the strength of my life, of whom shall I be afraid? When the wicked come against me to eat up my flesh, my enemies and foes, they stumbled and fell. Though an army may encamp against me, my heart shall not fear!"

What a wonderful reminder. Mitch could sometimes get caught up in the list of tasks they needed to complete at the Haven. The logistics to work out. The problems to solve. It was good to be reminded that, regardless of the sense of urgency he felt, the feeling of the world closing in around them, God was there protecting them and providing for all of their needs.

Mitch closed his eyes and let the words he had just read soak into his soul. He thought about all that had happened the last six months and knew that he would have never made it through without God's strength and guidance. Whenever he thought he was at the end of his endurance, God made a way. Whenever he started to fall down the tunnel toward fear, God would put someone in front of him to encourage and support. Everything was so different now, but Mitch knew that God was in it, so it was as it should be.

Mitch slipped out of the house quietly before anyone else had awakened to tend to the chickens. Mary was used to it by now. It was a rare occasion when Mitch stayed in bed until she woke. It wasn't that Mitch wanted it that way. He simply could not sleep in. He had always awakened early, and he did enjoy the quiet of the morning before the day started. It was a time he could pray and reflect on the day ahead. He had forgone his usual habit of checking the news online in the mornings. He now spent his mornings reading scripture and praying, and he felt so much better because of it. He did still check the news of the world, but later in the day. As he entered the barn and made his way to the coop, he wondered what this day would bring. He lifted his eyes and prayed, *Lord, what do you have in store for our little group today?*

When Mitch came back inside the house, the quiet was gone, replaced by the warmth of a house full of people who loved each other. Mary, Denise, and Betty were busy cooking breakfast. Dave, Jim, and Joanna were sitting at the table drinking coffee and talking about the day's chores.

"Good morning, Mitch," Dave called. "How are our feathered friends this morning?"

"Doing good, Dave. Actually, very good," Mitch remarked as he raised the wire basket they used to collect eggs. "Ten today. Not bad for the middle of winter."

"Excellent." Dave grinned. "The ladies are keeping up with the demands of the house."

"Yes, they are. I wish we had more, so we could share with others. But I guess in this kind of weather, trying to deliver to our families would be treacherous."

Dave replied, "True. Not worth the risk at this point." He paused and glanced at Jim and Joanna. "Say, Mitch, we've been talking and we have an idea."

"An idea about what?"

"Well, it is the middle of winter and there aren't that many chores to do around here. We need to keep busy, so we were thinking we would take some of the lumber out in the barn and build some beds."

"Build some beds? Why?"

"We call this place the Haven, right."

"Right," Mitch answered wondering where Dave was going with this.

Dave continued, "So, if it is a haven, isn't it reasonable to think that others will be joining us here?"

"Like who?"

"I don't know who. But I think God does."

"Okay, I can't argue with that. But where are we going to put these beds? All three rooms upstairs are full. Where would they go?"

"Down in the basement," Dave replied.

"The basement?"

"Yes. I know you and Mary have your offices down there, but you don't use them anymore. You're both now retired. You moved your computer to your bedroom, so they're sitting empty."

"You make a good point, Dave, but we don't have mattresses for these new beds. What would these people sleep on?"

"We figured that out too. We have all the cornstalks and wheat straw in the barn, right?"

"We do," Mitch replied hesitantly.

"And we have more than enough sheets here since we all brought all we had from our homes. We sew them together and stuff them with straw and corn husks. There should be enough for two full-sized beds."

"Dave, that is a great idea. Did you come up with this?"

"No, Joanna did."

Mitch turned to Joanna and smiled.

She shrugged "Well, it just made sense. We were talking about the possibility that more people would come here. I remembered that, when I was a little girl, my grandmother had beds with corn husk mattresses. I slept on one when I stayed at her house and it was comfortable. So, I said why not do that here?"

"I say, let's do it," Mitch replied. "We can set you up in the garage to build the beds. That will be much warmer than the barn."

Just then, Mitch's cell phone rang. He looked at the display and saw it was Matt. He hadn't heard from Matt and Kate since Christmas and was starting to worry about them.

"Hey, Matt, good to hear from you. How's the weather down there?"

"A raging winter storm. Same there?"

"Oh yes. About four inches on the ground and continuing to snow hard. What's up?"

"Mitch, things are getting crazy down this way. Kate lost her job because they are now requiring everyone to be vaccinated. Erica is still at the hospital, but we expect that to change any day now. And the people around here are starting to get desperate. Several houses in our neighborhood have been broken in to. They aren't looking for valuables. They are looking for food. I'm afraid it won't be long until they hit us."

"That's a shame, Matt. I assume you've done what you can to stay safe."

"We have. I have secured all the doors and windows as best I can. But I'm concerned that the thieves will get more brazen and try to do something during the day when we are going in and out."

"Matt, it sounds like it is getting too dangerous to stay there. Why don't you and Kate come up here? We have the room."

"That's exactly why I called. Kate just got off the phone with a neighbor who was telling her that they saw a group of characters driving through the streets yesterday. She said they were driving slowly and looking at every house as they went by."

"Ouch! Doesn't sound good at all. As soon as this storm breaks, why not come up?"

"We will. In the meantime, say a pray for us, Mitch. Ask God to place a hedge of protection around us."

"We will, Matt. All of us will." Mitch hung up the phone.

Mary observed, "It sounds like something is happening down there."

"It is. People are getting desperate and dangerous in their community. They plan to come here as soon as the weather breaks. We all need to pray in the meantime that God will deliver them safe here to the Haven soon."

"Done," Mary responded.

Later that morning, the new beds were progressing

rapidly. Knowing that two more were headed to the Haven soon created a sense of urgency. Dave and Jim were in the garage building the frames while Joanna and Betty were making the mattresses. Maggie helped Mitch bring in all of the straw and corn husks from the barn for the mattresses. By lunch time, the beds were almost done.

After lunch, the group worked together to rearrange Mary's and Mitch's offices to accommodate the beds. They did not feel like bedrooms, but they would be functional. Mitch knew who one room was for but wondered about the other. Could it be for his brother, Steve, and his wife, Lydia? He hoped so.

36

JANUARY 9

AFTERNOON

The new bedrooms all set, the group settled in the living room for the afternoon. It was important they enjoyed some restful time every day. In a couple of months, it would be spring, and their days would be filled with many chores inside and outside. As they so often did, they shared stories from their lives. It was a way to take comfort in times past when life was more normal, and the memories helped them cope with the reality that they were now living in. Maggie shared humorous stories from her days as a teacher. The stories of the kids' hijinks were always good for a laugh. They also reminisced about their days back in Wadesville, remembering great times going to the local arts festival, attending the community concerts, and the many cookouts in the summer. As Joanna was telling one of her funny stories about the dog she once owned, Mary's phone rang.

She rushed into the kitchen where she had left it and

answered, "Hello?" Mary listened, then continued, "Hi, Kate. I did not expect to hear from you today. Is everything okay?"

The group stopped talking and turned their attention to the call.

Mary continued, "Oh my, that's awful! Are you both okay?"

Mary listened for several minutes, then said to Kate, "All right. I understand. You are doing the right thing. But please be careful. It will be dark soon." More listening. "Yes, I will tell them. No, don't worry about that. We have that taken care of. Goodbye."

Mitch asked, "What's up, Mary? Are Kate and Matt all right?"

Mary walked back into the room. "They're okay. Kate says that one street over from them two houses were broken in to while the people were home. The thieves didn't hurt anyone, but they took everything they had to eat."

"That's terrible," Joanna said.

"They were elderly couples and retreated to other rooms to hide. Kate said that they knew, if they came to their house, it might be a different story. Matt told her he could not stand by while their house was robbed. So, Kate told him that they needed to leave now."

Denise asked, "They're on the road now? In this weather?"

"Yes," Mary replied. "Kate says they took all their food except a few emergency items over to the two couples. She said they told them they should be safe now as the thieves think they have no food. Then they packed up everything they could fit in their truck and are headed this way."

There was a pause in the conversation as everyone contemplated the gravity of what they had just learned. Things had deteriorated to the point that it seemed all societal restraints were gone. Lawlessness had taken hold of the nation. Mitch thought about the treacherous journey ahead for Matt and Kate. He knew Matt would stay off the main highways as best he could to avoid trouble. His big four-wheel drive truck would help. But it would still be a risky trip in the storm.

Mitch also thought of their neighbors to the North. He knew that it was only the winter weather that was keeping the Garretts inside. With spring, the risk of their neighbors causing mischief again would come back.

Maggie broke the silence, "Can there be any doubt that God knew this would happen today? Why else would we be prompted to make more beds? Joanna, I think God specifically put that memory from your childhood in your head so we would be ready for Kate and Matt."

Joanna responded, "Maggie, I think you are absolutely right. Now that we know they're coming, let's see what we can do to one of those rooms downstairs to make them more comfortable."

The ladies set to redecorating Mitch's office, now guest bedroom. Down came Mitch's paintings and framed prints of historical events. His desk was moved to the corner and end tables were used as nightstands. Mitch and Jim brought down a chest of drawers from his and Mary's room that they didn't really need. By the time it got dark, they had Kate and Matt's room ready. It had been three hours since Kate had called to say they were on the way. Mitch knew the two-hour drive would take longer in the storm, so he was expecting them any time.

Two hours later, Matt and Kate had still not arrived. Mitch and the others were starting to get worried. They had planned on the two new residents of the Haven to join them for dinner. Mitch kept looking out the window, watching for Matt's white truck coming up the main road. The storm still raged and spotting a white truck would be difficult, but, thankfully, the road was all but empty in the storm. Glancing at the clock once again, he saw it was almost 9 p.m. Seven hours since they knew Matt and Kate had departed. Mitch looked back out the window just in time to see Matt's truck turning onto their road, then into the driveway.

"They're here!" Mitch called out.

Everyone hurried into the living room, looking out the windows as Matt brought the truck to a stop. Slowly, Matt and Kate emerged from the truck and plodded through the blowing snow to the porch. Mitch opened the door and ushered them into the house. They both looked exhausted.

As Matt pushed back the hood of his coat, he looked at his best friend and exclaimed, "Thanks be to God. He is the only reason we are here." With that, Mitch and Matt embraced. The two men felt the stress fade away as they were reunited.

Mary rushed over to Kate and gave her a tight hug, only letting go to help her off with her coat.

Kate said, "I should leave this on. We have so much to

unload from the truck."

Mary replied, "Don't worry about that. Come in here and sit down. You must be totally worn out. Tell us about the trip. What took so long?"

"Matt can tell you about it," Kate said. "I just want to sit here for a while and relax. I am stiff all over."

Mary led Kate to the couch and got her comfortable while Matt started to tell of their journey.

"Well, once we decided it was time to go, we started packing everything we could think of that could be useful. We packed enough clothes for all four seasons. Some bed linens. Towels, toiletries, cleaning supplies, and whatever food we didn't take to the neighbors. We still had room in the truck, so I started throwing in anything else that made sense. Camping gear, tools, hardware, kitchen utensils. A little bit of everything."

Betty said, "That was smart. But why did it take so long? Did you run into trouble?"

"Quite a bit, actually. I took along my gas cans from the garage. They were mostly empty, but for some reason it made sense to bring them. I'm glad we did. We took off up the state route out of town. I didn't want to go over to the freeway. Getting stranded there in this storm would have been precarious. We had driven about an hour and came upon a small gas station in a little village. It was one of those with the old gas pumps, not the new digital ones. I thought it might be good to fill up the gas cans in case we needed them. The owner was a nice older gentleman. He asked what we were doing out on such a terrible night. I just told him we were heading toward home but were several miles away and wanted to fill up. I said we would pay cash. I did not know if he would ask for my vaccine verification or not. But he did not even mention it. So, I topped off the truck tank and filled the cans in the back."

Denise had been making a fresh pot of coffee and brought a cup each to Matt and Kate.

After taking a sip, Matt said, "Thank you. I've never tasted anything so good!"

Mitch asked, "So, what then? That does not explain what took so long. Did you get stuck in the snow?"

"No," Matt replied. "Nothing like that. We kept coming north on the state route until we got to Chester where we had to turn right to start coming northeast. It was slow going in the storm, but we were making good progress. As we drove through Chester, there was a roadblock at the main intersection."

"A roadblock," Dave said. "A police roadblock?"

"No," Matt replied. "Not the police. It was three pickup trucks. It did not make sense. At first, I thought it was an accident, but as we got closer, I could see it wasn't. What I did see were men standing next to the trucks. I could not see their faces because they were bundled up against the cold. But I could see they were all armed. Rifles and shotguns it looked like. I could see that there was only one more intersection ahead before we reached the trucks. So, I turned left to avoid the roadblock. Before we rounded the corner, I could see men scrambling into two of the trucks and then start in our direction."

"They came after you?" Maggie asked.

"Exactly. I realized we could be easily followed

through our tracks in the snow, so I had to do something. I was familiar with Chester and knew they didn't have a police department. So, we were going to have to outrun them or outthink them to get away."

"Which did you do?" asked Denise.

"A little bit of both. I figured the best way to get away was to hide in plain sight until they gave up looking for us. I knew I could make a swing around the perimeter of the town out of sight of the main intersection. We did that and then came back toward the center of town one street over from our original route. By then, we had lost our pursuers —I had been driving without my lights on and the white truck helped shield us from view. As we approached the center of town, I neared a car dealership I had seen before and we eased into one of the empty spots and shut off the truck. I could just see through the buildings the one truck still at the roadblock. After about twenty minutes, the other two trucks came back. So, we just settled in to wait them out. Our truck was getting covered with snow, so there was little chance we would be spotted. I thought that these guys would eventually get tired and bored and leave. Well, that took almost two hours. When they finally left, we waited another half hour to be certain they were gone and eased out of the lot and down the road, lights off, until we were out of town."

"Oh my," Denise commented. "You must have been cold sitting there."

"I was never so cold in my life," Kate said. "We couldn't even move around to try to stay warm. We didn't want to take a chance at someone seeing us."

"After that," Matt concluded, "It was just a matter of staying on the road. The blowing and drifting snow was getting pretty bad. My biggest concern was getting past the state capitol. I thought about taking the outer belt to save time, but we decided it was best to avoid the city altogether. So, we came up the rural routes to the west, then headed east once we cleared the city."

Mitch looked at his friend, saying a silent prayer of thanks. "I for one am very glad you are here. I wish your trip had been more pleasant, but regardless, welcome to the Haven!"

"Thanks, Mitch. It is good to be here. Kate and I have felt a longing to be here for these past few weeks. I know God is here." He reached over and took Kate's hand. "I can't think of a better place to be right now."

"Good to hear," Mitch said. "Now let's get your truck unloaded and get you settled into your room. I think you will like it, especially the bed."

Matt looked at Mitch inquisitively while Mitch gave Joanna a wink.

The entire group helped Matt and Kate unload their truck, taking the personal things to their room in the basement, food to the pantry, and the camping and other gear Matt had brought to the garage. Once they had everything in place, the members of the group made their way to their rooms to settle in as the storm outside continued to rage. They couldn't help but think of the storm as an expression of the state of things in the world. Out there was danger and the unknown. Inside the Haven, comfort and peace.

37

JANUARY 10

The people at the Haven awoke the next day to a world covered in white. As fierce as the storm had raged the day before, in the morning all was calm. While Mitch was not overly fond of winter and snow, the tranquility of the morning was moving as he trudged toward the barn to tend to the chickens. He stopped halfway to the barn and slowly turned, taking in the hushed beauty. The wind had blown the snow so it looked like waves on the ocean, frozen in place. The sun made the flakes sparkle like diamonds, sometimes too bright to look at. And the complete quiet, enhanced by the blanket of white was so peaceful. That is until Mitch's solitude was invaded by the loud racing of an engine to the north. He looked that way and saw that the Garretts were firing up their ATVs. He knew they would crisscross their property, playing in the snow for quite some time. *So much for a peaceful morning,* he thought as he continued to the barn.

When Mitch returned to the house, Matt was in the kitchen making coffee. Mitch smiled as he watched Matt, thinking back thirty years to when he and Matt met. It was in Virginia on a hot, humid May weekend. They had both joined the same Civil War reenactment unit and were attending their first event. The heat had been almost unbearable, sleeping on the ground did not lend to much actual sleep, and eating only what they had brought in with them was not exactly fine dining. They both had loved it and, as they got to know each other, anticipated the next event. For the next twenty years, Mitch and Matt attended reenactments all over the country. From Maryland to Mississippi to Pennsylvania and North Carolina, Mitch and Matt traveled together to the reenactments and became like brothers. As age and responsibilities brought their reenacting time to a close, the two spent more time on the golf course. Still enjoying the outdoors, but with less physical demands than playing soldier.

It was in those years that Matt and Mitch grew closer, sharing their deepest thoughts on life, family, and faith. The bond created wasn't strained by the fact they lived two hours apart. The past few years, as the world continued to spin out of control, the two talked more about the state of things from a biblical perspective. What did the events in and around Israel mean as far as prophecy was concerned? Where was the US headed spiritually and how did they respond to those events? How were they to think about these times? They had had many discussions about whether they were living in the end times. Matt thought so and made it clear he didn't think the world would last twenty years before the rapture and tribulation. Probably less, he had told Mitch. While it seemed possible to Mitch those things could happen quickly, he tried not to dwell on timeframes and argued that, regardless of when, being prepared spiritually and doing God's work were what mattered.

As Mitch entered the kitchen, he remarked, "For a man who used to not like coffee, you've become quite the caffeine addict."

Turning from the coffee maker, Matt responded, "Well, you are to blame. It was your camp coffee that got me hooked." He finished pouring the water in the maker, turned it on, and continued, "Those frigid mornings in camp are what did it. I was so cold, I just wanted something hot to drink. I then discovered the best coffee I've ever tasted. Still is."

"Thanks, Matt, it just requires patience to make good camp coffee." Mitch grabbed two mugs from the cupboard. "You know, those were such great days back then. I love how it taught us we could get by with very little, much less than we've got now."

"So true, and life slowed down when we were out there in the field. When you have to walk everywhere you go, your world gets really small. You find ways to keep yourself occupied without technology and all the rush of modern life."

"I also remember how quiet it was, besides the sounds

of hundreds, sometimes thousands of reenactors, horses, wagons, and such—but those were all natural sounds. They fit in with the land we were living on."

"Is that one of the things that prompted you and Mary to move out here? To get away from the noise of the city?"

"Yes, that and more. I realized there in the city we were much too dependent on modern conveniences, as well as our needs for everyday life. Not to mention, the expectation of keeping the lawn manicured and everything just so in an upscale suburban neighborhood. Here, things are more laid back and natural. Sure, we keep the place nice, but in a country way."

"I hear you. I was getting a bit bored with the constant effort to keep our place up, and a little bit tired too. It's hard work and you just get it all done and a week later you're right back at it."

"Some days I felt like a pet gerbil on a spinning wheel. Always going, but never getting anywhere. But now, here at the Haven, we live by the seasons. Planting in the spring, harvesting in the summer, and preparing for winter during the fall. It's like all the work I do here means something. It has tangible results for our living, not just for show."

"Well, I know Kate and I look forward to our new lives here. Horever long that will be."

"Are you two telling old war stories again?" Kate asked as she entered the kitchen.

"Not too many," Mitch responded. "How did you sleep?"

"I slept wonderfully," she said. "I didn't know a rope bed could be so comfortable. What is inside the mattress?"

"Cornhusks," Mitch replied.

"Cornhusks? Really?"

"Yes," Mitch said. "Joanna was the one who came up with the idea to build extra beds for downstairs. She remembered sleeping on a cornhusk mattress many years ago. So, since we had plenty of them here, it made sense to put them to use."

"Well, I am glad you did," Kate said.

Mary then walked into the room and greeted everyone. "So, what are we talking about this morning?" she asked.

Matt replied, "Cornhusk mattresses."

"Well, of course, what else?" Mary responded with laughter in her voice. "Let's change the conversation though, how about talking about breakfast?"

"My favorite topic," Matt responded.

Mary and Kate started on breakfast while Mitch and Matt headed for the garage to sort more supplies.

Matt started, "Mitch, this is an amazing operation you have here, and to have done it all in such a short time is quite the accomplishment."

"Thanks, we did work rather hard at it last year after we moved here. I didn't realize then why I felt a need to do things so quickly, but I am glad we did. I'm not sure how we would manage without everything this land has provided."

"It is indeed a blessing. So, now that Kate and I are here, we want to contribute in any way we can."

"No worries there. Everyone at the Haven contributes —according to their abilities. This winter it is mostly about cooking and cleaning, but come spring, the garden will keep us all busy. Cutting and splitting firewood for next winter will take all spring and most of summer."

"Looking forward to doing meaningful work. But tell me more about your ministry here. You've mentioned it some on the phone but give me the details."

"Let's have a seat. The telling will take a while."

Mitch pulled out two folding chairs, then continued. "Well, we started last summer. We donated some of our produce to a food pantry up in Evanston—that's about fifteen miles from here. The pantry is run by a local church and they feed about six hundred families a month."

"Six hundred? Must be a big church."

"Not really. The church is rather small, but the people there have big hearts and are dedicated to doing the Lord's work."

"Okay, but how did that lead to the work you are doing now?"

"As we got to know the pastor up there, he told us that, while they fed so many, there were many more they were not reaching. Mostly, he said, here in the southern part of the county, it's difficult to get the word to people that there are resources they can take advantage of."

"So, what did you do? Obviously, you were able to find out who needed help near here."

"We started with our local Bible study group. Someone mentioned a family that had just lost their income and were having a tough time. So, we contacted them and asked if we could bring by a few groceries. Matt, these were good people who just had some bad luck."

"That's usually the case. So, you started helping this family and that led to?"

"That led to building trust with people. After we had visited the family, the Hendersons, for a few weeks, they mentioned another family nearby that was going through a rough time. So, we asked them to call to make an introduction. They did and we started making weekly visits to the Jordan family."

"How many families do you visit each week now?"

"First, our visits are now every two weeks. There are far too many to get to every week. But I believe we are serving twenty-five families as of now. No, make that twenty-seven."

"Wow! I can see why you had to change to every two weeks. But with that many families, where do you get the food? Especially in the winter when the garden is fallow."

"Good question. When Mary and I started this last fall, we had built up a bit of a stockpile of nonperishable foods. At first, we were just thinking in terms of having extra for ourselves, with maybe a little more to help others."

"A wise thing to always have extra on hand."

"Yes, it is. But one day, as I stood looking at the shelves of food we did have, it became clear that, although we had enough to last a while, we had the space and the ability to do more. We did not want to be hoarders or preppers. That defies God's instruction to not worry about tomorrow. But we did feel called to create the ability to help those in need."

"So, how did you accumulate so much before the stores required vaccine proof for entry?"

"That was a concern. Mary and I went shopping almost every day. We would not buy large quantities of anything, just reasonable amounts. Over time, about five weeks, we had amassed a fairly good quantity of food. But it wasn't enough."

"So, what did you do?"

"We couldn't do much. When the restrictions hit, Dave and Denise were kind enough to buy fresh foods for us every week. That was back in October. But our stockpiling had to come to an end. We did have enough, we thought to help people get through the winter. I figured, come spring, we would figure something else out."

"So, does that mean you are getting low on food for others?"

"Actually, no. Our best estimate is, we can help feed twenty families for the next four months."

"How is that possible?"

"First, when Dave and Denise, Jim and Betty, Joanna, and Maggie arrived last November, we were able to do some serious work on our inventory. Once everyone saw what we were doing, they jumped in to help."

"Okay, so everyone else helped, but how in the world were you able to accumulate enough to feed twenty families for a that long?"

"That's where God came in. Everyone realized that we had the room to store more food. With six people now able to get into the stores, they started buying food every day. At first, we tried to be really organized. Mary keeps an accurate inventory, so we were able to maintain good lists of what we needed each week to keep our stock levels even on all items. But then, as the stores started having trouble keeping shelves filled, we had to resort to buying whatever was available."

"Mitch, this is all great, but it must have been expensive. I mean, food prices are up twenty-two percent in just the last six months."

"We talked about that last fall when we started. The fact is all of us are very blessed with resources. We realized that our previous planning for the future included shopping, travel, and other expenses that were no longer relevant. So, using those funds to buy food instead was an easy decision. I'll admit, at first it was frustrating to pay so much for things. It was irritating to pay almost double what we used to. But the truth is, it's just money. In Deuteronomy, we are instructed that it is God who gives us the power to get wealth. And that means it really is not ours anyway. God makes all things, including money."

"I've always tried to look at it that way."

"I know you have, Matt, and so, thanks to our friends and God's resources, we have been able to gather enough food to help others."

"I've got to see this for myself, and it's all in the basement?"

"Sure is. You remember the door at the bottom of the stairs in the room you and Kate are using?"

"Yes. I figured that led to your furnace and such."

"It does. The furnace, water heater, and a large freezer. That side of the basement is as large as the finished side. I'll take you through it after breakfast this morning. Speaking of which, we should probably be getting back inside before Mary sends someone after us."

———

AFTER BREAKFAST, Mitch and Mary took Matt and Kate to the basement to show them the "warehouse" as they called it. As they entered and Mitch turned on the light, the couple gasped.

Kate said, "Oh my! Look at all of this."

The unfinished side of the basement was about twenty-five feet wide and thirty-five feet deep. The furnace, water heater, and freezer were along the back wall. The walls on either side were lined with large shelving units, and each one was filled with food. Matt did a quick count, noting there were seven units on each side. Each one filled to capacity.

"Mitch," Matt exclaimed, "This is impressive, and it looks so organized."

"That's my doing," Mary said. "When we started, we just had four shelves down here. Then, when we got serious about stocking up and brought in more shelves, I realized we needed a system."

"I can see that," Kate said. "Can you explain what we're looking at?"

"Sure," Mary responded. "Each individual shelving unit has five shelves. The bottom shelf contains proteins.

Canned meats, peanut butter, and tuna. The next shelf up is all canned fruits. Next is canned vegetables. Then pastas, sauces, flour, seasonings, and rice. On top we have oats, cereals, granola bars, and cookies."

"Amazing," Matt said. "So, how do you keep track of how old the food is? With this much, seems like it would be hard to know that."

"It would," Mary said, "But I have a system. Walk down here with me." Mary stopped in front of a shelving unit that had a large red towel hanging on the front of it. "This is our next up indicator. We will pull from this shelf for our next deliveries, then move the towel to the next shelf."

"But this shelf behind it isn't empty." Kate said.

"Correct," Mary responded. "What you're seeing there is the process of refilling an empty shelf. Ideally, we like to refill a shelf within a day or two of it being empty. Sometimes it takes a little longer, especially this winter."

"So," Matt said, "You just keep moving down the line, starting back at the beginning when you get to the end?"

"Almost," Mitch said. "Since we have shelves on both sides, we go down the right side first, then we start at the front of the line on the left."

As they turned back to the front of the room, Kate and Matt could see more shelves on either side of the door they came in. But they looked different. Walking back toward the door, they could see the difference. There were four shelving units as large as the others but filled not with food. Each one was crammed with dish soap, toothpaste, toothbrushes, razors, shaving cream, and a myriad of other toiletries.

Mitch explained, "These shelves were Joanna's idea. We had been focused on food, and rightfully so. But Joanna pointed out that people need these other things as well. While being fed is necessary for survival, these items help people to feel better about themselves. To feel at least somewhat normal."

"Not to mention, it's good hygiene," Kate said. "Again, this is amazing. And I can't wait to help get these things to people in need. To do God's work."

38

JANUARY 17

The post-holiday economic slump was getting worse. It seemed the administration in Washington had no clue on how to fix it. Or perhaps no desire to do so. Instead of coming up with a plan to restart the economy, the press conferences were filled with empty encouragements that things would get better. "We live in a great nation that will come back from this temporary downturn," the press secretary claimed. But this didn't gel with that same administration's constant criticisms of the country. While serving up empty platitudes on one hand, the political leaders decried the very system they operated as one of inequity and failure. The irony was it was their own actions that had brought about such chaos. Inflation continued to soar, now in double digits. Housing starts had dried up. The recently ended holiday shopping season's dismal numbers had led to multiple chain stores closing for good. Food prices continued to rise. Gas had stabilized at $7.50/gallon, but that was due more to less demand as winter slowed travel. Most expected the upward climb to begin again in the spring. There was much anticipation for the president's State of the Union speech this evening.

The residents of the Haven settled in around the television awaiting the president's speech. It was a rare thing for the set to be on at all. So much of what was being broadcast now was unfit to watch. Violence, promiscuity, even foul language was commonplace. Not to mention the coercive commercials that insinuated you were a failure unless you possessed more and more meaningless products. Television had become a nonentity for the people of the Haven. They rarely had time to watch even if they wanted to. With the daily chores each had, what time they had left was usually spent in Bible study or simply enjoying conversation, and they were better for it. The manic consumerism of the world did not penetrate their world. Yes, they knew it was out there, but they had recognized it for what it was. A soul-destroying indulgence in worldly things that left a person feeling empty and frustrated. The promised happiness if you just bought what the ads pitched never came. It just led to an increased desire to fill an empty spot that never seemed to go away. Of course, Mitch, Mary, and their friends knew there was only one thing that would fill the emptiness. The love of Christ.

And it was with that knowledge they gathered to hear

what the president would say. Their attention turned toward the TV as they heard the House Sergeant at Arms say, "Mr. Speaker, the president of the United States."

The president entered the House chamber, not to the usual boisterous applause. The reception sounded more forced and without enthusiasm. The representatives and senators in the chamber looked worried, even those of the president's party. The game had changed for all of them. No longer could they manipulate the perceptions of the American people to their advantage. Things were beyond that now. They could no longer posture and pontificate. The United States and its people had real problems that were affecting everyone. Neither house had any answers. Even token bills had not been proposed to make it look like they were doing something to help. Every idea floated in committee was quickly recognized as ineffective and withdrawn. So, as the president strode to the podium, the applause quickly died out and everyone took their seats.

President Benjamin Jordan had been in office only a short time. He had been a part of Washington politics for decades but had done nothing noteworthy until being elected president. In fact, many would be hard pressed to describe his stance on political issues. That would all change this evening.

President Jordan stood at the podium and looked directly into the camera and began.

"Mr. Speaker, Mr. Vice-President, Members of Congress, the First Lady of the United States, and my fellow citizens, this evening I come to you during a most unique time in our nation's history. Never before have we faced such times of uncertainty. Not since the attack on Pearl Harbor in 1941 have we as a people faced such challenges. I would contend that the challenges we face today are even more daunting than those of World War II.

"For today, we are not faced with fighting a war to stop the reign of a few evil dictators. No, today we are faced with evil itself. An evil that has infiltrated every aspect of human life and livelihood. One that, if left unchecked, will continue on its path to destroy mankind. We do not face this evil alone. Indeed, the entire planet is now united against an enemy we must defeat.

"That enemy is one that pervades our homes and businesses. An enemy that attempts to influence our children. An enemy that must be defeated. Who is this enemy you ask? It is intolerance. It is narrowmindedness. It is a refusal to acknowledge scientific truth. An insistence on holding on to failures from the past and a hatred of this planet. People of America, our enemy today, perhaps the greatest enemy we have ever seen is all around us. It is your neighbors who blatantly ignore sound medical advice and gather in churches—many unvaccinated and none wearing masks. It is some of those same people refusing to acknowledge everyone's right to marry who they choose by denying them the services of their company. It is people who insist they have the only way to heaven and all other religions are false. These same people have no respect for women and violently protest against their right to choose.

"And now, as we face a world economic crisis, these people, our enemy, try to tell us we brought this all on ourselves. That we are responsible for the ills of the world. We did so because we refuse to follow what they call truth. As if they are the only ones who know what truth is. They say that we have turned from God and this is the result. They tell us we must go back to the way things were before and ask repentance. I ask repent from what? From finally recognizing that we all have the right to be who we want to be regardless of how we were born. Repent from pursuing the happiness our Declaration of Independence speaks about? And to pursue that happiness as we see fit without the former moral restrictions that persecute those who think differently.

"Ladies and gentlemen, we have nothing to repent of. Except perhaps for taking so long to recognize the value of each individual and the sanctity of their personal truths. But no more. From today forward, we must cast off the moral oppression of the past and forge ahead into the future to create new ways to exist on this planet as part of a global citizenry. A united people around the world capable of solving global problems.

"The only way we can see ourselves through this crisis and create lasting peace and safety is to join together with nations across the globe to create an order that is new. A world system that works for all people in all nations equally. Tomorrow, I will be presenting to Congress a bill that authorizes me to work with leaders from other nations on a one-world system of government. A system that addresses both economic and social problems in a wholistic way. A system that is larger than any one nation. For, it is clear to me that our focus should no longer be on the United States of America, but rather on all of humanity.

"Thank you."

As the residents of the Haven sat stunned by what they had just heard, a smattering of enthusiastic applause could be heard on the TV. The applause started to gather into a roar as the senators and representatives came to their feet. It wasn't that they agreed with the president's proposal. It was more a matter of survival. Joining a global government meant they were off the hook for solving the problems of the country.

As Mitch picked up the remote and turned the television off, Denise clasped her hands together and exclaimed, "Come, Lord Jesus, come."

"Amen," Jim agreed.

Mitch rose from his seat and stood before the group. "I think we all know what this means."

"No doubt," Matt added. "Clearly, this is a step toward the one-world government of the Anti-christ. I guess the only question now is, how long will it take for it to happen?"

Dave remarked, "A good question, Matt. Of course, we can't know God's timing. Whether this new world order is imminent or a year or two or three down the road, who knows? But it certainly gives a sense of urgency to our work here. We need to reach as many people as we can with the Gospel."

Mary responded, "I say we increase our visits and check in on as many families as we can. With it being winter, we need to do so anyway to make sure everyone has enough food and are warm and safe."

"Agreed," Mitch said. "Let's meet right after breakfast in the morning and map out a strategy for delivering more Bibles and helping those in need."

———

LATER THAT NIGHT, Mitch was checking the house, making sure the doors were all locked. As he entered the living room, he saw Matt sitting on the couch.

"Can't sleep, Matt?"

"It's not that, Mitch. Well, maybe some. But I wanted to talk to you."

"About what," Mitch questioned as he settled into his favorite recliner.

"You and I go back a long way."

"Sure do. Back when we were young and weren't afraid of anything."

"That's the point. Back then, we were so young and naïve. Traveling across the country at Civil War reenactments. Golf trips. Just enjoying ourselves and having a good time."

"Lots of great memories, my friend," Mitch replied, wondering what Matt had on his mind.

"Yes, some great memories." Matt paused as if he was somewhere else for a moment, then turned to look at Mitch. "I can't help but think of all the people we have known throughout the years. People from all over the country that we call friends, and many of them don't know the Lord. That weighs on me. I fear for their souls. That makes me think of everyone else as well. So many are going to make the wrong choice. Like now when things are rapidly heading toward the time when we are called home. But more so after the rapture and the decision to follow Jesus will be so much more costly. It keeps me awake at night."

"I understand what you're saying, Matt. It can be overwhelming to think about just how many are being deceived. I think about some of my nieces and nephews who don't even have a frame of reference for these times. My brothers and sisters were raised in the church, even though they don't go now, and their children haven't been taught anything about the Gospel. I am afraid, for them. What will they do when the time comes to decide whether or not to take the mark?"

"I just feel so helpless. Evil seems to be taking over everything and we are powerless to stop it."

"Yes, we are powerless, but God is not. Matt, we need to keep the faith and know that the work we are doing here at the Haven is making a difference. We may not see it, but I am confident that some of the people we are reaching with our Bible deliveries are turning to the Word and seeking salvation. We are planting the seeds and God is watering them."

"I'll keep reminding myself of that." Matt sighed. "You know me, I like to see a project completed. Trusting that it is happening outside of my knowledge is not my strong suit."

"Maybe not, but your faith and your witness are your strong suits. Just keep doing that and let God use you in the way He intends." Mitch rose, reaching to turn out the last light in the room before he added, "Now let's get to bed. We have a busy day ahead tomorrow."

39

JANUARY 18

After breakfast, the group returned to the table to discuss how they would continue their mission in light of the president's address the previous evening. They were a quiet group. As Mitch looked at each of them, he could see that there was a quiet resolve there. A determination that had been taken up a notch by the current circumstances.

Mitch held two sheets of paper in his hand. One contained a list of the families they had been helping for the past two months. The other was a list of families they had yet to visit. Looking at them, he spoke, "We have a total of twenty-seven families we need to do follow-ups with. I've arranged the list according to when we last visited, the ones that have been the longest since we've seen them at the top. This list..." He held it up to the group, "...is families we have been meaning to visit but haven't gotten around to yet. There are eighteen on this list. That's forty-five total."

"So, how do we do this, Mitch?" Maggie asked. "Do we get to the new families first?"

"I don't think we have time to do it that way, Maggie. It's winter and with a few inches of snow on the ground, the cold, and now everyone stressed over all that is going on—plus what was said last night, I think we need to start visiting both lists today."

"I agree," Denise said. "But how are we going to get to them all soon enough. I worry that some may be out of food by now. We know from our pre-Christmas visits that many of these families rely on us completely."

"Good question," Mitch replied. "I think we have to go all out in getting to these people this week. It is Tuesday and we should try to visit everyone on both lists by Friday."

"That's about eleven visits a day," Jim commented. "We're all going to have to get out there to visit everyone."

"Almost all," Mitch said. "We can't leave this house empty. It's too much of a risk that someone might realize no one is here and break in. Remember, these families we visit have been telling us they are seeing that happen in their neighbors' houses. The ones that have been abandoned. So, I suggest we go out in three teams of two, leaving four here to do what needs to be done to keep things going. The cooking, cleaning, tending the chickens, and all that."

"I'll volunteer to stay here," Kate said. "I've had enough driving around in the snow."

"I'll stay as well," Maggie added.

"Thanks, Kate, Maggie," Mitch said. "I think one of us guys needs to stay here as well."

Jim said, "Betty and I will stay."

"Great, thanks, Jim. So, that means, Matt, Joanna, Denise, Dave, Mary, and I will make up the three teams going out. I am assuming you and Denise will want to go out together, Dave?"

"That makes sense," Dave said.

"I'll ride shotgun," Denise said. "I've always wanted to say that!"

Mitch laughed, "Okay, Denise, but I think we'll have you take one of the pistols instead of the shotgun. It's less threatening to the families we visit and can be concealed."

"Agreed," Denise responded. "But I'm still calling it riding shotgun."

Everyone smiled at Denise's enthusiasm and Mitch continued. "Matt, why don't you and Joanna go out in your truck? Mary and I will take ours."

"Sounds good," Matt said.

Jim took his keys out of his pocket and handed them to Dave. "Here, take my truck. I am sure your SUV can make it through the snow, but the truck says strength and will maybe keep the bad guys away."

"Thanks," Dave said. "You're probably right about that."

"Okay," Mitch said. "We have time for two visits each this morning and three this afternoon. We'll break up the list geographically to be as efficient as possible. I'll have your assignments in a few minutes, so let's start loading up the trucks with supplies."

As the group started dispersing to their tasks, Mary piped up, "Wait. There is one more thing before we go."

"What is it, Mary?" Mitch asked.

Mary replied, holding out her hands to either side, "We need to ask the Lord to be with us as we venture out to do His work."

Around the table, the group held hands and bowed their heads as Mary prayed, "Lord, we come to you this morning asking for your protection as we seek to do Your will and serve others. Please bring us all safely back from our work and we ask for open hearts in the families we visit today. Amen."

Each truck was filled with a variety of dry goods, canned food, and Bibles. The group had developed a system for their deliveries that proved efficient and made the best use of their resources. New families received a standard amount and variety of foods based upon family size. Existing families were asked about their current food on hand to determine what was needed to last them until the next visit—about two weeks. The new families on the list had been vetted by the group already. Once they were given a new family in need, three members of the group would make a visit to meet the family and get to know them before adding them to the delivery list.

These interviews were thorough. Families were asked about other resources they had for food and other staples so the Haven group did not replicate giving, thus making sure they were extending what they had as far as possible.

Some of the families on the list lived near farms where generous farmers supplied them with fresh milk, eggs, and potatoes. Others had friends and relatives who were helping. Still other families survived solely on what was provided by the Haven. It was a monumental task to keep track of the now forty-five families. With supplies getting harder and harder to find, Mitch worried that their stockpile would dwindle down to very little. But for now, he thought what they had on hand would last until spring. Then, the produce from the garden would provide much of the food they delivered.

40

FEBRUARY 20

One of the certain things during a Midwest winter is, at some point there will be a brief thaw in the weather. Unusually warm and dry for a few days. Just enough to tease of the coming spring. The day before had been the start and this morning's bright sunshine promised an even warmer day.

When Mary walked to the barn to collect eggs, she noticed a beat-up pickup truck slowly driving by on the road. At one point the truck stopped just past the driveway. Mary tried to glance over without turning her head to see if she could identify who was in the truck. The sun cast too many shadows for that and made the incident more alarming. The brashness of whoever was in the truck to stop and stare was unnerving. Hurrying to the barn, Mary watched from the shadows inside the door. The truck continued to sit there for a few minutes until it slowly drove away.

Later that morning at breakfast, Mary shared what she had seen with the group. Everyone realized that the incident had the potential for trouble. The last thing they wanted was attention toward their home. With the economy still reeling from double-digit inflation and growing food shortages, people were getting desperate. It wasn't that the group was not willing to share what they had. It was their purpose after all. All someone had to do was ask and they would be given. No, the concern was for their safety. Desperate people were capable of doing things they never would have dreamed of in normal times. They worked to conceal that the house was a stockpile of food. That would make it a target for the raiders prowling the roads.

While breakfast continued, Mitch spoke, "I think it's time we took some steps to protect ourselves and to be less conspicuous."

Heads nodded around the table.

Mitch went on, "First, we have too many vehicles in the driveway. That alone draws attention to this place."

"But what can we do about it?" Maggie said.

Mitch replied, "There is an abandoned junkyard about a mile down the road. I suggest we take whatever cars we don't need here and stash them in the junkyard. If we need them later, we can easily go get them."

"That should work, Mitch." Matt said. "Do you think they will be safe there?"

"I think so. Like I said, it has been abandoned for some time, but there are still a lot of vehicles there. One thing we will need to do is make them look like junkyard cars.

We can throw mud on them and whatever else comes to mind. We will take the batteries out as well."

Jim said, "Seems like we should keep all the trucks here since we use them to make food deliveries."

"Definitely," Mitch responded.

Joanna added, "Maybe one car in the garage with a full tank in case of an emergency."

"But that still means we'll have three trucks in the driveway." Mitch said. "That alone will draw attention. We can put one inside the barn and the other behind it where it is less likely to be noticed."

The group went about carrying out the plan for the vehicles. It was not difficult to find a remote corner in the junkyard to stash the cars and they chose to hide Jim's truck behind the barn. Since it was black, it would be less likely to attract attention. Not so with Matt's white truck, so it went into the barn. The work done, the group settled into the living room to tune in to the news. They were met with the shocking news that the parliament in Canada had passed legislation declaring the Bible a myth and would prosecute anyone who teaches it, especially in regard to human sexuality and behavior. What did this mean for the United States? The rest of the world? They all knew that, once the pandora's box of religious persecution became rule of law, it would spread rapidly across the globe. There was little hope that any ground lost for religious freedom would be regained.

The news of the action in Canada was followed with an economic update for the US. Images of empty store shelves, food warehouses heavily guarded, and protesters in the streets bearing signs demanding access to food were hard to accept. How did the greatest country on Earth come to this? Yes, the crop failures and rising cost to produce food had contributed to the shortages. But they did not explain the rapid and devastating famine that appeared to be approaching. The government was mostly silent about the crisis. A few offhand remarks saying this was only temporary and would right itself soon brought no comfort to hungry people. They wanted answers and promises but received empty platitudes instead.

When Mary reached for the remote to turn the television off, Maggie asked, "I don't quite understand what is going on. How did this happen? Isn't there a reserve of food? How did that reserve run out so quickly?"

"Good questions, Maggie," Matt replied. "It is a bit baffling. However, I've been following this situation for a while, and it is not as sudden as it seems. Back when the virus first hit and everything was shut down, the fertilizer companies got behind in production. We actually got most of our fertilizer from Russia and they decided to cut off all supply to the West. The fertilizer that is available is selling for twice the normal amount. Many of the farmers, especially the smaller ones can't afford the cost increase, so they just didn't plant at all."

"I get that," Maggie nodded. "But is all that enough to cause this?"

"It is," Matt responded. "For many years, our economy has run on what is called the 'just in time' principle. That means we only make or grow what we need when we need it. It saves the companies a lot of money because they don't need the large warehouses or to tie up their capital in goods waiting to be sold. The downside, of course, is that any disruption in the supply chain has an immediate effect and it cannot be made up very quickly."

"So, what does this mean for us here?" Joanna asked. "I'm not worried about the ten of us, but what about all the people we help every week? Are we going to run out of food for them?"

"An excellent question, Joanna," Mary responded. "That is something I have been worried about for some time. Even before this news, I wasn't sure how we would find enough food for our ministry and, if we did, how much longer can we afford to buy it?"

"From what I see downstairs, it looks like you have enough for quite some time," Kate said. "I suppose the question is, how long will what we have last?"

"Exactly, Kate," Mary replied. "From the best I can figure, we can get by with what we have for three months —that is, if we cut back on what we deliver. That means cutting back here for us as well."

"I for one, could use some dietary restriction," Dave said as he framed his substantial mid-section with his hands. "Not to make light of the situation, but reducing the amount of food we eat, while not preferable, is not too much of a sacrifice."

Jim bobbed his head. "We have been eating pretty good around here and I won't complain if we cut back. I think the bigger concern is how are we going to restock the shelves—both in the kitchen and the pantry downstairs? Three months is not that long if we can't find food."

Betty suggested, "There is one solution to this, but I am not sure if anyone will like it."

"What is it?" Mary asked.

"Well, remember last week when one of our people we deliver to told us about the guys who came around trying to sell them food for ridiculous prices?"

Everyone in the group nodded.

Betty continued, "Of course, that family could not afford their prices and had to say no. Those gougers are obviously getting that food from somewhere. What if we found out where and bought it first?"

Matt said, "I hear what you're saying, Betty, but it is likely the supplier is stealing that food, rather than buying it."

"A likely case, Matt," Mitch said. "But Betty is right, we need to find a way to get to that food before the black marketers do. I suppose the first thing to do is to find out where they are getting it from. We'll send out two groups tomorrow morning, see if we can track them down, and do some surveillance. Jim and Denise, you two can go with me. Matt, you take Dave. We will head out right after breakfast and meet back here by noon unless we find something before that.

41

―――――

FEBRUARY 21

The next morning, the two teams headed out on their delivery routes, keeping a lookout on the roads for potential black marketers. As luck would have it, they did not have to hunt long. When Matt, Jim, and Dave pulled into the Fergusons' driveway with a load of food, an unfamiliar van was parked up close to the garage.

Getting out of the truck, Matt cautioned his friends, "Let's act like we're just stopping to visit. We don't want anyone knowing we brought food until we know we can trust them. Hopefully, it's just friends visiting."

As they strode up to the door, two angry men stormed out. With only glances, they brushed past the three. Then the first man, tall and a bit heavy, wearing jeans, cowboy boots, and a faded work jacket suddenly turned and hollered to the three.

"If you are lookin' to sell something to these people, don't bother. They got no money."

"Money for what?" Matt asked.

"Money for food, what else? That's the only thing worth buying anymore. No one needs luxuries or fancy things, just food and maybe some gas."

"You have both?"

"Maybe I do." The man eyed Matt suspiciously. "Why, are you a buying man?"

"Could be. Depends on what you're selling and how much."

"Follow me and I'll show ya."

They made their way to the back of the van and the man opened the doors to reveal boxes and boxes of food. Mitch could see canned fruit and vegetables, pastas, peanut butter, tuna, and more. *Just what we need for the pantry,* he thought.

"Wow," Matt remarked. "You sure have a lot of food there. Where did you get it? Not from a store I think."

"Why are you asking? Never mind where I got it. Are you buying?"

"Depends. How much?"

"I make it easy, ten bucks per item."

"Ten dollars!" Jim blurted. "That's crazy. No one is going to buy anything at a price like that."

The man responded, "They will if they get hungry enough." He started to close the doors and stated, "If you aren't buying, I'm out of here. I don't have time to stand here and talk."

"Wait a minute," Matt said. "It's not that we aren't

buying, but we don't have that kind of money on us. We'll need to go get it. Can we meet somewhere, say in about four hours?"

"I suppose we can do that. You got some place in mind?"

"Yes, how about the parking lot of the hardware store in Mt. Olive?"

"Sounds good. I'll see you there in four hours."

The man closed the van doors and started for the front of the van.

Matt called out, "Say, what's your name? I like to know who I am doing business with."

The man turned and said, "You can call me Sam. And yours?"

"You can call me George," Matt replied.

Sam and his cohort got into the van and backed out of the driveway. Mitch, Jim, and Dave watched them until they were out of sight, then went to the truck for the food they had brought with them. Inside, they talked to the Fergusons who told them that Sam and his friend were pleasant at first but turned mean when they learned the Fergusons had no money.

When the three returned to the truck, Dave started, "I'm assuming you have a plan here, Matt? I don't think we're willing to pay ten dollars apiece for food from these guys."

As Matt started the truck and backed out of the driveway, he said, "Yes, I do have a plan."

On the drive back, Matt explained that he believed Sam must have a supplier. While it was more than likely that his supplier had stolen what he was selling, he would be selling it for less than Sam and that would be their goal. Find the supplier and buy directly from him at a lower price.

"I don't like it," Mary protested. "It's too dangerous. You don't know what you'll be walking into if you find this supplier."

"Yes, it may be dangerous, but Matt's idea is a good one," Mitch replied. "And what choice do we have? We need to start restocking the shelves now or we'll run out of food. Any way we try to find more will be risky."

"Explain it again," Joanna chimed in. "How are you going to find this supplier without this Sam guy knowing?"

"It's simple," Matt replied. "We'll meet Sam at the hardware store and buy enough from him that he will need to restock his van. Dave and I will be in my truck doing the buying and Jim and Mitch will be in Jim's truck. After the buy, Jim and Mitch will follow Sam to his supplier. Once we know the location, we'll go straight there and buy the food from the supplier."

"But how will you get this supplier to sell to you?" Kate asked. "He won't be very trusting of someone he doesn't know."

"True, he won't. But we will tell him Sam sent us and, hopefully, that will be enough to get him to sell to us."

Maggie gave her two cents. "Matt, I think your plan will work, but only once. What about after that? Wouldn't it make sense to find a way to buy from this supplier again and again?"

"Good point, Maggie. I hadn't thought of that. But I

don't see how we can pull that off. We need to make the supplier think Sam sent us to get him to trust us."

"What if you did that, but then offered the supplier more than what Sam is paying him. Make it sound like you want to go into business for yourself and cut Sam out of it? He will probably go for that if it makes him more money."

"A brilliant idea, Maggie. I think that might just work."

That afternoon, Mitch and Dave waited in the hardware store parking lot while Jim and Matt took up post on the street within view. Right on time, Sam pulled up in his van and parked next to Mitch's truck. All four men got out and made their way to the back of the van.

Sam looked at Matt and Dave, "You guys ready to do some business?"

Dave replied, "Yes. Let's do this.

"So, you got the money? How much?"

"Enough to buy what we need. How many items do you have in there?"

Sam opened the van and Matt and Dave could see that not much had been sold since they had seen the stash at the Fergusons'. Mitch estimated there were perhaps two hundred food items in the van. He was glad that he and Mary had stockpiled cash for emergencies, it would take most of what he had brought to clean out the van.

Sam raised his eyebrows as he responded, "It just so happens I did an inventory before I got here and there are 212 items here. You aren't thinking of buying me out are you? You don't look like you got that kind of cash."

"As a matter of fact, we do. You see, there are several of us living in one house and we pooled our money for this. It's all we have. So, how about you give us a discount since we're buying it all?"

"A discount?" Sam laughed. "Mister, there aren't any discounts anymore. You want the food, you pay my price or I drive away right now."

"Okay, okay. We'll pay it." Matt said as he pulled two envelopes out of his pocket. Each held a thousand dollars. As he showed them to Sam, he said, "I got two thousand, so I guess you will have twelve left because that's all we have."

Sam replied, "You know what, I am feeling generous today. So, I'm going to throw in the twelve just to show I am not a bad guy. You want to have your man there get the food?"

"Maybe it would be better if your man got the food out. Mine here will take it from him and put it in my truck. I'll give you the first envelope before they load, and the second when they're done. Sound fair?"

"Yeah," Sam replied. "Sounds fair. Can't blame you for being careful. Lot of mean characters around now a days," he said with a sneer. "Hey, Charlie, start unloading this stuff."

Charlie got in the back of the van and started handing Dave the boxes as Mitch handed Sam the first envelope. Sam checked the envelope to verify the cash and smiled. When the loading was done, all four men started to get in their vehicles. Before Sam got in the van, he said, "Now I want you to pull on out of here first. I don't want you following me. That wouldn't be wise."

"No problem," Mitch said. "We just want to get home and take care of this food."

As Matt pulled away, he heard Charlie say to Sam, "Now that's doing some business! Nothing better than doubling your money, and the whole load too!"

Thanks, Charlie, Matt thought. *Now we know how much Sam pays for the food.* As he glanced in his rearview mirror he saw Jim and Mitch sitting in Jim's truck. Jim gave a nod to let Matt know they were ready. As Mitch headed back home, he said a silent prayer, *Lord, keep Jim and Mitch safe. We need the food, but not at the cost of someone getting hurt. Amen.*

———

LATE THAT AFTERNOON, Jim and Mitch returned to the Haven, having successfully followed Sam to his supplier. Mitch explained what they had found to the group.

"I don't think Sam was paying much attention to anything when we followed him. He was probably so happy about selling out to you, Matt, and he never noticed us behind him. Just like you expected, he went straight to his supplier for more food."

"So, where is it?" Matt asked.

"Somewhere you would never suspect. The fireworks store down Route Sixty-Two."

"It makes perfect sense," Jim said. "It is completely secure with that big fence all around it, and the building itself is rather large."

"Are you sure Sam was going there for food and not something else?" Dave asked.

Jim replied, "That is what we wondered. So, we went down the road a short way, found an abandoned homestead, and parked behind the barn. From there we could walk through the woods until we were across from the side of the building where no one could see us."

Mitch continued, "From there we saw men unloading semi-trucks of food and taking them into the building. Better yet, we saw Sam and his buddy, Charlie, bringing out cases of food and loading them into their van."

"Well, that tells us what we need to know. Now we just need to decide when we will go there and execute our plan," Matt said. "I think we should wait two days to go. Whoever is running that operation will not expect Sam to come back, or send someone in our case, for a few days."

Mary added, "Mitch, we used almost all our reserve cash to buy out Sam's van. What are you going to use for money?"

"I'll go to the bank and withdraw what I can from savings."

"Will that be enough?" Mary asked.

Dave suggested, "I think we should all get as much cash as we can. Who knows how long the banks will even be open? Much less dispensing cash."

"Good idea," Mitch responded. "Let's do that tomorrow."

The next day, the group split up and headed down to the city to empty their bank accounts. When they counted up their funds, they had almost sixty thousand dollars.

While it sounded like a lot, they knew the rising cost of everything would use it up very quickly. They had to buy not only food, but gasoline and other necessities. They doubted that the supplier would keep his prices where they were for long. Demand and scarcity would see them get more costly as time went on.

42

FEBRUARY 25

They decided to take Mitch's truck to the fireworks shop since it was the oldest of the three and would not arouse suspicions. Mitch, Matt, and Jim dressed in their shabbiest clothes to look the part of Sam's henchmen. Mitch and Matt would do the talking while Jim stayed near the truck as backup. As they approached the gate, two armed men appeared and stopped them. Each were holding a semi-automatic rifle and it was apparent they knew how to use them.

Mitch rolled down his window to talk to the men, but they ordered the three out of the truck.

"Out of the truck and keep your hands where we can see them," the first man commanded.

Following the orders, the three spread out in front of the truck. Earlier, they had discussed the importance of not getting clumped together and thus making it more difficult for someone to get an advantage.

"What's your business here?" the first man asked.

Mitch responded, "Sam sent us to get another load. Business has been good and he sent us to buy more."

"Sam has never sent anyone to pick up for him. How do I know he sent you?"

"He said you would need some proof. Sam drives a gray van and his partner is Charlie."

"Anyone could know that. What else?"

"Well, he said he pays five dollars an item, and not to let anyone charge more because he has a deal."

"Okay, good enough. We'll open the gate and you pull up to that door there on the side of the building. Honk your horn once and someone will come get you."

Mitch, Matt, and Jim got back in the truck, drove through the gate and up to the door as instructed. Mitch cautioned, "Let's try to look natural as possible. Maybe even bored and tired? We're just Sam's employees, doing our jobs."

Mitch honked the horn and a man, also carrying a rifle, came out the side door.

While two of them unloaded from the truck, the man remarked, "Ain't seen you here before. How'd you get through the gate?"

"Sam sent us," Mitch replied as he came around the truck.

"Sam, huh? He usually comes himself."

Matt replied, "Sam's up in the northern part of the county making deliveries. He knew he would sell out and wanted to get another load, so he could start selling again first thing in the morning."

"Makes sense. All right, follow me."

As Mitch and Matt followed the man inside the building, Jim stayed in the truck. He turned it around, so it would be facing back toward the gate in case anything went wrong, and they had to make a quick getaway.

Entering the building, Mitch and Matt were amazed to see cases of food stacked to the ceiling as far as they could see. Several men were walking around with clipboards, writing down what they assumed were inventory figures. *Quite the operation.* Mitch mused while the man took them toward the back of the building to a small office. Their guide knocked on the door, opened it, and motioned for Mitch and Matt to enter.

Inside, they found a neat office with two desks. The one to the side was occupied by a young man, perhaps in his early twenties, busy at a computer's keyboard.

Seated at a desk in the center of the room was the man in charge, Mitch assumed. Mitch wasn't sure what he had expected from the man who ran this operation, but it was not what he saw before him. Looking to be about forty, he was trim, well-kept, but not athletic. Mitch could imagine him as a teacher or insurance salesman. Anything but a black marketer.

When they approached the desk, the head man looked at them with some suspicion, questioning, "My boys at the gate tell me Sam sent you. That's not normal and I don't like surprises. How do I know Sam sent you?"

Mitch responded, "As we told your men at the gate, Sam and Charlie are up north making deliveries, so he sent us to get another load."

"That so? So, why didn't Sam call to tell me you were coming?"

Mitch wasn't sure how to answer. It made sense that Sam would let this man know of a change of plans. He had to think fast.

"Sam told me you don't do phone calls, too risky with the government able to monitor everything. He said you only do business face to face."

"That's true. So, maybe Sam did send you. One more question to prove you are on the up and up. What's my name? Surely Sam would have told you to verify he sent you."

Mitch was afraid of this and had no idea how to respond. Before he could think of anything, Matt spoke up, "No names, Sam told us. He said you like to stay anonymous."

The man looked for a moment at Matt, then shifted his gaze to Mitch. After what was too long for comfort, he relaxed. "That's right. No names. All right then, let's do some business. How much does Sam want this time?"

Mitch replied, "Three thousand dollars' worth. I know it's more than his usual, but business has been good and Sam wants to kick things up a bit."

"Deal,' the man agreed. "My man here will take you out to the warehouse and take care of you."

Mitch looked at Matt and said, "You go along with him and help get things loaded. I'll be right there." He then took the money out of his pocket and started to hand it to the man behind the desk.

"Not to me," he said. "Give it to my accountant over

there." Mitch did and the young man quickly counted the money.

As Matt left with the other man, Mitch turned to look at the man behind the desk who gave him a curious look.

"Something else on your mind?" he asked.

Mitch knew this was the moment of truth. Either he could strike a deal for future buys or the man would get suspicious and they would be in trouble. He had to play this just right.

"Yes sir, there is something else."

"Go on," the man said.

"Well, me and my boys been grunting for Sam a while now and we are getting tired of it. We are thinking we want to go into business for ourselves."

"You do, do you? So Sam sends you here for a pick up and all of a sudden you want to cut him out?"

"Not exactly. Sam works the eastern and northern part of the county. We were thinking we would work the western part and maybe even a little farther into the next county. No competition for Sam, so you make even more than you do now."

"Sounds intriguing. You got your own cash to do this? Money is scarce now a days."

"We scraped up enough to get started."

"Let me think on it. You go help your man get loaded and I'll let you know before you leave."

"To help you decide, we thought this through and realized, since we are new to the business, it's only fair we offer an incentive," Mitch said as he pulled a wad of bills from his pocket and held them up. "We'll pay you a premium just to show we're serious. Sam pays you five dollars per item, we'll make it six." Mitch held the money out and waited to see what the man would say. After a moment, the man motioned toward the accountant and Mitch handed the money over. Inwardly, Mitch sighed with relief, but outwardly, he remained stoic. As he turned to leave the office, he said a silent prayer, thanking God that their plan had worked. Their ministry to feed their neighbors was now secure.

When Mitch reached the truck, they were just finishing loading. The truck bed was full of boxes and half of the back seat as well. Jim was jumping in the driver's seat and Matt was making a final check of the boxes when the young accountant stepped out of the building and made his way to Mitch.

As he approached, he said, "My boss says he could use the expansion in the business and he will take you on. Just come back when you need more inventory."

Mitch replied, "Will do. Tell your boss thanks and we'll see him soon."

As soon as the truck exited the gate, all three men let their breath out. The gamble had worked and now they had access to an almost inexhaustible amount of food.

43

MARCH 1

The beginning of March meant that winter would soon be over and the group at the Haven could start working in the garden. Midwestern springs were unpredictable, so they would have to wait and see how soon things warmed and dried up. In the meantime, thanks to their new source, the group was able to expand their food ministry to help another ten families. Using the three pickup trucks and going out in teams of two, the group delivered food and supplies to one or two families per day. It wasn't the most efficient way, but the safest. Making only two deliveries meant less time on the road. Roving bandits were on the rise and the chances of encountering them increased the longer they were out. A second reason to use all three trucks was to avoid carrying too much on any one truck. Should they be stopped and robbed, less food would be lost.

That evening after dinner, the group assembled in the

living room to catch the latest news. What they saw was the American president advocating something that a year ago would have seemed impossible. Mary turned up the volume as the president began to speak.

"My fellow Americans, we live in difficult times. Perhaps more difficult than any other time in our history. Certainly more challenging when this country defended its freedom against the British in 1812. Even more challenging than when we engaged in a bloody civil war. There is more at stake than when we became involved in both world wars. What I'm referring to is the challenge we face today from intolerance, greed, and ignorance.

"There has been a growing evil in our country. It is an evil that threatens to undermine the very core of our republic, and this evil comes not from a foreign threat, but from within. It comes from those who refuse to accept that the world has changed. Our past views on nationalism and sovereignty are outdated. Sadly, these people vehemently, and sometimes violently, advocate a return to the way our country used to be. They talk about freedom, but what they really want is control. Control over the government and our society.

"We simply can no longer tolerate such dangerous views in a peaceful society. Many of these nationalists, as I call them, talk about the loss of God-given rights, and therein lies the problem. These zealots are using the Bible as their playbook. They contend that God created the Earth and all of us and the only way to live properly is according to the Bible. Such intolerance is an embarrassment to our great nation. We are a country of many faiths and beliefs. To suggest that there is only one true belief is in direct opposition to what this country stands for.

"And sadly, my colleagues on the other side of the aisle have adopted these beliefs and are working to defy the will of the American people. We are a people that are open to all views, regardless of their origin. Afterall, not one of us can say we are the holder of absolute truth. Truth is in the eye of the beholder. What is true for me may not be true for you. Federal legislation and Supreme Court rulings in recent years have advanced our belief in multiple truths, and of that we can be proud.

"But more legislation is needed. That is why I am introducing a new bill before Congress that will bring unity to the political process. A bill that will, once and for all, return our governing to one that serves all people. This new bill, entitled the Unity Party Bill will set aside our old, divisive political system in favor of a new, unified system. No longer will the old party hatreds get in the way of governing our country. With this legislation, we will truly be one in our service at every level of government. The old parties will not be recognized as valid this spring in the coming primaries. Only candidates of the new Unity Party will appear on ballots.

"I'm proud to be the first member of the Unity Party. I hope you will all join me and become a member of the Unity Party as we look forward to a new era of peace and security for our country and out world."

Much as they did after the State of the Union Address in January, the residents of the Haven sat stunned at what they had just heard. There was no doubt the president's bill would pass. His current party held a majority in both Houses and the president's signature was a foregone conclusion. No one at the Haven had been politically active with a particular party, but they had been civic-minded, kept informed and voted in every election. While they held no affiliation with a party, they recognized the danger of eliminating the two-party system. Debate on issues would disappear. More importantly, the president had singled out Christians again as being the problem. The ramifications of that were obvious. Current members of Congress that refused to join the new party would not appear on the ballot. Those that joined, but still kept their traditional views on politics and faith would almost certainly lose in the primaries. The shift from a vibrant political system to one that was no more than a rubber stamp for those in power was inevitable.

"I know this is serious," Maggie said. "But what does this mean for us? How will it affect us here in our daily lives?"

"Good question," Dave replied. "The president did not indicate that membership in this new party is mandatory for all citizens, just for candidates."

Matt said. "But I don't think that will be far behind. I suspect that, in order to vote, we will have to be a member of this Unity Party."

"That's ridiculous," Joanna said. "It's not constitutional."

"It is ridiculous, Joanna," Mitch responded. "But I think we moved past constitutional a long time ago. What concerns me more is the president tying the troubles of the country to our faith. He all but said Christians are the problem and this new party will take us out of the political process completely. It doesn't surprise me, but it is concerning."

"All true, Mitch," Kate nodded. "And Maggie's point is well taken. How will this affect us here at the Haven? It is hard enough to buy anything now. Will it get harder once all this comes about?"

"Probably so," Mary said. "It is a short step from a one-party system to total control of the population. The government has already taken away our right to assemble, especially at churches. This new party, with its condemnation of Christians, will label anyone who is not a member as a subversive and a troublemaker."

"I agree," Denise said. "I have often read of the persecution the early church suffered under Rome. I guess, now we won't have to imagine what it was like anymore. We'll be living it."

Dave said, "Just as Peter wrote, 'Dear friends, do not be surprised at the fiery ordeal that has come on you to test you, as though something strange were happening to you. But rejoice inasmuch as you participate in the sufferings of Christ, so that you may be overjoyed when his glory is revealed.'"

44

MARCH 6

itch and Denise were in Mitch's truck, heading home after making deliveries to families. They were in an isolated part of the county and in good moods. The Peterson family they just visited were new to the faith and eagerly asked questions of Mitch and Denise. The father, Ken, and mother, Janet, along with their three teenage children had been studying the Bible Mitch brought to them during the winter. Recent events prompted them to finally begin reading and they started where Mitch suggested with John's Gospel.

As they continued down the road, Denise remarked, "I can't express enough the joy of seeing such devotion as the Petersons have for the Word of God. It's certainly inspiring and reminds us how important our work is."

"It does indeed. The Petersons are like so many were when we started our deliveries last fall. We left a Bible, but didn't say much about it, figuring they would respond better if we didn't get in their faces about believing. Some started reading right away and some, like the Petersons, took a while to get curious."

"Well, with the state of things in the world, I imagine many are searching for meaning to get through each day. I'm just glad they gave their lives to Christ."

"Me to. Every person we meet who does that is one less that will be left behind to deal with the tribulation. As much as I am looking forward to seeing Jesus at the rapture, I can't help but think about all the people who will miss that opportunity."

"Yes, Mitch. When we came to the Haven, it was more about getting out of the city and its dangers, but the work we are all doing is such a blessing."

Mitch suddenly hit the brakes as he came around a bend in the road to see a truck parked sideways, blocking their path. Through his side mirror he also saw another truck appear and stop behind them about fifty feet away. The truck in front was about the same distance. They were trapped. Both trucks were dirty and had seen better days.

Mitch stated, "I don't see a way out of this at the moment. They have us blocked in. Let's get out and see if we can talk our way through."

Both climbed out of the truck slowly, leaving the doors open.

"Cover the rear," Mitch told Denise.

Denise did so, her hand on her gun as Mitch stood behind his door while a man holding a rifle got out of the truck in front. Mitch could see there was no one else in front besides the man.

"How many back there?" Mitch queried over his shoulder, not taking his eyes off the man with the rifle.

"Just one," she responded. "He hasn't gotten out yet, but I can tell he has a rifle or maybe a shotgun."

"Hopefully, a shotgun," Mitch said. "Shotshells won't do much damage from that distance. Let me see if I can get this guy in the front talking."

Mitch called out, "Good afternoon. I guess, since you're blocking this road, you want something. What is it?"

The man responded, "What have you got? Anything in your truck?"

"Just the two of us," Mitch said.

"Well, in that case, I guess we want the truck. You can just put the keys on the hood and walk away. Don't want to hurt anyone, just need your truck."

Mitch replied, "That's not going to happen. We need this truck too and, since my name is on it, I think I'll keep it."

The man shifted from one foot to another as if deciding what to do next, then said, "Listen, mister, I don't want to shoot you, but we are leaving with that truck. So, why not make it easier by doing what I said?"

Mitch slowly pulled his gun from the holster and brought it up aimed at the speaker. Denise noticed what Mitch was doing out of the corner of her eye and followed suit, aiming at the rear truck driver through his windshield. The driver sat up straight and Denise could see his eyes widen at the sight of a gun pointed at him. Denise knew the man was probably just doing what the other told him and didn't really want to shoot anyone. But things could get out of hand quickly and people could do things they normally wouldn't.

The man at the truck in front regripped his rifle, countered, "Mister, that isn't very smart. We got you covered front and back. Just put the keys on the hood and no one gets hurt."

Mitch replied, "I don't want to see anyone get hurt either, but you are not getting this truck."

The man yelled at his accomplice behind, "Troy, don't just sit there, get out here."

Troy slid out of his truck and stood behind the door with his rifle in his hands, but not aimed at Denise. He was young, probably no more than twenty years old.

Denise, realizing that Troy was as scared as she was, called to him, "Troy, I don't think you want to shoot me, do you?"

Troy looked down at the rifle, then shook his head. "I don't really want to, ma'am, but I guess I will have to if you don't do what my uncle says."

Denise responded, "Troy, is it really worth that just to get our truck. To kill someone?"

"We don't want to kill nobody," Troy said. "We're just trying to get some food and supplies. My uncle says, if we stop vehicles, we might find them carrying some. You see, we don't have any money. If we did, it wouldn't buy much these days."

Denise muttered, "Are you hearing this, Mitch?"

Mitch replied, "Yes, and I know what you're thinking."

"We could help them."

"Be careful."

Denise turned her attention back to Troy and said, "Troy, I can understand what you're saying about needing supplies. These are tough times and everyone is having trouble finding food and such. What if I told you we could help you out?"

Troy looked at Denise quizzically. "Help us out? You mean you would help us even though we ambushed you? Why would you do that?"

"Because, Troy, that's what we do. We're just coming back from taking food to a family. We do that every day. We can do the same for you and your uncle too. All you have to do is ask."

From the front, Troy's uncle called out, "Hey, Troy, what you doing back there? Why you talking to that lady? Just stand there and point your rifle. I'll do the talking."

"But, Uncle Henry, this lady says they'll get us some food."

"Yeah, right," Uncle Henry responded. "You know we don't got no money to buy food."

Troy looked back to Denise, "He's right. Like I told you, we don't got no money."

"You don't need any money, Troy. We don't charge anyone for the food we bring them."

"Hey, Uncle Henry, she says they don't charge for the food." He turned back to Denise, "Really? You just give it away?"

Before Denise could respond, Uncle Henry spat,

"Now that can't be so. Nobody just gives food away. She telling the truth?" He asked Mitch.

"The absolute truth," Mitch affirmed. "It's what we do every day. Bring food to folks who don't have any."

"Why would you do that?" Henry asked in disbelief.

"Because" Mitch replied, "People need food and we have a way to get it."

"It still don't make sense. How do I know you're telling me the truth?"

Mitch replied, "I guess you'll just have to trust me. Look, Henry, there are ten of us at my house. Denise here and some others came up from the city last fall and we all are trying to do the Lord's work. Delivering food is one way we do that."

"So you're a Christian then?"

"Yes, all of us are."

Henry remarked, "Now that I can make sense of. Sounds like something my dear-departed wife, Martha, would do. She was always talking about loving your neighbor and all."

"Exactly," Mitch replied. "So, why don't we all just put away our guns so we can get you and your nephew stocked up? We can bring the food to your house or meet somewhere neutral if you prefer."

Henry thought a moment before lowering his rifle. His shoulders sagged a bit as he looked back up and pleaded, "Mister, I'm sorry about all of this. Me and Troy just don't know how we're going to make it the way things are. Even if we had money, we can't go to the stores because we don't have that vaccine proof to get in. We hear tell of some guys going around selling food, but they are charging crazy prices, so that won't work either."

"Not to worry," Mitch said. "Really, all you need to do is ask and we'll put you on the list and deliver food and supplies every two weeks."

"Just like that?" Henry asked.

"Just like that," Mitch replied.

"All right then," Henry said. "Hey, Troy, put that rifle away. These nice folks are going to help us."

Troy let out a breath and lowered his rifle as he smiled at Denise. Denise holstered her gun and commented, "See, I told you we would work this out."

Henry gave Mitch his address and Mitch promised they would stop by with food later that day. Troy smiled again at Denise as he got in his truck, turned around and drove off. Henry continued to apologize as he got in his truck and drove away. Once they were gone, Mitch and Denise got back in their truck. They looked at each other and smiled.

"Now that was a God thing," Denise said.

"Yep," Mitch replied. "Makes you think there are angels watching over us or something."

Later that afternoon, Mitch and Denise traveled to Henry and Troy's with a food delivery. When Mitch offered Henry a Bible, he declined, telling them that he had his wife's Bible and that he thought maybe he should start reading it like she always wanted him to. As they left, Troy thanked them both at the door and told them his Uncle Henry was a good man, he was just getting desperate. Mitch told Troy not to worry, no hard feelings.

45

MARCH 10

It was a sunny and surprisingly warm day as Maggie, Joanna, and Kate sat on the back deck enjoying the sun. While they basked in the rays, all three were thankful to be outside. It had been a long winter and the hint of spring was a blessing.

Joanna remarked, "You know, I can't think of any place I would rather be than right here on this deck."

"Me too," Maggie replied. "I can't think of anyone I would rather be with than you two."

"I agree." Kate bobbed her head. "There is something about this place. It's special. I don't know how, but it just feels special."

"I'm with you on that." Joanna smiled. "I think it has something to do with the work we're doing here. It is so gratifying to help people the way we are."

"I know what you mean," Maggie said. "And I like that we have so much to do here at the house. Tending the chickens, milling and baking bread. It's like doing life simpler. Focusing on the things that really matter."

Kate exclaimed, "Hey look, deer!"

"Where?" Maggie asked.

"Back there along the fence between here and the neighbors."

As the three watched, four deer munched on grass at the back of the property. Two were on the Harrison's side of the fence and two were on the Garrett's property. They started to move forward until all four are happily nibbling grass at the Haven. Suddenly, a shot rang out and the deer scattered. The three looked to their left to see Johnny Garrett with a rifle blazing away at the running deer. Unfortunately, Johnny chose to shoot at the deer headed toward the three women. His last shot was uncomfortably close to the deck, the sound of the bullet passing was heard by all three.

Joanna jumped up from her chair and started toward Johnny as mad as a hornet. She was still fifty feet away when she started in on the young Garrett, "How dare you shoot at us! What were you thinking? Nothing, that's what. You could have shot one of us!"

As Joanna approached with Maggie and Kate following, Johnny looked indignant. "Well, I didn't hit you, did I? No reason to get so worked up. Just shooting at some food."

"And you thought it was okay to shoot at deer not on your property?" Kate demanded.

"I don't see why that matters. Times are hard and normal rules don't apply anymore."

"Oh really?" Maggie sputterd. "Does that include not shooting at people?"

Everyone turned when a door slammed open and Tom Garrett stormed out of the house yelling.

"What in the world is going on here? What is all that shooting and yelling about?"

Joanna replied, "All that shooting is your son here acting like a fool and almost shooting one of us."

"That true boy?"

"I wasn't shooting at them, Pa. I was shooting at some deer."

"Deer that were on our property," Kate said.

"Is that right," Tom responded. He turned to Johnny, "Son, you're going to hurt someone one of these days. Now give me that rifle and get in the house."

As Johnny handed his father the rifle and started inside, Mitch, Matt, and Jim come running up, guns drawn.

Mitch said, "What's going on here?" He looked at Tom suspiciously. "Who was shooting?"

"It wasn't me," Tom growled. "It was my fool son shooting at deer."

"He just about shot one of us," Maggie said.

Mitch angrily spat at Tom, "Garrett, that boy of yours is a troublemaker. I didn't say anything when he drove his ATV back here and rutted up my yard, and we haven't complained about the loud parties when you're gone. But this is too much. It's time you acted like a father and disciplined him."

Tom replied stiffly, "Listen, Harrison, he's my boy and

I'll take care of him. I don't need you telling me how to father my son."

"Just make sure you keep him in line. Things are tense enough as it is. We don't need someone around here with a rifle who doesn't know how to use it properly."

"I don't like what you are insinuating, Harrison. My boy might make a mistake here and there, but I taught him to shoot and he knows what to do with a rifle."

"Apparently, he forgot that today. Just don't let it happen again."

Tom Garrett stared at Mitch for a few moments, then turned and headed back toward his house. The rest turned to walk back to the Haven as Maggie observed, "Mitch, it sounds like you have had problems with these folks before."

"From time to time," Mitch responded. "It's usually more annoying than dangerous. Not like today. While Johnny is the troublemaker, his father doesn't help when he ignores how his son is acting up."

"Do you think he learned his lesson today and won't cause any more trouble?" Kate asked.

"I hope so. But if the past is any indication, I doubt it."

As they arrived at the house and entered, Mitch couldn't help but feel that Johnny Garrett would someday make a mistake his father couldn't ignore. He just hoped it was not a fatal one.

46

MARCH 14

As the food shortages and gasoline prices increased, people took to the streets again protesting and demanding their elected officials do something to relieve their suffering. The president and state governors continued to insist that the current shortages and inflation were temporary. Things would get better soon, they promised. This did not assuage those who were hungry and about to lose their homes. Many expressed their mistrust in government after so many lies and deceits. For too long, people had been told one thing while their lives proved something different. The president's recent announcement of the one-party system had sent thousands into the streets in protest. As the group at the Haven watched all of this on the television, they wondered just how long it would be until God called them home and out of the chaos.

That evening, the group at the Haven gathered in the

living room. Mitch had called a group meeting to discuss the most recent developments and how they should respond.

Mitch began, "Dave, would you please open our meeting in prayer?"

"Of course," Dave replied. "Our dear, heavenly Father, as we come to You this evening beseeching Your will in our lives, we ask nothing for ourselves. We seek only Your direction for this humble group. You have brought us here for Your purposes. Some we can see, some we have yet to see. I ask Your blessing on each of us. Keep us strong in Your Word and give us the courage to face what is before us with the confidence You provide through the Holy Spirit. Amen."

"Amen, and thank you, Dave," Mitch said. "It seems like each week there is some new revelation of Satan's evil plans that requires a response from us. Certainly a spiritual response to be sure we are not deceived and stay strong in our faith. But there is always a physical response needed as well. Like when food became hard to find and so costly. We pooled our resources, so we could continue to purchase food, unfortunately, on the black market, and have not had to cut back on how we serve others. I want to thank all of you for being so generous in that. I know it wasn't easy to clear out your bank accounts."

Joanna responded, "Mitch, it really wasn't that hard for me. It's only money and I think it's obvious to anyone with eyes to see that priorities have changed. I have everything I need right here, so the money means nothing to me now."

"I agree," Maggie added. "I can remember asking Jim last fall when he thought things would return to normal. I so wanted that to happen. But Jim was honest when he said they never would, and you know what? I don't want them to. When I really thought about it, life before all of this wasn't that great. Sure, I was doing well, as we all were. But the world itself was not."

"True, Maggie," Mary said. "That's why Mitch and I came here. We could see that evil was rising. And ever since then, our lives have become much simpler and more meaningful. Especially now with you all here."

"I can think of no better place to be, Mary." Denise said.

Mitch said, "Well, again, thank you all." He paused a moment, gathering his thoughts and then said, "We have done very well here and are truly blessed. It hasn't been easy getting through the winter. I suppose most would expect ten people living in one house to have some friction. But that has not been the case. So, I thank you for that as well."

"I have to admit," Kate said, "When we came here back in January, I was a little concerned about having so many people in one home. Not that I expected any real problems. It was just that, we all know what it can be like with a house full. Of course that is when we had our kids at home. But this is different. We are all on the same page and working for the same things every day. I just feel so comfortable and secure here with all of you."

Betty responded, "I could not agree more, Kate. I wasn't so sure about coming here last November. I mean, we could not stay down in the city. Things were getting too scary. But I liked my privacy and was worried I would feel claustrophobic. That has not happened at all."

"It is quite amazing," Mitch said. "And I think we need to focus on the togetherness we have in the coming days. There is no doubt in my mind that things are going to get much worse. So bad in fact, that it will require us to adjust everything we do. There will come a time when food will be harder to get. Our current supplier won't have inventory forever. What he does have will just get more expensive."

Mitch looked down at the legal pad he had written some notes on, then continued. "The dangers we face on the road and even here are not going to go away. They will get worse. So, I've jotted down a few questions we need to answer in regard to how things are now and taking in to account that normal is not coming back, ever."

"Fire away," Dave piped up. "Let's move forward attacking our challenges like we always have."

"Thanks. Our first question is, 'How do we handle the fact that food may start to disappear altogether and, secondly, considering that, how do we continue to serve the families who have come to rely on our twice-a-month deliveries? I've asked Jim and Betty to take an inventory of our current food stock with a look toward the possibility of making do without any substantial resupply."

Jim said, "I can tell you all, this was a sobering project. The idea of having our food supply cutoff is scary. But the good news is, Betty and I think we can do okay. At least for a while."

"How long?" Kate asked.

Betty responded, "At least until the end of the year. Now, this takes into account that the garden will provide a lot of food starting in June and all the way through the late harvests in October. We'll be able to replace much of the dry and can goods we currently deliver with fresh produce. Then we'll also be canning much from the garden and then also have a nice stock of potatoes. All in all, we think we can comfortably make it to the end of the year."

"That is good news," Maggie said. "But I sense there is bad news as well."

"Unfortunately, yes," Jim replied. "Two things in that line. First, we cannot take on any new families. If we do, we will run out of food very quickly."

"I don't like that," Mary said. "How can we say no to people in need?"

"I understand," Betty replied. "I feel the same. The best we can do is to refer those families to others in the area who are doing similar to what we are. We know they are out there and have made contact with some."

"Thanks for the update, Jim and Betty," Mitch said. "There are two more items we need to address. One is infrastructure here at the Haven. The other is security. Matt did some work on the infrastructure issue."

"Thanks, Mitch." Matt nodded. "So, by infrastructure we mean the utilities—electricity, propane, water, and sanitation. All those things are good for now, but there is the real possibility that any one of those, if not all, could become a problem in the future."

"Do you think that is a real possibility, Matt?" Joanna asked.

"If the last two-plus years have taught us anything, it's that anything is possible. Before all this, no one could have predicted our churches being shut down. Or entire business sectors closed. Or unchecked violence across the country. Of course, the food shortages are another example of the fact that the unexpected can happen at any time. Just as the supply chain has been disrupted to cause shortages, so can the supply chain for utilities occur."

"Is there anything we can do here at the Haven to prepare for such disruptions?" Mary asked.

"Yes," Matt replied. "There is a lot we can do. Fortunately, our most basic need, water, is not a problem. The well you and Mitch had put in last year means we will always have a good supply of water. The next utility is propane. This house uses propane for the furnace and cooking. We are coming into spring when you would usually only get the tank filled enough to cook with during summer, filling it full in the fall. I am recommending we fill it to its 500-pound capacity now. Plus, we should also prepay for another tank fill now."

"Why do that?" Denise asked.

"Because the price of everything is going way up and propane prices also rise each fall. If we prebuy now, then this late fall or early winter, we'll have paid less and, more importantly, we'll know we have it on reserve for this place."

"Good points, Matt," Dave said. "Your next item is electricity. I'm thinking that is a major concern."

"It is," Matt replied. "No way around it, we need electricity to run this place. Without it, we can't run the refrigerator or the big chest freezer in the basement, and that will be crucial as we are freezing vegetables from the garden."

"So, I take it you have a recommendation," Mitch said.

"I do. It will take some time and a lot of luck, but I think we can address this issue. First, let me say that any solution to the electricity problem will not include lights in the house or power to the electric water heater. It will be hard enough to generate enough for the essentials—refrigerator, freezer, furnace in the winter, and the sump pump in the basement."

"That makes sense," Joanna said. "I guess that means cold showers if the power goes out."

"Actually," Matt said. "If something goes down with the power grid, the water tower that pumps that water up into the holding tanks won't work. So, when the tank in the tower empties, no more water."

"That's what happened to us here last year," Mary said. "It wasn't a power outage, but a bad pump."

"Exactly," Matt responded. "So, in the event of an extended power outage, we will have no water pressure in the plumbing. All water will have to come from the well."

"Now, Matt," Maggie said. "How will we stay clean then?"

"We do it the old fashioned way. Mitch and Mary have a galvanized washtub out in the barn. So, we'll use that for bathing. We simply heat some water and do it the way our ancestors did a hundred or so years ago."

"Or even less," Mitch said. "I can remember as a boy at my grandparents' farm taking baths in a washtub. They did not have running water, so that's how they did it."

"Will we want to use the precious propane to heat water for baths?" Denise asked. "Seems like we would want to save it for heating the house."

"We would, Denise," Matt replied. "We will heat water out at the fire ring. We have plenty of access to wood, so that would be the best way to heat water for baths and for washing dishes or clothes."

"Oh, I hadn't thought about washing clothes," Maggie said.

"I think we'll get along okay," Dave said. "These are good plans, Matt. We'll just have to change our outlook on daily life. Matt, you indicated you had a plan for electricity loss. What is it?"

"I do. I did some checking, and there is a solar power business not far from here. I want to get what we need there to convert the house to solar power. That is, if they still have enough solar panels and other parts to do so."

"Won't that be expensive, Matt?" Denise asked.

"It will. I'm not sure how much, but Kate and I can make the contribution to the household."

"We would be blessed to do so," Kate said. "One of the things we did before we came here was get as much cash as possible. We figured we would need it and besides, it wouldn't do us any good sitting in our bank back home."

"Thanks to you both," Mitch said. "Matt, when do you want to go get the solar supplies?"

"The sooner the better. Let's go tomorrow."

"Done. Why don't you take Dave and Jim with you?"

"Good idea," Jim said. "Matt, what about sanitation? That was on your list."

"This is a tricky one," Matt said. "Well, part of it is. I suspect, at some point trash collection may stop if everything else breaks down. The solution to that is simple. Mitch and Mary already have a compost pile in the back of the property. We just make sure all organic material goes on that pile. As for paper-based trash, we save and reuse whatever we can, and use the rest to start fires in the fire ring. Anything that can't be composted or burned, we put in a pit we will dig at the back of the property."

"That all sounds simple enough," Denise said. "What is the tricky part?"

"The tricky part is the septic tank. Here is where we have to be disciplined. Normally, all water used in the house flows to the tank. The tank fills and the overflow goes out pipes in the back yard and filters into the ground. The problem is that solid materials build up in the tank and it has to be pumped out every three years. Mitch and Mary had the tank pumped out last spring, so we have two years left under normal use. I figure we can extend that to at least four years, maybe more if we're careful."

"Excellent work, Matt," Mitch complimented. "Any questions?"

There were none, so Mitch continued to the next item.

"Our last issue to address this evening is security. We have all been careful on the road making deliveries, so that has not been an issue yet. We will just need to stay vigilant and keep an eye out for trouble and not get trapped like Denise and I did earlier. Now to security here."

Mitch looked down again at his notes and said, "We all know that the Garretts behind us are a potential threat. Mostly the son, Johnny, but as things get worse, people will get more desperate, and desperation leads to bad choices."

"Do you really think the Garretts would do something terrible?" Maggie asked. "As mad as I am at Johnny for almost shooting me, it was an accident. He didn't mean to."

Denise added, "Yes, Maggie, it was an accident. But Mitch's point is that people who are hungry or scared have the potential to do harm."

"Exactly, Denise," Mitch said. "We still treat everyone with kindness and compassion but pay attention for signs of bad intentions or suspicious activities. Like that old truck Mary saw stopped out front. That was certainly suspicious and we need to be more aware of things like that."

"I agree," Matt said. "Just dealing with the black marketers for food shows us that there are some bad people out there. We can't be too careful."

"This is all too scary," Joanna said. "But I guess I have to agree we need to be careful. I never thought things would come to this. So, Mitch, I'm sure you have some ideas for how we can protect ourselves."

"I do, Joanna. Here's how I see things. The property is not so large that we can't see the property line in any direction. That's good. We also don't have a lot of trees, so no place to hide when approaching the house. I feel pretty confident we don't have much to worry about during the daytime, but to be safe, let's not go outside to the barn and elsewhere without a buddy. The rule of the day is to move about in groups of at least two."

"Makes sense," Jim said. "I doubt anyone would try anything in daylight, but better to be on the safe side. What about at night? Should we be concerned while we are all asleep?"

Mitch replied, "Yes and no. I think we are pretty safe inside at night. But let's have at least two people do a security check. Make sure all the windows and doors are locked before we turn in."

"What is the no?" Kate asked.

"The no is outside of the house at night. The motion sensor lights around the barn will help some. But if we're all asleep, we won't see the lights."

"Sounds like we need to keep watch at night," Jim said.

"Good idea, Jim," Matt said. "The person on the last shift has to make breakfast!"

Maggie responded "Well, that leaves me out. I can't even make coffee."

"Me either," Joanna said.

"Okay, Maggie and Joanna won't be put on the early morning shift," Mitch said. "Now, if you are on watch and something happens, no matter how small, do not investigate on your own, and do not turn on the lights. Quietly wake us all up and we'll investigate as a group. If something were to happen outside, chances are it could be dangerous. Understood?"

All nodded in agreement. Betty took the first shift, explaining that she usually was up late anyway. The night progressed without incident. With ten people to keep watch, members of the group only had to take a shift every third night.

47

MARCH 27

itch was deep in thought while he worked in the garden. Unlike last spring, this year, March was warm and mostly dry. He decided they should be able to start planting in a few weeks once the ground was tilled and ready. As Mitch followed the rototiller around the garden, Maggie and Joanna were following and picking out rocks the tiller had exposed. Denise and Mary were hanging clothes on the line to dry. Jim and Dave were cleaning out the chicken coop—a much-needed task after the long winter. Betty was busy tidying the flowerbeds around the house. Matt and Kate were in the kitchen preparing lunch for the group.

But Mitch was distracted as he tilled. He had talked to his brother, Steve, again that morning. He'd tried to convince him that things were not going to get better. That they were living in a time where evil was gaining, and God's patience was wearing thin. Steve did not argue

Mitch's contention that God was watching and probably was not happy. He did believe in God and in Jesus. He knew the stories from the Bible and accepted them. But he also did not think he had to go to extremes when it came to believing. After all, he and his wife, Lydia, were good people, and their children and grandchildren were too. They all believed in God and that was enough. Making yourself feel guilty was not something Steve agreed with. He did not like to talk about the details of faith. It was just too personal. Mitch finally conceded he would not convince Steve that time was short and repentance was the only way to avoid an eternity far worse than what the world was today. He hung up the phone and dropped his head in prayer. "How could his family ignore the obvious?" he prayed. "Lord, show me what to do to help them see." But no answer came. Mitch could not figure out why God would be silent on this. It was so important to him. He sighed, coming back to the garden and concentrating on his tilling.

When Mitch turned the tiller north to begin his next row, something ahead and to the right caught his eye. He stopped and peered at what looked like two people walking across the farm fields from the direction of the freeway. He shut off the tiller, which got the attention of Maggie and Joanna.

Denise and Mary looked over from their work, noticing the two people coming their way. As they neared, Mitch could see that the two were a young man and woman—mostly by the style of clothes they were wearing.

Mitch took off his gloves and approached the two as they came near the garden, Joanna and Maggie following.

"Hello," Mitch called.

The two stopped, seeming unsure about coming closer.

Joanna called to them, "Hi! Don't be afraid. Come on over. I'm Joanna, this is Maggie, and that there is Mitch."

With that, the two approached and the young man said hesitantly, "Hi. I'm Chaz, well Charles really. But everyone calls me Chaz. This is my wife, Chloe."

Chaz was about five-feet-seven and rail thin. He was wearing faded jeans and a t-shirt featuring a rock band. His haircut was not much of a cut, but more of a tousled look popular with the younger crowd. Chloe was shorter, about five-feet-four and equally thin. Her attire included skin-tight black jeans, boots, and a denim jacket over a bright green t-shirt. Chloe's blonde hair, unlike Chaz's was neatly cut and styled.

"Hello, Chaz and Chloe," Mitch said.

Chaz gave a hesitant wave and explained, "We were driving from up north down to the capital and our car broke down. We tried to call for a tow truck, but they said it would take hours, probably not until after dark. We didn't want to sit out in the car after dark, so we thought we'd see if there was a town nearby where we could hang out and maybe get something to eat."

"Sorry to hear about your car," Mitch said. "Mt. Olive is just on the other side of the freeway, about two miles from here. But no need to go there. You can join us for lunch. We were just about to take a break and go in and eat."

Chloe and Chaz look at each other uncertain if they should accept the offer.

Maggie said, "Come on. Join us for lunch and we'll get to know each other."

Chloe, speaking for the first time, said, "Okay. Thank you."

As the group entered the house for lunch, Matt and Kate looked inquisitively at Chaz and Chloe. Mitch said, "Kate, Matt, I would like you to meet Chaz and Chloe. Their car broke down over on the freeway and they walked here looking for someplace to get help."

"Chaz, Chloe, it's a pleasure to meet you" Matt said. "You are just in time for lunch. Just give me a minute to pull up a couple more chairs."

Jim helped Matt grab two more chairs to put around the table. Actually two tables. Mitch had brought up a spare dining table from his office area when the group from Wadesville arrived. With the two tables end-to-end, they could seat the ten of them comfortably. Twelve was no problem either as Mary and Kate brought out more plates and silverware.

After everyone was seated, Mitch explained to Chaz and Chloe that, before each meal they said grace. He looked to Jim and asked, "Will you please give thanks for us?"

"Certainly," Jim replied. Everyone bowed their heads as Jim continued, "Dear Father, we come to you again in thankfulness for all our many blessings. We thank you for this wonderful home we live in. We thank you for this land you have provided to feed us. We thank you for this food we are about to eat and for the hands that prepared it. Today, we also thank you for bringing Chaz and Chloe to us. We ask you blessings upon them and help with the challenges they are facing. Amen."

As the food was passed around the table, Matt asked, "So, Chaz, tell me how you ended up here from the freeway. That has to be three miles from here."

Chaz spooned mashed potatoes onto his plate and replied, "Our car broke down as we were on the way to the capital. Chloe has some relatives there we were hoping to stay with. We come from up on the lake in Clear Lake and lived in the city there. After the rough winter we had, we knew we needed to get away from all of the cold and snow, not to mention the craziness. The downtown is like a war zone. Most of the office buildings are empty, at least of businesses. Originally, that was due to the virus and people working from home. But lately, it's because so many businesses have been laying off workers. And then people started moving into the office buildings last fall. I guess because, with the power outages, they figured they could stay warmer in a big building. But with food scarce, many of them started breaking into restaurants and such and taking what they needed. The police tried to stop it at first, but eventually gave up because they were outnumbered. Now, nobody goes into the downtown at all."

"That's terrible," Joanna said. "So, were you living in the downtown?"

"No," Chloe replied. "But we lived close to it in an apartment building. I was afraid the squatters were going to start coming out of the downtown looking for food. But thankfully, they never came to our building."

Chaz said, "Yes, but we could hear gunshots not too far away and knew it was a matter of time."

"How did you survive then?" Denise asked. "Were the stores still open in your neighborhood?"

Chaz replied, "At first, yes. Then they started to close when the delivery trucks would not come that close to the downtown. The last time we went to the store in our neighborhood, the owner told us he was getting ready to close because his shelves were almost empty."

"When was that?" Betty asked.

"That was in early December, right after Thanksgiving."

"Then what did you do for food?" Maggie asked.

"We had a good supply stocked up," Chaz replied. "But not enough to get through winter. So, we started making trips south just out of town and getting as much as we could each trip. We always left at daylight so we could get home by noon. It seemed like all the trouble happened later in the day or at night. So, we were okay on food, but our real concern was paying the bills. Both of our jobs disappeared back in September, so we had no income, and we used all our savings to buy food and gas."

"So, what did you do?" Mary asked.

"That was the strange thing," Chloe said. "We were worried mostly about paying the rent. We didn't want to get thrown out going into winter. But we had no money, so we just stayed there waiting for an eviction notice. It never came. Early on, we tried calling our landlord to tell him our situation, but no one answered. Then we learned that our neighbors in the building were in the same fix and they too never heard from the landlord. We could not figure it out."

Dave commented, "It's likely your landlord had problems of his own and collecting rent was the least of his worries. He may well be in the same situation you were and was just trying to get by."

"You're probably right," Chaz said. "Anyway, when spring came, we decided we needed to get out of Clear Lake. So, we started out this early morning headed for Chloe's relatives."

"Quite the story," Mitch said. "Well, you're safe here and we'll try to help you get to your relatives as soon as possible."

Chloe and Chaz looked at each other and Mitch could see fear in their eyes.

"What is it?" He asked.

"Truth is," Chaz said, "We don't know if Chloe's relatives are even there. We have been calling since yesterday and no answer."

Chloe added, "I have been trying my aunt's cell and their landline all the way down. Nothing, and that's not like them. They are almost always home and why would my aunt not answer her cell? Or even call back. I left messages."

"Where does your aunt live, Chloe?" Mitch asked.

"On the west side, about a mile from the downtown in an area they call the Hillside."

Mitch closed his eyes for a moment, dreading what he knew to be true. "I'm sorry to tell you both, the Hillside is now much like what you described in downtown Clear Lake. Businesses all abandoned. A total breakdown of utilities from fires and vandalism. The fire department and emergency services won't even go in there. The mayor announced a few days ago that the city is abandoning the area. He said it was too far gone to save."

Chloe's hand went to her mouth to stifle a sob, but her shoulders shook with tears. Chaz tried to comfort her but was of little help. The group sat in silence, some bowing to pray, others simply waiting quietly. After several minutes, Chloe looked up and stared vacantly. Her next words were barely a whisper.

"Where will we go now?"

After a few moments of silence, Mary spoke. "You'll stay right here of course. You are welcome here as long as you want to stay."

"Oh, we couldn't do that," Chaz says. "You don't even know us. Why would you want us to stay here?"

"Because you need a place to stay," Mitch responded. "That's why. We have an extra room."

"How can that be," Chaz said. "There are so many of you here and you have an extra room?"

"I knew there was a reason," Joanna said.

"Reason for what?" Chloe asked.

Joanna explained. "Back in January, I got the bright idea, more correctly, I was given the idea that we needed more beds here. At the time, there were only eight of us and we each had a bedroom. One for each couple and Maggie and I share a room. But something kept telling me we would need more places for more people."

"What people?" Chloe asked.

"I didn't know at the time. But we no more than got them made and Matt and Kate showed up. So, there was one of the new bedrooms occupied." Joanna looked at Chloe and Chaz with a smile. "The other room has sat empty until now. I've wondered who it was for. It was for you."

"Wait a minute," Chaz said, "you built an extra bedroom for somebody you didn't know was coming? I don't get it."

"It's like this," Joanna continued. "Sometimes, if you listen to God enough, He'll tell you what to do. You may not know why at the time, but that doesn't matter. What matters is that you do it. That's exactly what we did, and here you are!"

"I don't know what to say," Chaz responded.

"Nothing to say," Mitch replied. "Welcome to the Haven."

48

MARCH 28

Breakfast at the Haven the next morning was a joyous affair. For some reason, the presence of Chaz and Chloe put everyone in a good mood. Another day of hard work in the garden and around the house was ahead, but this morning, the group simply enjoyed being together and knowing that two young people had found their way to the Haven.

As they were finishing their breakfast, Chaz asked, "So, tell me again how you all ended up here together. I'm still not clear on that."

Dave replied, "Now that I think about it, all of us being here is a bit unusual. But there is a good explanation. When Mitch and Mary moved here two years ago, they told us they wanted to build a place where they could be away from all the craziness of the city and live a more comfortable and peaceful life."

"That makes sense," Chaz said. "I can understand that."

Dave continued, "Yes, and it was obvious to the rest of us that they were comfortable here. But Mitch kept talking about how they had been called by God to this place, not just for themselves, but to create a haven for others when the time came."

"This is where I start to get lost," Chaz responded. "So, Mitch, how did that work? Being called by God? Did you hear a voice or something?"

"Not exactly," Mitch replied. "Although it was very clear to me, I would not call it a physical voice. I'll explain it this way. Have you ever had a strong sense, I mean really strong, that you should do something? Or maybe not do something?"

"Yes, I know what you mean. We got that feeling a week or so ago and knew it was time to leave Clear Lake."

Mitch replied, "So, Chaz, describe that feeling you both had. Was it a realization that it was time to leave? Or was it something more?"

"Huh. I never really thought about it much, just knew it was time to go. But, as I do think about it, I realize it was more than a feeling. It was like something was pushing us to leave. It was not in response to something happening. We just woke up one day and knew it was time to go."

"Sounds like God was leading you very clearly," Mary said.

"I think you're right, Mary," Chloe said. "It wasn't like Chaz and I talked about it. We just both knew it was time to get out of there."

"Exactly," Mitch said. "That's what it was like for us here. We just knew that we had to leave the city. It was crystal clear also that wherever we went, it would be a place of refuge for others."

Dave then said, "All the time Mitch kept telling me he knew this place would be a haven and that, eventually, Denise and I—and everyone else here—would come, it sounded a bit out there to me."

Chloe asked, "So, what changed that brought you all here?"

Joanna responded, "What changed was how we looked at what was going on around us. I will just speak for myself and say that I was doing my comfortable life in my condo, ignoring what was going on in the world and thinking things were not that bad. It was just all the news reports being sensational. It really wasn't as bad as some people said it was."

"And then?" Chloe asked.

"And then, one morning, I was reading my Bible, and it was like God smacked me upside the head and said, 'Wake up!' The wakeup call was in the book of Matthew, chapter 24. Just a minute, let me get my Bible and I will read it to you."

Joanna went to the living room and returned shortly with her Bible. Thumbing through the pages, she found what she was looking for.

"Here it is. Matthew 24, verses thirty seven to thirty nine. Jesus is telling the disciples what it will be like toward the end, just before He comes back. 'As it was in the days of Noah, so it will be at the coming of the Son of

Man. For in the days before the flood, people were eating and drinking, marrying and giving in marriage, up to the day Noah entered the ark: and they knew nothing about what would happen until the flood came and took them all away. That is how it will be at the coming of the Son of Man.'

"Who is the Son of Man?" Chaz asked.

Joanna replied, "Jesus. That is the term that was used a lot by the prophets in the Old Testament when they were talking about the coming Messiah."

"Okay, I understand," Chaz replied. "But what does Noah have to do with how things are now?"

Joanna responded, "Good question, Chaz. What Jesus is saying is that, during the last days, people will be ignorant of the times they live in. They won't be able to see that this world is winding down. Its time is coming to an end. To be honest, I didn't see it either. Not until that day when God showed it to me in this scripture. So, just like before the flood, most people are clueless about what is going on."

Chloe asked, "Did God warn the people before the flood? Or did He just decide to kill them all? I thought God loves everyone."

"He does love everyone," Denise affirmed. "He did try to get the people back then to turn away from their evil ways. It took Noah and his sons 120 years to build the ark. All that time, Noah stayed faithful to God and warned the people of the coming wrath. But they just laughed at Noah and went on with their evil ways."

"So, people could have gotten on the ark with Noah and not died in the flood?" Chloe asked.

"Sure," Joanna replied. "But they didn't because they had moved so far away from God they couldn't see the truth right in front of them. And it is just like that today. People have separated themselves from God so far, they can't see how evil and sinful the world has become."

"I can see what you mean," Chaz said. "It is pretty obvious when you look around just how bad the world is. Even before the virus, the violence, and the shortages, I could see that people had become so selfish and mean. Even our friends seemed different. It was like something was in them that was making them violent and scary."

"What you saw was Satan at work in your friends," Mitch informed. "When people decide to give themselves over to evil, to ignore the basic call to be good, they are inviting Satan to come into them and take over."

"Take over, that makes sense," Chloe said. "It did seem like our friends had been taken over by something. Something evil and dark."

"Darkness is a good description," Joanna remarked. "It was that darkness I finally recognized all around me. I remember, I called Dave and Denise to talk about it and they, too, had been thinking about the same thing. As a matter of fact, God had given them the same scripture in Matthew the night before."

"And they weren't the only ones," Jim joined in. "Betty and I came across the same verses in Matthew 24 about the same time."

"The same verses were in my daily devotional that week as well," Maggie added.

Chaz responded, "So, all of you read the same part in the Bible at the same time, and you thought the same thing too?"

"We did," Joanna said. "When we discovered that, we decided to get together and talk about it. So, we gathered at Dave and Denise's and tried to figure out what it meant —why God had given us that particular scripture at that time."

"That's amazing," Chaz exclaimed. "So, what did you decide?"

Dave nodded. "It was a long night of discussion. We talked about how the scripture aligned with the world today."

"I guess that seems obvious," Chloe said.

Dave replied, "Not at first, Chloe. To be honest, none of us wanted to admit that the world had descended into such darkness. Because, if we did that, we would also have to admit that things were not going to get any better. If we agreed that we were living in the days Jesus described, that meant we had to agree that the world was as evil as it was in Noah's time."

"That meant," Denise said, "We could no longer live in our peaceful little bubble and ignore what was going on around us."

Chloe mused out loud, "I imagine that was a hard thing to do. Didn't it feel like everything had changed? That nothing was the same anymore?"

"It did," Denise said. "But, in truth, the world didn't

change, we did. The world was already evil and full of chaos and lawlessness. We just finally realized it for what it was. That meant we had to change our lives."

"So, that's when you decided to come here?" Chaz asked.

"Not quite." Joanna shook her head. "That took a little more searching. After we talked that night, we knew things would change. At first, we simply thought that we had to pray more, read the Bible more, and just wait for the end to come."

"Explain that for me," Chloe said. "What does it mean when you say waiting for the end to come? Sounds really scary."

"It does," Joanna replied. "But only if you think the end of life here is the end of all things. For Christians, our hope and promise from God is that the end of life here on earth is just a transition to eternity in heaven."

"I grew up hearing that in church," Chloe said. "But how does that transition work? And were you all just going to sit and wait for it?"

Joanna responded, "The transition we were thinking about is what we call the rapture. It is when God decides to bring all Christians on earth to heaven. Sort of like when Noah and his family entered the ark. All believers will be taken to heaven before the world is destroyed."

"So, God is going to destroy the earth?" Chaz asked. "Like with a flood again?"

"Not a flood," Matt said. "God promised after the flood He would never cover the earth with water again.

That's where rainbows come from. God created them as a promise to us to never flood the earth again."

"So, if not a flood, how is it going to happen?" Chaz asked.

"That is a good question," Matt replied. "One that will take some time to answer. But the important thing is, you don't want to be around to experience what will happen after all the believers have been taken away. As bad as things are now, they will be much, much worse after the rapture."

"So much to think about," said Chloe. "It sounds like we have a lot to learn. Will you teach us? Will you help us understand all of this?"

"Of course, we will," said Kate, taking Chloe's hand and giving it a squeeze. "We will take all the time you need. We can get started this evening." Kate paused and looked at the two young people. "I have a question for you both."

"Okay," Chloe said.

"Until this evening when we talk more, ask yourself if you think God has brought you here to the Haven for a reason. Are you here right now because this is where God wants you to be? Will you think about that?"

Chaz and Chloe looked at each other, then Chloe turned to Kate. "I think we already are thinking about just that."

49

APRIL 6

Resurrection Sunday had a special meaning this year for the twelve at the Haven. Commemorating the death, burial, and resurrection of Jesus Christ was special for Christians every year. But this one held such significance for the group because of its promise. In the midst of chaos, immorality, and violence, the promise of a future of peace for eternity was like a lighthouse in a sea of darkness.

As the group gathered in the backyard to observe the day, Chloe asked Joanna, "Why do you call this Resurrection Sunday instead of Easter? I've never heard of it before?"

Joanna replied, "It's pretty simple. Like so many holidays, Easter has elements of pagan celebrations from the past."

"Pagan? What does that mean?" Chloe asked.

"It means not Christian essentially. Previous to what is

now called Easter, people around the world celebrated the coming of spring with festivals and such as a means of welcoming the new growing season. Many of them did so in relation to whatever god they equated with life. In second-century England, the Anglo-Saxons spring holiday worshipped their goddess of renewal, Eastre. Christian missionaries started to gradually convert the pagan holiday to a commemoration of Christ's resurrection. It then spread throughout the world and became a Christian holiday."

"That's amazing," Chloe said. "Are there other Christian holidays like that?"

"Sure, Christmas is a combination of the commemoration of the birth of Jesus, along with other traditions from before and after His birth."

"Makes you wonder what is true and what isn't," Chloe remarked.

"It can be a bit confusing," Joanna responded. "The important thing to remember is that our faith is not about traditions. It is about a personal relationship with Jesus. The truth is, no day on the calendar is more special than any other."

"Wow. I guess I have a lot to learn. I thought Christianity was all about going to church, celebrating holidays, and praying a lot."

Joanna patted Chloe on the knee and said, "My dear, all you need to do is pay attention to the last one. Prayer is the foundation of faith. Church is simply gathering together to worship and pray. Holidays are nothing more than traditions. Some good, some bad."

With that, Denise stepped to the front of the group with her guitar and they started singing.

As the Haven twelve worshipped that Sunday morning, around the world many churches, synagogues, and mosques held celebrations of a different sort. The growing desire for a unification of religious practices had coalesced into an effort to use Easter as a jumping off point for the melding of different faiths. Instead of celebrating the resurrection of Jesus in the Christian faith or the Passover for Jews, these churches, synagogues, and mosques celebrated what they called the new faith of the new earth. Their messages were about bringing peace and security to the world by uniting all religions. They called for a dedication to love the planet and care for it. They stated that no one religion represented absolute truth. Political leaders around the world applauded this new religion and boasted that, with it, the world could finally be united for common goals.

But not everyone was enamored with this new form of worship. True Christians around the world saw it for what it was. They knew the Bible teaches that, in the end times, a false prophet would arise and lead a false, world-wide religion. Those loyal to the Jewish faith rejected the message from whom they considered to be blasphemers. Many devout Muslims viewed the effort with a seething hatred, seeing it as an example of why all those not true to the teachings of Islam should be exterminated.

50

___

APRIL 9

Matt and Chaz had begun the installation of the solar power system at the Haven. They had completed installing the panels on the south-facing roof of the garage and were now running the lines to the electrical box in the basement. Chaz had been rather quiet all day and Matt figured it was just the upheaval of his and Chloe's lives. After tightening a screw, he turned to Chaz, "I can tell you have a lot on your mind. I may not have all the answers but I'm willing to listen. Everyone needs a good ear now and then."

"Thanks, Matt. I do have a lot of questions. So many questions."

"Go ahead."

"It's about what you all believe. About what is going on in the world. About what is going to happen next."

"I get it. It seems like everything has sped up, and nothing is the same anymore."

"Exactly. I don't know what to believe or how to even go forward. Nothing makes sense anymore."

"Why don't we just start with one thing? One question that keeps coming up in your mind?"

Chaz sighed as he looked around the room. "Well, I guess my biggest question is, why is all of this happening? And why now? Chloe and I had so many dreams for our future. Buying a house. Starting a family." He turned and looked at Matt. "But that all seems impossible now. So, what's the point? What do we have to look forward to?"

Matt paused for a moment as he considered how to respond to Chaz. He wanted to say the right things. Just as he had tried to do with his own sons. They had rejected his admonitions to come to the faith. He did not want Chaz to do the same.

"Chaz, first, I hear what you are saying. I know you're not the only one who is asking these questions. All around the world people are wondering the same thing. With all the chaos and violence and uncertainty, where do we put our hope?"

"Yes, what is there left to hope for? I mean, I can't see any way that things get better. It feels like the world is falling apart and no one knows how to put it back together."

"It does. But, Chaz, the truth is that the world has always been falling apart. Ever since Adam and Eve made their big mistake in the garden of Eden, the world has been headed in the wrong direction."

"That's not very encouraging."

"It may seem like it, but there is a real reason to be hopeful. Even in the midst of all of this."

"I can see that in you and the rest of the people here. But I don't understand it. Why do you have this hope when the world is going crazy? You and Kate came here and left your house, just like Dave and Denise and the rest. Don't you feel like you lost everything?"

"From a material perspective, I guess that is true. We left a lot when we came here. But we also gained a lot as well. Let me explain why we have such hope while everything is falling apart."

"I wish you would. I could use a reason to hope about something right now."

"So, let me ask you, did you understand what was talked about Sunday morning when we worshipped?"

"Well, yeah. I get the story. Jesus came to earth, was killed, and went to heaven. Then, those who believe that happened will get to go to heaven, eventually. But no one is there now. We're here on earth and it's not good. Why is God letting things get so bad? Why does He let all this killing and stuff go on? Shouldn't He be stopping it?"

"Good questions and the answer is pretty simple, but not easy to accept. I mentioned Adam and Eve making a really bad mistake, let me explain that. When God made Adam and Eve, He intended for them to live forever in the garden He had made for them. All they had to do was be content there and God had one rule for them to follow. That was to not eat from the Tree of the Knowledge of Good and Evil."

"Yeah, I remember that story. They did and God

kicked them out of Eden for it. But why would God set them up like that. I mean, why did He even put that tree in the garden where they would be tempted? It's human nature to want to do something that someone tells you not to."

"Yes it is, Chaz. If we look closely at the story of the creation of Adam and Eve, we read in Genesis that 'God created man in his own image.' Many people think this means we look like God. But that is not what it means at all. We are created to be like God in that we have free will to think and do what we want. You see, all the animals God created before Adam and Eve did not have that ability, and they still don't. Animals follow a God-given instinct for survival and procreation. However, God made man with the ability to think abstractly about the world in which he lives. He also made us with the ability to speak and to listen. Language is an amazing gift from God that no other creature has."

"So, you're saying that God made us like Him? But we don't have any powers like God."

"No, we don't. That's because we aren't God. In His image means we have the ability to observe, think, and decide. Unlike God, though we do not have the ability to make the right decisions all the time. God is inherently good, so He always makes the right decision."

"Okay, I think I understand that. But I still don't get why God would create a situation where Adam and Eve could make such a terrible mistake."

"Because He wanted to create us with free will. Not like the animals who have to follow instinct, but with the ability to make decisions. And that is because, God wants to love us and be loved by us. You can't love without free will."

"So, it is all about choices."

"Exactly."

"I think I get it. God created us in a way that we can choose to love Him or not, and also, so we can choose to do good or bad. That means God is not responsible for the bad things in the world, we are."

"Yes, we as the human race cause everything bad in the world. From Adam and Eve until now."

"Does that mean we're supposed to make only the good choices and if we don't, it's our fault that the world is going crazy?"

"Not really, Chaz. It simply means we are not perfect and make mistakes. You're not responsible for the choices others make, only your own."

"So, how do I fix that. My bad choices, I mean."

"You can't."

"That seems hopeless."

"You can't fix them, but God can."

"This is the part I never understood. I was taught that, if you were a good Christian, you always made the right choice."

"Sorry, Chaz, that is a lie. No one, not even the most devout Christian, always does the right thing. We're not perfect, far from it. That is why Jesus came. You see, God tried many ways to get people to obey Him and worship Him only. He spoke through the prophets to tell the people what to do. He gave Moses the Ten

Commandments so people would understand what to do, and none of that worked. People would not listen to the prophets. They took the Ten Commandments and added to them with other rules that confused people and God's original ten became secondary."

"Still sounds hopeless to me."

"And it did for people for a very long time. Until Jesus came. That changed everything."

"How?"

"In a nutshell, God sent His Son, Jesus, to Earth as a baby, born of a virgin, Mary. He grew up and when He was about thirty years old He began his ministry here on Earth. It was all part of God's plan to save a world that just could not get it right when it came to obeying God and doing His will, and that will was simply to love God and each other."

"That sounds simple enough. So, you're saying that, if people had just behaved and done the right things, Jesus would not have had to come?"

"Not exactly. That is because it is impossible for us to do God's will all the time. Back when Adam and Eve ate the forbidden fruit, it caused sin to enter into them, which they passed down to their children and everyone since then. So, no one was capable of doing the right thing every time. We are just too flawed. Because of that, we lost eternal life, which Adam and Eve had before they sinned against God."

"That I understand. No matter how hard I try, I make mistakes and do or say things I regret."

"We all do. But here is the great news. When Jesus

came, He did not just come to Earth to be a good teacher. God had a plan to save us from our sins once and for all."

"What was the plan? From what I have heard, you have to admit you are a bad person and promise to not do bad things again. Is that it?"

"No. If it were that easy, we wouldn't need Jesus. Besides, we're still not perfect, so no promise like that could be kept. God's plan was for Jesus to sacrifice Himself and take on our sin. You see, it was sin that separated us from God in the first place."

"That is what the cross is about? Jesus dying was the taking of our sins?"

"Yes, that was it, and on that first Good Friday, He was crucified, then rose from the tomb on the third day in fulfillment of God's plan for us."

"That had to be a hard thing for Jesus to do. Die for everyone like that."

"It was, but remember, Jesus is God as well. I know, that sounds confusing and we can talk about that another time. The important thing to remember is that Jesus died for us and all He and God ask of us in return is to admit we are sinners then ask Him to forgive us and come into our hearts and try as best we can to live our lives here on Earth according to His instructions."

"Those instructions are in the Bible?"

"Yes, everything we need is in the Bible."

"So, what about the part about being perfect if you are a Christian? Is that true?"

"Not the being perfect part. We are still human and flawed. But the wonderful thing is that, once we ask Jesus to save us and enter our hearts, we are changed. We want to do what is right all the time. We can't actually do it, but we want to. When we don't, we pray to God for forgiveness and ask His help in doing better the next time."

"Sounds pretty simple, but not easy."

"Yes, simple but not easy is the best way to describe it. There is one more thing that happens when you commit your life to Jesus."

"What's that?"

"You receive God's peace. As Jesus told the disciples when He gave them His peace, he said I do not give you the peace of this world, but God's peace."

"What's the difference?"

"God's peace is not dependent on circumstances. In fact, His peace gets better when things go wrong. The worldly peace people talk about is the absence of violence, hunger, and other bad circumstances. God's peace comes from the knowledge that, no matter how bad things get, this life is temporary and our life in heaven with God and Jesus is forever."

Chaz sat in silence for a few moments and it was obvious he was thinking about what they had discussed. He then stated, "Matt, this is a lot to think about. Thanks for talking with me. I'll let you know if I have more questions."

"You do that. Any questions you have I will try to answer. If I don't know the answer, we'll look in the Bible because that is where all the answers are."

51

APRIL 10

Joanna and Chloe were hanging laundry on the close line in the backyard. It was a sunny, warm day and everything around the Haven was starting to turn green. Mitch was cutting grass at the back of the property and Jim and Dave were cleaning out the barn. Chloe stopped hanging clothes and turned to Joanna.

"Can I ask you a question?"

Joanna stopped her own work. "Sure, ask away."

"Chaz was telling me he had a conversation with Matt yesterday about Jesus. He says it's something he needs to think about and maybe I should too. Chaz tried to explain what Matt said, but I'm not sure I understand the process."

"Chloe, I'm happy to try to explain what I can. Go ahead and ask your question."

"Well, it sounds like, from what Chaz said, all we have

to do to be a Christian is to ask Jesus to forgive us and be in our lives. Is it that simple?"

"Why, yes it is. Not easy, but it is that simple."

"Okay. Another question. Why? Why would Jesus do what He did for me? I can understand why for you and everyone else here. You're such good people and deserve to go to heaven. I'm not sure I do."

"Oh, Chloe dear, no one deserves what Jesus is offering. None of us. You see, Jesus' death on the cross was a gift. A gift to everyone who will accept it. We can't earn our way into heaven."

"So, if I accept this gift, what happens then?"

"Well, first off you will be changed. On the inside. You will look at the world differently. You will see other people differently, and you'll think differently."

"Will it take time to change or will it happen all at once?"

"A little of both. Once you commit your life to Christ, you will feel a comfort and peace come over you. But there is still work to do. Reading the Bible every day is part of it."

"I've tried to read the Bible before, but I just couldn't understand it."

"That's because it was written for those who believe. Once you believe, the words will make sense to you. They will jump off the pages with understanding and truths you could never see before."

"That sounds exciting." Chloe paused for a moment, then added, "Thanks, Joanna. This helps. I agree with Chaz, this is something we need to think about."

"You do that, Chloe. Normally, I would say take as long as you need to think about it. But with the current condition of the world, I would recommend not putting it off."

"I will do that. I can see why we shouldn't wait. I get the feeling something's coming and soon."

As the two went back to their task of hanging clothes on the line, Joanna smile and thought, "God is good!"

52

APRIL 20

Mary and Kate were washing up the dishes from dinner when the lights went out. Jim and Matt returned from the garage where they had been stacking firewood. Mitch came up from the basement while the rest of the group filtered into the kitchen.

Mitch remarked, "No storms, so I wonder what caused the power to go out."

"Good question." Matt nodded.

Mary commented, "I hope it wasn't another accident. Living in the country like this, it seems someone is running into a power pole every few months."

"I should get an email from the electric company in the next few minutes. They always send one explaining what happened and how long until it is fixed."

"Good thing we have the solar back-up," Chaz stated.

"Thanks to you and Matt," Kate added.

"Mostly Chaz," Matt deflected the compliment. "I couldn't figure out how all the components went together between the panels and the electric box. But this guy had it solved in minutes."

Chaz smiled modestly as Chloe squeezed his arm with pride.

"I should be getting that email any minute," Mitch said. "Mary, can you get on your phone and check the newsfeeds to make sure there isn't anything else going on?"

"Sure. Let me just pull it up." She tapped a few icons and the newsfeed from one of the television stations in the city popped up. When she saw the headline at the bottom of the screen, she turned up the volume on her phone so everyone could hear the newscaster.

"Repeating the latest on the reported widespread power outages here in the city and across the state. We are getting information that the power grid has been the victim of a cyberattack. We do not know if this affects just the state or is nationwide. Officials at the Statehouse tell us they are attempting to contact energy officials in Washington but have not been able to reach anyone.

"Stay tuned for updates on this and other news. We are currently operating the station on emergency generators which should keep us on the air for at least ten hours."

Then the signal was lost and Mary's phone went blank.

"This is bad," Chaz said.

"How bad?" Maggie asked. "There have been cyberattacks before. Usually, they don't last all that long."

"That's true," Chloe responded. "But attacking the power grid is different than a company's website or a refinery."

"How so?" Denise asked.

Chloe looked at Chaz and he motioned for her to go on. "First off, getting far enough into the programs that run the power grid takes a hacking ability that is far beyond the capability of some hacker sitting at his laptop. To do something like this, it has to come from someplace big. Like the military or some kind of government agency."

"What country would want to do this? Isn't it trackable?"

Chaz jumped in, "I don't know who did it, but no, if the hackers are good enough, it can't be tracked. Whoever did this is that good."

"We don't know yet that it is that big a problem. The news said it was just within the state," Matt said.

Chloe responded, "That's all they know of now. It is likely it goes much farther. The electrical grid in the US is all interconnected. Like that big regional outage that happened a few years ago in the Northeast and made it all the way to Cleveland before they could stop it."

Joanna said, "I don't understand. Exactly what does a cyberattack do and why can't they just reboot or something?"

"I wish it were that simple," Chaz replied. "Basically, a cyberattack is someone inserting a software virus into a secure system. It corrupts all of the instructions in that system, making it stop working. Most of the time, the only way to fix it is to start with all new hardware and backup software. You have to disconnect any computers that have been infected."

"But here's the thing," Chloe added. "If you don't act fast enough, the virus can travel to other computer systems and infect them. The power grid management is interconnected just like the wires carrying the electricity."

"So," Dave questioned, "It is possible the virus could travel fast enough to infect power grid computers in the entire country before it can be stopped?"

"Exactly," Chaz replied. "And getting them back online will take days, if not weeks."

Mary asked, "How is it you two know so much about all of this?"

Chloe replied, "Mostly professional curiosity. Chaz and I used to work at a company up north that developed manufacturing control programs. You have to learn about how hackers work so you can design programs that they can't get into."

"So, we had to keep up on the possible impacts of cyberattacks on all kinds of things to do our jobs," Chaz added.

"Well, we're certainly blessed to have you both here to help us understand what's going on." Mitch looked at his phone. "But why did Mary's phone go out? It is battery operated."

"Check you phones," Chaz said. "You should still have power, but no signal. When you have a local outage, it is something that has impacted your local grid. Cell towers run on a separate, special grid. This is hitting the entire grid, so even cell towers are without power."

"Life without cell phones!" Joanna said. "I guess that isn't so bad."

"Probably so," Denise said. "It does feel strange to be so disconnected though. To not know what is going on beyond our little world here."

"So true, Denise," Mary agreed. "But, until less than a hundred years ago, people did okay without all the information we were used to. I guess we'll get by as well as they did."

"Good point, Mary," Mitch muttered. "In the meantime, let's all check our rooms and other areas to make sure our emergency lighting is in place. Matt, can you and Chaz switch us to the solar generator?"

"Sure. Come on, Chaz, let's turn it on and see if it really works."

It took Matt and Chaz less than ten minutes to get the solar system online, and the refrigerator started humming again. Mitch instructed everyone to make sure the lights were off throughout the house. He didn't want their home to stand out while all the others were dark. They would only use the solar power for the essentials—fridge, freezer, water heater, and the furnace if it became cool enough at night.

Once all the tasks had been completed, the group gathered in the living room for the evening. The room had an intimate feeling being lit by candlelight. Once everyone got settled, Maggie asked, "So, I understand what happened, but why did it happen? Who did this?"

"That's a good question," Mitch replied. "It could have been anyone, I suppose. Any ideas?" he asked the room.

"I have one," Jim said. "But it's kind of crazy. Maybe it's not worth mentioning."

"Please, tell us," Mary pleaded.

"Well, it seems to me that something like this had to come from one of our country's enemies."

"You mean like Russia or China or North Korea?" Kate asked.

"Maybe," Jim replied. "Probably not North Korea because they don't have that level of sophistication. Russia or China would make sense. And there is another possibility. That's the crazy part."

"Who?" everyone asked with their eyes.

"A group that isn't part of any one country. Perhaps people who have a bigger plan for the world, and they can't implement their plan while the United States is strong."

"I can see that," Matt said. "There are people out there who have been talking about a new global economy, and new monetary system, and even a global government. And the US has been the one country standing in the way of something like that."

Jim responded, "Exactly. So, if these people crash our economy and create chaos, it will be easier to go ahead with their plans."

"But what about when the grid comes back online?" Chloe asked. "Things will get back to normal then."

"Somewhat normal," Jim replied. "But the damage will be done. People in our country have lost a lot of confidence in our economy, the government, and each other. A major disruption like this will act to push us closer to the edge toward complete chaos."

"That's a scary thought," Joanna stated. "Well, I know one thing we can do to make it better. Pray. Pray for those who are fixing the grid to do a good job. Pray for people to not panic and remain calm. Pray that the Lord will see us through this."

"An excellent suggestion," Mitch nodded. "Let's do so now."

While each of the members of the group prepared to pray, Mary noticed that Chaz and Chloe were the first to bow their heads. Mary thought, *And I will pray that these two would come to know the Lord.*

53

APRIL 26

I t took five days before the power grid was restored. It did not happen all at once, but gradually. Power came back on at the Haven after only three days. The rural areas were much easier to get back online than the cities. The restoration of power brought with it the news that crime had skyrocketed in that short time. Robberies, theft, assault, and murder had proliferated as people panicked and those with evil intent realized the loss of power meant nine-one-one systems were down.

Martial law had been declared throughout the state, but few knew about it without any form of communications available. The group at the Haven were not too affected by the loss of electricity. Their days prior to the outage had not relied on it much, and the solar system kept the basics running in the house. When the power came back, they went back to life as they had been.

Not that they were not grateful to be able to take showers again.

One thing they did keep from the time without electricity was to use candles during their evening gatherings in the living room. They liked the feel of the flickering light and how it made them feel closer.

As they settled in for their time of Bible reading and discussion, Chaz stood. "Chloe and I have something we would like to say." At this, Chloe stood up beside him.

"By all means, please go on, Chaz," Mitch said.

"We have talked about this a lot the last few days, even more when the power was out, and we've decided we want to become Christians. Am I saying that right? I mean, is that what you call it?"

"Oh, Chaz, you are saying it just fine!" Joanna said. "I am so happy for both of you."

Chloe said, "We're happy too. It feels good to just make the decision. It's like this weight has lifted off of me. I didn't really even know it was there until it was gone."

"This is wonderful news!" Mitch said as he rose from his chair. The others followed and surrounded Chaz and Chloe with loving expressions.

Chaz asked, "So, what do we do now? Is there some sort of promise we make or something?"

Dave replied, "Yes, a promise and an admission. If you're ready, I can help you with that."

"I'm ready," Chaz responded.

"I'm ready," Chloe joined.

"Bow your heads and repeat after me.

"Dear Lord Jesus, I know that I am a sinner, and I ask

for Your forgiveness. I believe You died for my sins and rose from the dead. I turn from my sins and invite You to come into my heart and life. I want to trust and follow You as my Lord and Savior." Dave finished the prayer.

The entire group exclaimed in a loud, jubilant voice, "Amen!"

54

MAY 8

It was planting day at the Haven. The chances for frost were over and the group was busy planting tomatoes, peppers, cucumbers, beans, melons, sweet corn, potatoes, and, of course, sweet potatoes. Denise and Chloe were planting the sweet potatoes. Denise explained how much she enjoyed eating them. Mary was overseeing the planting of the tomatoes, making sure there was room for the plants to grow. Maggie and Joanna were planting the green beans, while Betty and Jim were laying out the sweet pepper plants. Matt and Chaz were planting the potatoes, and Mitch and Dave filled their own rows with sweet corn seeds.

Mitch was so grateful for having so much help with the garden. The previous year, the same task had taken him and Mary several days to complete. But now, with so many hands, it was all done in a matter of hours. Just in time for lunch.

When the group sat down to the noon meal, Matt told them he had something to share with everyone after lunch. Once the dishes were cleared, Matt pulled out his tablet and said, "I got a message from a friend of mine with a link to a news story that is rather interesting. Scary in fact."

"What's it about?" Maggie asked.

Matt replied, "It's about the effort to unite all religions in the world."

"That sounds ominous," Dave said.

"It does," Matt agreed. "Let me just read part of the article for you.

'Under the guidance of Pope Francis and many other religious leaders, the One World Religion complex in the United Arab Emirates will open in 2022. The website for this initiative describes it as follows:

The Abrahamic Family House will be a beacon of mutual understanding, harmonious coexistence, and peace among people of faith and goodwill. It consists of a mosque, church, synagogue, and educational center to be built on Saadiyat Island, the cultural heart of Abu Dhabi in the United Arab Emirates. Through its design, it captures the values shared between Judaism, Christianity, and Islam, and serves as a powerful platform for inspiring and nurturing understanding and acceptance between people of goodwill. The vision for the Abrahamic Family House originated after the signing of the Document on Human Fraternity by Pope Francis and Grand Imam Ahmed Al-Tayeb in February 2019.'"

"Wow!" Betty said. "They make it sound so pleasant. So nice. It says they will capture the values shared by the three major religions. But if you take away the things that are different between them, there isn't anything left of substance."

"Like what?" Chloe asked. "I don't know much about Islam and Judaism. Well, or Christianity either, but I am learning."

Betty responded, "The main difference is how you get to heaven. Briefly, Jews believe you get to heaven by following Jewish law as revealed from the prophets of old and that the Messiah has not yet come. Muslims, by following the rules in the Koran, and of course that Mohammed was the true prophet. We Christians believe it takes salvation through Jesus through repentance and a direct relationship with Him. Not something you earn by good works, but by accepting the free gift of Christ."

"So, if you take those basics out, what's left?" Chaz asked.

"Not a lot," Denise said. "What's left is a belief that there is a God and that we should do good works."

"Isn't there a word for that?" Chloe said.

"There is," Matt said. "It's called agnosticism. An agnostic believes God exists, but we can't know Him or know what happens to us after this life. It is a belief system that basically says, 'God is probably somewhere, He may have something to do with us, and maybe there is an afterlife.'"

"That sounds pretty worthless," Chaz said. "It isn't believing. It's just idle speculation for no purpose."

"For someone so new to the faith, you sure have a

profound way of seeing truth, Chaz," Mitch complimented.

Chaz shrugged his shoulders, a little embarrassed at the compliment.

Everyone rose from their seats and started for their afternoon tasks. Mitch stood and wondered where this new religious project would lead. Nowhere good, he thought. He was reminded of an old saying, "Those who believe in nothing will fall for everything."

55

MAY 20

As Mary and Betty went out to collect eggs and opened the door to let the chickens outside, Mary noticed that the chicken run door was open. The run was attached to the back of the barn and covered on the sides and top with wire mesh. A small sliding door could be raised and lowered for the chickens to come out during the daytime. *That's odd,* she thought. *I know that was closed last night.* She stopped, holding out her arm in front of Betty.

"Someone has been here overnight. Look at that door."

"That isn't right," Betty said. "We always make sure that door is closed and the latch secured with a carabiner. Someone has been in here."

The two went back to the house to report what they had seen. They returned with Mitch, Jim, and Dave to investigate. In addition to the door being open, the cable to the sliding door was hanging free outside the run. That cable was always secured to a hook, whether opened or closed. Dave stayed outside with Mary and Betty while Mitch and Jim entered the barn to check out the inside. As they went around to the front, they checked the large double doors, finding them secure. The same was true for the front door. Mitch unlocked it and they entered to find everything in order. The coop, a six-by-ten-foot room built in the back corner of the barn had not been disturbed. All fifteen chickens were safe and the nest boxes were full of eggs.

Mitch and Jim returned to the back of the barn and Mary asked, "Is everything okay in there?"

Mitch replied, "Yes, no sign of anyone trying to get into the barn. Chickens are all safe."

"So, what do you think happened?" Betty asked.

"I'm not exactly sure," Mitch replied. "My guess would be that someone tried to get at the chickens through the chicken door inside the run. When they realized the door was too small to get through, they must have given up and left."

"Anyone can see you can't get through that door." Betty said. "It's only about a foot wide and high."

Jim responded, "True, but desperate people will do crazy things. At least they didn't get in."

"We can be thankful for that." Mitch said. "Mary, why don't you and Betty go on in and get the eggs. Looks like the hens were busy this morning."

After Mary and Betty left, Mitch stood looking at the open door with concern.

"Do you think they will be back?" Jim asked.

"Probably so," Mitch replied. "The only questions are when and what will they try next?"

That morning at breakfast, the twelve were quiet. Someone had invaded their home. Their Haven. All of them had a good idea of who it was. It was just the sort of thing Johnny Garrett would do. The question was, what should they do about it?

Breakfast finished, Mitch said, "Can everyone please stay seated for a few minutes? I want to talk about what happened at the coop and what we should do."

"Good idea," Jim said. "Do you have a suggestion?"

"I do, but it is something we'll have to agree on because all of us will have a part in it."

"Whatever it is, I'm more than willing to pitch in," Dave said.

"Thanks," Mitch responded. "Here's my plan. There is not much more we can do to secure the barn inside and out. The locks on the barn are good, and as we saw this morning, getting in from the chicken door won't work. However, if someone is determined, they will find a way in."

"What do you think they're after, Mitch?" Kate asked.

"Hard to say exactly. Could be the chickens themselves or it could be something in the barn."

"Probably not my truck," Matt said. "It would be hard to steal that with all of us here in the house."

"True, Matt," Mitch responded. "It could just be the chickens. If it is Johnny Garrett, that means our neighbors are hungry. We can certainly help them with that."

"Of course we can," Denise said. "We could take some food over to them today."

"Thanks." Mitch grinned. "Maybe not today. I want to have a talk with Tom Garrett first. I would prefer you not go over there until we make sure your visit will be welcomed."

"Why would he have a problem with a gift of food? Seems like a simple thing."

"It is, but some people get sensitive about receiving charity. They think it implies they can't take care of themselves. Besides, I want to feel Tom out about Johnny. I don't know if I can get over there today, we have a lot to do in the garden and still have our deliveries to make."

"Okay," Denise said. "I'll wait until you give the go ahead."

Jim piped up, "Mitch, you said you had a plan. Can you explain it to us?"

"Sure, it's pretty simple. I think we need to post guards at the front and back of the house overnight. The inside watch obviously has its downside as we can't keep our eyes on everything outside all the time. With one on the front porch and one on the back deck, anyone approaching can be heard coming, and if not, the motion lights will expose them. We will do two-hour shifts starting at ten p.m."

"That will mean eight people each night to cover if we guard until 6 a.m." Jim pointed out.

"Yes, so that should mean no one will have to guard more than three nights in a row. Now, if anyone doesn't feel comfortable doing this, just say so and you will not be put on the schedule. No one will think any less of you at all. A job like this isn't for everyone."

"If you don't mind," Maggie said, "I will pass on the guard duty. Sitting out in the dark at night, I would be so nervous I don't think I would do a very good job."

"No problem, Maggie," Mitch said. "Anyone else?"

Chloe raised her hand hesitantly and said, "I don't think I should do it either. Like Maggie said, I'd be too nervous too."

"Again, no worries, Chloe. So, that gives us ten people to work with. I will work up a rotation for the next two weeks and, hopefully, things will settle down and we can drop the guard duty."

———

THAT EVENING, Mitch shared the guard rotation he had developed. He made it clear to the group that the purpose of the guards was to watch and sound the alarm if anything suspicious happened. When the first shift began at ten p.m., all the lights in the house would be off so the guards could take their posts in the dark. Lights would stay off during shift changes for their own safety. Guards could choose the weapon they were most comfortable with, a pistol, rifle, or shotgun. Mitch felt uneasy about Dave taking a shift unarmed but respected his decision.

Mitch decided he would take the two to four a.m. shift as he felt that would be the most likely time for the thief to return. The first shift had Matt on the back deck, with

Joanna on the front porch. At midnight, Dave would be out back and Jim in the front.

Later, as Matt sat on the back deck, peering into the night, he heard the door behind him slide open and close. Dave whispered, "Been quiet?"

Matt responded, "Yes. Haven't heard or seen a thing. Hopefully it will stay that way."

"I think it will. While I agree with Mitch on the necessity of guards, I have a good feeling about this. I don't think anything will happen tonight. The thief probably got scared by his failed attempt and won't come back."

"I hope you're right, Dave. Still, it is good to know we have eyes up all night looking for trouble."

"Indeed. Well, you go on in and get some rest. I will see you in the morning."

"Okay. Good night, Dave and be safe."

On the front porch, Jim had relieved Joanna and settled in to one of the rockers, shotgun laying across his lap. As he peered into the darkness, he said a silent prayer that no harm would come to the group.

Inside, Mitch had been tossing and turning, trying to get to sleep. He needed to get some rest as he would have to be up a little before two a.m. to relieve Dave. He had just finally drifted off a few minutes after midnight when he bolted up at the sound of a gunshot outside.

"What was that?" Mary exclaimed, waking up next to him.

"A gunshot. Sounded like a rifle," Mitch informed as he hurriedly got dressed, grabbed his pistol off the nightstand, and hurried toward the back of the house. He was met by Matt, Denise, Chaz, Maggie, Chloe, and Kate.

"What happened?" Denise asked.

"Not sure," Mitch replied. "But we need to find out. Matt, you and Kate go out the front and investigate. I'll take Denise to check the back. Maggie, you take the back door and Chloe the front. Lock the doors and wait there to let us back in. Don't unlock the door unless you know it is one of us. Let's go."

Matt and Kate went out the front door to the porch, Chloe locking it behind them. They immediately saw that Jim was not there, so they hurried down the steps to look around. Mitch and Denise eased onto the back deck as Maggie locked that door behind them. Immediately, Mitch noticed that the motion sensor light at the back of the barn was on, but Dave was nowhere in sight.

"Where's Dave?" Denise asked with concern. "He should be here on the deck."

"I don't know," Mitch replied. "He could be over by the barn. Let's go check but be careful. Whoever fired that shot may still be around."

As the two made their way off the deck and toward the barn, Matt and Kate came around the east side of the house also headed toward the barn. The light was drawing both pairs to it with an anticipation of danger.

Matt and Kate went around to the right as Mitch and Denise headed for the near side of the barn. Circling toward the back, Matt and Kate got to the chicken run first. Mitch heard Kate gasp and say, "Oh no!"

They quickened their pace as Matt called out, "Mitch get over here, but tell Denise to stay back."

Mitch turned to stop Denise, but she ran around him toward the barn too quickly for him to stop her. He scrambled to catch up and, once there, from the light from the barn, he saw Dave lying on the ground motionless. Denise was already hugging his limp body and sobbing. Jim stood there in shock, Matt and Kate beside him.

Mitch's worst fears had come true. While he knew there was always the possibility one or more of them would be hurt or even killed, he thought it would happen while they were out making deliveries. Not here at the Haven. Not Dave, the one who refused to carry a gun. Mitch knew he should have insisted Dave be armed or at least not let him do a guard shift.

Mitch asked Jim, "What happened?"

"I'm not sure. I was sitting on the front porch and everything was quiet. Then I heard Dave holler out, 'Hey there, what are you doing? If you need food or something, all you need to do is ask.' That's when I heard a shot and took off around the house. When I got here I saw Dave lying there. I knew he was gone. The shot hit him right in the chest and he wasn't breathing. I was about to come get you when Matt and Kate showed up."

"You didn't see or hear anything?"

"No. By the time I got here, nothing."

Mitch turned to Kate and Matt. "Kate, can you please go back to the house and tell everyone what happened? Turn on all the lights inside and out and gather some flashlights so we can look around and try to find something that will tell us why this happened."

Kate nodded to Mitch and turned to walk toward the house. After a few steps, she broke into a run. As Mitch watched her go, he could see the others looking out through the sliding doors. He knew the news would devastate them.

Turning back to the scene, Denise's sobs had quieted, and she was simply holding Dave's head in her lap, staring off into nothing. Mitch's heart wrenched at the sight and he wanted to go to Denise and comfort her. But there would be time for that later. For now, they had to figure out what happened, who did this, and why. The outside lights coming on at the house caught his attention and he turned to Matt and Jim.

"We need to do a search around this area to see if we can find anything helpful. When Kate gets back with the flashlights we'll start."

Just then, Kate returned, along with Mary and Joanna. The latter two handed the flashlights they had brought to Matt and Mitch and went to Denise. Kate held up two walkie talkies and said, "I brought these too. I figured we could use them while we search."

"Good idea," Mitch said. Let's do this in pairs. Matt, you and Kate go toward the left, heading north away from the barn. Take ten steps forward, then turn left and search for twenty steps. After that, turn right and do the same in reverse. Jim and I will do the same to the right. This way, we should be able to methodically search the area quickly. If we don't find anything, we'll broaden our search area."

The two pairs started out, flashlights to the ground, eyes probing. As they did so, they could hear Denise crying again. As much as Joanna and Mary try to console her, the pain and loss was too deep. Mitch hoped Denise would find the strength to get through this. He hoped he would as well.

He and Jim were on their third turn searching when the walkie-talkie crackled, and they heard Matt's voice.

"Mitch, we found something over here."

"What is it?"

"You better get over here and see for yourself."

"Okay, shine your light our direction, so we can see your location."

Matt did so and Mitch and Jim followed the beacon to a spot about fifty yards from the barn, angling toward the left. As they approached, Matt moved the flashlight to his left and down on the ground. Lying there was a rifle as if it had been dropped. It was a rifle Mitch knew very well, a Ruger 450 Bushmaster, popular for deer hunting. Mitch looked back at the barn, then turned 180 degrees and looked out to where he could see the Garrett house 200 yards away. The rifle lay in the direct line between the two.

"That is Johnny Garrett's rifle, isn't it?" Jim asked.

"Yes, it is," Mitch replied.

Agitated, Jim said, "Let's go over there right now and settle this!"

"Jim," Mitch started, "As much as I would like to do just that, we would not know what we would be walking into. It's dark and I suspect everyone over there is on edge.

No doubt Tom Garrett has figured out what happened and is prepared for us to come for vengeance. All that will do is get more people hurt or worse. No, we wait to confront them later. Right now, our only concern is Denise."

Jim responded, "Of course, Mitch. You're right, I'm just so mad right now, I want to do something."

"I understand, Jim. I do too. I'm more angry right now than I've ever been in my life. But if we're who we say we are, we will remember that vengeance is the Lord's. Let's pick up that rifle and get back to the barn."

Matt picked up the rifle as Mitch added, "Matt, can you take that around to the front of the barn and stow it in the loft? Make a wide swing around the barn. We don't want Denise to see it."

"Sure, Mitch," he replied.

Matt and Kate headed for the front of the barn while Mitch and Jim returned to the back. Joanna was on the ground with Denise who was still holding on to Dave. Mary was standing a few feet away, tears streaming down her face. As Mitch approached, Mary asked, "Did you find anything?"

Mitch led Mary several steps away from Denise and quietly replied, "Yes, we found Johnny Garrett's rifle laying on the ground about fifty yards away."

Mary gasped and said, "That doesn't surprise me, I guess. But why would he shoot Dave? He was unarmed."

"I don't know, Mary. Best I can figure, Dave surprised Johnny and he fired in a panic. When he realized what he had done, he must have taken off running for home. He probably dropped the rifle as he didn't want to touch it anymore. Ironic. Him dropping the rifle is the only reason we know what happened."

"What are you going to do, Mitch? We can't let him get away with this."

"No, we have to do something. I'll call 911 and report this. Hopefully, the sheriff will take some action. We do have the rifle to prove it was someone from the Garrett place."

Mitch called 911 and a deputy came, along with the coroner. Mitch showed the deputy where they had found the rifle and Matt brought the rifle itself from the barn to hand it to the deputy. Denise had been convinced to go back to the house so the coroner could do his job.

The deputy stood holding the rifle. "I wish you wouldn't have picked this up. Removing it from the crime scene was a mistake."

Mitch replied, "I'm sorry we did that. I guess we weren't thinking straight. But four of us saw the rifle lying right here, that matters, doesn't it?"

"Well, yes it matters. But it might give a defense attorney an opening to create doubt about this being the murder weapon."

"Won't ballistics tell you that?" Matt asked.

"It will if we can find the bullet. The crime scene folks should be here soon. Hopefully, we can find it."

With that, the three walked back toward the barn. As they arrived where the coroner was doing his work, Mary walked up to Mitch and pulled him aside.

"Mitch, I know the coroner is going to want to take

Dave's body away, but Denise says she doesn't want Dave to leave here. She insists she can't stand the thought of him lying in a cold morgue and she wants him buried here at the Haven."

"Okay, I'll see what I can do."

Mary returned to the house as the crime scene unit arrived. After talking with the deputy, they started setting up lights in the backyard to search for the bullet that had killed Dave. They searched all night and at dawn before giving up. The deputy explained that the crime scene leader figured the bullet was not likely to be on the property. Since the shot was made at close range with a high-powered rifle, it would have passed through Dave and traveled some distance before hitting the ground. Perhaps as far as a quarter mile. Without the bullet, the evidence of the rifle was mostly circumstantial.

"You are still going to arrest Johnny Garrett, aren't you," Mitch asked.

"Not just yet," he replied. "We'll take the rifle to the lab to see if the caliber matches the one with which the deceased was shot. We will also check to see if we can determine who owns the rifle. If we can tie it to the Garretts, I will pursue an investigation in that direction."

"And if you can't identify the owner?" Matt asked.

"Unfortunately, without determining ownership, there won't be much we can do."

"But what about witnesses? Several of us saw Johnny Garrett with that rifle a few days ago. We know the one we found is his."

"Do you?" the deputy said. "Can you positively

identify the rifle you found as belonging to the Garretts? Can you describe any distinguishing marks? The model number? Anything?"

"Well, no," Mitch replied, feeling helpless. "I suppose not."

"Look," the deputy said, "I agree with you. It seems apparent that someone from that house over there was here and shot your friend and dropped the rifle on the way back to that house. It seems apparent. But in a court of law, logic does not convict. Evidence does. Once we get the lab work back and ownership determined, and if it leads to the Garretts, I'll do all I can to find out who did this."

Mitch shook his head in disbelief. Was it possible that Dave's murderer would escape justice? Especially when it was so obvious what had happened and who had done it. He wanted to challenge the deputy. To demand he go over and arrest Johnny Garret right now. But he knew that wasn't possible. He also knew the deputy would do what he could. He had to rely on him to do his job.

Sighing, Mitch said, "I know you'll do your best, deputy. Just let us know if we can do anything to help."

———

MITCH AND MATT convinced the coroner that they had made arrangements for Dave's body. He was somewhat hesitant to agree, but told them that all the evidence they needed had been gathered, so he relented. Mitch, Matt, Jim, and Chaz carefully moved Dave's body to the barn and constructed a simple wooden coffin for him. They then dug Dave's grave on the northeast corner of the property. It was a perfect spot as that corner had a small grove of trees with wildflowers growing around the edges. As the four finished the grave, they looked across at the Garrett house. No one had come outside all day. No cars left for work. No one checked the mailbox. It was as if they were waiting inside for something to happen. Mitch only wished he could make something happen. But he was powerless to do so and it ate at him. Denise deserved justice. They all did.

After a few minutes, the four men made their way back to the house. Mitch started to ask God why this had happened but stopped himself. Death was a part of this broken world. God didn't cause it. What God did do was welcome Dave home. That was something they would all have to help Denise remember if they were to be any comfort to her.

56

MAY 22

They decided to have Dave's funeral the next morning. Denise had not eaten the previous day and was showing signs of fatigue. That and the grief seemed to consume her. Always the cheeriest of the group, it almost felt like a double loss. Dave physically gone and Denise not the same person as before. Mitch had asked Denise if she had any requests for the funeral. She answered with only a shake of her head. So, Mitch, together with Joanna and Mary discussed what they should do and decided on a simple service. Some readings from scripture and inviting any who wished to say a few words. Singing was not even contemplated. Denise was their musician and singer and it somehow didn't seem appropriate to try without her.

As the eleven gathered near the grave, Mitch saw out of the corner of his eye movement at the Garrett place. Without turning his head to draw attention away from the service, he looked and saw Tom Garrett standing on his back porch. Mitch could not say why for certain, but he could tell Tom was upset and was paying his respects by standing there. Mitch wondered how respectful Tom would be if the sheriff came for his son. *Enough of that,* Mitch thought. *Time to focus on saying goodbye to a dear friend.*

Mitch cleared his throat to start. "We are never truly prepared to lose someone. No matter if it is from a lingering illness, or suddenly. Our brain can try to convince us we are ready to say goodbye, but our heart knows better."

Denise began to falter and Mary and Joanna, standing at her side, held her up. The tears were falling again and Mitch had to look away to continue.

"Yes, our heart knows better and that is the way it should be. We should never be ready to face loss. Especially, one like this. Even knowing that Dave is now with Jesus in heaven, we still miss him terribly. The wise counselor. The jolly fellow. The man of deep faith." Mitch paused, looked at Matt and nodded.

Matt said, "In Ecclesiastes chapter three, verse four, Solomon writes, 'A time to weep, and a time to laugh; a time to mourn, and a time to dance.' We are weeping now while Dave is laughing. We are mourning and yet Dave is dancing. Picture that for a moment. Our dear friend dancing? Anyone who knows Dave would like to see that."

Everyone chuckled at the image of Dave in heaven dancing. Even Denise broke into a bit of a smile. Matt continued.

"The twenty-third Psalm is often read at funerals, and with good reason. It is a reminder to us that God is with us always. It says,

'Even though I walk through the valley of the shadow of death, I will fear no evil, for you are with me. Your rod and your staff, they comfort me. You prepare a table before me in the presence of my enemies. You anoint my head with oil, my cup overflows. Surely goodness and mercy shall follow me all the days of my life, and I shall dwell in the house of the Lord forever.'

"The shadow of death can be a terrifying thing. We usually focus on that in the Psalm, but I don't think that is what Dave intended for us. Nor God. I believe, we need to look to the end and the promise that we will dwell in the house of the Lord forever. That is where Dave is now. That is where we all are looking forward to going. He just got to go before we did."

"Thanks, Matt," Mitch started again. "If anyone would like to say a few words, please feel free."

After a few moments, Joanna looked at Denise, still holding her arm and offered, "I never had a brother, but Dave was like one to me, and Denise a sister. I don't just mean like a sibling. I'm talking about a brother and sister in Christ. Dave was always taking care of me. I can't tell you how many times he was over at my condo fixing something. And he never complained, no matter how late or early it was. It was like he enjoyed crawling under my sink or on the roof. I loved that guy more than you can a brother."

Denise gave Joanna a hug and whispered something in

her ear the others couldn't hear. Mitch's eyes fell on Chaz who looked like he wanted to say something.

Mitch reached out, "Chaz, I can tell you have something to say. Go ahead."

"I don't know if I should. I mean, we haven't been here that long and maybe it's not my place."

"Of course it is," Denise said. "Please say what is in your heart."

Chaz looked down at his feet and shuffled a bit before looking up at Denise. "I haven't said much about my family to any of you, but I didn't have a dad growing up. And my mom didn't care a whole lot about me." A lump caught in his throat and Chaz looked away for a moment before continuing. "So, honestly, I did not know what it was like to have parents. And then we came here and Dave and Denise, and everyone, were so kind and caring. Dave especially. He taught me things about doing stuff around the house and he taught me what it means to be a good husband. I could see him doing that every day with Denise—being a good husband."

Chaz paused to collect himself as he fought back tears. "I want to be the kind of husband to Chloe that Dave was for Denise. I want to be the kind of man Dave was to everyone. I know I will never be what he was, but I am going to try."

As he finished, Chloe enveloped Chaz and the two stood there holding each other.

Mitch waited a few moments to see if anyone else would speak, then added his words, "For those without hope, those without Jesus, a time like this is tragic. While the circumstances that took Dave from us were evil, the tragedy itself is for the one who killed him. We can't call Dave's death a tragedy, for if we do, we're saying his presence in heaven is also a tragedy. Yes, we will miss our dear friend and mourn his absence. And at the same time we will rejoice in his new, eternal life with the Lord. As we rejoice, we will wait to join him when our time comes. Whether through a natural death or the rapturing of the church, one day soon we will be with Dave again."

Matt said to the group, "Let's bow our heads and pray for the soul of our dear friend and husband and for God's strength in this time. Dear Father in heaven, we know You can see us standing here grieving the loss of Dave. A husband, a friend, a mentor, and, most of all a servant to You, Lord. We pray for Denise that You may wrap Your loving arms around her and comfort her. We pray for strength for all of us as we face this broken world without one of our strong advocates. But we know, the strongest advocate for us is Your Holy Spirit. We ask that You give us a double portion of the Spirit while we grieve. And Lord, we end this prayer with the words of the great revelator, John, 'Surely I come quickly. Amen. Even so, come, Lord Jesus.'"

The four men slowly make their way to the barn to get the shovels and bury Dave's body. They waited patiently on the barn porch as Denise lingered to say her last goodbyes. Mitch looked and saw Chloe standing halfway between the grave and the house looking in Denise's direction. She stood perfectly still, her face like stone with her hands to her sides. Mitch had never seen anyone stand so still.

After several minutes, Denise turned and, with the help of Mary and Joanna, made her way back to the house. As they passed Chloe, Denise stopped and motioned for Mary and Joanna to go on ahead. She turned and embraced Chloe for a long time. It seemed they were giving and taking strength from each other equally. They finally separated and Denise took Chloe's hand and led her toward the house. They did not go in but went around to the front porch. Mitch lost sight of them as they climbed the steps.

Mitch, Matt, Jim, and Chaz returned to the grave where they gently lowered the wooden casket down, then covered it with earth. It was hard work and not a word was spoken until they were done when Jim said, "I have to say, I feel somehow satisfied that we were able to do this for Dave and for Denise. It is so different than going to a funeral home or church where professionals do all this. Does that make sense?"

"It does, Jim." Matt nodded. "There is something about taking responsibility for doing what needs to be done. I agree, it is not pleasant, but I feel honored to have been able to say goodbye all the way to the end."

"What about you, Chaz?" Mitch asked. "How are you feeling?"

"Not like I thought I would. I have been to funerals before, like for my grandparents. But never anyone I was close to. This was hard and it hurts. And I'm with Matt and Jim, it was an honor to know Dave and also take part in this. I just hope we don't have to do it again."

"Amen to that," Mitch said. "Let's get back up to the house and clean up."

———

THAT EVENING AFTER DINNER, the group sat in the living room and told Dave stories. Some were funny, some serious, but all were soothing to hear and to tell. Jim showed Denise a marker he had made for Dave's grave out of a large stone tile he had found in the barn. On it he had engraved Dave's name, birth and death dates, and on the bottom an inscription that read, "He has passed through the shadow and into an everlasting light in the darkness."

57

MAY 28

Over the next week, the group of now eleven tried to go back to their daily routines. The deputy stopped by to say he had talked to the Garretts and everyone in the house swore that Johnny was in the house the night Dave was killed. Mitch tried to get angry about the lack of justice, but he could not bring himself to it. Especially after Denise had asked them all to pray every day for Johnny Garrett. She said that Dave was not the one who lost that night, it was Johnny with his sinful deed and justice was less important than Johnny's soul. So, Mitch prayed for Johnny every day, as did the others.

Slowly, in steps, they returned to their routines. They had to increase food deliveries to catch up from the days lost after Dave's murder. The garden required daily attention. Everyone kept busy, partly from all that needed done, and partly to keep from retreating back into their grief. Denise and Chloe spent most of their time together. It was obvious to the group that Chloe was as shaken as Denise by Dave's death. So young and tenderhearted, Denise recognized Chloe's fragility and stuck close to her. Each day, Denise got a little better. Perhaps it was from focusing on Chloe instead of her own pain. Whatever the reason, Mitch was glad to see Denise start to recover.

Mitch didn't know what lay ahead for them, but he knew life would not get easier at the Haven. Especially with all that was going on in Washington and in government capitals around the world. The president had announced new requirements for vaccine identification. Even though the virus was starting to recede, and new cases were falling every day, it seemed there were those who would not let go of the concept of permanent identification systems. The embedded microchip program that had started in Sweden several months before as a permanent vaccine ID, was recently expanded to include all medical records for an individual and there was talk of also using it to make purchases. Now the US president revealed that the government would begin exploring the use of chips in Americans starting July 1. Participation, he said, would be completely voluntary. *Somehow*, Mitch thought, *it would not take long for the voluntary to become mandatory.*

Mitch had begun to end his daily prayers with the scripture Matt had shared at Dave's funeral, "Even so, Lord Jesus, come."

58

MAY 29

There were still a few hours of daylight left after dinner and all but Mary and Mitch were in the backyard sitting around a campfire. The hot, humid days were late this year and Maggie suggested they build the fire and enjoy the evening. Chloe and Joanna were chatting quietly, while Matt and Chaz tended the fire. Kate and Denise were discussing dinner for the next day—it was their turn in the rotation to make the meal. Jim was in a chair with his back to the house, facing the back of the property. He had the rifle in his hands. Ever since Dave's murder, Jim never went outside without the rifle. He had still not forgiven himself for what had happened to Dave. Logically, there was nothing he could have done, but it still weighed on him.

Inside the house, Mary had finished tidying up the kitchen and walked into the living room where Mitch was sitting on the couch deep in thought. Sitting down next to him and wrapping her right arm around his left, she said, "You look troubled Mitch. What's going on in that head of yours?"

Mitch's attention was brought back to the living room . He looked at Mary and patted her hand, sighed, then answered, "Troubled is the right word. I've been thinking about what will happen July first. I know we've prepared as much as we can, but I just don't think it will be enough. Not with eleven mouths to feed. What if someone else comes? We won't turn them away, but where will we put them?"

"My dear," Mary responded, "You've always been a worrier." She stroked his hair. "And, to your credit, all that worrying was well founded. If it hadn't been for your insight into what was coming, how much worse off would we be? Last year, even when I thought you were maybe getting carried away with the garden, the well, and overstocking the pantry, it was a comfort to know that you were taking care of us."

"Thanks, but I never envisioned this. I thought things would get bad, but not this bad. Not this personal. I figured the world would continue to decline, but not this fast. I guess I wanted to believe that the immorality and violence would be something we would observe at a distance. I never dreamed we would be burying one of our best friends right here."

Mary responded, "Yet, here we are. In the midst of a broken world that's falling apart. We've watched it happen and knew it was coming. But Mitch, think about all we have done. What you've done. It was a year ago that you told me you felt God had brought us here for a reason. There was a purpose for us, even though we didn't know at the time what that purpose was. Now we do. This place has been and will continue to be a haven for us as long as God leaves us here. I truly believe it will be a haven for those who come after. None of this would be possible without you listening to God and following what He wanted us to do."

"I can't argue with any of what you are saying, Mary. It's just that there are so many people counting on us right now. Our friends sitting there outside. The families around us who rely on what we produce. In a few weeks, everything will change with this chip. How long can we hold out here and still help those in need? If anything goes wrong with the garden; a late frost, too much rain, a drought, we won't have enough food."

Mary patted Mitch on the shoulder before she stood. "Hold that thought. I'll be right back."

Mitch watched her go into their bedroom and wondered what she was up to. Mary returned in a moment and sat back on the couch with her Bible. She started flipping through pages until she found what she was looking for.

"I wanted to look it up to make sure I got it right. This is in Matthew six, verses thirty-one to thirty-three. 'So do not worry, saying, "What shall we eat?" or "What shall we drink?" or "What shall we wear?" For the pagans run after all these things, and your heavenly Father knows that you need them. But seek first his kingdom and his righteousness, and all these things will be given to you as well.'"

"A good reminder, my love. Thank you."

"Mitch, I think it is good for you to think about our future, and you have a gift for doing the right thing so we're prepared. But don't worry so. Who knows, maybe tomorrow will be the day Jesus calls us all home. We won't have any worries then."

"No, not a one. Actually, I've been wondering about that. Not worrying, just wondering. Of course, we don't know God's timing, even though it looks like events are moving faster toward the end. But again, this chip plan could be delayed and may not happen this year. I guess that's what has me worried. I don't want to go down the road of planning for the rapture in a specific timeframe. That seems wrong. So, I plan as if it will be a while. Doing the math on the food is unsettling."

"I understand. But all we can really do is our best. As a wise man once said to me, 'It is what it is.'"

Mitch put his arm around Mary and smiled. He thought, as he had so many times, *What did I ever do to deserve such and amazing wife.*

———

OUTSIDE, the sun was getting lower, and the group would have to go in soon. It was simply too dangerous to be out at night. Even with the motion detector lights Mitch had installed around the house and barn, no one wanted to be caught in the darkness. They had moved the night guards inside, figuring it would be much safer, and the lights outside would warn them of approaching trouble. If not, they had learned it was not worth the risk to be outside. All but Chloe and Denise had gone inside.

As the fire began to die down, Chloe asked Denise, "I get the basics of what you're saying, but I am still having trouble understanding what you call absolution. Is it really true that being saved means all of your past sins are wiped away? Like erased from a chalkboard. If that is true, why do I still think about things I've done in the past and regret them?"

"That's a very good question," Denise replied. "I'll use your example of a chalkboard. Even when you erase the board, the chalk is still there. But, instead of words or numbers on the board, it is just chalk spread out evenly. It's like that when our sins are forgiven. The remnant is still there, but now it is pushed to the background. We can then write new things on the board. Like love and joy and peace."

"That makes sense, but I guess I was expecting that my past life would kind of disappear. At least, I was hoping it would."

"I understand, Chloe, and I used to think so too. When I was a young Christian, I expected God to make me a new person and none of the old would be left."

"Exactly," Chloe said. "The new heart I have in Christ, I thought would mean the old me would be gone completely."

"And, in some ways, it is. You do have a new heart.

That heart has totally changed your life. You don't want the same things you used to, do you?"

"No, I don't. I even wonder why those things were ever important to me."

"That is the point. We can't forget who we were before we were saved, but we can recognize the change in us and never look back."

"That is something I will never do, look back. I feel like I wasted all of those years of my life. So, will we ever forget about our old selves?"

"Oh yes, we absolutely will."

"When?"

"When we go to heaven. The Bible tells us, when we get to heaven, we will wear robes of pure white. Those robes signify the new, heavenly us. Without sin or even the thought of it. All we will ever think about will be God and His glory."

"And that's what Dave is doing now?"

"Yes, he is."

Chloe smiled. "I am so happy Chaz and I found this place. And I'm very happy to have found you."

Denise hugged Chloe and said, "I am too, my dear."

59

JUNE 3

The front porch of the Haven was a perfect place to watch the sunrise, especially on Sunday. As Mitch sat in the rocking chair sipping coffee, he felt at peace. While some might have been disturbed by the lack of traffic sounds, Mitch soaked it in. He thought to himself, *This is what God's creation should sound like.* He turned as he heard the screen door open to reveal Maggie stepping onto the porch. She sat in the other rocker and greeted, "A beautiful morning, Mitch."

"Yes, it is. You're up early. Couldn't sleep?"

"I slept well. In fact, I've been sleeping better than ever since I came here."

"I'm glad to hear that."

"Something woke me up. It was like I had this feeling that today is going to be special, and I wanted to be awake for it."

"Of course. This is the day the Lord has made, let us rejoice and be glad in it."

"Yes, that, but I think there is something more."

"Maggie, you've always had a listening heart. I'm certain God is giving you, giving us a hint of some kind. We'll pray during this morning's service that we see what He wants us to see."

"I don't know that God is talking to me, you maybe, but not me."

"Maggie, God talks to many people in many ways. He sometimes pushes our thoughts in the direction He wants us to go. Sometimes, it is His still small voice. Sometimes He shouts at us in our heads, and sometimes the Holy Spirit speaks to us by creating a feeling in us. I've seen Him speak to you in all of these ways because you are listening." Getting up from his chair, Mitch added, "Come on, let's start breakfast for the sleepy heads in there so we can have church early this morning. I've a feeling God has something planned for us today too."

The people of the Haven wandered into the kitchen and dining room as the sun continued to rise. It was going to be a beautiful day. The warmth of the sun was already promising it would be pleasant. Chloe and Chaz came in and Chloe immediately asked, "What can we do to help."

Mary responded, "Chloe, can you slice the bread for me? Chaz, can you help Jim arrange the chairs out back? We're going to have church outside this morning!"

"Sure," Chaz replied and headed out. Chloe stepped into the kitchen and gathered the cutting board, bread, and knife and started her task.

While Chloe sliced the bread, she debated with herself whether to ask Mary a question that had been on her mind lately. Life here at the Haven was so nice and she was grateful the group had welcomed her and Chaz so warmly. She didn't want to spoil the good feelings of this place, but it just wouldn't go away. "Mary," she asked, "How long do you think all of this will continue? I mean, can it go on much longer like this? It seems like every day evil gets closer and closer to swallowing us all up."

Mary turned from the stove to look at Chloe. The young woman had become like a third daughter to her. She loved her as much as Elaina and Abbigail. Her daughters, she wondered how they were up in Tipton. It used to feel like not that far way. But now, it seemed like they were on the other side of the world. With all communication sporadic, she had no idea how they were doing. Were they safe? She knew Mitch was worried about his family too. Their refusal to listen and to come to the Haven or to God was heavy on his heart.

She sighed and refocused on Chloe. "I have no idea how long. But we must remember, God has promised us all that we will not have to suffer through the Tribulation times. In 1 Thessalonians chapter five, verses nine to eleven, the Bible says, 'For God has not destined us for wrath, but for obtaining salvation through our Lord Jesus Christ, who died for us, so that whether we are awake or asleep, we will live together with Him. Therefore encourage one another and build up one another, just as you also are doing.'

"Our job as believers is to not be deceived and to

follow Christ no matter the cost. But we have that promise that, even though it has been hard, we will not be subjected to the worst of what is in store for this earth."

Chloe nodded in understanding, but the look of concern was still there.

Mary came close to her and put her arms on her shoulders. "My dear Chloe. Look at you! Look at what God has done in your life. He has protected you and Chaz and brought you here to be with us. He has opened your hearts to His Word and you have been a blessing to us all. Don't you think He is going to keep His hand on you, even as things get worse?"

"Of course. I know all of this, but sometimes it just gets me down. Sometimes I just feel worn out from the tension and stress of the situation. I have faith that God will take care of us, but the darkness feels so close."

"My dear, it is close. I feel it too. Sometimes I wonder why Jesus hasn't come for us yet. But in God's timing, not ours. His ways are not our ways. Even through all of this, we know His plans for us are good."

Chloe smiled and the tension relaxed a bit in her shoulders. Mary gave her a quick hug and said, "But until that time, we still have to eat, so let's finish up breakfast for this crowd before they start growling."

———

Sunday breakfasts at the Haven were special. On the other days, breakfast was part of the workday. On Sundays, the meal was the start of a day of thankfulness and worship. The dishes had all been cleared and people were moving out to the back lawn where the chairs had been set up in rows for the service facing east toward the still-rising sun. They had no set time for church on Sundays. They had learned to let God make things happen when He wanted them to. Sometimes the service didn't start until almost noon. But this morning, it was earlier than usual. No one knew why nor thought much about it. They just seemed to flow naturally toward their worship.

Mitch walked to the front with his Bible as Denise was preparing her music for the service. Her guitar was on a nearby chair, and she was arranging the songs in the order she had planned them to sing. Mitch looked at Denise, seeing something different in her. Since Dave's death, Denise had been pensive and quiet. She still was the same compassionate, caring person she always was, but the boundless joy she carried with her had lessened. Understandably so. Dave's murder had shaken the group. They had come to believe that God was protecting them, and no harm would come here at the Haven. Looking back, that idea seemed arrogant to Mitch. Being here wasn't about God keeping them from harm, but about God bringing them together to support each other as evil swirled around them. No one doubted they would see Dave again, but his strengthening presence was sorely missed by everyone.

"You seem different this morning. I haven't seen that smile so bright in a while."

Denise looked up from her papers and responded, "I

don't know what it is. When I woke up this morning, I had this overwhelming sense of peace and contentment." She looked out over the garden at the sunrise, then back at Mitch. "Every morning since it happened, I wake up to this terrible empty feeling. It takes a lot of prayer just to get motivated to start the day. But this morning, that feeling wasn't there. The hole in my heart was gone. I don't understand it. I figured the mourning would gradually fade away. But it's like it was lifted from me all at once."

"Well, that's amazing. I wonder what it is God has for you that He would take away your grief."

"I don't know, but I'm looking forward to finding out."

"Me too. I think it's about time we start our worship."

They had talked about having their Sunday service outside last fall before it got too cold. But the traffic noise from the highway would have made that difficult. Now, it was a rare sight to see a car or truck on any roadway, so they had moved their services outdoors since the weather warmed.

Mitch made sure everyone was seated and ready, then moved to the front and began to speak. But he couldn't say a word. He tried to open his mouth, but found it clamped shut. The group looked at him curiously, Mary with a bit of concern on her face. As Mitch looked out over these people who were closer than family, and at the home they shared, the garden they worked together, the colors before his eyes seemed deeper and richer than ever before. It was as if everything looked brighter and more intense. He couldn't find words to describe it, but it felt complete.

Like he was seeing everything in front of him for the first time.

When he looked at Mary, he could somehow see her inner beauty more clearly than ever before. His gaze moved to Denise, and there, too, he saw her more clearly, like he was seeing inside her—her soul. Mitch shut his eyes and wondered what was going on. When he opened them, he surveyed the group. Jim and Betty smiled at him and he could see their humble, servant hearts on their faces. He turned toward Maggie and Joanna. There, he saw something he had never seen in either. Gone was the underlying loneliness that lived under the surface. Instead, he saw pure joy. What was going on? Had he been so caught up in running the Haven he had failed to see these people?

Then he looked over to Chloe and Chaz. The young couple the entire group had adopted and cared for. Ever since they had arrived several months ago, Mitch had been worried about their faith. Whether they would hold strong in the face of a world literally falling apart. He had seen the worry on their faces every day. But today, that worry was gone. It had been replaced with a serenity that seemed to surround them. Finally, Matt and Kate. Gone was the concern for their children and the stress of not knowing where they were and if they were safe. Matt, Mitch's closest friend and brother in Christ, had the unbridled smile Mitch remembered from when they were young, when they still had their lives in front of them. He met Mary's gaze again. Was God giving him eyes to see what he had never noticed before?

His eyes drifted upward, drawn there for some unknown reason. The rest followed too, compelled to raise their faces heavenward. Their sight had revealed the full beauty before them and, like Mitch, they wondered in awe at the strong feeling of such peace. Then the sky itself seemed to brighten to a light beyond white. Not from a single source, but the entire sky glowed brilliantly with a shine that held no color, or maybe all the colors at once.

Then they all began to realize, it was time. Jim and Betty, Maggie, Denise, Joanna, Chloe and Chaz, Matt and Kate, and Mitch and Mary gazed upward and raised their arms, hands open in anticipation. The feeling was one of such extreme joy that they could not believe their hearts could hold it. A warmth enveloped them, making everything around them recede out of sight and awareness until nothing seemed real except the awareness of His presence. In that moment, they were gone.

The music sheets Denise had been holding floated gently to the ground. Mitch's Bible fell too, landing softly in the grass. A gentle breeze blew through the backyard of the Haven and turned the pages of the Bible. A stillness then settled over the yard, not even the birds were singing. The Bible, worn from use and full of bookmarks lay open to the sixteenth chapter of the Gospel of John. Verse thirty-three had been highlighted.

"I have told you these things, so that in me you may have peace. In this world you will have trouble. But take heart! I have overcome the world."

EPILOGUE

Steve sat at the kitchen table staring at the envelope. He was still numb from what had happened two days ago. So many gone in a moment. He was not really surprised. Deep down he knew such a day was coming eventually. He had just ignored it, just like he did everything else he knew to be true. Why had he been so stubborn? He knew why. He did not want to think about hard things. Especially when that meant the possibility of embarrassment. Believing was easy for his aunts and uncles, and his parents. They were from a different generation. One that expected you would go to church, pray over meals, and obey the rules. But his was a generation that focused on having a good time. Doing what they wanted and avoiding the un-fun things in life. Besides, if you were a good person, didn't steal, hurt others, and were mostly nice to people, God was probably going to let you into heaven. None of that made sense anymore. Everything that was three days ago was gone. The world was going crazy, and he knew why. He knew what was coming next.

Steve took another sip of coffee and slowly reached for the envelope. He turned it over in his hands. He read the front, printed in Mitch's precise handwriting,

To my family. Only to be opened in the event I am no longer here.

He slid open the flap, pulled out two sheets of paper, and began to read.

"Dear family,

If you are reading this, it means I am no longer here on this earth. If I am gone due to illness or accident, know that I am now in heaven with Mom and Dad and Jason. If Mary is still with you, please look out for her and the girls.

If we are both gone, along with millions of others, we are still in heaven, but I pray for all of you and what is to come. Some of you already know what happened to all of us. We were called home by our Lord Jesus. Most people refer to it as the rapture. I simply think of it as the time when Jesus said, 'Enough.' The Bible tells us that God will not let his people suffer through the evil times. You may wonder, 'Why now?' I don't know the answer to that question as I write that but I may find out in heaven. What I do know is that there is still a way to be where Mary and I are now. It won't be easy. In fact, it will be dangerous. Before we left, being a Christian meant not hiding your faith. We were to live our lives as an example of God's love and power.

You can't just do that now. But you still must believe. Even when you are scared and want to give in to what the world tells you, stay strong. Do not get the chip. Once you do, all hope is lost. Don't be deceived by the lies telling you the chip is for your health and safety. It has one purpose and one purpose only. To forever mark a person as belonging to Satan.

We have always been a close family and you all will have to be closer than ever to get through these next few years. The only way to survive is to withdraw from the world. Leave everything behind and live isolated from the evil and the madness. So, gather together as quickly as you can and go to our house in Mt. Olive. I hope you are reading this in the spring or summer when the garden is planted, so you will have food to eat. If it is winter, there will be plenty of canned goods and food in the freezer. There are seeds for planting the next season. Go during the day when you can see trouble coming.

Most importantly, read the Bible every day. Everything you need is there. We may not have one for everyone, but there are several in the house. Start with Revelation so you can understand what is going on now, then the Gospels, especially the Gospel of John. As time goes on, things will get worse. But, in the end, it will all be worth it. God wants every person to go to heaven, even now.

Your brother and uncle,

Mitch"

Steve held the letter for several minutes, staring at the words. He knew his brother was right about everything and it scared him. Everything scared him right now. He had no idea what to do next. Steve looked up as he heard gunshots not too far away and wondered how long it would be until they reached his street. He thought of his mother and father, his brother Jason, Mitch and Mary, all of his aunts and uncles, and his grandparents. He knew where they were. In heaven. He had always believed his parents were there and Jason, too, when he died seven years ago. But what he had never thought about was whether he would be there with them. It was something he had put off thinking about. Until now.

He bowed his head and, more with his thoughts than words, asked God to help him. There was too much to say, too much to think about. Somehow, he knew God understood, could read his heart. After several minutes of praying without words, in barely a whisper he said, "I believe."

As Steve lifted his head and opened his eyes, he felt at peace. He didn't understand it, but it was there. He looked at the envelope on the table. He picked it up and examined it. He noticed a bump in the bottom corner and turned it over. Out dropped a key with a small tag that simply said, "The Haven." He looked at the key, turned it over in his hand and recalled his brother talking about how he and Mary had worked to make their home a haven. Steve didn't really understand what Mitch meant at the time. Now he understood.

He now knew what to do. He also knew what was ahead. It would be difficult. More difficult than he could ever imagine. But what choice was there? Stay here and wait for the evil to come? He was grateful that his brother had prepared a place for them. A haven.

He had some calls to make. It was time to gather the family.

ABOUT THE AUTHOR

Mark Holbrook spent twenty years in the television and radio news business before switching careers to oversee the marketing efforts of Ohio's state Historical Society. He also acted as the Civil War historian for the organization. Now retired, Mark enjoys country life with his wife Melissa on their mini farm north of Columbus, Ohio.

Always interested in sharing stories of the past, Mark has appeared in three films, Ambrose Bierce: Civil War Stories (2006), The Light of Freedom (2013), and Wings of the Wind (2015). Mark is also a long-time member of the Ohio Humanities Speakers Bureau. He has also appeared in an episode of Mysteries at the Museum (2014).

With experience as a news reporter, anchor, radio host, and public speaker, Mark continues to help people and organizations better themselves through his consulting firm History is Personal. Mark's previous writing efforts include freelance projects for tourism organizations and is the editor of the book *The Buckeye Vanguard* about the 49th Ohio Volunteer Infantry.

You can learn more about Mark and sign up to subscribe to his blog page at historyispersonal.com.

THE HAVEN: FLIGHT TO FREEDOM
PREVIEW OF BOOK 2 IN THE HAVEN SERIES

This was taking far too long. Steve Harrison fidgeted as he awaited the arrival of his sister, Rachel, and her daughter, Savannah. It was now two in the afternoon and they needed to get on the road soon. He wasn't worried about running out of daylight during the trip. It would not get dark until almost nine. His real concern was getting to his brother's house early enough to figure out what was going on and to get everyone settled before the sun went down. The drive, normally only forty-five minutes, would take about an hour and a half. They would avoid the freeway and use the backroads to stay away from potential traffic jams and dangerous situations.

Steve looked down the road again and wondered if maybe something had happened during his sister's drive from Whitney in the southern part of the state. He was also worried about drawing attention to his home. With family members arriving and the loading of vehicles, the risk that they would be noticed by the roving bands of criminals was much higher than Steve would prefer.

Ever since the worldwide disappearance of millions of people four days ago, order had broken down and with it, a rise in crime and violence. President Jordan had declared martial law with a curfew from dusk to dawn. Among the millions were Steve's brother, Mitch, and his wife, Mary. Those two, with their friends from the city who had moved in with them the previous fall had vanished four days ago. Also gone were children. All the children under about ten years old had disappeared. Including several of Steve's grandchildren.

Mitch had given Steve an envelope to open only after he was gone. Inside, Mitch had explained what had happened—the rapture had taken him and Mary and all believers to heaven. In the letter, Mitch begged Steve to gather the family and head north to his and Mary's home where it would be safe. Steve had not needed the letter to know what had happened. Having grown up in the church where his uncle was pastor, he knew that the disappearances were the rapture of Jesus' church. Steve just wished he had not left that church years ago. If he had not, perhaps he and his family would not be facing the coming evil now that would dominate the world for the next seven years.

Steve had forgotten about the envelope the day of the vanishings. He was too preoccupied with the disappearances of his grandchildren. His son's youngest daughter, five-year-old Helena, and his daughter's four-year-old Ariana had disappeared with all the others. Gone, too, were four-year-old Chase and two-year-old Dylan, the two sons of Lucy, Steve's wife's daughter. Trying to console them had proved fruitless. How did you convince a parent that their child is in heaven when they had not been taught anything about the Bible? Did not know that something called the rapture was coming?

Steve had finally convinced his children, along with two of his three siblings, to pack everything they could and head to Mt. Olive and Mitch's house. It was not difficult to do so once everyone realized staying in the city would be dangerous. Faith, the youngest of the Harrison siblings, had arrived an hour ago with her daughters, Morgan and Kinsley. Lucy and her husband, Brett, had been there since the morning. The two were still in shock and had not wanted to leave their home initially. They wanted to be there in case their children returned. Once Steve convinced them what had happened, they agreed to go along with the rest to the place that had become known to the family as the Haven.

Walt, Steve's younger brother, along with his wife, Amber, was not coming. They would not believe the rapture had occurred and decided to stay put. Even with Steve, Rachel, and Faith all begging them to join, Walt simply refused to budge and said it would all blow over. No amount of arguing was going to change his mind. Steve knew that one factor to Walt's stubbornness was the fact that his five children were scattered throughout the city and had no interest in leaving. Steve could understand Walt's desire to protect his children. He just hoped doing so would not lead to making the wrong decision about who to believe in the coming months.

Finally, Steve saw Rachel come around the corner and head toward his driveway. To his horror, following just a few car lengths behind was an SUV that looked like it was full of passengers. He could see a few gun barrels as his attention went from the SUV to Rachel's car. He waved frantically for Rachel to hurry as he called out for his son, Randy, and son-in-law, Gary.

"Rand! Gary! Out here now!"

Randy and Gary came flying out the door in answer. Gary had Steve's shotgun in his hands, Randy was unarmed.

Steve had already pulled his 9mm Glock from its holster and had it in the ready position as he turned to Randy and said, "Randy, what did we say?"

"Always armed, Dad." Randy replied contritely.

"Go get it and hurry."

When Steve turned back to his driveway, Rachel had pulled in and was looking at him with fear in her eyes. Steve motioned for her to stay put. He looked to do the same with Savannah, but she had already gotten out of the car and taken a position behind her open door with a rifle pointed at the oncoming threat. The SUV had slowed as it approached Steve's house, ready to turn in and stop. At the sight of Steve, Savannah, and Gary with guns drawn and ready, the driver sped up and drove on past the house.

Steve waited until the SUV had turned the corner at the end of his street to holster his pistol. Gary and

Savannah relaxed as Rachel called out from her open window to Steve.

"Can I get out now?"

"Sure, Coast is clear."

As Rachel came up the driveway, she asked, "What was that all about?"

"Bad guys, Mom," Savannah replied as she approached as well. "I noticed them when we made our last turn. And then when I saw Uncle Steve with his gun out, I knew something was up."

"That was quick thinking, Savannah," Steve said. "Your rifle made the difference. Gary and I were vulnerable out in the open in the yard and I think those guys would have tried it except you had them covered from the side."

"No problem," Savannah responded, hurrying toward the house as Randy charged out with his pistol.

Steve said, "It's all over, Randy."

"Gee, I'm sorry, Dad. I guess I panicked a bit and forgot."

"Randy, it's okay. This is new territory we're in. It will take some getting used to. Just keep your holster on with the pistol in it and you won't have to worry about it."

"Will do," Randy said as he turned to follow Gary back into the house.

Steve turned toward Rachel and asked, "How are you holding up?"

"I am doing okay, I suppose."

Rachel's husband and Savannah's father, Mike, had died the day before the disappearances. He had been in declining health for a while and his passing was somewhat expected. It still irritated Steve that he and the rest of the family could not attend the funeral. Rachel and Mike lived an hour and a half south in Wellesley. With the world in turmoil, it just wasn't safe to make the trip.

Steve put his arm around Rachel. "You know I would have been there if I could."

"I know, Steve. You made the right call. It wasn't worth the risk and you needed to stay here and take care of your family."

"Well, we're all together now." He sighed and added, "Almost all."

"Walt is still being stubborn?"

Steve nodded.

"I don't understand him. He was ready to drive down to Wellesley for the funeral until I told him not to. And now he won't drive less than an hour to Mitch's house where it's safe."

"I know, Rachel. He says it's because he doesn't want to leave the children and I get that. But I think it is more about denying what has happened. All we can do is hope he and Amber come around and join us up there soon. Speaking of which, we need to get on the road. Let's go inside and get things moving."

ACKNOWLEDGMENTS

I seriously doubt my grandparents ever thought about their grandson Mark being an author one day. Even so, much of my faith foundation was developed from them while spending summers on their respective farms. I learned to appreciate the growing of food, tending to livestock, and being closely tied to the land. I thank them, Vincel and Alma, Leonard and Ethel for their investment in my upbringing and my education as a person and a Christian.

I would also like to thank the many people who have walked alongside me as I have tried to grow in love and wisdom. Specifically dear friends Dan and Deb who counseled, supported, and cared for me in difficult times.

I also thank my brother Jeff. Taken too young, my older brother (by only ten months!) was more like a twin. We shared so many likes, not the least of which was reading, gardening and antiquing. I will see him again one day and know that we will have a lot to talk about. My parents, Hobert and Wilma provided a loving home that I realized as an adult is a rare thing today. As parents, I could not ask for better ones.

Many thanks to my beta-readers Mike, Linda, and

Mike. Their insights and observations were invaluable in refining the story.

I am thankful to the people of Zamiz Press. Marie, Eliza, and John have been great to work with. The Haven was not just another project book to them, but a story they appreciate and want to help share with the world.

To my wife, Melissa who encouraged me all through the writing and publishing process. Her faith in me is humbling and inspiring.

And finally, to our Father and God who early one morning sat me down at my computer and began to put the words on the pages. I did not see it coming, but once started I had no choice but to complete the story.